EVERY RISING SUN

EVERY RISING SUN

◇◇◇◇◇◇◇◇◇◇◇

A NOVEL

◇◇◇◇◇◇◇◇◇◇◇

JAMILA AHMED

HENRY HOLT AND COMPANY

NEW YORK

Henry Holt and Company
Publishers since 1866
120 Broadway
New York, New York 10271
www.henryholt.com

Library of Congress Cataloging-in-Publication Data is available.

ISBN: 9781250887078

Our books may be purchased in bulk for promotional, educational, or business
use. Please contact your local bookseller or the Macmillan Corporate and
Premium Sales Department at (800) 221-7945, extension 5442, or by e-mail at
MacmillanSpecialMarkets@macmillan.com.

First U.S. Edition 2023

Designed by Gabriel Guma

Printed in the United States of America

1 3 5 7 9 10 8 6 4 2

To Abbu, who told me stories, and
to Ammi, who taught me how to write them

But all this world is like a tale we hear—
Men's evil, and their glory, disappear.

FIRDAUSI, SHAHNAMEH

Shahrazad turned to King Shahryar and said, "May I have your
permission to tell a story?"
He replied, "Yes," and Shahrazad was very happy and said,
"Listen."

THE ARABIAN NIGHTS

Before the Nights

◇◇◇◇

It is said that in the province of Kirman, a land of green pistachios and dusty mountains, reigned a Seljuk Malik called Shahryar, who wed a pearl-skinned beauty named Fataneh. Great men and women of the empire gathered to fête the newlyweds, and among the many, perhaps the least, was Shaherazade, the daughter of the Malik's vizier.

Against the ring of brassy trumpets and deep-bellied drums, the bride and groom processed toward the citadel. Shaherazade's black braids bounced against her back as she leapt, each jump bringing a fleeting moment in the air that allowed her to puzzle a piece of the wedding scene: *Jump.* The silk-clad shoulders of the wedding guests. *Jump.* Palanquins bedecked with silver bells. *Jump.* The bride's glittering robe of vermilion and jade. *Jump.* Her necklaces of gold, earrings of emerald.

Shaherazade landed.

"Calm down, Shaherazade." Her father stayed her with a gentle hand. "You will see the Malik and his bride soon enough." Vizier Muhammad smiled, removing the sting from his admonition. He brushed a kiss on top of Shaherazade's rose-scented head. "There's a good girl."

Self-consciously, Shaherazade straightened her palm-green robe, which she had thought quite becoming, but which now, after seeing the bride's regalia, seemed childish. Sullen, she scuffed a curled slipper against the flagstones.

She could not sulk for long as the crush of wedding guests swirled from the bailey into the grand hall of the citadel, following the bridal procession and carrying Shaherazade and her father with them. Turquoise tiled arches swooped like snowy swan necks, and silver and gold lanterns glowed overhead with a soft, firefly light. Shaherazade smelled something light and herbal—angelica, nigella—and more eye-watering scents— esphand and frankincense.

Blinking away tears, Shaherazade pushed toward the Malik and Fataneh Khatun, who now sat cross-legged beneath a white canopy. Briefly, the Malik's hand covered the Khatun's, but her eyes remained demurely downcast. A silver mirror between them reflected two luminescent candelabras, a Qur'an, and a half dozen other daily items that had borne significance in Persia since the time of Zarathustra.

Over the strum of tars and the rumbling verse of Turkic song, Shaherazade whispered to her younger sister, who had appeared at her shoulder, "Are they not so sweetly in love?"

Dunyazade plucked at a stray scarlet thread from her tunic and responded with marked disinterest. "Very much." Sighting servants unloading hare spiced with thyme, saffron-scented rice, pullet stew simmered in ginger and rose water onto squat tables, Dunya exclaimed, "Let's go!"

The children threaded past the silken legs and belted waists of the mass of viziers and emirs, generals and courtiers, philosophers and poets, maliks and khatuns. Even the Malik's suzerain, the young Sultan Toghrul III of the Seljuk Turks, shadow-eyed under a heavy crown, was in attendance.

As Shaherazade bumped, nudged, and forced her way through the illustrious crowd like an oiled goat, she stepped on a pearl, a luminous full moon, smooth and white, one of many scattered by careful servant hands. She stumbled, flinging out her arms and striking a green-robed potentate, who whirled away like an angry top.

Flushing, Shaherazade cast about surreptitiously, hoping no one else had seen her, *her*, ten years old and practically a woman, trip like a child. To Shaherazade's dismay, she caught the kohl-lined eye of Fataneh Khatun. The Khatun's lips parted in not unkind amusement. Her pale hand trembled as she nudged the Malik, whispered in his ear. He grinned at Shaherazade, neat white teeth flashing bright. Hotness drowned Shaherazade's cheeks, humiliation slicking her stomach. Before she could flee, hide beneath a table, or better, in an empty courtyard or abandoned room, the Malik beckoned her.

This was an order from her ruler, her Baba's master. How could she but obey? Tentatively, Shaherazade stepped forward. She wished Dunya would find her and pull her away.

Her fist to her chest, Shaherazade genuflected from the waist as she had seen her Baba do.

"Assalamu'alaikum Shaherazade." The Malik's mouth twitched with humor. "How well you look."

Shaherazade nodded but could not speak—she had never felt more a coltish, foolish girl than in the face of the couple's blossomed beauty. The Khatun's ebony hair, barely obscured by a sheer storm-blue veil, cascaded past her hips in fine plaits. The emeralds and gold of her diadem picked out the sunshine-on-grass color of her eyes. If it were possible, the Malik was even more beautiful, with coal-black hair, tilted dark eyes, high cheekbones, and a nobly curved nose. When he glanced at his bride, who flushed obligingly, he glowed. Shaherazade knew, just knew, that theirs was a love that would be sung down the ages, like the sagas of Leila and Majnun, Vis and Ramin, Khosrau and Shirin.

"What do you think of my new wife?" The Malik stroked Fataneh's hand, the brawniness of his all the more apparent for the delicacy of hers.

He did not wait for Shaherazade to reply. "I was lucky to find her, you know." He turned to Fataneh. "Is it not so, *jaanem?*"

"Yes, O Malik." The Khatun's voice was soft, the chirp of a dove.

"You must not call me 'Malik.' I would have you call me 'beloved.'"

"Yes, jaanem." Her smile stretched her lips tight.

The Malik returned his attention to Shaherazade, his grin filled with the sum of his youth and innocence. "Indulge me, little Shaherazade, and let me tell you of the moment I fell in love." He caressed Fataneh's fingers. "Three months ago, I visited the governor of Ganja, Fataneh Khatun's father. There, I saw those gleaming green eyes—have you ever seen such pure and true green, like spring leaves, like Nowruz?—peeking from her veil. In that moment, I fell in love, as though we had been made from one soul cloven in half in the Therebefore. Then and there, I asked her father for her hand." He kissed Fataneh's fingers, stained red with bridal henna. "Now, tell me little Shaherazade, is she not the fairest woman, the kindest, the sweetest, the gentlest in the land?"

Shaherazade dropped her head to restrain her giggles. She wished she could think of a clever response, but her words ran dry.

Spying her taut lips, the Malik mockingly scolded, "Now, you know you should not laugh at your Malik. You are lucky I am feeling magnanimous, little Shaherazade, that my wife has made me so happy. Today, I forgive you. But go play before I change my mind and take your head!"

Ducking that head, still attached by the Malik's grace, Shaherazade walked away, attempting stately grace.

As folk dancers twirled to Oghuz song, Seljuk nobles and luminaries toasted the newly married couple into the velvet night, whispering how well matched they were, the union's divine blessing, the long and happy fate awaiting them.

How could they have predicted fortune's course, the shredding of this shining marriage, and the empire, in less than a decade—and Shaherazade's hands stained red, not with bridal henna but with blood?

PART ONE

◇◇◇◇◇◇◇◇◇◇◇◇

587 After Hijrah

1191 After the Death of 'Isa

One

◇◇◇◇◇

There are words and then there are *words*. Words that can bind hearts, break a marriage, rupture an empire. Words that burn in your mouth like black peppercorn, that crack the soul like bone, that linger in the air until the Day of Reckoning's trumpets shred mountains to cotton and break the earth like an egg. Words created the dizzying spiral of our worlds—*The Creator of Heavens and Earth . . . He but says "Be" and it Is*—and so too, will they destroy it.

But for now, I call out my sister's name and hope it draws my quarry nearer. "Dunyazade!" My slippers skid across the time-polished floor of Bam's citadel. "Dunya!"

As my call fades around a corner, I hear a protesting voice. ". . . The Khwarezmid forces and Oghuz armies have each been expanding into Persia. Seljuks are falling before them in battle. Your wife's father, Sultan Toghrul, and the Seljuk Empire itself stand on the brink of defeat."

"Do not forget the Franks, calling themselves Crusaders, still besiege Acre. Sultan Saladin has appealed again for aid."

I can make sense of only about half of what is being said. We have heard that the Franks have renewed their assault on the Muslims of Jerusalem, but that is a drama so far away it might as well be another world. The Oghuz and the Khwarezmids, though, are twin menaces much closer to our hearts, wild people rapidly gnawing away at our Seljuk Empire—although they are yet parasangs north of Kirman, each occupied with defeating Sultan Toghrul and his emirs.

"We shall see to it that my father-in-law receives aid. My wife will have it no other way."

I recognize this voice immediately. The Malik.

Rounding the corner, I collide with a knot of men. Papers fly as my feet skip, my slipper slides, and I claw at the faience wall behind me for support. The Malik steadies me, his fingers curling around my shoulders. Behind him, his advisers' faces twist in disapproval. A pair of scribes scurry to gather the sheaves drifting down like snow.

A furious blush heats my cheeks. I step away from the Malik, my shoulders hot and cold where he touched them.

"Apologies," I mumble.

The scribes dart veiled glares at me.

"Are you searching for your sister, Shaherazade Khatun?" The Malik tucks a lock of black hair, jostled loose by our collision, into his jeweled turban. The impulse to tug it forth again, feel its cool silkiness slide against my palm, suffuses my fingers. I clench my hands tightly.

I drop my eyes. Nod.

Even nine years after his wedding, over eight years living alongside him in the Arg-e-Bam, and knowing him for each of my nineteen years, I still struggle to articulate myself in his presence. Before his majesty and kindness, I feel my veins blossom and hot blood dissolve my muscles and bones. I could be left for a formless heap at his feet.

He laughs fondly and I feel foolish. I wish I had turned the corner and careened into anyone else, or better yet: glided past the Malik, demurely inclining my head.

"Halt your search. You will not find her until she wants to be found." He gives me a knowing look. Dunya's reluctance to my lessons is infamous, a joke that apparently has risen to the Malik's ears. "But do me a favor and find Fataneh Khatun."

I nod, trying to recover the grace I have lost. Judging from the councillors' eyes, the effort is not well received. I am sure Baba will hear of this. Still, the Malik's eyes twinkle with gentle amusement.

"Your father told me part of a story you told him," the Malik calls as I retreat.

I whip around, my heart hammering.

He smiles. "I should like to know the ending, someday."

"I—I . . . I should find Fataneh Khatun."

How could Baba have told him? I duck and flee, and the drumbeat of my heart drowns all sound.

✳ ✳ ✳

I must admit: the Khatun frightens me. The Malik can praise her sweetness and beauty to Paradise and she can win the people's hearts by endowing mosques and madrasas, but since her earliest days in Bam, she has held herself aloof, aware that she is a creature of ground pearls and gold dust, too fine to associate with those of us formed of clay.

Still, at the Malik's order, I search narrow halls and wide chambers, the cool, dim baths and the sun-hot gardens, the harem's shaded corners and the wide-open polo fields. I even hesitantly knock at the door of the quarters Fataneh Khatun shares with the Malik, as a pair of guards, armored in shimmering chain mail, look on stonily.

I trail from one end of the Arg-e-Bam to the other, passing servants and clerks and secretaries, all those who power the citadel, until finally, I stand before a door of sweet cedar etched with interlaced stars. I push into the room.

Empty, save for scattered rugs and dusty benches.

A closed door stands in the back. A bubbled glass window looks onto a courtyard where pink flowers and green leaves are aflame against an adobe wall. From the courtyard garden, I hear leaves rustle, wind sigh.

Once, there was a pari *queen, fair as the moon, who possessed all she could desire. She possessed one more thing: a festering secret that could destroy all she held dear . . .*

A thud against the courtyard door snaps me to the present.
And another.
A woman's satisfied breath and a man's relieved groan. Of its own volition, my hand pushes the door, and a man and woman tumble at my slippers. In the sunlight's eager glare, they are a conjoined entity. I catch the woman's smooth shoulder, the man's dusky thigh. Shame sears me.

I smile politely at the floor, damning myself for opening the door. I am on the verge of offering greetings, but the woman glares at me. And her eyes. A distinctive green famed throughout Kirman. Squeaking, I close my own and back into the room.

I try to repress the scene, but it unfolds before me again and again. I wish I had tried any other room, opened any other courtyard door. Or had not, like a simpleton, opened this one, when it was volubly clear that I was not meant to see what was occurring behind it.

I examine a pore in the floor, the minuscule puckers and shimmering mica flecks, but I follow their movements out of the corner of my eye. Neither the man nor the woman attempts to explain as they tighten their trousers, pull down their robes. They do not even look my way. As if I am nothing. A landed bird, a blown leaf. I wish I were.

The man I do not recognize. He appears generic enough: dark hair, dark eyes, dark skin, a handsome cut to his cheekbones, a sharp nose like a hawk's. I cannot determine his pedigree or rank. He could work in the kitchens, toiling in smoke and fire, or be a visiting emir, traveling from province to province to offer his sword. But the woman . . . this woman, rutting where any passerby could discover her, is the Malik's wife, Fataneh Khatun.

They exit. First him, and after several moments, her. They pass me, smelling sweet, of flowers and musk. Their footsteps trail down the hall.

A gust slams the courtyard door shut and finally, I breathe. When the tap of their slippers fades, I step into the hall. An iron-hard grasp clamps around my arm. The Khatun's face looms, not remorseful as mine would have been, but angry, defiant. Her gold rings gouge my flesh. I pull away, but her grip is unyielding. My mouth dries at the manic glint in her eyes.

Despite her small stature, she strong-arms me into the room and kicks the door shut.

She grabs my chin, no gentleness in her touch, her full lips steely. "Shaherazade." She drawls my name, elongating the alif near the end.

I do not know which I fear more: being alone with her or being discovered by someone who would wonder what was passing between us. I do not know whether I would be able to lie—whether I *should* lie.

"Clumsy Shaherazade. Little Shaherazade, the girl who stumbled at my wedding, tripped gracelessly on pearls before the Malik."

My face reddens. For a moment, I am a child again and the Khatun is the embodiment of all I could never hope to be.

Fataneh Khatun smiles and her voice silkens, a soft rope around a softer throat. "The daughter of Vizier Muhammad, a widower with two daughters? I am sure he worries about finding husbands for you and your sister. Perhaps I could arrange suitable matches to ease his mind? Or I could slip to the Malik how deserving your father is of a few new landholds and *iqta'*?"

She releases my arm and the blood tingles back. She pats my head, ringing my skull. "Let me make myself clear, *jaan*," she hisses. "If you speak of this to *anyone*, your head will be the *first* on the chopping block, followed by your sister's and your father's. That, I vow to you by Allah."

I drop my eyes and nod. I hope that is enough, that she will leave me alone, that this will ebb into nightmare. My family's lives are not worth divulging what I have seen.

"Good girl." She pats my head again, *pat-pat-pat*, as if she would drive me into the ground like a nail into wood.

My skin jumps as new footsteps fall on the floor. The stride is heavy, the sole thick. Fataneh's breath catches.

The Malik, finally free of his retinue, enters. "I thought I heard voices." His grin is easy. A small measure of relief trickles through me: he is not suspicious. Lighting on the Khatun, who watches me grimly, his eyes shine with pleasure. "Well done, Shaherazade! You have found my wife!" As though I have pulled off a particularly daring *shataranj* maneuver.

Smiling weakly, I murmur, "Yes," and rush into the hall, away from these trapdoors. Behind me, the Malik and Khatun laugh. I do not know at what.

It was a dream. It was a dream.

I wind up the Fire Tower and burst onto the rampart. Mountain wind cools my brow. I wish the sun's glare would scorch my memory. I try to fold away what I have seen, to press it into a tight bundle, seal it in a box, tie it with a cord, and tuck it away in the dark creases of my mind.

I open my eyes to a blue sky above and the earthen warren of the town of Bam below—its bazaars, mosques, and madrasas, the verdant cotton fields and pistachio groves rimming the town's walls, the Jebal Barez Mountains and desert beyond.

Then, like a knife, a fear darts through the dark and cuts my careful packaging: What if the Malik finds out? What if he discovers his wife's unfaithfulness, learns that I knew of it and, like an accomplice, concealed it? I gulp down ice-cold panic and begin wrapping the memory away again, more tightly than before.

TWO

Morning sun spills through lattice shutters like clarified butter, warming my freshly bathed skin. With a surreptitious glance at Gulnar, my maid, I slip into a tunic to hide the plum-colored bruises left by the Khatun's rings. Despite concerned probing by Dunya and Baba, I have managed to keep the Khatun's secret for more than a week, but it squirms in my stomach like a cat in a sack.

I sit on a floor cushion, a clouded silver mirror propped before me. As Gulnar plaits my hair into dozens of fashionable braids, a knock sounds against the door.

"Come in!"

Baba swoops in. "*Kafi*," he says to Gulnar. She bows her head and departs.

My father sits behind me and begins expertly weaving my hair, parting and combing and twining. Closing my eyes, I remember the months after my mother's death when I would allow only him to touch my hair as she had. His fingers still retain the old skill. My throat grows hot with memory.

"O Baba, don't! You'll ruin your fine suit!" My father, in readiness for court, is garbed in the finest of fulgent blue linen, which glistens like silk.

The mirror reflects his smile. "Shaherazade jaan, you have been avoiding us. What is the matter?"

I meet my father's gaze in the mirror and see in it a profundity of understanding and kindness. I cannot meet it for long. "Baba . . . I have a secret," I whisper into my lap.

"Can you not tell me?" he asks patiently, selecting another lock and splitting the strands in three.

"I'm afraid, Baba."

His fingers tighten on my braid. "Of what?"

I pause. As much as I long to unburden myself, this knowledge is combustible, a chimera of Greek fire. "I can't tell you." My fingers lace tightly in my lap.

He looks at me with patient, world-weary eyes. "Is there anyone you can tell, jaanem?"

Thinking of Shahryar, I flinch. It is a heavy burden to deliver heartbreak, especially when the Malik has lost so much already. "No, Baba."

"Now that is untrue," Baba says to mirror-Shaherazade.

My reflection arches an eyebrow.

"Pray on it, Shaherazade. When we mortals can find no counsel among our own, it is to Allah we must turn." Finishing the last braid, he rises and dusts his brightly striped trousers. "I must meet with the Malik, but I will pray that Allah helps you find a solution." He stops before the door. "Know this: so long as I am here, you have nothing to fear. My attention is always yours."

My smile, put on for Baba's benefit, dissolves as he departs. The secret sinking in my bowels, I turn my choices like a silver dirham. The Khatun is a sinner who threatens my family and betrays a husband who would pull down stars to weld a diadem for her hair if she asked. She deserves no protection. And if I am discovered as an accomplice to her treason? She can damn me but she cannot protect me, not then. I would be a fool to place my life in an adulteress's hands.

I drum my feet. From a chest, I retrieve a leather-bound book, *The Incoherence of the Incoherence*, assiduously calligraphed in Córdoba and shuttled along routes through the Maghreb and Cairo and Jerusalem and Baghdad to sit in my hand in Bam. I brush my fears away. Nothing will happen. The Khatun will stop, the Malik will never discover her, she will never tell him. No one will ever know I was involved.

Unless . . .

Unless I am not the only one who has discovered her. Unless there's a cabal of servant girls and sweeper boys who have encountered Fataneh and whom she has bullied into silence. But that silence can break, an egg dropped from a nest, and the secret can spread, quick and viscous. What did she do with her lover? Rip off his head like a spider finished with its mate? *The Incoherence of the Incoherence* slips from my hand and falls open, red and black ink swirling across its pages.

"Are you well, little Shaherazade?"

I leap up. The Khatun leans against the doorjamb.

"Yes, O Khatun, thank you for your concern." I try to shrink myself and pray that Gulnar will return to disrupt whatever game the Khatun has come to play.

Her slanted green cat's-eyes watch me, a mouse struggling in her paws. She taps a finger, the nail stained ocher with henna, against her lip. "I have not forgotten my promise, O *dokhtar-e-vizier*. I have thought—why should you not marry the Malik's brother? You would be a second wife, but he *is* the Malik of Samarkand. Believe me, Vizier's Daughter, I keep my promises."

She is so close that I can smell her attar of roses, the cloves on her breath. "Have you lost your tongue? Why don't you speak? Or have you already spoken?"

Sharp tiles dig into my back. I wish the wall would turn to vapor and let me slip through. "I do not know what you speak of, ay Khatun, but I have said nothing."

She pinches my cheek. "*Shad bash*. You will like Samarkand, Shaherazade. And we will be sisters, bound by law and blood."

✳ ✳ ✳

Standing on the citadel's walls, I consider the Khatun's offer. Marrying Shahzaman would not be the worst outcome. After his and Shahryar's father, Turanshah, had rebelled, been captured, and ignominiously killed himself, Sultan Toghrul had sent Shahzaman to be fostered by Samarkand's childless malik before I was born. If Shahzaman is anything like his brother, good-naturedly kind and cheerily handsome, I could be happy. This would be a good match, one I would be lucky to make. The sweetness overripens. Why is the Khatun offering me such a prize? At her word, I could be married to some no-name, backwater emir.

She's scared. She's scared of me.

The idea is absurd.

I lean over the crenellated wall toward the excited cries of men below. Across a ground kept verdant by underground pipes, the Malik and his companions play polo, their horses sailing beneath them and the ball zipping between thwacks of their mallets. Town children cheer their Malik as he executes a particularly gallant goal. He grins at them and looks up, catches me watching from my perch. Before I can drop my eyes, he raises a hand to his heart and bows from the saddle. My own heart slides into my stomach, burning all the way.

"What are you looking at?"

"Dunya! Nothing! I was looking for you." Red-cheeked, I wave *The Incoherence of the Incoherence* under her nose. "You didn't enjoy al-Ghazali, but perhaps you will like ibn Rushd."

Ignoring me, Dunya peers over the wall. Her dandelion brocade robe shines against her long black braids. "Oh. The Malik." She takes

The Incoherence of the Incoherence, flips the pages, pausing on this page and that, cocking her head as if in a serious assessment of its arguments, and returns it. "Stop it, Shaherazade. You will make the Khatun jealous."

"Of ibn Rushd?"

"Shahera . . ."

"I don't know what you're talking about."

There was once a boy who could only tell lies. He was not a bad boy, but the truth refused to pass his lips. His teeth would build a dam, his mouth a tight seam, and the truth would stopper behind. Only when lying would his words fly like swallows . . .

"Come to tonight's feast with me. Fataneh is fêting this month's favored poet."

The Khatun is a great patroness of the arts: poets, philosophers, and calligraphers, musicians and artisans. At her invitation, they flock to Bam, filling the citadel with sweet words and strange new thoughts. They say the court in Bam rivals that kept by Sultan Toghrul in Hamadan. But I am not sure I can stand an evening of a poet extolling Fataneh's gazelle gait and lion heart. Confession bubbles on my tongue, but I bite it back. Who would I be to bow my little sister's shoulders with it?

✳ ✳ ✳

With everyone at Fataneh's feast, the citadel is mine for the taking. I walk through the empty halls, lit by sweetly burning olive oil torches that pool shadows in corners, and catch drifts: shivery strains of a tar, the poet's soulful intonation.

I turn away from the great hall and toward another long hall. The faience wall gleams like pearls, and as the din of the party fades, I feel isolated in this shimmering oystershell world.

The Arg-e-Bam has thirty-nine watchtowers for guardsmen to look out for Oghuz raids or caravans of arriving maliks. I enter at the base of the Fire Tower, where once stood a Sassanian temple to their god of fire. Although it is late winter, the air in the tower is warm and dense. Stone stairs, eroded to nubs, scurry to the top. I hitch my robe past my knees and dash upward. My breath heaves, but I open the door to a cool gust and a million silver stars above. In the town below, lamps and candles glitter, a small galaxy itself.

Here, Shahryar's father's atabeg took the corpse of Shahryar's father after his suicide and cut it into forty pieces for his rebellion.

I stand here, at the edge of the citadel's highest point. Soft breaths behind me. The Malik stands at my shoulder. Even in the dim elucidation of stars and lamps, I can tell he is angry: his mouth is rigidly set, his eyes hard, his expression so at odds with his normal cheeriness. That I have wrought this change nauseates me.

"The Khatun has told me what you knew."

"What do I know, O Malik?"

"Of her adultery."

I say nothing. What can I say?

He steps closer and I smell sweat and musk. "Don't worry, Shaherazade. I forgave her. I love her." He caresses my neck and shivers dash across my skin. "But you. You I cannot forgive." His hands close around my neck and stars burst in my eyes.

I slap the wall, and the sting burns away the nightmare. He won't know. He can't know. I will forget this by next week. It will be as if nothing happened.

I descend from the Fire Tower, away from the ghastly ghoul of Shahryar I conjured. Whom do I fear more? Before this evening, I would have said Fataneh. At her best, she is queenly, untouchable. At her worst, she is ice and wrath. And Shahryar? He is sunny and generous, but he grew in the shadow of a father diced like an onion. Where did that settle in him? What did it sprout?

As I wend back to our quarters, drums and laughter ring from the Khatun's feast, although the poet's declamation has stopped.

The Arg-e-Bam is quiet here, away from the tumult of festivities. I am poised to push the door to our wing when I hear it again—a familiar sound. The sonorousness of one voice resonates with me: the poet. *That's imagination.* I hover at the threshold. I cannot follow these sounds again. Did I not regret it the first time? At best, I make enemies of two strangers. Another moan, the woman's this time, and I follow it. *Just a little closer.* I leave my slippers at the door and the floor is chill against my bare feet.

At the far end of the deserted hall, someone has snuffed the torches so only I am illuminated. The breaths louden.

This is quite enough. I retreat as quickly as I came, but all at once, three things happen: I hear the poet cry, "Ay Khatun!" The torch behind me flares and illumines, for the briefest moment, the Khatun encircled by the poet. The Khatun's eyes meet mine.

A fourth thing happens: I know that very soon I will be dead.

* * *

I wake up pillowed by foreboding. It muffles my head, constricts my waist, presses my shoulders down. It stuffs my throat and trembles at my fingertips. My eyes don't want to open. I open my eyes. The sun dances on my face, warm and radiant. I force myself to sit.

She knows. She knows I have seen her doubly. She knows, and the Malik knows nothing. The Malik knows nothing, but I know.

She is an indecent woman. Shameless. An adulteress and a sinner who threatens my family. A woman whose lies deserve to be exposed.

I bolt the door and retrieve a mahogany box of paper from the Papersellers' Street in Baghdad. The paper is skin thin and the sun shines right through. When my tales are especially good, I write them on this paper for Dunya, Baba, and my cousin Laila. Once or twice they have even been parroted to me in the harem as though they were well-known stories of old.

I lay the paper out and dip a reed pen into the bronze inkwell shaped like a lion wreathed in roses and thorns. A present from my mother at whose knee I learned distich after distich of the *Shahnameh*, my mother who always had poetry on her tongue.

The domed lid rings as I replace it. I carefully write:

O Malik-e-Kirman, you would be wise
To wonder if there is more to your wife than you surmise.

I cringe. Verses at which Firdausi would weep. I repeat the couplet a dozen times to taste its rhythm. The pen scratches across paper.

She holds your heart, this is true
But whom does she hold, away from you?

It is not verse for the ages, but it will do. I rewrite it in clean, sloping calligraphy, dotting letters with diamonds. I cut away the message and after the ink dries I roll the sliver around my smallest finger like a ring. After I burn the draft, I collect its ashes in my palm. The soft gray mound trembles as I walk to the window. I blow, and the ash flies past Bam's minarets and domes, its cupolas and crenellated golden walls. Those words are now nothing, the sand of the Dasht-e-Lut, the snow of the Kuhbonan Mountains.

I pull on a deep-necked green gown, edged with thick bands of gold and overlay it with a purple *farajiyya* embroidered with coruscating red and orange flowers. I bind the robe at the waist with a fringed sash. My long trousers trail past my ankles and I crown myself with a diadem, a pear-shaped garnet swinging in the center. The normalcy of the routine distracts from the weight in me.

The hand clutching the note is tight and sweaty. I try to forget where

I'm heading. The hall buzzes with the busy chatter of scribes and sweepers, clerks and cooks, who pass me without a glance.

Two Turkmen mamluks, physical links to our tribal Turkic ancestry, flank the Malik's door. Their helmets rise to domed peaks, and their armor of overlaid iron scales gleams dull silver, like fish slapped and shining on a market stall.

I cannot slip my note to the Malik like this. The guards will not forget that. Then, the fingers will point. *An unmarried girl of a certain age becomes bored, stirs up scandal. The vizier has been neglectful in his duties to see his daughters wed. Nineteen and unwed, ay Khoda.*

I turn away.

✳ ✳ ✳

I carry the paper for four days, until it is as soft as linen and the script is blurred from rolling in my nervous palm. Yesterday, unseen, I watched Fataneh walking the gardens hand in hand with the Malik and the sight filled my mouth with the taste of soured milk. But she avoids me, and this quiet is more frightening than her threats.

For the second time, I approach the Malik's door.

The mamluk on the left smiles. His teeth are crooked and gapped. During battle, chain mail veils their faces, but while guarding the Malik's quarter, their faces are bare. *Shamshir* blades hang at their sides, shields strapped across their backs.

"Shaherazade Khatun." He and his companion bow their heads, their chain mail jingling like tambourines.

Beginning to unfurl the paper from my finger, I smile. "Is my father in the Malik's chambers?"

"The Malik is not in his quarters."

"Oh." *What if Fataneh sees this paper before the Malik?* "Is the Khatun within?" I hope I sound guileless but the question feels strange in my mouth, sounds strange on the air. The paper hangs loosely in my hand and fear of the Khatun sticks in my mind, a thread too thick to pass through a needle's eye.

"Is all well?"

I force myself to raise my eyes. "Yes, yes."

The guards do not notice the hollow waver in my throat.

"Do you know when the Malik is expected back . . . so that I might know when to expect my father?"

"The Malik will be back in two hours, after he prays Zuhr in the Congregational Mosque. He will lunch in the great hall. As is always done."

Right.

"And Fataneh Khatun?"

"In the evening."

And then, the impossible seems possible.

They need to be distracted. I could pretend to see an intruder or . . . "Have you heard the tale of the guardsman who became a caliph?"

When they do not stop me, when they wait expectantly, I speak.

"It is said by those who know and Allah knows best, that in Baghdad, the City of Peace, where djinn act as humans and if you are not careful . . ." My throat feels dry. I try not to think of how much depends on this. I try not to imagine the mamluks laughing me and my tales away, the Khatun appearing over my shoulder like a djinn. I swallow and press my hand against my fluttering heart. ". . . and if you are not careful, your soul can be stolen from you on the street, lived a humble guardsman named Rais."

The paper is hot in my hand.

"Rais was a wise and honest man. When he returned home every night from his day of guarding the Caliph, he would find men and women waiting to hear his judgments on their quarrels.

"The Caliph was unlike Rais in every regard. He funneled money meant for the poor, for their mosques and madrasas, toward maintaining his harem and palaces. He levied tax upon tax so that he and his companions could dine richly on lamb and drink deeply of wine. But to Rais, it did not matter whether the Caliph was good or bad. He had sworn to protect the Caliph, and protect him he did.

"Every year, the Caliph processed through Baghdad to bathe in his subjects' adulations. Playing the magnanimous ruler, he tossed dinars to the crowd, which men and women took home only to discover they were yellowed nickel. This year, however, as the glossy sedans swayed through the usually rowdy streets, the people were silent, their eyes narrow, their faces hollow."

The mamluks are taken. I can see it in their wide eyes and parted lips.

"Rais followed the Caliph, his senses pricking at each corner. The procession did not falter, and if the people were grim, they were also passive. But just as the litters passed under the shadow of the palace, a tall, thin man hurled himself at the Caliph, passing through the guards as though they were mist. He was a Hashashin, one of the secret sect who train in the mountains to kill as easily as breathe and then disappear, like vapor in sunshine."

The mamluks' arms hang loose—a Hashashin could tumble through the window and slice me through and they would notice nothing.

"Rais knew his duty. He threw himself at the assailant, but the man had Shaitaan's luck and Hashashin training. He found that hairsbreadth sliver where Rais's armor was weak and slipped his blade into Rais's heart."

I can still leave. Crumple the paper in my hand, burn it to dust, blow it away. Turn around and leave the secret to fester between Fataneh and me alone. But then—there is goodness and rightness in telling true, in speaking out against wrong.

Ay Khoda.

The paper slips from my fingers and flutters like a feather to the mosaic floor.

"Before the other guards could strike, the Hashashin snaked like lightning and stabbed the Caliph until his gold robes were red as madder."

My robe covers the quatrain.

"—The Caliph's limp body rolled out of the palanquin."

I step closer to the door, the paper dragging behind me.

"Before the guards could capture the Hashashin—"

I raise my robe above my ankles.

"He turned the knife on himself, falling into the bloody heap of three on Baghdad's streets."

Bismillah. I flourish my robe and knock the paper into the space between floor and door. My hands float up, weightless.

"But this is Baghdad, and in this city, humans are not alone. The tumult attracted a passing djinn. He glanced at the Caliph and knew he was dead: no breath whispered, no heartbeat quickened. But he knew something the others did not.

"Rais was alive.

"The gathered guardsmen shivered as the djinn, invisible and incorporeal, slipped between them and hovered over Rais. Rais, who, so near to death, could see dimensions the others could not.

"'I know who you are, Rais ibn Kabir, and I will save you.' The djinn reached into Rais's heart and pulled out something silver that was molten one moment and mist the next. The djinn knew Rais's soul to be good and pure, untainted by the avarice that had marred the Caliph. He floated to the Caliph, raised Rais's soul, and blew it into the Caliph's mouth. His touch sealed the Caliph's wounds as life glimmered in his brown eyes once more.

"In Baghdad, they said the Caliph's brush with death reformed him. He lowered taxes, lived more simply, and founded mosques and schools and foundations for the people. He even invited the slain guardsman's family to live with him, eventually marrying the guardsman's wife, poor as she was. And if the Caliph sometimes spoke late into the night with someone no one could see, what did it matter in the face of all the good he did?

"And that is how a guardsman became Caliph."

The mamluk on the right starts, and the one on the left gapes as though waking from a nap.

I leave the guardsmen, light with relief. Something foreign flushes through me. I struggle to place the feeling until I realize it is *power*, small and startling, this ability to captivate with my tales—and achieve my ends. It sits on my tongue, strange and sour at first.

Slowly, it sweetens.

Three

The muezzin finishes the Maghrib *azaan*, heralding the evening prayer. As yet, I have heard nothing—no rumors rising like steam from the harem or slipping from guard to guard, servant to servant. Instead, I have spent my day curled in bed, pleading an upset stomach and plagued by worry. What if the note were swept away by breeze or broom? What if no one read it? What if the Malik did read it? What if Fataneh found it, read the thin script through narrowed eyes, and knew that I had betrayed her?

I wish I had said nothing.

The Malik holds my furled note, fury and fear twin fires in his eyes. The Khatun stands straight-backed, confident.

"Fataneh jaan, what does this mean?" His wavering voice tells Fataneh that he will believe her denial, for he wants to, more than anything.

"What is this?" She extends her hand. Reluctantly, he drops the quatrain in.

A quiet outrage draws over her perfect features. "I cannot believe that you would believe these lies, azizem."

He lowers his head, ashamed. "I knew it was untrue, but . . ."

Fataneh shreds the note. She takes Shahryar's hand, rubbing his thumb with her own. "I understand. Jealous people will stir fitnah. *And I know who it was—Shaherazade, daughter of your vizier. An envious, hateful girl. An Oghuz agent. Perhaps her whole family is."*

The Malik's face tightens with rage. "Then she will be punished!" He summons his mamluks. "Arrest Shaherazade. And if you must, arrest her father and sister as well."

"Shaherazade!"

The room spins, and I nearly fall off my low bed. Baba stands in the doorway, grim faced. "Gulnar tells me you have been ill."

"I'm fine, Baba." I follow him to his desk where he inspects papers, tucking a few beneath his arm.

"Good, good." He raises his head and I see his weariness. "There's bad business with the Malik. I will be busy tonight. Try to get better. I shall send for a doctor."

"What sort of business?"

But I know. What else could it be? My father has faced wars and famine unshaken, but here he is, sentences no more than bites.

His face closes. "Issues with the Khatun. I must go before the Malik acts . . . rashly. Just . . . keep Dunya safe. And yourself."

Once Baba leaves, I smooth my braids and rise to go to the harem. Since her marriage, it has been Fataneh's domain, a court within a court, where women incubate power and weave plots. If there is news to be had, I will find it there. As I walk through the citadel, it is awash in whispers—the chamberlain hissing with a minister, a clerk talking softly with a scribe. A serving boy dodges past me, almost bowling me over.

"O Shaherazade, have you heard anything from your father?" a minister asks, looking up expectantly from his conversation with the chamberlain. I scurry away.

I arrive at the harem's great wooden doors, which are guarded by two austere eunuchs. Recognizing me, they pull the heavy doors open, revealing a hall tiled in blue and green and thronged with women—cousins and concubines and courtiers. The hall is warm with their breath and their bodies, despite the spraying fountain and slaves slowly waving fans. I recognize Hanna, a councillor's daughter, head bent close with other noblewomen. Spotting me, she stretches out her hand.

"I heard that the Malik's mamluks came to the harem an hour ago," Hanna says. "To bring the Khatun for questioning."

I cannot believe it. But here it is: my words, knotted into reality.

"Have you heard anything from your father, Shaherazade Khatun?" The questioner is a young noblewoman whose curls fizz in a dark halo.

"He only said there was trouble with the Khatun. Nothing more."

"The Malik found a note," offers a concubine with almond skin and lines around her dark eyes. She sits apart on a peacock silk divan. "Accusing the Khatun of adultery. He went searching for her, this note in his hand."

I choke. "Is it known who wrote it?"

"No, but it sent the Malik hunting: he looked in all the courtyards and gardens and hidden stairwells and corners. Finally, he found her, entwined with a slave, like a pen dipped in an inkwell, just as the note warned." At the responding gasps, the concubine preens with the satisfaction of a story well received, but she is not yet finished. "The Malik ran the slave through with his shamshir."

"And Fataneh Khatun?" My voice is little more than breath.

"She begged for mercy and is now locked in a cell."

***

Dunya and I sit across a checkered shataranj board. She moves her alabaster vizier and my granite chariot scoops her up. It is almost midnight. Baba has not returned, and we have had no word of Fataneh

Khatun's fate. Dunyazade and I are not the only ones awake—outside, lamps still shine in the town windows, small fires burning.

"What do you think deserves to happen to the Khatun?" Dunya's fingers, nails shiny and pink, little half-moons peeking at the beds, dance over the pieces' heads—elephant, horse, foot soldier—before pushing the elephant diagonally.

What deserves to happen to a woman who was so reckless? An adulteress. Who did not stop after being caught once, after being caught twice?

My stomach clenches as I tap one foot soldier and then another and then skip my elephant across the blocks. "Mercy will make him look weak."

And this is not an empire founded on mercy. Mothers put out their princes' eyes, sultans poison wives, and atabegs force maliks to spin to their command.

"Will no one speak for her?" Dunya's horse checks my shah and I cannot move him without placing him in checkmate.

I'm killing her.

But what can I say? The Malik has more than my note: he has the sight, the smell of the Khatun with her lover. He will transpose her sin on every dark corner of the citadel until his last days.

I knock my shah over in surrender, send him clattering to the floor.

∗ ∗ ∗

Gulnar is trying to rouse me with a hot glass of tea; my eyes open reluctantly. I still feel the soft edges of my dream.

"Wake up, Shaherazade," Baba whispers.

"Che?"

"You need to get ready, jaanem."

What is it? The question emerges a mumble.

"The Malik has decreed that the Khatun will be executed this morning. She demanded that you attend, and the Malik has granted her wish.

I could not dissuade him. He would not even grant her a trial. Get Shaherazade ready, Gulnar."

The door closes and Gulnar, still in her simple cotton sleeping tunic, pours a pitcher of cold water into a ceramic bowl. Washing my face, I feel a chill.

He is doing it.

Gulnar hastily weaves my braids and fastens a misty veil to my hair with a pearl diadem. Wrapping me in a squirrel-lined overmantle, she binds my gray robe with a deep-crimson sash: dawn gray, bloodred.

"Courage," Gulnar whispers in Oghuz as I follow Baba.

It seems that the entire citadel—from clerks to concubines—waits at the Fire Tower's base. Baba guides me inside with a hand on my shoulder. Behind us, the murmurs swell as the crowd realizes that I am joining him. We emerge into the cold morning at the tower's top. Thin white light illuminates the crenellations. I can puzzle out the faint outline of the still-sleeping city, the Cimmerian luster of desert and mountains at the horizon.

Winds buffet the veil across my eyes, glazing the raised platform and the councillors, administrators, and bureaucrats a gauzy gray. The Malik stands beside the executioner, his hands folded grimly behind his back. I grip Baba's hand.

The tower door swings open and Fataneh emerges, flanked by two guards. Clad in a white-and-silver robe, she holds her chin high. The light of the ascending dawn haloes her hollowed cheeks and shadows the sullen half-moons under her lashes.

I look for Shahryar to soften, but his gaze is unflickering, unfocused. He does not see her. He refuses to see her. Fataneh's back stays straight. She is unveiled, and her hair has been swept up to ease the executioner's work. Her pulse bobs in her throat, a white sail in a white sea.

She stands before the block. Her hands are untied, and she stares above the crowd, into farmland and sky. For a moment, her eyes meet mine and I wish that the floor would open and ricochet me past the stairs, away from her. Then she looks away, as if I am no one at all.

"By Allah, I swear that I have seen you commit adultery." The Malik repeats the oath four times. "I take upon myself the wrath of the Almighty if I testify falsely. Will you deny it?"

She says nothing.

The air petrifies.

"Then you are guilty of fornication, adultery, and treason," the Malik intones. "The punishment for these crimes is death."

I expected some tremor of emotion, some evidence of the love he had borne for Fataneh, but there is no hint that he is destroying his beloved. As if he had never said, *Is she not the fairest woman, the kindest, the sweetest, the gentlest in the land?*

As if she is nothing to him.

"Kneel," he commands, cold and flat.

She folds to her knees like a step in a dance. She bows her head, closes her eyes, and waits. The call for morning prayer, the muezzin's husky proclamation, otherworldly in its power to summon men and women to face their Creator, binds us together, shatters the stillness. I half think that she will beg him to spare her life, send her into exile, remember his love for her. But she remains kneeling, her head bent over hands cupped in prayer.

As the azaan fades, the executioner swings his scimitar. For an infinite second, the steel blends with the low clouds. Despite Baba's heavy hand on my arm, I cannot look away. The blade slices through her skin and then her flesh. I hear the hard grinding of metal against bone, flinch as the blood sprays, like a fountain in a garden courtyard, and finally gape as the still-limpid green eyes stare from the basket. Her body crumples over the block, the white-and-silver robe crimson with her warm, fresh blood.

I bury my head in Baba's warm shoulder. I have done this. I wrote four lines and took a woman's life. I try to remind myself that she was a sinful woman who deserved this end.

Inna lil-lahi wa inna lahi rajioon, To Allah we belong and unto Him we return.

The Malik's lips move with the same prayer. He closes his eyes. Opens them. Looks at my father. "And now, Vizier Muhammad!" My blood chills at his cheer. "Let's begin the search for my new wife!"

Four

◇◇◇◇◇◇

The Malik's strange new mood pervades the citadel. When I glimpse him, he is sharp and bright and brittle, with a smile wider than ever and eyes that glitter hard.

Two weeks have passed since Fataneh Khatun was toppled.

And the people of Bam? They mourned their Khatun, despite how she was found. They mourned her for her generosity, for the mosques and madrasas she established, for her patronage of musicians and poets and artists. They mourned her despite Shahryar's rage, draped their homes in black, beat their chests in grief until Shahryar sent soldiers to silence them, to rip crepe from doorframes, to scratch Fataneh's name from the mosques and madrasas she had held in trust. A poet Fataneh had patronized wrote a quatrain in her honor that circulated among the townspeople.

Two days ago, Shahryar's soldiers crucified him before a furious crowd.

Fires have been set near the citadel; one burned even in the gardens, crisping roses and hyacinths to ash. Last night, someone set an abandoned shop ablaze, the conflagration erupting into a flaming tower that lit the city a hellish red.

Baba has demurred and promised to comb through Persia and Arabia and India looking for a suitable bride. But the Malik is impatient, and his clerks drew up a list of the men of Kirman who are most in debt and have comely daughters. To these fathers, the Malik offered relief for their debts and the honor of becoming the father of the next Khatun. Fathers with connections at court balked, but the most desperate opened themselves to the Malik's terms. His clerks visited each house and finally, on this balmy night, they are returning with the woman destined to be the Malik's next wife.

I lower the hand-painted cards with which we have been distractedly playing, as the high music of flutes pipes through our window. Dunya's eyes widen, and our friend Mahperi piles her cards on the table, tapping and sorting until they are evenly aligned. We rush to the window to see what we can in the dim torchlight. A small procession of horses flickers through, and an old palanquin, in a style popular when my mother was wed, bobs on the wide back of a brown horse.

"That must be her," I whisper.

"What will happen to her?"

Mahperi forces optimism through tight teeth. "Perhaps the Malik will love and cherish her. He is doing a good thing in helping her father meet his debts."

Neither Dunya nor I respond, and even Mahperi lets the hope die as it leaves her lips. The Malik may love her, it is true. The moon may split in two and fall like a star.

✴ ✴ ✴

The bride, Altunjan, has been brought, and now the duty falls to the citadel's women to surge into the harem and prepare her. Forced merriment stalks the torchlit halls. Musicians play flutes and drums, and although the music is meant to sound joyous, it feels ominous. The girl has no mother; one of Shahryar's aunts stands guard as the Malik's concubines, female relations, and noblewomen bind the bride's hair with jewels, adorn her hands in henna.

Altunjan sits in the center of the harem, arms outstretched, fifteen years old but possessed of utter calm. Even as sweat beads her face, her black eyes remain still. I hold her hand to sweep the wet, green henna paste across her palm, and feel her heart racing.

Gesturing for a maid bearing a silver tray, I take a cool glass of pomegranate nectar and bring it to her lips.

"Mutashakaram." Her voice is coolly melodious, the kind of voice a storyteller would wish for. The pomegranate stains her mouth red.

"What is your name?"

"Shaherazade, O Khatun."

The henna we had striven to save smudges between her fingers as her hands tremble. "I am afraid, Shaherazade," she says softly so that the other women, least of all the Malik's aunt, cannot hear. "I fear that . . . something will happen to me. Like Fataneh Khatun."

I wipe the smear from her soft palm and meet her great oryx eyes. Hold them. What can I say to this girl that would be both true and comforting? I feel anger rise at her father who would trade her for dinars, at the Malik who tears a girl from her home, and at all of us who swarm around her like bees but do nothing to guard her against the dark spirit that moves in the Malik. But I say, "You have nothing to fear. Fataneh Khatun was a bad woman. She was proud and foolish. Be kind to him and he will be kind to you." I smile. I hope. "There. Now, how does the henna look?"

She examines the intricate pattern that blooms like a flower in the center of her palm and climbs like vines over her fingers. "It is beautiful. Mutashakaram."

***

Through the hazy blue of my dream, I feel hands on my body.

I bolt upright. Dunya materializes, perched at the foot of my bed.

I press a palm to my racing heart. "Ay Khoda, Dunya. I thought you were an *ifrit*."

"I haven't been able to sleep."

Last night rushes back. Altunjan in the harem, her hennaed hand quaking beneath mine. Altunjan, resplendent in an emerald farajiyya, signing her wedding contract beside the Malik. A surprising, shameful envy mushrooming in me. And among the too-loud guests and frenetic music, the Malik glowing darkly, the farce's black heart.

"I heard noises. A woman weeping."

I feel a chill. "A dream, Dunya." I push open the lattice shutters—stars still prick through the sky, but light lines the horizon, signaling Bam's muezzins to wash their hands and feet and climb spiraling minaret steps to call the azaan.

Dunya shakes her head, unconvinced. "Come with me."

I pull a fur-lined mantle over my tunic and follow. Baba's door is closed, his usual snores silent. I try not to think anything of it.

The torches have guttered out in the night, and Dunya and I slink through shadow to the Fire Tower. Unlike the dawn of Fataneh's execution, no crowd bides.

"See, Dunya? All is well. The Malik would not—" I struggle. "He would not hurt her."

Dunya leans her head heavily on my shoulder. "You're right."

As we turn back, I hear steps. We squeeze ourselves tighter against the wall, stop our breaths.

A pale Shahryar appears.

No.

He strides from the tower, without looking back.

Then, Baba, his face a storm of grief and anger and fear, and something I have never seen before: powerlessness.

No.

I clutch Dunya, suffocate the scream in my lungs.

The black-garbed executioner stomps out. Gingerly, he hefts a basket. In the quiet, I can hear a *drip-drip-drip* onto the flagstones. The drops are red, no, they are black, and each strikes like a drum, rings like thunder.

* * *

Did I lead Altunjan to her death, a lamb to slaughter? I had not known the Malik would execute her, sweeping her to the top of the Fire Tower without even the ceremony of the court in attendance. But I comforted her. I should have seen that the Malik was dangerous, that I had twisted open a bottle and let a *shaitaan* take over his soul. I should have sneaked her from the citadel, into the mountains. Did she curse me as the scimitar whistled toward her neck? Perhaps I did what was best: the Malik would have had his way, and at least Altunjan died in hope.

I knead my stomach. I cannot shake the fear that I have killed not one Khatun of Kirman but two.

It is only hours after Altunjan's beheading—only hours since Dunya and I watched the headsman carry away the girl whose hands I held only yesterday. The Malik has already announced his quest for a new bride. The citadel's halls echo with a dearth of young women. I would wager that if I walked through Bam, I would find marriageable girls being hastily wed or hidden deep in the country.

I wish I could believe that Altunjan was a last violent farewell to Fataneh before the Malik returns to himself.

The sun in the courtyard feels too hot. My diadem clatters to the adobe floor and my veil flutters to a shadowy corner, but I still feel tight. I pull at the neck of my robe until the seams threaten to rip.

I stand at the core of this betrayal and blood. Me and a light-dappled courtyard. With a sharp pen and fine paper, I have wrought blood and madness.

✳ ✳ ✳

The wind catcher whistles and I smell sweet, woody smoke. A low chant, almost musical, vibrates through the air. I cannot discern what is being said. I fly from my bed and open the shutters. My eyes sting. A dark, snaking crowd encircles the Arg-e-Bam. The citadel has been set afire!— but no, it is only the guttering torches held by the crowd in the night. The chants grow louder. *Return her! Return her to us!*

Tonight's bride was a girl from Bam, a *diqhan* girl of the middling land-owning class, found by the Malik's clerks only two weeks after Altunjan's death. Her name is Shideh, and her night with the Malik is not up. Can she hear this?

"Vizier Muhammad!"

My heart stops. The voice is high. A woman's. *Her mother's?* I try to spot the speaker, but I am too far and the light too low.

"Vizier Muhammad! Vizier Muhammad! You have daughters! Return us ours!"

I run outside my room to Baba and Dunya who stand at the window. He eases his arm from Dunya's shoulders. "I must go."

"They know us," Dunya says after Baba departs.

It is a cold thought.

Baba appears on the ramparts with two mamluks. The throng is thick and angry, as if all of Bam rises to demand Shideh Khatun's return. Baba has drawn a stately kaftan over his sleeping tunic and the silver spangles spark in the oily light. He holds up a hand, and the crowd falls miraculously silent. "You want your daughter, Shideh Khatun, returned. You say I have daughters and implore me with their names on your lips. For them, and for your own daughter, I will go to the Malik and beg him to return her."

Jubilant cries fill the night, but even in the twisting shadow, I can tell Baba is not optimistic.

Dunya voices the fear that twinges in my chest: "Do you think it is dangerous for Baba to intervene?"

I lean on the window ledge. "Baba is a good man. He must do as a good man does. And . . . and by doing so, he tells the people of Bam that they have an ally. He is giving them hope."

"And if he fails to deliver?"

I sigh. "I don't know."

Baba has returned to the ramparts. I calculate—he has not had enough time to reach the Malik's chambers. Dunya and I grasp hands and suddenly the ramparts are bright, as though a hundred stars twinkle on the walls. The Malik strides forth and pushes forward a woman—Shideh Khatun, who wears pearls in her black hair and bridal robes of gold. She trips against the train but catches her balance with outstretched arms.

"Is she crying?" Dunya asks, and I think I see the sheen of tears on the Khatun's cheeks. I cannot bear the desperation in her mother's face, the fear in Shideh Khatun's. What did her mother do when she learned that her husband had sold Shideh's life to pay his debts? I draw a sharp breath. In her place, I would have murdered him.

"Take her," the Malik announces. "I am not a monster."

I feel a swell of relief. He remembers himself. The madness is over, and he is once again the kind and kingly Malik of my childhood.

But then he continues.

"Take her tonight. But these mamluks will come with her and they will return her in the morning, for I am the Malik and she is my wife and I may do with her as I please." He kisses her cheeks and pushes her again, gently this time, toward the steps. A cloud of mamluks follows as she descends into her mother's arms. The townspeople do not cheer their victory, but they retreat and douse their torches, leaving the ramparts dark once more.

But I lie awake until night deepens into dawn and the earliest rising birds begin their song, unable to erase the sight of Shideh Khatun's terrified face, the warm, trusting feel of Altunjan's hands between mine, the memory of writing the note revealing Fataneh Khatun's sins, and my satisfaction at successfully slipping it beneath the Malik's door under the cover of a story. Two—perhaps three—women are murdered because of me. How many more unless the Malik is stopped?

Five

◇◇◇◇◇◇

Shideh fled into the countryside, guarded by her two brothers. The Malik's mamluks captured them, imprisoned her brothers, and returned to the Malik his recalcitrant bride. But townspeople, armed with stones and knives, confronted the soldiers bringing Shideh back. The soldiers killed two citizens outright and, at the Malik's order, strung them up to fester on the walls. Shideh was executed the next day. I did not attend, but the wailing from the town rose to my room. That night, more of Bam burned.

As Bam burned, I plotted.

Tonight, servants lay a *pilau* of rice baked with meat, *kofteh*, fried fish, juices of pomegranate and citrus sprinkled with saffron, fruits chilled on ice, and honey-sweet *halva* onto the brocade tablecloth in our wing. At my gesture, they retreat, leaving my family to dine in private with Ishaq and his daughter, Hanna. Ishaq is one of the Malik's most-favored councillors, a Jew, and my father's closest friend.

Bald pate gleaming, Ishaq reaches for the plate of fried fish I push before him. "Now, Muhammad, you know this is my favorite; and the halva! The kofteh! Am I being bribed? Is this politics or friendship?"

"He has barely eaten in the last few weeks," Hanna whispers to me. I notice the dark circles under Ishaq's jovial eyes.

"My friend, the invitation was not mine but Shaherazade's. You will have to ask her," Baba says with a smile.

"Well, Shaherazade jaan, which is it?"

I bite my lip. But I don't want to seem an uncertain girl. My mouth firms. "Politics."

Chuckling, Ishaq claps his hands in anticipation. He turns to my father. "O Abu Shaherazade, what is brewing in your daughter's mind?"

Baba gives me a sharp look. "The politics, like the invitation, are entirely hers."

"Go on."

I straighten. Take a breath and recite my prepared speech. "How long will the Malik be able to rule if he continues to behead new brides? He has already taken two. Each time he beheads a bride, Bam revolts. On warm days, we can smell the crucified corpses on the walls.

"Sultan Toghrul cannot help the Malik. He fights the Khwarezmids and his own atabeg for his freedom. And if the Khwarezmids or Oghuz hear of the unrest in Bam, they will pluck it as easily as a cherry. Another Seljuk ruler eating himself alive. Will the town stand with him? How long before his soldiers, tired of fighting their own neighbors, mutiny?"

Ishaq gathers a piece of fish, the meat white and flaky at the edges, with his fingers. "What do you propose?"

I draw courage from the serious way Ishaq regards me. "To stop the revolts, the Malik must stop beheading brides. To stop beheading brides, the Malik must stop marrying. To stop marrying, he must either remain unwed *or* remain married to one woman."

"Good thing the Malik has never been one for polygyny," Dunya whispers to Hanna.

"Both your father and I have attempted to persuade the Malik to those ends. He has failed to be convinced."

"It is easy to say what should be done," Baba adds, "and difficult to make sure it is."

Stung, I reply, "You failed to include the Malik's brides in your machinations. He wed girls who could not resist him."

"Those women were entirely in the Malik's power," Hanna says. "You cannot blame them."

"I don't, but a girl with support, who can maneuver—and plan—could break the Malik's cycle. She may even be able to bring the Malik back to himself."

"And who will be the bride to do this?" Ishaq asks.

Dunya squeezes my hand.

"Me."

"Shaherazade!" Baba exclaims. "This foolishness has gone on long enough." His voice softens. "I understand the desire to act—these are dark times—and it is brave and honorable of you, but this is madness."

"Baba, who better than me? I am not a young girl who has never left the countryside. I grew up in the Arg-e-Bam. You are not some debtor with no influence over the Malik—you are his most trusted vizier. We are not a family with no friends. I know Amu Ishaq will aid us, will you not?"

Ishaq pales. "Shaherazade jaan, I am always your servant, but . . . but you don't understand what you are risking. Even if you have support, what is your plan?"

I draw a breath. "I will tell him tales." I swig from the saffron-laced quince *sharbat*. Ice chips burn against my teeth.

No one speaks.

"On my wedding night, I will begin a story, but cut it off at dawn. I will tell him that the resolution will have to come the next night. So I will continue, night after night, wrapping him in tale after tale, until curiosity lulls his bloodlust, until stories of honor and goodness and bravery return to him his humanity."

"What if he demands that you finish the tale right then?" says Baba. "Or if the tale fails to catch his interest?"

Yes, what then? What happens if I am not as talented as I had hoped, if the guardsmen's interest in my tale was a fluke, my father and sister's praises a product of love? The blind bravado sheltering my scheme begins to slip.

"We turn a few of the Malik's servants our way," Ishaq offers. "Should it appear that Shaherazade's stories are not catching the Malik, we can smuggle her out."

"We would all have to leave," Baba says.

"How can you *still* continue to advise the Malik, Baba?" Dunya asks.

Baba sighs heavily. "You girls don't understand. I have cared for him since he was a boy. He is as a son to me. If I did not love him, I would have left him after he killed Altunjan."

"Don't you miss the man he was, Baba?" I say.

"With all my heart."

"Then give me this chance. We will not rush into it. We can decide on the kind of tales the Malik will enjoy. Amu Ishaq can make arrangements for our escape, if that time comes. I am not a martyr, Baba. But I must try."

"The allegiances of servants can change," Dunya says.

Dunya! I punch her knee beneath the low table.

"Yes, what happens then?" Baba sounds relieved, shaken of temptation. "What happens if the servants fail to do their duty?"

Dunya returns the punch on my knee. "Servants may prove disloyal, but I could attend Shaherazade. I could help prompt her storytelling, and if the Malik were displeased I could slip away and inform you."

My little sister, my protector.

Baba buries his face in his hands. "Instead of one daughter, you suggest I send two?"

"Who better to protect one of us than the other?" Dunya says.

"You two are all I have in this world."

My chest tightens, and I reach for his hand. Dunya grasps his other. One imagines bureaucrats with hands soft from soft living, but Baba's hands are firm with work. I don't think he has had a full day of rest since he was a small child.

"Baba, I will be safe. You and Amu Ishaq will keep Dunya and me safe. I vow to you, by Allah, I will not die at the Malik's hand."

My father lets me read the displeasure, grief, and fear carved into his fine wrinkles. Lets me see how old this conversation has made him.

"I will think on it. I can promise no more."

✳ ✳ ✳

Two days ago, at the top of the Fire Tower, the Malik executed a third new bride named Inanj. The night before, Inanj had sobbed through her wedding as her guests stood silent. The Malik did not spare his weeping wife a glance. The afternoon of Inanj's execution, townspeople clashed again with soldiers, leaving injured on both sides.

The longer Baba stalls, the more my resolve slips. Perhaps that is what Baba wants. But I refuse to be lulled into forgetting that I took the first step toward this destruction. And I can imagine how it will be if I spin the Malik's soul out of occultation: his kindness and good humor unearthed and shining once more through the citadel, his fingers surreptitiously sweeping over my neck, sending charges down my spine, our eyes so full of love that we drown those around us with it.

I find Baba in the citadel's library, a book open in his lap. I shut the door.

"Durood, Baba." I kneel and peek at the book's leather cover. "Ibn Fadlan's travelogue? I haven't read that yet. Is it any good?"

"I can hardly think on it."

"Oh, Baba."

He snaps the book shut and it spits air back at him. "The Malik has two new bridal prospects. He asked me to help choose. I suggested he look to the country for his new wife, since his last two were from Bam. He asked for names. I told him I would reflect and provide them tomorrow."

Me.

It heats my ears and my lips. Let me do all that I have promised. But standing at reality's precipice is different from proposing it. Is it craven to say no? Will Baba be happy to have me safe, or will he be disappointed that his daughter is a coward? His daughter a coward and the man he loved as a son mad, a fine legacy for Vizier Muhammad.

"Don't do it, Shahera."

He pleads but does not command. Is it because he knows as well as I that a mad Malik, with a pile of dead girls at his feet, endangers Kirman? That no one will fight for him when the Oghuz or Khwarezmids come for him, as they have for every other Seljuk ruler? That worse, his own people may rebel? Persuasion has not worked, and murder has not cooled his ire. Perhaps he could be assassinated or imprisoned—but Baba would never do that. If Baba refuses, someone else will. And those who resist coups do not live long.

"What other way is there?" I ask.

He cannot think of one and neither can I.

Even so, I cannot say it. "Give me the night, Baba. To think on it."

Baba clasps my cheeks and kisses my forehead, his mustache bristling at my hairline. "You don't have to do this. You are more precious to me than all of Kirman."

Yet, I do not think that a whole province, full of people, is more precious than one life, even if it is mine.

* * *

Lukewarm water from the ablution fountain runs over my right hand thrice and my left hand thrice. I splash it on my face and swirl it in my mouth. As the water slides to my elbows and washes the dust off my feet, I hear crickets sing. If I tilt my head and stare at the sky, creamy with stars, I can lose myself in sight and sound.

There is a ritual, a teaching of the Messenger, a prayer to beg the Creator's guidance on the eve of a great choice. Wet footprints trail behind me as I walk to my bedroom. I spread a red prayer mat with a dark-blue center westward, toward Mecca. I cup my hands against my face and smell brackish water mixed with the ambergris of my morning's perfume.

Ay Khoda, I seek Your counsel, for verily, You are the knower of the Unseen. Ay Khoda, if you know that wedding the Malik is good for me, for my religion, for my family, for Kirman, for the Malik himself, then decree it for me, bless me with it, and make me satisfied.

I drop my hands to my breast and murmur the Arabic prayers my mother taught me. Once finished, I unpin my veil, extinguish the lamp, and wait to dream.

* * *

I see Baba in the morning.

"I dreamt of your mother and she told me to forbid you."

"I dreamt of Mama and she told me I must."

Baba's mouth is hard, his eyes drawn, and I wonder, is that truly what the Mama in my dream meant. But I awoke determined to stanch this flow of blood and I cannot permit doubt to couple with weakness and breed inaction. "I must, Baba."

He leaves without a word.

* * *

I leaf through *Travels to the Volga Bulgars*, which Baba left last night. Although I am almost halfway through the travelogue, I cannot recall a single incident. Baba enters the library, ashen.

His voice shakes. "I nominated you, Shaherazade."

I bury my head in my hands, and the book thumps to the ground. *It is done.* Now that it is done, now that it is real, I do not think I ever wanted it. I do not want this. But it is done. I have done it. I must do it.

"I nominated you, Shaherazade.

"How could you make your own father, the one man in Kirman who could protect his daughter, send her to slaughter?" He kneels before me, and tears drip to his cheeks like dew. "Before I offered your name, I asked if he would keep his next bride safe. He demanded the name and I gave him yours. I asked if he would treat you gently, if not for your sake then for mine."

"What did he say?"

"He said he would be honored to wed you, to join our lineages."

I feel warm. "O Baba! *Zabardast!*"

He shakes his head. "But he said that for my sake, he would not lie. I tried to withdraw your name, but he would not let me speak further. I did not think—" He clears his throat. "I thought that you being my daughter would be enough to make him stop. Have I not been a father to him?"

My throat aches at Baba's pain and I remember: Dunya and I in a courtyard. In the Arg-e-Bam, soon after Mama's death. Footsteps echoed. Shahryar, with a package. His teenage cheeks still rounded at the apples like a child's, his eyes warm, voice hesitant, half expecting a rebuff. I remember swelling with the desire to wrap my arms around this fatherless boy-malik's neck and press my child-soft cheek to his.

He sat cross-legged and produced a circular board with quadrangles of ivory and obsidian and divided into five concentric circles. The black-and-white squares against the courtyard's blue-and-white tiles created a dizzying whirlpool. A game, a Byzantine variant of chess called citadel. Patiently, he taught us its vertigo-inducing rules. Gifted us the board and pieces, a present for two motherless girls, and played with us for months and months, letting us best him, laughing at our delight.

Can that boy be so gone?

"Baba, I promise, I will be fine." I wrap my arms around him and wish it were true. "You and Dunya will keep me safe. You are the only man in the province who could winkle his daughter from underneath the Malik's nose."

"We can set you free now, Shahera," he says urgently. "The majordomo has been given two weeks to plan the celebrations: we can orchestrate an escape in that time."

I cannot let such weak thoughts grow. Not while I might still prevail. "Do you think he has really gone mad, Baba?" The Malik does not seem taken by madness—madness is hot and swirling, while the Malik is cold and far.

"*His* father, Turanshah, went mad . . . What did Turanshah do after his rebellion was lost? Did he let me counsel him to flee with his wife and children deep into Daghestan? No, he met disaster with disaster and took his own life. And so his son creates his own disasters too. This is their family's madness."

"And our family's madness is to try and save these maliks who don't want to be saved. If I were a boy, would I not have grown to be a vizier too?" I imagine: a young boy, a face broader than mine, hair cut short, swaggering around the citadel, the strut of someone entitled to space. "Since I am not a boy, I must be a wife."

Baba smiles hollowly. "Within the year, you will have more power than me, insh'Allah."

"Everyone bends to the will of a Seljuk Khatun."

In every other generation, a wife of a Seljuk malik or sultan rules her husband completely, and through him the land itself. This generation gapes for a Khatun. It was not Fataneh.

Perhaps it will be me.

✳ ✳ ✳

I will never voice my doubts. If I balk, the plot will crumble. And so I remain silent as envoys carry invitations to Seljuk emirs, to Saladin of the Ayyubids, and to the Malik's brother, Shahzaman of Samarkand. However, our messenger to the Great Seljuk Sultan Toghrul III has returned with disturbing news: Toghrul, attempting to gain independence from the commander of his armies, the atabeg Qizil Arsalan, has been imprisoned. The atabeg now reigns in his stead.

In the shadow of the wedding, my father and Ishaq have managed to direct the Malik's attentions to matters of state—to this news of Sultan Toghrul, to the Khwarezmids and Oghuz Turks who skulk in the shadows, sniffing for their chance to take yet another bite of the Seljuk Empire, to Sultan Saladin's pleas for aid against the Frankish assault. If the Malik is less attentive to business than he was before, he is at least beginning to show concern, to see a life beyond Fataneh's betrayal.

It bodes well.

Six

◇◇◇◇◇

On the eve of my wedding, I sit in the harem, surrounded by women. They thrum their tambourines and clap in time with Turkic wedding songs in a celebration that has become rote. There, in the corner, Altunjan, Shideh, and Inanj lurk, phantasmic. Deep in the shadows, Fataneh smirks. *Are you satisfied, Shaherazade?*

My hands shake as Leila, the daughter of my mother's sister, squeezes henna into an elaborate pattern of flowers and crosshatches across my palm. Leila is an incarnation of my mother: large, liquid Persian eyes and a mouth like a rose. Longing for Mama grips me, tight and sudden. I feel the comforting press of her body against my shoulder, the cool silk of her hair tickling my cheek. Whatever my dreams said, if my mother were alive, she would not have permitted me to marry the Malik. There is a reason the heroes and heroines of tales are orphans.

Leila tsks as her line wobbles and I am transported to gilding Altunjan's hands just weeks ago. The henna cracks as my hand clenches.

I could flee now. Dunya sits on my right; I could set her to fly with a message to Baba. Hanna sits in front of me; I could send her with a missive to Ishaq. Leila, with Mahperi's help, could create a commotion, while I slip away to Baba and let him bury me in a wagon carrying baskets of pistachios to Baghdad. I could open a bookshop, visit the library of the Bait al-Hikma when the sun is the hottest and the stores are closed, and listen to street-corner storytellers after the day cools.

I could flee now and leave Baba, Dunya, Leila, Ishaq, Hanna, and Mahperi to bear the brunt of the Malik's wrath. Leave the girls of Kirman trapped in a cycle of marriage and murder. A cycle I started. I refuse to think any further.

A concubine with a wide crimson mouth approaches us. "Shaherazade Khatun, I know it is the place of the women of the harem to entertain you tonight, but I have been asked to put forth this request: Would you tell us a story?"

"A story?"

One of her copper plaits smudges the henna on my hand. She winces apologetically.

Practice before an unfamiliar audience will be useful.

"Very well." I pause, Mama's voice in my ear: *See how Gorgani builds the tale so you weep with Ramin and share Vis and Ramin's love even as they betray each other. Unlock the heart, Shaherazade jaan, and you unlock storytelling.* I try to find a point of inspiration, gauging the interest of my audience. Suppressing the tremble in my voice, I say:

"O my sisters, it is said that in Esfahan there was a young woman wed to a merchant. Her husband was a wealthy man, who traded in fabulous jewels of unbelievable beauty. Emeralds as large as your fist, diamonds that sparkled like raindrops, goldwork so fine that its full sense could be gauged only through touch, rubies that gleamed like the bloodred sun, pearls that outshone the moon. Despite this, he dressed his wife in tarnished silver, for he believed that jewelry of value should be sold to increase his own wealth. And he kept his home bare, believing that wealth should only be poured into investments.

"But oh, how his wife yearned . . .

"Just to hold a piece. To frame it against the sun and watch the colors refract and dance upon her skin. And maybe, oh just maybe, wear it, if only for a moment.

"One afternoon, while her husband caroused with friends at a tavern, Mihri dismissed the servants from the day's housework and crept to the bedroom she shared with the merchant, where he stored the least of his jewels in a chest. The lock was simple, and with a hairpin Mihri toggled it open.

"The jewels were paltry, unremarkable: cloudy sapphires and chipped turquoises, but it was the first time she had beheld such treasure without her husband's oversight. One piece particularly caught her eye: a hollow gold brooch that curled like a leaf, polished aquamarines scattered throughout. A perfectly spherical ruby dotted the center. The gold was light, the gems small and unremarkable. The piece was, in other words, unexceptional.

"Except it was not.

"Breathlessly, Mihri pinned the brooch to her plain cotton robe. Thinking she had heard a step, her head whipped up, but it was nothing. When she looked down again, she could not believe her eyes.

"Her simple blue tunic and faded cinnamon trousers were nowhere to be seen. The dress she now wore was sumptuous. Only the brooch had held steady. Disbelievingly, Mihri stroked the Badakhsani blue silk robe, soft as water, and marveled at the sunshine brocade trousers.

"'What magic is this?' she breathed, but before she could ponder the mystery, she heard her husband's familiar footfall. Panicking, she stripped off her new robe. With the brooch still attached, she folded it into a dusty corner beneath her bed and pulled on another homey robe. At the last minute, she remembered to lock her husband's chest.

"Her husband, who was disinclined to notice her, did not register the glimmer of excitement in his wife's eyes. As was his habit, he ate his dinner, went to his study to review the accounts his clerk had prepared, and went to bed. Mihri, too, fell asleep.

"When she awoke the next day, she thought she was still in a dream. Their room—undressed brick walls, rough-hewn wooden furniture, cushions and rugs of coarse wool—had transformed. Their bed was now a behemoth of delicately carved rosewood, the hangings on the walls were finely stitched silk, and the rugs could have graced a sultan's palace. Humming, Mihri prepared her husband's breakfast. But her peace was short-lived.

"'What devilry has come over our room?' her husband demanded, his eyebrows twisted in anger.

"'How can I know if you don't?' she replied.

"'Why did you not wake me when you saw what had happened?' he asked.

"'I thought that you had done me a kindness at long last.'

"Her words stung, as intended, and her husband blinked, once, twice. Without speaking, he left. As soon as Mihri was certain he had gone, she rushed up the stairs and unfolded the dress. The brooch was still there, and although it looked no different, she recognized its magic. And she waited.

"Just as the Maghrib azaan rang through Esfahan and the sun sank like a gold dinar into the sea, her husband came home and beheld the new wonders that had overtaken his house. The golden touch of the brooch had spread: soft cushions with dancing Damascus embroidery piled on new colorful silk rugs for which their city was famed; even a fish-shaped fountain spouted at the entrance.

"'What is this new bewitchment?' he demanded.

"Mihri shrugged and answered, 'Bewitchment? I call it a blessing.'

"That night, her husband went to sleep with a pensive smile on his face.

"Some mornings later, her husband woke, just as the dawn light touched their new fineries. He jostled her awake. Blearily, Mihri stared at him, but it was his words that drove the sleep from her.

"'Talaaq, talaaq, talaaq.' I divorce thee, I divorce thee, I divorce thee.

"She became, in that moment, a repudiated wife.

"'Karim . . .' she murmured in shock.

"Without looking at her, her husband explained, 'Allah has seen fit to bless me with a fine home, the kind of home I find I deserve. However, you . . . are not the sort of wife to grace a home like this. I have found another, a young, beautiful creature. Her father states that she will enter no house as a second wife. You may take your things and leave.'

"Mihri had seen only twenty years, yet here she was, too old for her husband, ten years her senior. As her husband departed, he instructed, 'Be out of my house by the time I return.'

"She wasted no time in discarding her plain robe and dressing in the new blue one. She pinned the brooch to her gown. Head high, she marched through the dusty streets of Esfahan.

"Her mother welcomed her, and when her father and brothers returned from their butchering business, blood caked so deeply in their fingernails that even the most vigorous scrubbing could not dislodge it, they vowed retribution against her faithless husband.

"But Mihri smiled. 'Just wait,' she counseled. She locked the brooch in a chest and let it appoint her parents' simple home with blue and orange tiles, silk tapestries, and fine Fezzi leather poufs.

"They did not wait long. That *jummah*, the jewel merchant, banged on Mihri's door. Frantic, he asked to see her, but Mihri made him wait until the sun was well past its zenith. As she approached, he took in Mihri's gold and emerald robe.

"'Mihri jaan,' he began, all sugar. He proffered a bag of sweets and another containing fine pearl earrings.

"'What brings you so shamelessly to my home?' Mihri asked.

"Surprised by her ferocity, he answered, 'When I brought my fiancée's father to show him my home, the house was changed. The ornaments, the carpets are all gone. *What have you done?*'

"Quietly, Mihri said, 'I have done nothing. It is you who made me miserable with your miserliness, you whose grasping drove me from my home. It is your punishment, for the magic is in me. It has always been in me. And without me, it cannot exist.'

"The merchant considered for a moment. 'Very well. In that case, I shall marry my fiancée, and she shall be my first wife, and you shall be my second.'

"'You have divorced me triply. You will need my consent again for marriage, and I shall not give it.'

"The merchant shrugged. 'Triply? I divorced you once and I can take you back after a single divorce.'

"'You would lie then?'

"The merchant deflated. 'In all the years we were married . . . you never spoke to me like this.'

"'*You* never spoke to *me*.'

"Lips pursed, the merchant left. Mihri considered the matter settled and herself victorious.

"But it was not so, for her former husband visited her day after day after day, each day bringing gifts more resplendent than the last. The rubies and sapphires she had so admired now graced her arms, her ears. Her home smelled sweet with jasmine and roses, and her family dined on fine food provided by their erstwhile son-in-law.

"First, Mihri ignored him, although Karim tarried in front of her home for hours. Finally, at her mother's insistence, she met him—but only for a few minutes. It felt good to be the one denying favors, and Mihri began to look forward to gloating at these meetings.

"Mihri could not pretend that her former husband's attentions were not flattering. But she knew his intentions, and that kept her feet on the ground and gave free rein to her tart tongue. She ignored the bubble of disconcertion at his smiles at her sauciest replies or his silence about his new fiancée.

"One day, many months after Mihri had moved out of her husband's house, he came to her as was his habit, more regular than the sun. The merchant was downcast, and for the first time, Mihri's heart was tugged. To mask her reaction, she demanded, 'What is it?'

"The merchant sat. He stood. He paced. He counted the veins on his hands, glanced at his curled slippers. Mihri watched, perplexed. Finally, he said, 'Mihri jaan, I know I have done you great dishonor, but I have asked your father's permission once more to wed you, and he has agreed. Now, I ask you for yours. If you say no, I will trouble you no further.'

"'I will enter no house as a second wife.'

"The merchant was confused. 'Second wife?'

"'Yes, second wife,' Mihri snapped. 'Recall why you divorced me!'

"'I am sorry, Mihri, for the hurt I have caused you. The husband I failed to be to you,' the merchant said. 'But I never wed the other girl. I could not when you held the whole of my heart.' His simple words carried the weight of his guilt and the acknowledgment that neglect is its own unkindness. But what truly struck Mihri was that his apology carried no expectation of forgiveness.

"Now, the merchant's confusion was Mihri's. Tears stung her nose. 'Leave,' she commanded. The merchant slumped as he walked away, and Mihri called, 'Come next week.'

"She passed the week in deliberation, kneading and stretching her thoughts like dough. Finally, the merchant arrived once more at her door.

"'If,' Mihri started, her mouth dry. 'If I were to marry you, I will not bring my magic. It shall stay with my parents. You will have to treat me well, with kindness, with attention and care. Only if you accept me as I was, before I brought wealth to you, will I wed you. If not, I will know that your affections have been false and we will part.'

"Mihri's heart felt heavy at the prospect of never seeing the merchant again. She enjoyed, more than she would admit, freely speaking before him and seeing Karim's shocked smile. He was no longer the dour miser she had wed—but she knew it was an act and had girded her heart.

"Karim opened his mouth to answer.

"She closed her eyes.

"'Yes.'

"Mihri could not believe she had heard the word from the merchant's lips.

"'Yes. I have neglected you and from now on I shall treat you with the love and kindness you deserve. *You* are far more than *I* deserve.'

"And so, Mihri wed her husband in a grand wedding he paid for and entered as a bride once more into their now well-appointed home. And no wife was treated better, for in truth, there is no greater treasure for a husband than his wife."

———————

I reemerge from the trance of the story. The visions of Esfahan—the merchant's jewels, Mihri's exultation at adoration, the liquid feel of her robe—fade from my senses.

To my surprise, I see tears brimming, lips quivering.

"That was . . . lovely," the copper-haired concubine says, her throat hoarse. She kisses my cheek. "Mutashakaram for the gift of this story."

The rest of the women follow her lead, embracing me gently with thanks. Their tears are sticky against my face.

And I understand. They are saying their final farewells. They look at me and see a girl who will lose her head, unable to save herself or anyone else. To them, I am already a ghost.

***

I sway in a gold and ruby litter, held high on broad shoulders, as my wedding procession winds from the South Gate of Bam to the hilltop citadel. Holding the rosy tasseled curtains back with shaking hands, I peer at the townsfolk. Despite the mimes and minstrels, the men, women, and children of Bam stand somber. Some shopkeepers have strung festive lanterns above their doors—or perhaps they never took them down. Other arcades stand dark, blackened with ash in protest of the executions. The sight makes my stomach drop. The Malik affects not to see the black archways as he and my father, surrounded by a thick knot of mamluks and the Malik's boon companions, lead the procession. A troop of camels and silver-belled mules, bedecked in Byzantine brocade and bearing silver chests of jewels and silk, jingles behind us. This and vast fiefs and *iqta'* lands are my *mahr*, the bride-gift paid to me by the Malik. The inheritance my family will receive on my death.

None of it feels real.

In the central bazaar, players have tied large bolts of cloth, molded to scatter shadow giraffes and elephants on walls. The delighted laughter of children ripples forth, the first warm sound I have heard all day. Those happy sounds are replaced by the beat of *tombeks* and tambourines as we cross the Chelekhoneh River and pass through the Worm Gate, approaching the citadel.

I clutch at the litter's poles as the men descend to their knees to allow me to step down before the Arg-e-Bam's great gates, where, only a few weeks ago, a mob demanded Shideh Khatun's return. Taking my hand, Baba leads me inside. Dread tightens his eyes and his hand shakes around mine. Musicians trail behind us, each beat sounding increasingly ironic. My violet bridal robes weigh more with each step, until they grow so heavy that I want to sink to my knees and insist that I can go no farther. But this decision was mine, and I will not sully it with cowardice.

Now, in the golden glow of the great hall before the silver-white marital canopy, Baba's grip tightens. He pulls my palm close to his beating heart. His eyes are red with grief. "Do not do this, my child."

To witness Baba pleading cracks me in two, but I choke down my fear. "I must, Baba. You know I must."

I break his hold and sit under the brocade canopy to await my husband.

The smell of good food—saffron-scented pilau, chicken cooked with lemons and fenugreek, lamb roasted with apricots and raisins—makes me queasy. The musicians strum their gut-strung *komuz* and pipe their flutes, while a poet recites his verse about the election of a bird king, compensating for the hush in the hall. I wish they would stop. I wish we could all be silent and let me do this stark, dark thing without masking it in joy.

I recall the glory of the Malik's wedding to Fataneh, the scattered pearls, the Malik's infectious joy, the luminaries in attendance—Sultan Toghrul himself! But who will journey to attend the fifth wedding of a man who has murdered four wives in less than two months? Even the few guests in attendance—the men who run Bam and their richly dressed wives, who have known me my entire life—regard us grimly.

I whisper to Baba, "When will he arrive?"

"The longer it takes, the happier I'll be."

But in response to an unseen cue, the musicians' fingers and hands dart furiously against dulcimer and drum, the quick melody echoing into my bones. I clench my father's hands.

The drums stop.

The Malik enters.

I cannot breathe.

The Malik pauses to embrace his younger brother, Shahzaman of Samarkand, before striding to the dais, ducking beneath the canopy, and seating himself upon his squat ebony throne beside me. How mundane this must be for him. His attention does not so much as waver in my direction. Even in the implacable stillness of his expression, he is arresting. He wears a gold turban-like cap, a *boerek*, over his shoulder-length hair. His crimson wedding coat highlights the black of his beard, even managing to soften his brown eyes. Against all odds, warmth tingles through me and I know myself to be a fool.

"The contract," the Malik commands.

Dressed in sober olive-green robes, the *qazi* steps forward, scroll in hand. With great care, he unrolls the contract on the low table before the Malik. The text is framed by a rendering of an archway, each intricate curve of the stonework painted exquisitely in turquoise and gold. A servant lays out twin bronze inkwells on a plain table. Another puts pens into our hands.

The qazi reads the contract aloud. I receive a significant dower payment from Shahryar upon its signing, and should the contract be terminated "by divorce or death," I, or my father, will receive the remainder of the mahr. Hearing the qazi say *death*, seeing it written in the contract, an all-but-certain eventuality, makes me feel faint. I hope no one notices how the pen trembles in my hand.

The qazi turns to Shahryar. "Are these terms acceptable?"

"Qubool ast."

The qazi addresses my father. "O Guardian, ask your daughter if these terms are acceptable."

For a moment, this spectacle fades. I remember being a girl, pulling out my mother's fine silks and jewels, garbing myself like a bride, and my mother finding me, equal parts amused and angry. When I grew older, I dreamt of a great wedding to a man I loved whose eyes shone like the Malik's, a man with whom I shared a happiness so deep it could not be measured.

I could say no. I could shed my finery and flee. I look at the guests, many with daughters of their own. I think of the townspeople, who watched me today with fearful eyes, and of the ash and fire that foretells mutiny. I think of Baba, so close to the Malik that any harm that befalls the Malik will fall on my Baba just as hard.

Loud enough for the entire hall to hear, I announce, "Qubool ast."

Baba proclaims, "She accepts!" and his voice shakes.

"Sign the contract," the qazi says.

Shahryar leans over the table first, scribbling his name carelessly. What is this to him but the fourth time he has signed such a contract only to sever it within the day?

With the same hand that sent Fataneh to her death, I sign my name.

"*Mubarak,*" the qazi congratulates as he looks at me sorrowfully.

***

As the guests feast, Shahryar distributes robes of honor to notables: my father, Ishaq, and a bevy of emirs and bureaucrats. I can keep nothing down save for a bit of stewed pullet. Baba and Dunya are no better. Shahryar partakes deeply of his food and drink. A chorus of a Turkic wedding song rings out, one I remember from Fataneh's wedding, long ago.

The guests and their falsely hearty congratulations pass in a dim, perfumed blur, until the crowd thins. The Malik, too, has departed, cheered by his boon companions. I am alone with Dunya and Baba.

My legs are unwilling to raise me, to walk me to the Malik's quarters. As I meet Baba's eyes, tears bead on my lashes. "Baba," I wail softly. My speech is fuzzy, my mouth heavy, as if stuffed by a ball of damask. The desperate fear that I have been quelling crushes my chest.

My father pats my head, but he shakes so badly that my teeth are knocked together. Seeing tears in his gentle eyes cracks my heart. "Shaherazade jaanem, azizem, my heart, my liver, my eyes." He wipes my tears with his hands, his retreating fingers inky with kohl. "Do not cry. I will see you in the morning. And the morning after that—" But he chokes, and the rest suffocates in his throat.

Dunya rises and pulls my father and me up. Dipping the sleeve of her new gown in a cup of water, she wipes my cheeks until my grief stains only her dress. I cannot manage to speak as we walk toward the Malik's rooms.

Well-wishers crowd the Malik's door: Leila and Hanna and Mahperi, Ishaq, and even Shahzaman, all but the last smiling at me with purposeful force. Musicians bang tombeks and rattle tambourines with little rhythm, just desperate excitement, as if by pounding loudly enough they can dispel the specter of death. I give Baba a final smile through my tears, like any bride leaving her natal home.

Because I have no mother, Leila breaks off and joins me as Dunya closes the Malik's door, silencing the cacophony behind us with a decisive thud.

Dunya peels away the layers of my wedding finery: fringed green sash, ruby-and-diamond diadem, violet farajiyya of ciclatoun, amaranth tunic of Dimyati brocade embroidered with gold, until I am left in only a fine white chemise.

From having stumbled upon the Khatun, I am perhaps more knowledgeable than other well-brought-up virgins, but my face burns as Leila whispers hurried counsel. "Lie back, that is easiest at first. Put your knees around his hips and try to relax. It will hurt more if you do not relax."

"Will it truly hurt?"

"Oh yes. And you will bleed. But it is not so much pain and it is not so much blood."

Then I recall what happens if I fail in my design and it seems foolish to fear the pain of losing my maidenhead.

"Remember," Leila continues, "that pain and blood are the witnesses of your purity."

"Do you like it?" I think of Fataneh, hiding in corners of the citadel for it, losing her head for it. Surely it cannot be all pain and blood. Or is this for women as war is for men: a source of only pain and blood to which they keep returning for reasons unknown?

Leila smirks, and I remember her ribald and joyous wedding night, crowded with games and laughter. "Then, no. Now, yes."

Dunya, unusually quiet, has finished daubing attar of roses and ambergris onto my wrists, neck, and knees. She buries her face in my braids and we stand together for an endless moment. As she steps away, I lose something.

"Khoda hafez, Shahera. May Allah keep you safe," Dunya murmurs. Leila echoes the blessing and kisses me softly on the forehead. Dunya opens the door, and the sliver is enough to let in the rattling music, the cheers of my friends. The door shuts softly and I am alone.

Sitting on the carved bed, I await my husband. Crushed rose petals release their spicy fragrance into the cool night air. Silver sparks, like metal struck in a forge, bright and combustible, dance through me.

These could be my last few hours on this earth.

The thought is overwhelming. Eyes closed, I breathe deeply and unravel my plaits. As each braid falls apart in my hands, my pulse steadies.

The door creaks, and my heartbeat ricochets once more. There, bigger than I ever realized, stands my husband, Shahryar, Malik of Kirman.

"Salaam." My voice is an embarrassing squeak.

Smoothly, he decants bright red wine into two silver chalices. He offers me the second, but I shake my head. The Malik downs the first glass and then the second. The wine tints his mouth like bright cherries. Too late, I think that wine would have helped in what is to follow.

"Disrobe," the Malik commands, reclining against the pillows.

For a moment, I don't understand. Then, as he waits, I unlace my chemise, letting it puddle around my ankles. Unbraided, my hair falls in crinkled waves about my shoulders. Fan-shaped earrings and thick gold bangles are my only adornments left.

"Stand over there."

With misgiving, conscious of every sway of my hip, the length of my leg, the peaks of my breasts, all exposed for his judgment, I walk to the center of a large indigo rug. The bracelets clink against my arm. Determinedly, I fix my attention on the intricate crimson kilim hanging behind him.

He lazily rotates a finger, and I awkwardly spin. I flush a furious barberry red, but my expression remains immobile. I feel as common as a whore. I wish I were anywhere else.

"Come to bed."

Mouth dry, I return to the bed, folding my legs beneath myself.

He surprises me then by kissing me. His breath tastes sweet, like cloves, and yeasty like wine. I wonder if his lips can feel my inexperience, my uncertainty. Undressing, he presses me back, but he is gentler and slower than I expected. I close my eyes and hold his shoulders and briefly, I marvel that I am touching a man's shoulders, that I am cradling a man's body between my thighs, that all that has been the most forbidden is suddenly lawful. He deflowers me softly, and but for the initial gasp of pain and surprise, I grit my teeth and think, *This is what this is? What men are mad for, what women must at all costs protect?*

At the due moment, he tenses against me, squelches, "Fataneh," and falls into me.

He has burned her clothes, turning dinars of fabric and labor into ether, has melted her jewelry and discarded the gold into Kirman's treasury, has set her books ablaze until the words she loved turned to ash, has taken her head, and yet, he has not been able to kill her.

He rolls over, and I shift so he can see my maidenhead dotting the sheet, the same color as the bridal henna decorating my hands and feet.

My voice barely a whisper, I ask, "Malik Shahryar, may I call my sister to help bathe me?" I wait for him to refuse and leave me truly defenseless. Instead, he flicks his fingers disinterestedly. Taking this as assent, I wrap my robe and call to the mamluk outside. "Please send my sister Dunyazade."

Hovering at the door, I avoid looking at the Malik. Does it matter to him what he intends to do to me tomorrow morning? Take one head tonight and the second with the dawn? Does it matter to him that he called his dead wife's name on our wedding night?

Before I can dwell too long, Dunya barges through, bearing refreshments. Bowing before the Malik, she places the silver platter on the bed. The shining metal obverses his regal features.

I whisk Dunya behind a lattice screen that some thoughtful servant has placed to shield a washbasin. Embracing me tightly, Dunya touches my cheek. "How was it?" she asks quietly. She dips a washcloth into a bowl and squeezes out the lukewarm water before handing it to me.

"Uneventful," I whisper back. As I sponge the blood from my inner thighs, I flinch at the tenderness. I drop the cloth in the bowl and it rusts the water. Dunya helps me slip a gilt-and-white nightgown of Dabiqi linen over my head. I grip her forearms, take a deep breath, and nod.

As we approach the reclining Malik, I ask, "Malik, if it pleases you, may Dunya join us as we eat?"

I hold my breath. *Ay Khoda, let him permit this.*

"She may."

Suppressing a victorious smile, I pour the tea, handing the first cup to the Malik, and then one to Dunya, before pouring a last cup for myself. I drink deeply. Tonight, I will need every ounce of wakefulness.

"Sister?"

"Yes?"

"Would you tell us a story?" Dunya dimples at Shahryar as though he is not the Malik but a boy who can be charmed like any other. "Shaherazade tells such wondrous stories." Her dark eyes are wide and guileless. Dunya can be a force to be reckoned with on the measure of her charm alone.

I drop my voice. "If the Malik agrees." It already sounds huskier, more melodious. Altunjan's harmonious voice trills in my memory.

I meet Shahryar's indifferent eyes for the first time. My anxiety unfurls again, reminding me that I have never been able to string together more than two words in his presence.

He has seen all there is to see of Shaherazade. I attempt an inviting smile although I fear it is more of a grimace.

"Very well."

A shot of success spreads through me. Discreetly as I can, I squeeze Dunya's fingers. My mouth is already dry, but I know my voice will sound strong.

In the Name of Allah, the Most Gracious, the Most Merciful. May my Lord increase my knowledge and untie the knot in my tongue.

I begin to weave for my life.

Seven

I n the Name of Allah, the Most Gracious, the Most Merciful. O Malik, they say—and Allah knows better—that there is a story of past times and past peoples, that is best suited to men of intelligence and understanding. It concerns a boy, a servant in the household of the 'Abbasid governor of Egypt. He was a poor boy, an orphan from the streets, but he was lucky. He had the grace, which many lack, to be thankful for what he had.

"His chief duty in the palace was sweeping the cool marble floors of cavernous, empty halls, and his broom became his partner. Sometimes it transformed into a fair maiden to dance with or a brother with whom he voyaged to fight pirates. His broom even doubled as a sword if plot permitted.

"Sometimes, the princess, who was the daughter of the governor, would catch him at his play and he would blush pansy-pink. He thought the princess an incarnation of a *houri*, a beauty of Paradise. Soraya was not really a princess of course, but that did not matter. He was only a servant boy and could not speak to her anyway.

"But he could hear.

"And oh, what he heard. Plots and whispers and lovers' sighs. Jokes and schemes, gossip and tales. But he picked up only fragments and even then he dismissed most of it. He knew that men, like gales, are largely full of wind.

"One afternoon, just as the sun ripened in the sky, casting tall orange shadows across the white marble, the boy heard a whisper. The windows were wide and open, and the boy thought he heard the stirrings of a muggy Nile breeze, carrying the odors of al-Askar: ripe fruit and roasting meat and the salt of the sand dunes past the djinn-built pyramids. He heard a piteous mewl. And a clinking. Curious, the boy followed the sounds.

"He had thought the noise close, yet each time he neared it, it slid just a few lengths beyond. Clutching his broom and letting his ears lead, he pursued the mysterious mewls past lively fountains and blooming gardens, burning kitchens and quiet pools, until he hunted the sounds up a spiraling tower.

"When he had begun his search, the sun had hung in the sky like a voluptuous peach. When he reached the final door, it had sunk into the earth. Behind the door, he could hear mewling. He hesitated, but before his caution could outweigh his curiosity, the door swung into his face. Nimbly, he slipped behind it as a tall man dressed in crisp white walked out. The man did not see the concealed boy, but the boy recognized him: the vizier. The boy stood stock-still. But absorbed in his thoughts, the vizier paid no mind to the lumpy shadow behind the door.

"Sighing with relief as the vizier vanished down the steps, the boy vowed to never risk his wages like this again. He made to follow the vizier, but the mewling started again, more piteous than ever. The door was slowly closing, as if propelled by an invisible hand, and the boy, making a flash-quick decision, darted into the black chamber.

"As the boy's vision adjusted to the gloom, he beheld a strange sight.

"A dimly glowing golden birdcage hung from the rafters. It held what appeared at first to be writhing black snakes, enough to fill the cage from top to bottom. But no scales gleamed and no eyes glimmered, nor did they hiss or flick their tongues to taste the air. And they keened in high-pitched mourning, like wailing widows tearing their clothing. The boy's mouth was dry with fear, and goose bumps pricked his nape. Brandishing his broomstick like a scimitar, he retreated slowly.

"Then the mass of fat, twisting shadow spoke."

———————

"Allahu akbar! Allahu akbar!" The muezzins recite from their minarets, exhorting the faithful to leave their beds and join them for Fajr. Dunya's head lies dozily in my lap, but at the azaan, she sits up. Dim light seeps into the room.

My mouth is dry. Whether from fear or a night of narration I cannot say. (Of course I can say. It is fear, fear, fear. I am dizzy and ill and I want to weep. My head feels light, as though it is already separating itself from my body.)

I recite the muezzin's next words with him, a prayer. "Ashahud'anna la illa ha il'Allah." I bear witness that there is no God but Allah. *Save me, save me, save me.* Panic beats its wings against my ears.

"Finish your tale."

This is a game of shataranj, and I have but one move to save my shah.

"Your Majesty, the muezzin has sounded the azaan, and I'm afraid that there is more left than I can relate in the brief minutes before prayer. And after prayer, you will need to rest before attending to your day's business."

There. Let him not say that I begged to be spared, that I forced him into it. If he spares me, it will prove that something in him, somewhere deep, is still kind and curious. If he executes me, as he has Fataneh, as he has Altunjan and Shideh and Inanj . . . may Allah save us all.

I want to close my eyes against the panic, but if the Malik is to sentence me to death, he can meet my eyes. And I will meet my death with eyes open.

He opens his mouth.

I forget how to breathe.

"We shall continue tonight."

As if it means nothing to him. Without another look, without another word, he leaves for his ablutions.

I could float to the painted ceiling. The air is mine for another day.

Dunya and I squeal in each other's arms.

"You did it! You did it! You did it!" Her face glistens with tears.

My laughter booms through the room. "It could not have been done without you, Dunya jaan."

I clasp Dunya's hand and together we walk out into a throng of awaiting courtiers. Murmurs move like wind through the crowd. *She has been spared. She has been spared. Allahu akbar!*

Baba, eyes red and ringed dark, rushes to me and kisses my forehead. "O my liver, o my heart." The gathering parts as Baba leads us to our apartments. I clutch his arm, grateful that I still can.

Baba closes the door, and Gulnar, Hanna, and Leila rush to envelop me. I rest my head against Gulnar's soft shoulder, heavy with the sleep that fear had chased away. Before I sleep, however, I must give thanks. Dunya and I perform our ablutions and draw veils over our hair and turn toward Mecca as Baba leads the prayer.

At Fajr's conclusion, I greet the angel on my right shoulder and then my left, the angels that record my graces and my sins, and beg Allah: *Keep my stories beguiling to him, keep my head on my shoulders, help Shahryar become once more the Malik I knew. And thank You, thank You for sparing my life this day.*

✳ ✳ ✳

am jostled awake. "Shaherazade, Shaherazade." I crack an eye open and light bleeds through the curtain's edges. Dunya rolls over beside me. Baba's concerned face hovers above me.

"Shaherazade jaan." He pulls me from the bed. "I don't know how to say this . . ."

I sink to the floor. He does not need to say it. My stomach is on fire and I bury my face in my hands. The world zips, flashing black then white then black. "What of the escape?" I gasp.

Two guards storm in, their scimitars ringing with each step. I recognize them. They are the two I told the story to that long-ago afternoon.

One grabs my arm. "Did you think we were so stupid we would not see you slip the note? Did you think you were such a good storyteller that you could deflect our notice?"

"What does he mean, Shaherazade?" Baba asks.

The other guard frees his curved scimitar. "Who gave you right to speak to the prisoner?"

"How dare you speak to the vizier so?" I exclaim.

The man spits onto the blue-and-white-tiled floor. "Treachery runs in families, doesn't it?" The blade gleams in his grasp.

"What is the meaning of this?"

The Malik smiles at me kindly. I smile back. Of course this is a misunderstanding. He wants to hear the tale's end. He has given his word.

The Malik smiles again, showing his teeth, and they are carnivorous and sharp. I retreat until my back thumps the door.

My knees quake, but I do not crumple. I am Shaherazade, daughter of Vizier Muhammad and his wife Niloufer, who traced her lineage to Sassanian emperors. I try to remember that as I keep my back straight, head high.

Shahryar has led me to the base of the Fire Tower, its dark staircases curving endlessly upward. I debate whether I should measure my steps and exact every moment of my remaining life or if I should run, run, and end the game now.

I stand before the dark-eyed headsman and I recognize his eyes—he is the one who dropped Fataneh's beautiful head into a basket, who carried Altunjan's dripping body through the Arg-e-Bam. He spins his sword weightlessly. Thick wind whistles against my bare neck and the midday sky is night-dark. The crowd is immense; the wedding party has regathered, dressed in the same bright finery. I pick out Leila, Dunya, Hanna, Mahperi, Ishaq, Baba, crying, crying, crying.

The headsman beckons. I kneel, and bricks dig into my knees. I keep my eyes open. I try to pray, but I cannot remember the words. The blade chimes in the air, cold steel presses my neck, and finally—

Eight

I gasp awake, my hands flying to my neck. My fingers run along its intact contours. My heartbeat races, rabbit-fast, beneath my palms. The room is stifling, and I run to the window, open the shutters, breathe until my nerves steady.

I thought it was real. I thought it was all real. I stuff my hands in my mouth and laugh and laugh, laugh until I gag.

* * *

Tonight, I go to Shahryar adorned as a new bride in a crimson robe with trailing sleeves and long blue trousers. Leila has illuminated my lids and cheekbones with borax. Hanna has rubbed my lips red with carmine and darkened my eyes with kohl, while Dunya has perfumed my unbraided hair with a sandalwood comb. Not a tear is spilled tonight. The question is no longer whether I can do it, but rather, whether I can do it again. It may be less frightening for them, but only I know the black fears that carom around my heart.

Collared in gold and rubies, a matching diadem circling my forehead, I am accompanied by Leila and Dunya to my husband's door. Leila and Dunya kiss me on the cheek.

"There will be a dinner tomorrow night in your honor at my father's palace," Leila says cheerily. "We shall see you there!" The last sentence brooks no argument.

I enter the room most women see only once, at the very end of their lives. Shahryar is napping, his face peaceful in repose. At the chime of gold at my ears and the whisper of silk against my thighs, his eyes flicker open.

"Disrobe."

I obey, but slowly. Although I flush, my nerves are calmer. After all, this is a feat I only have to replicate, not discover anew. My gaze demurely downcast, I draw out my undressing, stretching seconds into minutes, a storyteller unspooling suspense. I flush as the Malik watches, but I let each piece slip: first the trousers, then the farajiyya, followed by my chemise. The bangles I slip off one by one; I unclasp the heavy necklace. The diadem I remove last. The silk sighs, the jewels jingle.

He pulls me toward him, his strong fingers encircling my wrist. Save for that touch, our coupling proceeds as it did last night. I am still sore, but I do my best to conceal my discomfort. Shahryar is tightfisted with his own emotions as well, and no sigh betrays whether he draws pleasure. He does not utter Fataneh's name again.

Once he is finished and we have shrugged back into our robes, we lie side by side in silence. His eyes are closed. I use his seeming somnolence to catalog the man I have wed, a man whose face I have seen only through stolen glances and upturned lashes. His nose is nobly curved. His lips emerge from his trimmed beard, sweet as dates. His cheekbones are cut sharp and his smooth skin is the color of new parchment, the face of a poet's hero. In repose, he reminds me of the happy bridegroom whose wedding I attended, with whom I spent my childhood half in love.

There was a time, not long ago, when nothing would have made me happier than to be his wife.

I remain quiet, afraid to rouse him. *I will wait patiently,* I think, resisting the easy lure of sleep. I watch the moon rise, a lily-white maid waking to greet her attendant stars.

In Peshawar reigned a Sultana of famed beauty, her face moon-pale and moon-round, eyes starstruck, and hair as velvet and black as night. Despite this, she was no stranger to grief, for her husband had vanished years before, swallowed into the earth itself.

One day, a Sufi arrived at court, bearing an immense jar.

"Fair Sultana, I carry news of your husband!"

While the Sultana had heard frauds before, she, like many bestowed with great luck, trusted easily. "What proof do you have, good brother?"

The man presented the vase, which came to his hip, unremarkable save for some gilded glyphs around its lip.

"Step into the amphora, O Sultana, and you shall find your husband."

Torn between suspicion and curiosity, the Sultana had her guards bring it closer. "How am I to fit in here, Brother?" she inquired, peering inside. But before he could respond, the glyphs hummed and a silver light enveloped the Sultana, gulping her whole.

Shahryar stirs, and opens his sleep-soft eyes.

"Might I call Dunya to attend me?"

He eyes me, unreadable. "You may."

Dunya arrives, followed by a pair of servants carrying kebabs, quince, and decanters of *sekanjabin*, a vinegar drink sweetened with sugar and mint and soured with lemons.

Reclining on the large bed, Shahryar sips his sekanjabin. True to its name, wrinkles pop up on his forehead. While Dunya curls at my knee, I sit straight-backed, cross-legged. Sekanjabin burns my lips, but physicians recommend it for its heartening qualities. And tonight, I need heart. *And luck.*

"Sister dear, would you continue the wondrous tale you began last night?"

"Only if the Malik permits."

I steal a glance at him. He is remote, an eagle untouchably high.

"I do." There is no warmth in his words, but neither is there ice.

"O Malik, it is said that a girl's voice sounded through serpentine shadow, betraying the accents of Fustat, the old city to the south of al-Askar. 'Who are you?' she asked the servant boy. A dozen more voices, of old men and young mothers, of strong youths and flower-frail maidens, chorused her question: 'Who are you? Who are you?'

"The servant boy stepped backward, wishing he had remained downstairs, wrapped in his imagination, away from whatever this was.

"'I am—' His voice cracked, so he started again, stronger. 'I am 'Omar, a servant of the palace. Who are *you*?'

"Once more, he heard the girl's voice. 'We are wraiths, captured by the man who visits this room.'

"'What do you mean?' 'Omar asked, aghast.

"There was a sigh. It was small, but echoed by the other shades until it sounded like a breeze. 'Perhaps if I tell you my story, you will understand,' the girl-shade said.

"'Fifty years ago, when Egypt was under Umayyad rule and Fustat was their capital, I was a girl, who played pretend, living out dreams and exploring the crannies of my city.

"'One day, I explored too far. My mother had warned me, but I'd spurned her worries. What could hurt me? I imagined cutpurses and slavers that I could outrun. I had been quick, as much cat as girl.

"'The evening was overcast as I wandered the bazaar. My tongue longed for sweetness, and when the stallkeeper's back was turned, I stole a handful of sugared almonds. A handful, that's all. Their pointed ends dug into my palms and I scampered to an old date tree, licking the sugar from my fingers under the sepulchral shadow of sprawling fronds. The Maghrib azaan had sounded minutes before, urging devout women and men to pray and inviting spirits into our world to play.

"'My mother had warned me against standing beneath trees at dusk, as light surrenders to dark, as day and night bleed together. They come together only to be pulled apart, and in this flux, demons walk. My mother had warned me, but I had not listened.

"'A man approached as I finished my almonds. He was tall and thin, more shadow than human. "Come, child," he said, and his voice was like satin. "I see you like sweets. I do too. Come, and I will provide you with plenty, and yes, enough for your mother and brothers too."

"'As I hesitated, he smiled, and his teeth were white as sugar, white as almonds. They were the whitest teeth I had seen and they dazzled in his mouth. *His teeth might be white, but mine are little and sharp,* I told myself. So, I took his hand. It felt hot and as if my fingers had slid through his flesh. But the world solidified as his grip tightened, and I dismissed the sensation.

"'As we walked down the street, he described the sweets we would eat: sugared dates, plums crystallized in honey, sweetmeats made with cream and molasses, tahini halva light as a cloud. My mouth watered, but my heart grew suspicious. A child does not survive long on Fustat's streets by trusting.

"'Night was almost upon us, and I thought of my waiting mother. "I need to go home," I said, yanking my hand. But though I pulled, he would not release my hand, and I saw that my palm was fused to his. I screamed, and the man's chest swelled, inhaling my cry. I leapt, determined to sink my teeth into his neck as I knew lions did, but he turned me aside as if I were no more than a gnat.

"'"Come, child," he chided. "'Is that any way to treat a friend? I shall return you to your mother before 'Isha, never fear."

"'I believed him. I had no other choice.

"'My voice in his chest, my hand glued to his, he wound me through the tangled streets until even I, who could have mapped Fustat like the lines in my palm, could not tell up from down. Finally, we arrived at his nondescript lair, shoved in a morass of identical homes. It smelled of clean, burning olive oil as my own home did. If I closed my eyes, I could imagine I was with my mother once more.

"'I was still attached to the man, who grew less shadowy while I . . . faded, and something inky leaked from my skin. When he picked me up, I was as you see me today, a shadow-snake, nothing more than the shade of my soul.

"'"What have you done?" I cried as the man sealed me into this golden cage. I threw myself against the wires, but they would not break; I tried to slip through and was repelled. The last of this world I saw was his smile, his sugar-white teeth twinkling, brighter than before.

"'I asked, "What *are* you?" to which he answered easily, "An ifrit."

"'Over the centuries, he trapped more soul-shades, luring them by their hearts' deepest desires: brides and dowers; wealth, power, and love. Soon, we moved from Fustat into the Umayyad palace. There, the ifrit, clothed as a man with the power of our flesh, connived his way into becoming the Umayyad governor's most trusted adviser and then turned his whispers to destroying that dynasty.

"'And we who listen know that he is whispering again, spinning webs to now destroy the 'Abbasids. He is a demon and in place of a soul, he harbors mischief.'

"The girl's plight moved 'Omar. He too had had a sister once, long gone in the fire that had taken his family, who had loved to eat sweets in the shade. 'I vow I shall help you.' He clutched his broom handle as though it were indeed a scimitar and he truly their champion.

"'Take the key! Take the key,' chirped the shades, like birds in a nest.

"It glinted, small and gold, beside the cage. He secreted the key into a pocket and ran down the steps. Evil was stirring in Egypt and 'Omar knew he had to stop it."

Dawn is beginning to peek through the window, a thin colorless strip announcing day.

"What a wondrous tale, Shahera." Dunya's eyes are heavy lidded, her head on a pillow next to my leg.

Kneading my back, I glance at Shahryar. As night has passed into morning, some of his stony reserve has faded, and I glimpse eagerness, tiredness, humanity. It all winks away when I meet his eye. Before I can answer, muezzins take up the azaan, the calls reverberating against Bam's adobe walls and brick houses.

"I'm afraid my time is at an end." I wince. The sentence sounds too close to a proclamation of death. I banish the thought before it seeps into the air and from the air into the Malik's mind.

He looks at me for the briefest instance and then his gaze falls to Dunya. Does he sense the trap we are laying?

My breath catches.

"We shall continue tomorrow."

✳ ✳ ✳

Leila's mother, my Ismat Khaleh, has laid a sumptuous repast in her city palace, aware of the honor of hosting the Malik and his latest wife at their first public dinner. The gilt wooden table threatens to crack under the weight of lamb and date kebabs, meatballs fried with pistachio and sweet with honey, spit-roasted chicken marinated in sour pomegranate juice and fragrant thyme, tender lamb in caraway-spiced onion sauce, sausage aromatic with cilantro and rue, accompanied with hot nan and sweet-and-sour apple sharbat.

Kirmani aristocrats recline on the silk cushions circling Ismat's table. Lamplight quivers on the turquoise faience walls, casting guests' faces alternately into shade and light.

"All is well, Shaherazade jaan?" Leila's eyes flick toward Shahryar.

"I'm sitting beside you, aren't I?"

"Alhamdulilah," she murmurs, squeezing my hand.

The agreeable chimes of enameled dishes and polite conversation are interrupted by a tight knot of heated men, none older than thirty, seated at the far end of Ismat's table. One, a round-faced youth, calls to Shahryar. "What do you mean to do about the Khwarezmids, O Malik? Even as we speak, they attack Khorasan, the empire's heart."

Leila's father, Goktash, who is known for his cold reason, snorts. "The rule has long been each Seljuk for himself. We are too divided, our brethren too crumbled, for Kirman to stake its peace on helping failing cousins."

"Such cowardice is dishonorable in a man of your birth, Amu Goktash!" exclaims a young man in a richly woven persimmon kaftan, pearls stringing his neck. "Do you think if the Khwarezmids—or Oghuz—defeat the other Seljuks, they will leave us standing?"

The hall resonates with angry protests as guests jump to their feet. Even the musicians' flutes and beating tombeks cannot drown them out. Goktash looks ready to slap the boy, but Shahryar's lips twist with interest.

Bejeweled hands fluttering, Ismat begs, "This is no conversation for dinner." When the men do not heed her, she raises her voice. "I have heard that my niece tells beautiful tales. Perhaps she will grace us tonight."

Through the mist of my emerald veil, I risk a sidelong look at Shahryar. He is weighing and watching. I shift, tracing the red and apricot threads of my new robe. "If my husband permits."

"I cannot deny a lady in her own home," Shahryar says, a smile flickering. My heart stops. Did I truly see that? I am dizzy, a drowning man catching a last glimpse of the sun.

But the first, round-faced youth is not so easily distracted. "Do you not have an answer, O Malik?"

Shahryar takes a long draft of his wine, eyeing the boy above his chalice. "The Khwarezmids will be occupied with Khorasan for years yet, aided and abetted by the Caliph in Baghdad. Goktash has the right of it. Kirman will not fall easily to the Khwarezmids nor to the Oghuz, no matter how they scavenge our villages. If you feel that your sword would contribute to Khorasan's defense, then by all means, join their efforts."

His dumpling cheeks reddened, the youth lowers his eyes. "As you say, O Malik."

Ismat sighs with relief, but her respite is short-lived.

The young man with the pearl necklace calls, "Perhaps you are right regarding the Khwarezmids and the Oghuz, Malik Shahryar, but what of Sultan Saladin's fight against the infidels attacking Jerusalem?" He slaps the table emphatically.

Nudging Leila, I whisper, "Who is that?"

"My father's cousin's son, Faramurz." Her eyes darken with worry, darting between the brazen boy and the Malik. "He should take care."

But Faramurz does not share Leila's apprehension. "Were we Seljuks not once caliphs of the *ummah*? Did we not raise our swords in its defense? Should we not rise to defend the ummah now?"

I exchange a look with Dunya.

"Last I heard, Acre is ripening, ready to fall at the slightest shake into Frankish hands," Baba notes mildly. I'm surprised, but there is a calculating cast to his mien.

"The Franks will not be content simply with Palestine," Goktash predicts. "They are as greedy as they are barbarous. Do not forget that just ten years ago they attempted to desecrate Mecca itself!"

The guests hiss.

"Should they defeat Saladin, they will spread like a plague," Goktash continues. "First to Damascus, then Baghdad. Soon enough, they will pass through the Zagros and arrive in Kirman. They will burn and rape, they will bleed our children and wives in our holy places. Distance will not save us. Only action."

As he speaks, I can smell the smoke of burning houses, taste the iron tang of blood, hear the desperate shrieks of women and children. Goktash seems as startled as any by his speech.

The hall falls silent, the air too tight to dare move.

Faramurz leads the first cheer, but the rest of the guests quickly take it up: courtiers, military men, and bureaucrats. My ears ring and in my mind tumble flaming crosses emblazoned across Frankish shields, the masonry arches of Masjid al-Aqsa, tall walls defended by Saladin's armies beside the glittering White Sea . . .

And we could focus the Malik on a noble cause. Leave Fataneh's shade in Bam and ride into a shadowless world. Suddenly, I understand Baba's calculation.

"Should we not answer Saladin's call, O Malik?" Faramurz demands, his handsome face alit with a zealous glow. Men, both young and old, whoop while their wives and mothers look on, dismayed.

Baba weighs Faramurz. Shahryar opens his mouth, ready to say something sharp, but Baba places a gentle hand on Shahryar's *tiraz*-banded sleeve. "Mutashakaram, son. We will consider your . . . arguments . . . most carefully."

Ismat unhappily twists her gold-printed farajiyya. Catching his sister-in-law's distress, Baba says, "Perhaps we should honor our gracious hostess's request and Shaherazade Khatun might share a tale."

The fleeting dream of Saladin, the Franks, and far-off Palestine dissipates. My dry tongue sticks in my mouth. I wish I could sink beneath the table and slither away. I swallow, and my tongue unglues itself.

"I am in the middle of a story right now that I could continue . . ." No one objects and my voice gains resonance as I sketch out the characters and events.

Ismat's guests dim, and only Shahryar remains.

———————

"O Malik, it is said that the servant boy returned to finish sweeping, losing himself in the swish-swish of the broom. Here he was, with a secret that could topple one of the most powerful men in Egypt. Imagining challenging the vizier to single combat, 'Omar flourished the broom and lunged. His stomp reverberated in the air and a giggle echoed through the hall.

"'Omar jumped and resumed sweeping, hoping the giggle was just another lost sound. The approach of the governor's daughter doused that hope. 'Omar's mouth dried as he beheld her. Never before had he been so close to her. Had he dared, he could have touched the cinnabar satin of her robe. Had he ventured, he could have brushed the black silk of her hair from her blacker eyes. His fingers trembled.

"'What were you doing, boy?' Soraya asked amiably. She raked him over with her eyes and 'Omar reddened like a maiden.

"Despite the depth of his mind, 'Omar was not clever with words, and with the governor's daughter watching him, 'Omar found his tongue tied.

"'Well! Speak up! Do you need help?'

"*Help*. 'Omar latched onto that word. Softly, he told the governor's daughter what he had seen. He did not know if she would believe him or betray him, but if he could not convince her, how could he convince Governor Mansur?

"Her eyebrows, lush and dark and joined in the middle, crinkled in disbelief. 'Can you *prove* it?'

"'Omar deflated. He could not take the governor's daughter to the vizier's tower. It was too risky, and he was only a servant, not a noble whose word was worth its weight in gold. Then it struck him: *gold*. From his pocket, he withdrew the tiny gold key. 'This is the key to the shadow cage,' he said.

"'How do I know you haven't stolen that?' Soraya asked.

"'*Why* would I show it to you if I had stolen it?' he replied. 'I beg you, O Sitti, tell your father about this.'

"The governor's daughter weighed his plea and finally said, 'Very well. I shall speak to my father, but I cannot guarantee that he will believe me.'

"The servant boy offered her the key, but she shook her head. 'A gold key in your hand is much more compelling than a gold key in mine.'

"Soraya left the boy to seek her father. 'Omar did not know it, but sometimes, Soraya watched him from the mezzanine. She had noticed him, years ago, dancing in the halls as he performed his chores, and something about his lightness made her smile. He was tall, and broad, and although she called him *boy*, he was almost a man, albeit young and uncertain. Still, his story was absurd, and she wondered if this boy she liked so well from afar was a bit slow—or quick and a thief. Nonetheless, she had promised she would speak to her father, and she would not renege. Her word *was* worth its weight in gold.

"She found her father hunched over papers that crackled beneath his fingers. When she entered, he had a smile ready for her. 'Good evening, *babibti*,' he said, straightening. 'What brings you?'

"She answered, 'O Baba, I have spoken to a servant boy named 'Omar, who sweeps the hall. He has told me the most strange tale.' She related everything, concluding with the accusation against the vizier.

"Her father was unconvinced. 'Soraya, I would not insult the vizier with such a wild accusation from a sweeper boy.'

"'Then see it for yourself!' Soraya exclaimed.

"'Even if I wanted, how could I?' the governor replied.

"Soraya had her answer ready. 'Command the boy to tail the vizier and alert you when he visits his tower. You can head toward the tower, but have someone else summon the vizier. As the vizier leaves, slip through the tower door. If the boy lies, then by all means, flog him. But if he speaks true, then punish the vizier and reward the boy.'

"'If it will please you, Daughter, that is exactly what I shall do.'

"At the governor's command, 'Omar spent the day following the vizier. If the vizier was in one chamber, 'Omar was sweeping in the next. If the vizier walked through the gardens, 'Omar was brushing spider-veined leaves from the path. The vizier did not notice 'Omar. After all, who was a broom boy before the Vizier of Egypt?

"Finally, as the sky began to deepen, the vizier returned to his tower and 'Omar returned to the hall where he had first heard the mewls. Through palace echoes, he heard the lock *snick* shut. It was time to tell Governor Mansur.

"Soraya was waiting with her father in his study when 'Omar approached nervously. 'H—he is in the tower, ya Said.' Soraya's father had her black eyes, and 'Omar could not meet either pair.

"A firm hand clapped him on the shoulder. 'Very well, boy.'

"The governor strode from the room and, finding the chamberlain, said, 'The vizier is in his tower. Summon him, but wait a few minutes.' The governor marched to the tower, certain still of the falsity of the boy's accusations against his steadfast councillor.

"Hidden at the tower's base, the governor watched the vizier fly off to answer the summons. *See what a loyal man he is*, the governor thought, climbing the steps. As the vizier's door swung shut, the governor hurled himself through. After his vision adjusted to the dark, he registered a gold glint. A domed cage presented itself. Stepping closer, the governor saw the coiling shadows.

"'*What* are you?' he whispered, although he knew.

"'Shades!'

"'Souls!'

"'Spirits of those who once lived and are now dead,' responded a girl's voice grimly. 'Spirits who were parted from their bodies and corrupted to give the ifrit vizier human form.'

"The governor fainted."

Finishing, I apprehensively peek at Shahryar, but he is far away and his eyes glisten like grease.

* * *

As we enter through the Arg-e-Bam's great peaked doors after dinner, I make to head to Shahryar's chambers. He stops me with a heavy hand on my shoulder. "I do not require your company tonight." He glows like oil fire, a strange shine skittering across his skin.

My mind cannot fix on anything. Is this it, then? I had thought he was pleased or, if not pleased, appeased. I swallow dryly, my skin tingling with a half-formed expectation that he will order his mamluks to drag me to the tower or wrench me there himself.

He does not give me another look. Instead, he shouts, summoning a few sodden boon companions and the grooms with their horses. He shakes off Baba, who tries to tug him back into the citadel. Clumsily, Shahryar and his companions mount their horses.

Standing together, Baba and I watch as they unsteadily gallop out of the Arg-e-Bam, their ringing blades and drunken laughter cracking the still dark of the night.

Nine

This is the tenth night Shahryar has left me. I should be grateful. The Malik's neglect means that my life does not dangle on the skill of my flawed tongue. But the citadel gossips about where he goes instead.

He carouses until midnight and then, with a party of equally drunk boon companions, raids Oghuz mountain encampments, a weevil of violence burrowing in his mind since Ismat's dinner. Baba cannot constrain him. The emirs cannot constrain him. Night after night, I hear the flurry of hooves and watch the torches fly from the citadel. He will return, stinking of Oghuz blood and wine, laughing as he and his companions string Oghuz heads along the walls. How could I have mistaken this new turn of his madness for incipient humanity? Have my tales somehow made it worse?

The worry leaves me sleepless.

An aureate line gleams beneath Baba's door. I knock.

"Enter."

Baba's room is small, with plain adobe walls. Books and ledgers and letters, all ordered by topic and date, line the room. He sits on the rug like a scribe: one leg folded to his chest, the other tucked beneath him, as his *qalam* scratches across the paper.

"The Malik is gone again, Baba." I sit beside him, cross-legged. I try to peek over his shoulder, but he lowers the paper before I can decipher it.

He sighs. "I know."

"What have the emirs said?"

"What everyone in Bam says. That if Shahryar continues, the Oghuz will attack Bam itself. And who can blame them?"

Is the Malik's bloodlust not quenched? Because he has not murdered me, must he take his anger elsewhere? Take it to our enemies, put them to the sword, and draw their eye onto Bam with its increasingly faltering ruler?

"He is mad, Baba. The emirs, the townspeople, the Oghuz—someone will assassinate him if he does not stop. How can he not understand this?"

Baba taps the paper. "His attention must be diverted, and Bam must be given time to settle down. I received another letter from Sultan Saladin requesting aid in Palestine. I have placed Faramurz in the Malik's company. Let the boy's passion infect him."

The night's quiet is disrupted by clomping hooves and yelling men.

Baba looks tired. "Your husband has returned. You should sleep."

I return to my room, but instead of falling asleep, I drape a blue veil over my unbound hair and slip to the citadel's entrance. Only a few bronze lanterns are lit, and drunk men stumble as the hostlers take their mounts. They are bloody and wounded but laughing. I wonder how they can laugh, these men who butcher for fun. They are not strangers to me: we have grown up together and this is what they have grown into. Baba's cat's-paw, Faramurz, stands apart, his hands clasped behind his back, looking to the floor.

An eagle-nosed emir with skin brown as palm sugar holds the drunk Malik upright. Like Faramurz, he appears uncomfortable with the debauchery. The Malik's eyes are bleary, his lips curling in a smile, but his arm dangles unnaturally. The man spots me. "Girl, fetch a doctor for the Malik. He has been wounded."

I hesitate, and the Malik raises his flushed face. "That's no servant, Atsiz. That's my wife, Shaherazade Khatun."

Atsiz blushes beneath his beard. "*Bebakshin*, O Khatun." He is handsome, I realize. Feathers brush my stomach.

I follow Atsiz and Faramurz as they carry the Malik to his room. The Malik's companions call for more wine, but at my gesture a quartet of mamluks escort them from the citadel, leaving it quiet once more.

Atsiz and Faramurz lay the Malik on his bed and leave. Dirt and blood stain the sheets. The Malik's eyes are half-closed, although I don't know whether that's from pain or drink. A sleepy steward fetches a doctor, who flushes the Malik's wounds with hot water and wine and slips a small dose of opium beneath his tongue. As the blood washes away, I can see the whiteness of the flesh and skin beneath. I suppress a gag, but when I rise the Malik mumbles something. I do not catch it. He tries again, through clenched teeth: "Remain."

The physician, a bald man with a long white beard, glances up from stitching the Malik's arm. "Distract him."

The Malik hisses as the physician's needle punctures his flesh once more.

I rub my face and begin.

"O Malik, it is said that when the governor awoke again, he saw his daughter, starlit eyes wide with fear. She was bathing his brow with a cool washcloth. His wife, Sabine, stood behind her, her face regal even when tight with worry. Heartening camphor and mint filled the room and cleared his mind. Soraya looked over her shoulder. Following her gaze, the governor saw the sweeper boy standing awkwardly by the doorway.

"'What happened?' the governor asked.

"Soraya explained, 'When you did not return, I became worried. 'Omar found you on the ground and carried you here. But the physician says you will be fine.' Soraya paused. 'What did you find?'

"The governor addressed the boy. 'You were right. He is an ifrit, an infernal djinn. I will . . . speak to the vizier immediately.' The governor made to rise, but Sabine pushed him down. 'You must rest.'

"The governor's world spun. 'Very well, but after Maghrib, I will have my say.'

"'O Governor, if I may speak?' 'Omar said timidly.

"'Of course, my boy. You have earned the right to speak freely.'

"Drawing confidence from that kindness, 'Omar said, 'I think it would be unwise to confront the vizier after Maghrib. Demons are strongest at twilight, and by the shadow's account that is when he strikes. I suggest that you wait until clear daylight, immediately after the noon prayer, when the sun burns out shadow. Gather learned men and women you trust and prepare them to recite the Chapter of the Djinn to drive the demon away. Your vizier is an evil not to be underestimated.'

"'Listen to the boy, Mansur,' Sabine said. 'He may be a servant, but he speaks wisely.' Sabine plumped her husband's pillows and began quenching the lamps. 'We shall inform the 'ulema that you wish to see them tomorrow after prayer.' Sabine shut the door, ushering the other two out.

"Sabine slipped a heavy jeweled ring off her finger and into 'Omar's hand. She whispered urgently, 'Now, boy, take this ring and tell the 'ulema to come to the palace tomorrow. 'Isha will begin soon. Start with the Mosque of the Banner Holders and go from there. Hurry!'

"The next day, the sky bloomed a deep blue and the sun's glare pounded away all shadow. The governor sat enthroned, flanked by his wife and daughter, their features obscured by translucent veils. Many of the gathered 'ulema were startled to notice last night's messenger standing beside something large and draped in black. Oddly, this morning he was dressed in a rich tunic, striped violet and yellow, and his turban was secured with an impressive cluster of rubies and amethysts. They were too far away to see 'Omar's discomfort as he stroked the scimitar at his side.

"The vizier entered the throne room, a genial smile on his face, which although narrow and sharp was pleasing. The vizier was the only one who did not perspire in the noon heat. 'Omar felt suddenly cold and slipped his hand on the sword hilt.

"Disregarding the crowd of bearded men and veiled women, the vizier swept up, tall and proud, bowing at the base of the governor's tiled throne. 'Governor Mansur,' he purred. His voice was silky, but beneath that, 'Omar heard venom.

"Governor Mansur smiled. 'Omar thought that if the governor ever smiled at him like that, he would faint. The vizier, however, was unperturbed, until the governor gestured for 'Omar to draw back the cloth. The golden cage sparkled, even as the wraiths within turned sunlight into shadow. The assembly pushed closer to examine this queer object. The vizier's lips whitened.

"The governor announced, 'In this cage, you see the shades of souls, consumed by this . . . demon . . . to imitate humanity as he plotted against us, a spider lurking in the shadows—'

"Before the governor could continue, the ifrit leapt and expanded. He grew taller, until the top of his turban brushed the ceiling, and larger, until he filled every corner of the room, suffocating all with his massive girth. Cries of 'Audhubillah!' and 'May Allah protect us from evil!' rang out.

"The ifrit continued to inflate, pressing into 'Omar until he thought his spine would snap, but 'Omar squirmed and squeezed and unsheathed his scimitar and struck blindly. He could hardly miss. When his point struck its target, the djinn deflated slightly, enough for 'Omar to dizzily inhale the sulfuric fume the ifrit leaked. 'Omar struck again and again, joined by guards, who hacked at the enormous demon until he smiled, a man once more.

"'Well,' the ifrit said.

"'Recite Surah ad-Djinn now!' quick-thinking Soraya ordered in the lull. The voices of the learned women and men rose in otherworldly harmony: 'In the name of Allah, the Most Gracious, the Most Merciful. Say, "It has been revealed to me that a group of the djinn listened—"'

"'Silence!' cried the vizier, and suddenly, everyone gagged for air. Soraya fell to her knees, clawing at her throat. The vizier spoke, impervious to the pained gasps. 'I am not unreasonable. I shall take my cage and depart, but once I leave the city boundaries, all here will perish.'

"As the ifrit made his pronouncement, 'Omar stealthily removed the golden key from his vest pocket. Black bubbles burst in his vision as he sidled to the golden cage. His hands shook and the key clattered against the lock, drawing the vizier's attention.

"'What are you doing?' the vizier snapped.

"In a blink, he was beside 'Omar. 'Omar gasped and stabbed the lock one last time: the key and cage began to glow and hum. With a mighty swing, the ifrit flung 'Omar to the other side of the hall, but it was too late: the door squeaked open and the snaking shades wrapped around him like leeches. As the shades attacked, the vizier transformed: his skin tightened, bones and veins protruding. His whole matter thinned to translucence. Still, he would not go. It was Soraya who restarted Surah ad-Djinn, and as the learned men and women chorused after her, the vizier erupted into a twisting flame that left 'Omar seeing inverse.

"When 'Omar regained sight, only the ifrit's faintly smoking robes remained.

"'Omar could only stare at the robe on the marble floor that he had swept just this week. He jumped when someone touched him. It was Soraya.

"Before the guards and the learned women and men of Egypt, the governor said, 'Well, my boy, you have rendered Egypt a great service. Anything that is in my power to grant you, I will.'

"Against 'Omar's will, he glanced at Soraya, who, behind her veil, was suddenly very pink. He averted his eyes and murmured, 'It was an honor serving you and Egypt, ya Saidi.' How could he, a street brat, think of wedding the governor's daughter? He felt cold with shame that the thought had even crossed his mind.

"Hiding a smile, the governor shook his head. 'I would be remiss if I failed to reward such bravery. Perhaps my daughter can think of a suitable reward?'

"Soraya ducked her head to conceal her burgeoning smile.

"'Ah, my daughter is modest,' the governor said. 'Well then, permit me, as her father, to speak in her stead. If Soraya will consent, I propose that you take her as your bride.'

"'Omar had never felt so overwhelmed. 'I—O Saidi, you could not wed your only daughter to a *sweeping boy*.'

"Governor Mansur stroked his beard. 'You are right, you clever lad. As it happens, a position has recently opened. I insist you take it.'

"A sneaking suspicion dawned on 'Omar. 'No. *La la la la*.'

"'Why not?' demanded the governor. 'I have faith that you will improve upon your predecessor.'

"Although 'Omar resisted, Soraya's pleas and her father's commands wore him down. He became the governor's vizier and some time after that Soraya's husband. What he lacked in fine bloodlines and education, he more than made up for with his willingness to learn, his honesty, and his loyalty. Egypt flourished with him at the helm.

"Many years later, when the governor died, 'Omar took his place. In time, Soraya delivered him ten sons and daughters, one of whom they named Jauhara. Upon her birth, the court astrologer charted the stars and foretold, his voice shaking, that this newborn daughter would unmake Egypt and then remake her anew. But 'Omar and Soraya placed no great stock in astrologers, dismissed his prognostication, and soon forgot it altogether.

"The stars, however, do not forget.

"The sun rises, and I fear that Jauhara's story will have to wait until tomorrow night."

———————

As the night has deepened, Shahryar's head has drooped, but he has nonetheless paid rapt attention. Rising, he kisses me on the cheek. Perhaps he is still intoxicated or delirious with pain or opium.

"Go to bed. I will see you tomorrow night."

I hover at the door. Shahryar lies in his bloodied bed, his hair greasy, the skin under his eyes gray. This is the great terror of the girls of Kirman, of the Oghuz encampments.

When a wound is infected and the humors imbalanced, the physician pierces the skin and lets the black blood spill until the veins run clean again. Can a man not do the same to his soul?

"There is talk, O Malik," I say, my speech tripping, "that we are journeying to Palestine to fight the Franks alongside Sultan Saladin."

"As the vizier's daughter, you must hear a great deal of talk," he says flatly.

"You are a great Malik: Why do you fight these Oghuz fleas?" I press. "Fight the Franks and write your name in history."

His hazy eyes snap with choler. "Did I ask for a woman's counsel?"

I back away, the wound pulsing hot beneath my fingers. "No, O Malik, you did not."

***

The Malik has not summoned me for weeks—nor has he embarked on drunken Oghuz raids. Since recovering from his injury, he sleeps soundly and alone from 'Isha until Fajr and meets with his councillors behind thick wooden doors. From the harem to the kitchens, the citadel is swept with the rumor that the Malik plans to march to Palestine and join Saladin.

I find Baba taking his leave of an Indian emissary and leap behind him. "Salaam, Baba!"

Baba clutches his heart. "Ay, Shaherazade. You will kill me."

"Baba, is it true? Is it final? The Malik is going to join Sultan Saladin?"

We walk into a small courtyard with blue-and-white tiles, a palm tree growing in its center. Baba's violet kaftan with silver tiraz bands shimmers in the bright light.

Baba removes the green-and-yellow-striped *kuleh* capping his head and wipes his damp brow. "It is near done. The emirs are presenting plans for the journey."

I think of a father distracting a crying child from his distemper by waving a long-tailed kite.

"Baba, won't the Malik leaving make us vulnerable? If I were the Oghuz and the Khwarezmids and I had not been thinking about attacking Kirman before, I would certainly think about it now." I shade my eyes to better read his face.

"Part of the army will remain to guard against the Oghuz and Khwarezmids. Behind Bam's fortifications, even halved, we are stronger than their rabble. Shahzaman will also stay."

"Will you go with the Malik, Baba?"

"I must remain. Shahzaman does not know the province and will require my hand to steady the courtiers and guide the army."

"Then who will advise the Malik?"

"His emirs, of course."

His emirs . . . and his idiot boon companions who egg on his violent mischief against the Oghuz—even when Baba is present to steady him. And without Baba? Who knows what unscrupulous adviser could thrust himself beside the Malik, injuring an already-hobbled Kirman?

But . . . if it were me, the whisper in his right ear guiding the Malik toward justice? The thought shivers like mercury in my belly, grips my neck with a hard leather glove.

"Baba, if he goes to Palestine, I must go with him."

A vision erupts: the great cities like Baghdad we will pass through, the luminaries—caliphs and sultans, poets and princes—whom we would encounter, the chance to live that which I have only read in books. I think of the wide world and its wonders that extend far beyond the suddenly small province of Kirman.

Baba rolls the kuleh between his palms. "Think, Shaherazade: if the Malik leaves you behind, you would have months without him. Maybe years. But if you join him? I would not be there to protect you. You would be alone."

The dream of peace and safety tugs at me: breath in my chest, sunshine on my eyelids, my neck secure. It is a world that is still, but it is a world that is small. The other *promise* still clutches me. "He will need an adviser who can act in your stead."

"You are not wrong." Baba replaces his cap atop his thinning hair. "But will he heed your counsel?" His tone indicates not.

"He heeds my tales, Baba. Already." And though the Malik sniped, I do not miss that the wheels toward Palestine began to turn only after our conversation at his sickbed.

Is that enough to wager my life on?

Baba settles his hands on his belly: his pose for argument, for diplomacy, for delivering news that will be ill received. His rings, silver and garnet, twinkle in the sun. "You have been Khatun for a month. I worry that you are overconfident."

As if doubts do not already crowd my mind. "Baba, I married him not only to guard Kirman, but also to retrieve him from his madness."

He does not have a quick response.

"This is not a request, Baba. I want to be your voice in Shahryar's ear, but to do that, you must arrange this for me."

I walk away before he can say no, before he can chide me as a father and I submit as his daughter, no longer a Khatun commanding a vizier, but a child once more.

Ten

◇◇◇◇◇

Today is the new year, the first day of spring, green with promise. I sit beside the Malik in the great hall to celebrate Nowruz in honor of the world's fourth ruler, Shah Jamshid, king of angels and demons who defeated an endless winter to usher in spring. Tomorrow, Shahryar will depart for Palestine to join Sultan Saladin's fight against the Frankish invaders, Baba's stratagem to distract the Malik from Kirman and Kirman from the Malik having found soft soil and taken root.

And I will go with him.

Singers, musicians, and poets fill the hall with merry music. Laden with sweet fruit and pistachios, gold and silver plates wink brightly, and Kirman's nobles glitter in fine new robes. In the shimmer and strum, I feel time blur between the present and the Malik's wedding to Fataneh. The sense of unreality compounds. Last Nowruz, the Malik was jubilant, bantering with his boon companions, slipping pieces of halva through Fataneh's parted lips, and cheering singers and poets. Today, he sits beside me, serious, almost a statue, watching the festivities indifferently.

The court astrologer, Qutlumush, approaches the throne in spangled robes of deep green, his beard so long that if he so chose, he could tuck it into the red sash at his waist. "O Malik, I come to congratulate you upon the arrival of the New Year. I have studied the movements of the stars and the planets, and this year will be the most successful year for Kirman yet. The planets have aligned so you will be victorious in war. The stars sing of the great wealth that will flow into Bam." Qutlumush nods to me. "And I believe that this year will at long last bring an heir to your line."

Shahryar appears unmoved by the flattering predictions, but the nobles chant "Allahu akbar!"

Baba side-eyes the court astrologer, who also predicted for many years that Fataneh would deliver an heir to Kirman and that the Seljuks would defeat the Khwarezmids and once more dominate Baghdad. Qutlumush may be something of a charlatan—although my mother once told me that he had predicted she would birth queens.

Now, a poet replaces the astrologer, presenting me a bouquet of hyacinths with a flourish. I bury my nose in the purple and blue flowers, feel their velveteen petals caress my face, and try to preserve this memory of my home.

* * *

As midnight nears and the beeswax candles melt low, the Malik stands. The court rises with him, their vestments radiant against the faience tiles limning the walls.

"For those who can continue to feast and still sit a horse tomorrow, feast, but I retire for the night. At dawn, we march. Insh'Allah."

"Insh'Allah!" The emirs and nobles cheer, giving vent to the anticipation that has been vibrating like a plucked tar string through the hall all night.

"Come, Shaherazade."

My neck twitches. Have I misheard? But the Malik regards me expectantly, even though we have exchanged no more than two words since I sat beside his sickbed. Panicking, I grab Dunya. Mulberry wood tanburs trill as we depart.

Behind the Malik's back, Dunya raises her eyebrows.

"Stay with me," I mouth, as his mamluks open his doors. His chambers have been hollowed for departure: trunks are packed, the wardrobe sealed.

Primly, I sit at the edge of the Malik's bed, Dunya beside me. I sweep out my long robe, the embroidered jade and ruby flowers gleaming in the lamplight.

Before Dunya can prompt him, Shahryar says, "Tell me of the broom boy's daughter . . . Jauhara."

Shahryar reclines against his silk pillows, his brow unruffled, a clear, glacial lake. On the surface, he does not seem a man about to lead his army across worlds. Does he, in the cistern of his soul, feel pain at departure, knowing that his advisers clamored for it because he could best serve his province by disappearing?

"O Malik, it is said that Jauhara grew into womanhood hearing of her father's bravery and her mother's courage. She was the youngest daughter, protected, sheltered, and coddled, all that youngest daughters should be. No silk too fine, no candy too sweet.

"But Jauhara was her father's daughter. While she was expected to soon marry, that thirst for adventure, that imagination that had catapulted 'Omar from sweeper to governor sang in her blood.

"And within a palace as storied and old as Jauhara's, things lurked from which even her father's worried eye couldn't guard her.

"One day, in the palace library, Jauhara discovered a tattered volume wedged between a book on herbal simples and rolled scrolls depicting human anatomy. It dusted her fingertips as she opened it to reveal the picture writing she recognized from statues dating back to the time of the pharaoh who was cursed in the Qur'an. On the book's back was writing in an older Arabic script. Jauhara could make out one word: *sehera*. *Magic*.

"Jauhara slipped the book into her sleeve, tiptoed to her room, and remained locked within for three days and three nights. The servants reported to Soraya and 'Omar that they heard strange chanting. One woman claimed to have smelled burning sulfur, while another swore that billows of pink clouds had squeezed through the door. On the fourth day, 'Omar and Soraya knocked on their daughter's locked door, but they received no reply. When the steward unlocked it, the room stood empty, Jauhara long gone.

"While her parents entered her room, Jauhara strode through an al-Askar bazaar, her breasts bound, her hair wrapped in a turban, a leather satchel in her hand. The book, the key to her freedom, was packed safely within. She spared little thought for her parents' worry.

"Had she known what she had awakened in the palace, she would not have been so sanguine.

"In the square, players thronged: men ate fire, swallowed swords, lay on beds of nails. An old man unraveled a tale for a group of spellbound children, and costumed men acted exaggeratedly for an applauding audience. For a decidedly smaller audience, a young man made an apple disappear, eliciting *ah*s. He made the apple reappear from a man's trousers to scandalized giggles.

"*Oh, but I could do that*, thought Jauhara. She approached the young man, deepening her voice. 'O esteemed saidi—'

"He gave her a look of profound loathing.

"Jauhara announced, 'I would show you some magic of my own, I, who have studied the magical arts of our ancient forbears.' Jauhara said a word, and earth exploded at the man's feet, coating him with dust. The crowd laughed, and Jauhara, although queasy, grinned. But the man raised his fist, exclaiming, 'Leave before I backhand you across the plaza!'

"Jauhara, who had been reared tenderly in her parents' palace, was stunned. Fleeing into an alley, she squeezed between two carts and wept until she was interrupted by a squawk.

"'Don't weep, dear girl.'

"Jauhara choked back tears and remembered her ruse. 'I don't know who you are, but I am no girl!'

"'You are a girl,' the voice said patiently. 'The daughter of Governor 'Omar and the old governor's daughter, Soraya.'

"'Who are you? Where are you?'

"'Lift the canvas.'

"Jauhara spotted a cream-colored canvas draping something dome-shaped. With misgiving, Jauhara lifted the cloth, uncovering a brass cage. Within perched a green-and-red-winged parrot with a lemon-yellow crest. Jauhara looked around, bewildered. 'Where are you?'

"If Jauhara had not seen the pink bill move, she would not have believed it.

"'In the cage, Sitt Jauhara.'

"Jauhara clutched her throat. 'Ya Allah! What magic is this? How do you know my name, my family . . . ? What are you?'

"The parrot sighed. 'I am a parrot, bewitched to know more than it should. Should you persuade my master to sell me, I could convince the players to let you join them.'

"Jauhara could not believe how easily the parrot had read her soul. 'How . . . ?'

"'Perhaps you should stop asking *how*, Sitt Jauhara.' Jauhara could hear a smile in the parrot's voice and, beneath that, silver music.

"Though the silk merchant grumbled, he sold the parrot, unaware of the creature's power, and Jauhara carried the unwieldy cage back to the square.

"'What shall I do?' she asked quietly.

"The parrot spread his red-tipped wings. The feathers glowed gold in the sunlight. 'You could return home.'

"Jauhara thought of home, safe—and suffocating. Here was an all-knowing parrot, the start of an adventure. Jauhara shook her head.

"'Then, you will tell the man in pink that you wish to join his troupe. You will say that you have a parrot who can read men's souls.'

"In the shade, Jauhara waited until the man descended from the stage before she approached him. 'Kind saidi, might I have a moment of your time?'

"The man smiled. Something about his face, the tilt of his head perhaps, reminded her of her favorite brother, Bishr.

"'I recognize you, boy!' he said. 'You made the earth explode at Bilal's feet. That was a neat trick.'

"Jauhara tried not to blush. 'Yes, saidi, that was me. I did not mean to offend. I have a request: I wish to travel with your troupe.'

"'You seem like a good boy, but Bilal already performs little tricks.'

"Jauhara was too quick for his brush-off. 'Oh, but saidi, see my parrot here. He is the rarest of all parrots. He does not merely imitate what he hears. Upon seeing a man, he knows his very truth. Go on, ask him anything.'

"Amused, the man asked, 'Very well: what is my name and where do I hail from?'

"As the parrot spoke, the man's jaw slackened. 'You are Qasim bin Qais. Your father is a miller in Basra, at the confluence of the Tigris and Euphrates. You were the youngest and always a scapegrace. You joined this troupe when you were no older than my master here.'

"Qasim laughed. 'Quite a trick! But to join us, you need something more. A parrot who can speak intelligently is astonishing, a parrot who knows your history a marvel—but I already know my father's job and my own reputation. What can you tell me that I do not know?'

"Jauhara's heart sank, but the parrot spoke: 'You worry you will not see your mother again. Her heart is fragile. In a few years, it will consume her. Go to her in the winter. It will bring her ease and you closer to the paradise beneath her feet.'

"Qasim's mouth shook and then steadied. 'Ya Allah. Truly, truly a marvel.' His voice thick, he turned to Jauhara. 'You may join us. What is your name, boy?'

"Jauhara faltered before answering. 'J—Jauhar, saidi.'

"'Come with me, Jauhar, and we shall travel east. I shall take you to splendorous cities: from Baghdad to Kirman, to Multan and farthest Cathay.'"

"Now, O Malik, the night's tale is done, but what is this compared to what befalls Jauhara—or shall I call her Jauhar?—next?"

* * *

The Fajr azaan seeps into the gray corners of my dreams. As more muezzins join, it grows too loud to be ignored.

Today.

Fully awake, I push up against my bed. We depart for Palestine today. Excitement buzzes through my limbs. I can hardly believe this is real. I wish I were staying in Bam; I cannot wait to leave.

I poke Dunya, who rouses sleepily beside me. "Up! We leave today."

She rolls to the other side and pulls the blanket over her head. I open the lattice blinds, breathing the sweetness of wet earth, the salt of the desert, and the incense musk of my room. Below, Bam stirs with preparation—the caravan of camels and horses lining up, servants maneuvering to load them with mountains of packages—food, clothing, arms, all the wares an army needs for a march.

Dunya dozes while Gulnar garbs me in a lemon-and-cream-striped gown, a purple farajiyya, pale pink trousers, and a fringed sash, all hardy cotton grown in Bam's own fields. I slip into a squirrel-lined overcoat.

"How do you feel, Gulnar?" I ask, for she too will be traveling with us.

Gulnar's dark brown hair is twined into neat braids that are finely stranded with silver, although her face is still young and unlined. She has been in my service since I was a little girl. While I have always thought of her as so much my senior, she must be no more than a decade older. "I already know I'll miss the citadel's comforts. And war. Well." Her voice quiets. "War is no light thing."

"No, no it is not."

Seeing that Dunya has buried herself even deeper into the blanket, I tug the covers off and jostle her awake. "Rise. Or the caravan will leave without you."

With an ill-humored look, she stumps to the basin to wash her face.

I recite, quoting Omar Khayyam,

"Awake! For morning in the bowl of night
Has flung the stone that puts the stars to flight:
And lo! The hunter of the east has caught
The sultan's turret in a noose of light."

"I'll catch you in a noose of light," Dunya yawns irritably.

I laugh and then stop, thinking of Baba who taught me that verse long ago. "Dunya, do you think we should stay? Or you should stay? Now that it is upon us . . . I do not like leaving Baba alone."

Dunya stretches her arms as Gulnar deftly layers tunic, trousers, robe, and sash onto her. "Baba is the one sending me with you. He does not want you alone."

"But I do not want him alone."

"Shall we stay?"

There swings temptation. Leave Shahryar to burn himself out on a faraway battlefield. Why would I care? I could live here safely with my Baba and my sister.

And then what?

Shahryar's foolishness leads him to die afar or fall under evil influence, leaving Kirman without a ruler, limping prey for the circling lions?

Who could Shahryar become beside me? Who could I become away from home?

"I must go, but you must stay."

At a rap on the door, Gulnar opens it. Baba's face is drawn, and my heart cracks. I embrace him in a rush, my head against his warm chest, my ear filled with the sound of his heart. "Subh bikhair, Baba," I say, but my throat is tight.

"Oh, my pigeons," he cries, his arms circling my shoulders and pulling Dunya in. I breathe him deeply, cedar and verbena, the memories of adoration and absolute safety.

As he breaks away, I notice Mahperi. Seeing my bewilderment, Baba says, "Mahperi will be joining to attend you. She is in your charge, Shaherazade."

Mahperi, who is a perfect Seljuk beauty with a round, pale face, slanted eyes, and a small mouth, smiles at me. "It was just decided that I could accompany you so long as I submitted myself to your care as the Khatun. How exciting, Shahera!"

I peer at Baba, still confused. He purses his mouth.

Ever delicate, Mahperi steps back as Baba clasps my and Dunya's hands. "I will miss you girls dearly, and every day I will pray for your health and safety and for your return. Pray for me as well, beloveds."

"Oh Baba jaan!" Dunya flings herself to him. Tears cling to her lashes. "Shahera and I have decided: I shall stay."

I nod. My face is wet. "How could we think of leaving you alone? Forgive me, Baba."

Drawing himself up, Baba regards us seriously. "I forbid it. Shahera, you must go and be a gentle voice to the Malik. Dunya, you must remain with Shahera, her best ally at every turn. I will be home and I shall be fine."

He pats my cheek, but I cannot share his resolve.

"Baba . . ." I whimper and think of the months and years I will be away from him. What am I without him near?

As we walk through the Arg-e-Bam, I try to memorize it: the gleaming green-and-blue faience tiles, the time-smoothed floors, the great gold adobe walls, the feel of Baba's hand in mine. As we step into the cool morning, I see shrieking, dark-haired children dodging between double-humped camels and perched on the battlements like radiant birds. An emir yells for the children to pull back. Doctors, orderlies, and merchants clot at the Worm Gate's pointed arch.

Mounted cavalry and soldiers, a force of four thousand, thick with armored Turkmen and mamluks, march from the garrison in precise rows, arraying themselves for the Malik's inspection. I cannot see where the caravan ends, but at its head, I spy the Malik presenting his four emirs, Emir Atsiz, Emir Ildegiz, Emir Özbeg, and the eunuch, Emir Savtegin—Baba whispers their names to me—with robes of honor for their part in raising this army and leading it west. Despite my nerves, a thrill surges through me.

Baba raises his voice over the crowd's cheers. "Do not worry about me, jaanem." I place his hand against my cheek and his voice softens. "I will write often. And Gulnar." He regards her with kindly eyes, while she ducks her head. "Watch over the girls. I trust your wisdom and your care for them above all else."

"By my life, ay Vizier."

Baba leads us easily through the mêlée of horses, soldiers, and scurrying children: seeing us, the crowd respectfully parts. He guides us toward the head, near Shahryar and the emirs, where a groom awaits with a matched pair of arch-necked black horses. "My gifts to you."

The mares are beautiful, with intelligent, liquid eyes that a poet would write about. I approach one, gingerly petting her velvet nose. Like any Turkman, I know how to ride, but it makes me uneasy to trust myself to a creature with its own mind.

As if reading my thoughts, Baba adds, "The Bedouins I bought these two from said they are the mildest sisters of a sweet-tempered mother. Too even-tempered to be useful in desert raids. Shaherazade, yours is called Andalib. Dunya, yours is Shaheen."

A nightingale for me and a falcon for Dunya. Somehow, it fits.

Three sharp bursts of a horn cut through the crowd's chatter, and silence descends as if all of Bam has decided to hold its breath.

"It is time to go, azizem," Baba says.

Clutching him, I decide I do not want to leave. Baba gently unclasps my arms and looks at me intently. "Shaherazade, my beloved. You are my great and glorious daughter." He runs his thumb over my forehead. "Allah has marked you for destiny. You must follow that. You must follow the Malik. Keep your faith in Allah and bring good, not harm, to His creation: you will do well. You will bring me great honor. You already have."

He kisses my forehead, where he marked my destiny. I catalog the moment: the paper-thinness of his lips, the shine in his eyes, the fine silver linen of his tunic. The love for me and Dunya that suffuses his face. His faith in me.

"I love you, Baba jaan," I say, as the groom offers laced hands to lift me onto Andalib. I find I cannot say more.

Baba holds Dunya tightly and I cannot hear what he murmurs to her, but she does not weep. She stands steady, kisses Baba on his cheeks, and floats onto Shaheen beside me.

Even as I feel the strings tying me to Baba tighten, I force myself to kick Andalib forward. *What if I never*—no, I will not give that thought life. I look back and Baba smiles at me, so sweet and warm that I want to jump from the horse, run back to my room, bolt the door, and never leave Bam or my Baba's side. But the promise of sinking my fingers into the strange lands beyond hardens my resolve. I wipe my tears, and leave my father to join the Malik, the emirs, and the *sareban*. It feels like betrayal.

Seeing me and Dunya, the Malik gestures for the horn to be blown again. Its long, drawn blast raises the hair on my arms.

"Bismillah," I whisper as Shahryar urges his white mount through Bam's winding streets, beneath the shadows of its immense watchtowers. The crush of the caravan follows. I wave to Baba until he disappears behind a forest of camel humps, and my tears blur the world around me.

The townspeople, joyous and excited as I have not seen them since before Fataneh's death, rain rose and tulip petals on us. The promise of war erases months of acrid burn between them and the Malik. The red and yellow petals cling to Andalib's black mane like dewdrops and flutter into the Chelekhoneh River, floating away on cold mountain water. The procession marches through wide squares bursting with fountains, past bazaars with empty stalls and mosques with tall brick minarets. The city dwellers' blessings ring in my ears (and my name!—they call my name and call it with love!).

As the *nawba* drums strike, the caravan surges from the wide South Gate onto the road leading into the mountains. Around us, cotton fields are just beginning to green and pistachio groves are in incarnadine bud. The caravan flows from Bam until finally the city has emptied itself and the giant South Gate shuts decidedly behind us.

PART TWO

Eleven

The sareban has guided the caravan west from Bam through the Jebal Barez Mountains. The mountains rise against the clear sky, bare and rocky except where grass has managed to burst forth in a triumph of spring. At the highest peaks, snow crisscrosses with gray stone. Gazing at the Jebal Barez as I ride, I think that five days' journey—especially at the laborious pace set by our caravan—is not such a distance from Bam, but save for our winters in Giroft, this is the farthest I have been from home.

"What do you think of our adventure, Shahera?" Dunya asks wryly. Mahperi laughs. From the dark circles under their eyes, I can tell that they, like me, are still acclimating to the realities of travel—cold tents rattled by wind that carries every sound and smell, thin mattresses through which I can feel each pebble, and never, ever enough sleep. It is hard not to be tempted by how close we still are to home and all its comforts.

I sniff and regret it instantly. The stench of manure and perspiration, of horses and men, clings to the caravan. "Five days and I doubt I'll ever be clean again. Thanks be that we are arriving at the caravanserai tonight. Imagine—a proper bed!"

Beneath my cheer, anxiety ripples. For the last five days, the Malik has ignored me, caught in a maelstrom of war, plotting routes with the sareban and exchanging battle stories with his emirs and boon companions. A wife doesn't fit easily into this camp world. But tonight, with the comfort of the caravanserai's clean blankets and soap, he may remember his wife. And I will be far from Baba and Ishaq's net.

* * *

We pass beneath a tall, peaked gate to enter the caravanserai. Looming walls, pocketed with an arcade of pointed arches, surround an immense, rectangular courtyard, open to the night sky. The caravanserai is almost festive, with music and singing and the chatter of merchants and other travelers. Within the arcade's niches, there are pens for animals, chambers for visitors, stalls selling roast chicken and warm rice. My stomach grumbles. As I descend from Andalib, I wince at the pain in my back, the chafing between my thighs. Shahryar, evincing no stiffness, swings from his horse and peers with interest at the bustling caravanserai.

A short man, whose portliness marks his success, approaches Shahryar with a magnificent bow. His bald pate gleams in the torchlight. "Assalamu'alaikum, Malik Shahryar. I am called Tawfiq ibn 'Uthman. I am a spice merchant," he says in fluid Arabic. "I would be honored if you and your company would dine with me tonight."

Shahryar replies easily, "It would be my honor."

* * *

After scraping the filth from my skin in the caravanserai's rough-hewn baths, I, with Emir Atsiz, Emir Ildegiz, Emir Özbeg, and Emir Savtegin, join Tawfiq ibn 'Uthman at a low table, surrounded by cushions, in a small stone room. The spice merchant is a generous host: servants load our plates with a vegetable and herb stew, heavy with parsley and leek, roasted chicken stuffed with sugar and Kirmani pistachios, large beef kofteh, rice cooked with chickpeas, and plush nan.

"Please," ibn 'Uthman says unctuously. "Eat, enjoy." He draws Shahryar into a complex conversation about trading privileges in Kirman and taxes on his goods, while Shahryar fends him off with noncommittal grace. The emirs, led by Emir Atsiz, talk among themselves, not of battle or politics but, surprisingly, of the verse of the famed poetess Safiyya al-Baghdadiyya, the wonder of the world, the ravisher of hearts and minds.

Before I can make up my mind to join, the merchant pauses for a breath and Emir Atsiz asks, "Where have you come from, friend?" Each word slips from his lips ponderously slow. His baritone catches in my chest.

Shahryar shoots Emir Atsiz a grateful look.

"I have come from Jerusalem and praise Allah I departed when I did."

"What have you heard?" inquires Emir Savtegin.

"Richard of England, Malikric, whom they call the Lionhearted, has conquered Cyprus, subjugating its ruler, a fellow Christian." Ibn 'Uthman shakes his head with pious sadness. "The men of the west are brutal, little better than animals. What care have they of someone's faith when they stand to gain wealth?"

My mouth contorts of its own will as I think of the Oghuz and Khwarezmids, members of our own ummah who aim to conquer us. Fellowship in faith is no barrier to the power-hungry.

"And," the merchant adds, "Isaac Comnenus of Cyprus had close ties with Saladin. I doubt Malikric liked that very much."

"What do you know of Malikric?" Shahyrar asks.

"I have heard that the Franks hold Malikric to be a man of high honor and chivalry. He promised not to put Isaac in chains of iron, and being a man of his word, he bound the Emperor of Cyprus in chains of silver!" Ibn 'Uthman guffaws.

Atsiz snorts. "I should like to see the men Franks hold to be base criminals."

"If you travel to Palestine, you will see such men and worse," ibn 'Uthman says. "But there is even more grievous news. The Frankish king Philip has arrived with his fleet on the shores of Acre and is throwing his weight behind the siege there. Saladin's men are weakening."

Sipping cinnamon-garnished carrot juice, I consider the possibility that we will lose against the Frankish barbarians. When they first stepped on our shores a century ago, the ummah was aghast at their brutality, which left the holy places in Jerusalem ankle deep in blood. Now, commanded by a king renowned for his cleverness in battle, who can say the Franks won't do the same again? The cinnamon tastes bitter in my mouth.

We finish the meal, thanking the merchant for his hospitality. I avoid the Malik's eyes and hope I can slip into the warm room shared by Dunya and Mahperi. But the Malik says in a low growl, "Shaherazade." As I trudge behind him, his emirs do not look at me, but the merchant watches us, a greedy sparrow pecking for morsels.

* * *

The Malik's steward, Yaghmur, has lit the oil lamp in the room. A red and black blanket covers the soft bed, and thick rugs conceal the flagstones. I carefully perch on the edge of the bed where Shahryar reclines, his scrubbed skin glistening. I feel a flutter low in my body and I almost expect Shahryar to pull me close. Instead, he says, "Tell me what happened next."

Trying to smooth the tremor in my voice, I say:

———————

"O Malik, it is said that Jauhara traveled with the entertainers' troupe from Egypt to ancient Aleppo and cinnamon Damascus, to the holy cities of Mecca and Medina, to Baghdad and Esfahan.

"The caravan now rested in a caravanserai in the high Himalayas, each peak a silver dagger piercing the sky. Exploring the caravanserai's small bazaar, Jauhara admired crystals excavated from mountain caves and glittering beadwork stitched into caps and vests. Still disguised as a boy, with her breasts flattened and hair wrapped in a turban, Jauhara enjoyed the liberty of androgyny. The parrot sat on her right shoulder and she liked his weight there, too.

"She bought a bowl of tea from a toothless woman. It was stronger, sweeter, and lightened with more milk and spiced with more cardamom than she was accustomed to, and she found that this too was something she liked. Jauhara crumbled sweet cake for the parrot to peck at. Jauhara summoned the courage to ask something she had been wondering for all of the months of her journey: 'Are there other parrots like you?'

"The parrot rolled his head bonelessly. 'I think not,' he said.

"'Then how did you come to be?' Jauhara asked.

"'I am only a parrot because I fell in love.'

"'I did not know that parrots could fall in love!' Jauhara exclaimed, but then she was embarrassed. Had her parrot not proven that his intelligence and feelings were as acute—perhaps even more so—than a human's, time and time again?"

The Malik's face is lax in sleep. Quietly, I douse the light and lie beside him. Pulling me close, he curves around me, a feeling so intimate that my heart pounds. I pass the night, pinned beneath his arm, wondering what it means that he wanted to sleep with me nestled into him.

* * *

The caravanserai and its comforts are days behind us, and the mountains have flattened into desert. I feel myself habituating to Andalib's swaying gait, my muscles hardening like those of my Seljuk forebears, who swept through great lands and made them their own.

The setting sun brings out the roses in Dunya's cheeks. Somewhere during today's journey, she lost her veil, and her braids swing freely past her hips, tangled with windblown sand. "Tell us a story as we ride."

"We're about to stop for the night," I point out, knowing that the lagging caravan will catch us shortly and then we will drop from our horses, raise our tents, and dine on meat and bread. After, the Malik may summon me to his tent or leave me with Dunya and Mahperi, as suits his temper.

Mahperi pokes shyly at my elbow. "Oh, do! While we wait."

I smile. "Oh, all right then.

"It is said that there was once a farmer with two sons born of two wives. Each son was the apple of his mother's eye, both sweet, cherry-cheeked boys who grew to be strong, kind men. Each was a mirror of the other. Because the boys were so alike, the wives loved both as their own and both boys called each woman 'Mother.'

"The boys grew in peace, but when they were twenty, war swept through their father's homestead, collecting them both and depositing them, at the end, far from home . . ."

A broad-shouldered figure appears behind Dunya on a cantering white horse. Shahryar circles us as if we're sheep being herded. We fall silent. The Malik's eyes dart from me to Dunya to Mahperi. "Why are you so far from the caravan?"

I swallow a sudden lump at this Malik, who seems so far from the one who curled around me just nights before.

But Dunya says with absolute sunniness, "We were begging Shaherazade for a story." Although we are honest, I can feel the nervous performance in Dunya's brightness and in Mahperi's wide-eyed innocence. And if I can sense it, surely the Malik can too.

"Go on then, Shaherazade," he says placidly, but he offers the invitation as if he has set a trap and somehow I am ripe to walk into it. "Tell us your story."

Ducking my head, I smile my obeisance and remind myself that we have done nothing wrong. "O Malik, it is said that once the war was over and its spoils divided between kings, Nuruddin and Shamsuddin journeyed back to their father's home in an Anatolian valley famed for its apricots."

I raise my voice above the loudening wind that harries my braids and plucks at my coral veil. "When the boys returned, they learned that their father had died some months before. His estate, which should have gone in equal pieces to his sons and smaller, equal pieces to his wives, had been swallowed by his brother, the village qazi.

"But Nuruddin and Shamsuddin did not suspect their uncle of wrongdoing. Their first night, their uncle welcomed them into their father's home. He served them a rich meal of lamb kebabs and caraway-roasted chicken and invited his nephews to regale him with tales of war. Not until a servant woman briefly touched Nuruddin's hand did he look up and recognize his brother's mother—"

Shrieking wind devours my words whole. To the north, the sky has bruised, dark and violet, like the marks the Khatun left on my arm. Red sand engulfs the horizon, as though Prophet Musa had stamped his staff and raised a wall from the desert to cover the sky. The wall roars toward us and the world darkens. My teeth chatter and I hear Mahperi shriek.

A *habub*. One that rises out of nothing (*"Be!" and it is*) and can decimate a town, a caravan, leaving corpses and destruction in its wake. Cheeks pale, Dunya, Mahperi, and I stare at the Malik.

"We must race back to the caravan," he instructs, suspicion forgotten. Quickly, he ties our sashes together, binding me last on the train. "You are the rear, Shaherazade. Do not lose sight of me."

As he ties the last knot, the habub falls on us, umbral and screeching like a hundred ghouls. The sand whips so furiously, stinging my skin like ground glass, that even though I tie my veil around my eyes, they can't stay open. I feel a tug at my waist and push Andalib forward, clutching her against the strong wind that threatens to knock us both over. Blindly, I follow the pull on my waist, take comfort at the steady pressure, the knowledge that Shahryar is at our head and will lead us to safety.

The sash slackens. Before I can secure it, the gale spins it away and it disappears in the gloaming.

"Dunya! Dunya! Shahryar!" The wind throws my cries back at me, fills my mouth with sand. It is no use.

They are gone.

I cannot discern anything save for Andalib under my thighs and the cold, hard wind that thrashes my body. I do not know what to do. Maybe, if I stay here, where they lost me, they will find me again. I dismount and bury my face in Andalib's side, praying that Allah keep me safe and trying to forget tales of the dead swallowed by the desert.

The habub weeps ceaselessly, swallowing all sight and sound, until seconds, minutes, and hours lose all meaning.

If these are my last moments, I try to remember those I love most: Baba and Dunya and Mama and Laila and Hanna. I beg Allah to forgive my sins, so that if I am to meet Him, I will do so with my soul feather light, so when Israfil blows his golden trumpet and I must cross the needle-thin bridge of as-Sirat to enter Paradise, the breeze blows at my back and I pass, unmolested by thorns and hellfire.

Ay Khoda, forgive me, forgive me for the deaths of Altunjan and Shideh and Inanj, for throwing Greek fire onto a house of straw.

I wait and wait for the wind to stop, for the world to clear, to open my eyes and find myself in the middle of the camp, safe and surrounded by Seljuk soldiers, my sister at my side.

There was once a girl who only had to say the name of the place and there she would be . . .

Where would I be? With Dunya and Mahperi, safe and warm. In my chamber in Bam, Baba bustling close by.

Anywhere.

Anywhere I was not alone.

* * *

At last, the wind abates and sand falls to the ground like snow. I brush it from Andalib's mane and her long eyelashes. She takes my ministrations patiently. Hours must have passed.

Above me, the sky clears, revealing gleaming stars and a pearlescent moon that glows above an emptiness that stretches until it is swallowed by darkness. The glimmer of the caravan is nowhere to be seen. Above me, I recognize some of the shimmering constellations: the Shackled Woman, the Bearer of the Demon's Head, the Snake Charmer, but I do not know how to use the stars to mark my location or guide me back.

Blood-drinking, shape-shifting ghouls, sired by Iblis himself, inhabit desert wastes like this. *If it were daylight and you were with Dunya, you would not be thinking of ghouls*—but in this eerie emptiness, my imagination brushes away the boundaries of reality.

Something—fear—grips my throat.

"Help!"

My cry vanishes into a vast vacuum. Nothingness and darkness melt together.

A tall shadow looms over me, reaching its arms toward me. I scream. The shrill sound breaks the glassy stillness of the night. A single palm tree with a spreading top. My pulse calms, and I loop Andalib's reins around its trunk.

"Is anyone there?"

I am not sure I want an answer. I tighten my robe and curl beside Andalib.

* * *

A fine line of light marks the horizon. East. I draw a breath. My mouth is dry and my head pounds; I shake my plaits and sand rains down. Scanning the desert, I look for a sign of the great caravan snaking along a road. Nothing. My thighs ache as I pull myself onto Andalib's leather saddle and we head toward the blackest part of the sky. A sea must be like this. An impossibly endless expanse, no borders, just horizon, devastating to those foolish enough to find themselves lost in it.

As the sun rises, I give the remaining water in my flask to Andalib. The harder I try to ignore my thirst, the more persistent it grows. I do not know what I will do when Andalib cannot continue. When I begin to grow mad, to see ghosts and mirages. When we ride for days and do not see a village, an outpost, or a caravanserai because the habub has blown us into deep barrenness. When we ride for days and are found by mercenaries or marauders, men of no mercy. Will Shahryar even send someone to search for me, or will he consider that the sandstorm has done his work?

This is the price I pay for Fataneh's death.

And although I married a man famous for killing his brides, it hits me now with physical ferocity: I do not want to die. I think of my great collection of sins and of how little I have done to offset their weight.

***

The wind whistles in my ears, sounding like someone calling my name. "Shaherazade Khatun! Shaherazade Khatun!" The cry is stronger now. I could almost believe it real, but I will not surrender so quickly to madness. I ignore the cries and focus on what is true—Andalib's hooves pounding against the dry ground, my own heart beating in my chest. Andalib rears, turning the world upside down. I hold tightly and lean forward, and her hooves thump to the ground.

Before me is a mirage. A man on a horse, with a scarf covering the bottom half of his face.

"You are not real."

But when I try to push Andalib through him, she stops and he pets her nose.

He pushes the scarf down, revealing a prominent nose and berry mouth.

"Emir Atsiz?"

I touch his face and he feels real: his beard soft, skin warm. I want to collapse with relief. He hands me a leather flask. As I gulp, the water dribbles from the corners of my mouth and splashes onto my farajiyya.

With the back of my hand, I wipe my mouth. "How far are we from the caravan?"

"A half day's ride." He hands me a kebab and nan. The kebab is cold and the nan dry, but I scarf it like a beggar.

"Is anyone else looking for me?" The words are crushed under meat and bread.

His eyebrows rise. "You are the Khatun. The Malik is deeply worried. Your sister and friend are hysterical."

Emir Atsiz makes a trough with his hands before Andalib, and asks me to pour the remaining water. I keep refilling his hands until the flask is dry, but even so, Andalib looks weary. Atsiz pats her softly. "She's had a hard night. If you keep riding her, you may ruin her." He ties Andalib's reins to his gray stallion. "You will have to ride behind me."

Seeing my hesitation, Emir Atsiz says, "If you ride her, you will kill her."

If I ride with you, he will kill me.

But I do not resist as Atsiz lifts me onto his horse and mounts in front of me. I wrap my arms around his muscled waist and feel a wave of exhaustion. Although I try, I cannot resist the allure of closing my eyes and laying my cheek against his broad back. He smells comforting, like nan and tea. I feel his torso vibrate with the hum of Oghuz song, quieting my worries.

***

feel a nudge. Blearily, I blink and lift my head from the warmth of Atsiz's back.

"We're close."

Straightening, I see the approaching blur of the caravan—horses and mules and camels and carts. I wipe the sand from my eyes and rub my face vigorously. From the caravan, a horseman darts out and careens to a halt, sending sand flying. Shahryar's eyes shift from me to Atsiz. Although I hold my body away from Atsiz, I can almost read the algebra whirring through Shahryar's mind.

There was once a girl named A'isha, beloved of the most powerful man in Arabia. While traveling through the desert with her husband and a party of traders, she bedded for a night beneath a palm tree. When the caravan departed the next morning, she realized, just steps away from the camp, that her necklace, a gift from her father on her wedding day, had fallen from her throat. Quietly, she slipped from her palanquin to retrieve the necklace, which she found easily in the shade of the palm tree.

But when she looked up again, the caravan, her husband and his companions, had disappeared.

She remained beneath the blistering sun with only the tree's broken shadows to protect her. She knew better than to set out alone and unguided through mountainous dunes. She knew someone would notice her absence; she was the wife of the Prophet Muhammad, the daughter of his esteemed companion Abu Bakr.

She waited. She waited hours, until the sun was past its zenith, but still she prayed and refused to be afraid.

At last, she heard the soft thud of hoofbeats. She sprang forward and for a moment, she was crestfallen. Her rescuer was not her husband or her father. It was not even her brother. He was a nomad named Safwan and he was handsome: dark hair, a noble face like an eagle's, and arresting eyes, the color of honey, the color of a cat's.

But in her relief, A'isha saw none of this. With the courtesy due any woman, but especially the Prophet's wife, Safwan offered her water and they rode silently back to Medina together on his horse.

A'isha had expected joy and tears and relief at her return. But A'isha had forgotten that she was a beautiful woman in the company of a handsome man who was not her husband.

Instead of jubilation, Safwan's rescue was seen as evidence of adultery: she was decried as a whore; the Prophet was advised to divorce her. Among the foremost calling for divorce was the Prophet's beloved nephew. Despite A'isha's protests of innocence, despite Safwan's denials, even after the intercession of the Prophet's adopted son, her name was dragged through the streets of Medina.

Still, her husband remained silent.

Her devotion to her husband and her faith was suddenly meaningless. She was not safe. No woman was ever safe, anywhere in this world. It was an injustice she had never fully grasped.

Then, at last, at last, at last, where men had failed, where her family had failed, Allah saved her, sent a revelation, Qur'anic verses, censuring, yes, censuring His Prophet, for not trusting his wife. And He, where so many had remained quiet, upbraided those who had wrongfully accused her:

"THOSE WHO BROUGHT FORWARD THE LIE ARE A BODY AMONG YOURSELVES: THINK IT NOT TO BE AN EVIL TO YOU," HE SAID. "WHY DID NOT THE BELIEVERS—MEN AND WOMEN—WHEN YE HEARD OF THE AFFAIR—PUT THE BEST CONSTRUCTION ON IT IN THEIR OWN MINDS AND SAY, 'THIS IS AN OBVIOUS LIE'? WHY DID THEY NOT BRING FOUR WITNESSES TO PROVE IT? WHEN THEY HAVE NOT BROUGHT THE WITNESSES, SUCH MEN, IN THE SIGHT OF ALLAH, STAND FORTH THEMSELVES AS LIARS."

Allah and only Allah returned A'isha to her position. Later in her life, she would become known as the Mother of Believers, a respected scholar, a fearsome war leader. But she never forgot that if her fate had been left to her people, it would have been very different indeed.

"When they have not brought the witnesses, such men, in the sight of Allah, stand forth themselves as liars," I murmur, sliding from Atsiz's horse.

Atsiz glances at me, but Shahryar does not move. He recognizes the verse. I know that Baba drilled him in the Qur'an as much as *Mirrors for Princes.* I meet his gaze, hope that he can see my exhaustion and fear and honesty. Then, I drop my eyes again in proper wifely deference.

He does not ask how Atsiz found me, if I am well, if I need anything. Instead, he says, "Go to your sister. We shall speak at dinner."

I nod, thank Atsiz quietly, and try not to compare how any other newlywed husband would have greeted his bride's rescue from certain death. After all, this is Malik Shahryar, the greatest murderer of brides Persia has known.

* * *

My tongue sticks to my mouth, and my back is cramped from sleeping like a curled leaf in Dunya and Mahperi's round tent.

Dunya shakes my arm. "Wake up. Shahryar wants to speak to you." I can hear the worry in her voice.

Mouth taut, Gulnar presses a cup of lukewarm water to my lips. Taking the cup from her hand, I push the tent flap aside to reveal a camp lit red and shadowed in black by small campfires. "What's being said?"

"Of you? Nothing."

"Don't lie."

Dunya sighs. "You were seen close to Emir Atsiz on the horse. There's a rumor that before this, the emir told someone that he admired you greatly. When he heard you were missing, he raced into the dawn to search for you without a second thought. But that is it. There is nothing else to say. The camp is giving thanks for your return."

Chewing a sprig of mint offered by Mahperi, I ask, "And the Malik?"

I consider yesterday from his viewpoint, of coming upon my sister, my friend, and me in a conspiratorial huddle, away from the camp, of me returning after a night alone accompanied by a handsome man.

Walking to Shahryar's tent, I feel the soldiers and merchants and medics watching. Perhaps I should be afraid, but instead I feel hot anger that somehow being lost in the desert until I went mad from thirst is not the worst outcome.

Chalice of wine in hand, Shahryar sits cross-legged on a thick crimson rug. Beside him stands a familiar-looking, hard-muscled mamluk. Pockmarks dust his nose and cheeks. At his hip, his shamshir glints silver.

"Sit, Shaherazade."

I sit across from the two men, watching Shahryar carefully. Surely he would not execute me like this, in a tent on top of a rug that would drink my blood and be forever stained. Then, I bite my lip at the absurdity of thinking that fastidious housekeeping would stay Shahryar's hand.

"This is Fakhruddin." Shahryar gestures toward the mamluk.

I clear my throat. "Durood."

Fakhruddin is tanned from a life of marching and camping. He is old for a mamluk—closer to Baba's age than Shahryar's. Beneath his receding hairline, his dark eyes are humorless. He seems a man who would obey his master without question.

"We were concerned by your disappearance. You are my wife and the daughter of my vizier. Your safety and whereabouts are of the utmost importance. For your protection, I have assigned a regiment of six mamluks. Fakhruddin here is their commander."

I shake with relief.

Fakhruddin nods. "I look forward to serving you, Shaherazade Khatun."

Few women have received the honor of a guard of mamluks at their command, mamluks who are trained from youth to be fearsome fighters and upon reaching manhood are freed by their master to whom they owe utmost loyalty. The last was Turkan Khatun, who led armies on behalf of her young Seljuk sultan son—but she was poisoned more than a century ago.

"You may leave, Fakhruddin."

As he exits, Shahryar's plump steward, Yaghmur, appears with a pretty slave girl and they quietly serve our dinner of simple chicken pilau and beef dumplings with yogurt. The girl refills Shahryar's wine with a simper. I fall on the food ravenously.

After I have cleared my plate, Shahryar says, "The last time you ended by saying that Jauhara's parrot had not always been a parrot."

A surprised satisfaction at his interest wars with tiredness. But of course, pleasing Shahryar wins.

"O Malik, it is said that Jauhara was stunned when the parrot claimed he had not always been a bird. Her surprise quickly passed, for after all, was it so strange that this parrot, who spoke and knew things that no one else could, was not what he appeared?

"'What were you before?' she asked. 'And how did you come to be a parrot?'

"The parrot said: 'Before time had begun to stretch in this universe, Allah formed me of white and gold light. I was one of His servants. I did His bidding in the heavens, on this earth, and in the worlds that lie within and past the infinite universes. I was an angel. Then, I fell in love.'

"'But I thought angels could only do as Allah ordered,' Jauhara protested.

"'Just so,' the parrot said equably.

"'But then . . .'

"Ignoring her, he continued. 'I fell in love with a woman whom I saw from the heavens. Her every movement was grace, the lift of her foot more beautiful than a dozen sunrises, the tilt of her head like the song of a nightingale. Her skin was brown, richer than rosewood, and striking light scattered on it like a dusting of stars. Her hair rose in the softest black curls and her long neck would have shamed a swan. Never in all the eons has such radiance walked your earth.

"'But I could not make myself known to Aminata. I followed her as she went about her business through Ghana, a city of twelve mosques, which, for its piety, had been blessed with gold and salt that grow in the rock like grass in the plain.

"'I followed her and tried, in whatever small way I could, to ease her life: I comforted her before her marriage, prayed beside her in sickness and in childbirth. Aminata could not feel or hear me, not as I was then, but sometimes, she would sense me and smile. Those smiles were the rarest of pearls, and for them, I would follow her until the Day of Judgment. But in doing so, I neglected the duties Allah had assigned me long ago.

"'Soon, she reached the middle of her life—it astounds me how quickly you humans live. It was as if I drew a breath and there Aminata lay, a newly made mother; I blinked, and here she tended her stone-and-acacia home, her children grown and gone. Yet you place such importance on them, as if there has not stretched an eternity before you and an eternity after you.

"'Yet, I began to understand that importance. Something shifted, perhaps Allah took mercy upon my heartache, and Aminata began to be able to hear me, a whisper in her ear.

"'One day, her husband heard her speaking to me while she worked at her loom. When he asked her whom she had been talking to, she replied honestly that she did not know. Her husband, however, was a jealous man and did not accept his wife's word. Aminata tried to explain that there was no evil, no sin, only good. But he did not like it, and believing something evil had overtaken his home and seduced his wife, he summoned a magician, who lived in the thickets surrounding the king's city, to settle the matter once and for all—'"

"The husband, then, is a villain because he did not want his wife speaking to a stranger in their home?" Shahryar's ears are apple-red, the edges of his speech soft with wine.

Careful. "He is not a villain, but the parrot brought comfort to his wife, and if her husband had understood he would not deem it untoward."

It's too late.

"Is that what you think? That there was nothing untoward with Fataneh and her lovers?" His fingers wrap into a shaking fist, and I can easily imagine his hands tightening around my throat. Imperceptibly, beneath my voluminous robe, I rise to my haunches, ready to propel myself through the tent so he will have to drag me back by my braids in full view of his men.

"I do not mean that. If you will let me finish the tale, you will see—"

"I see how you all regard me. Your father treads around me with care, but I see his disdain. He, you, all of you, think me a monster, think me broken, think me weak."

I want to say: *You are weak! Men and women before you have been betrayed, and men and women after you will be betrayed. But to be betrayed is not to be broken, and to be broken is not to become a killer.*

Shahryar rolls like a thunderhead, snapping with lightning. "For all your imagination, you do not understand love. Let me tell you of love, little Shaherazade."

I freeze like an antelope in an archer's sight.

"When I was a boy, my father hanged himself. My mother and brother were exiled to Samarkand, where she died before I ever saw her again. I was abandoned, forced to grow to manhood alone, with courtesy but without love.

"But one day, I journeyed to Ganja to meet its emir, and in its gardens, I beheld Fataneh. My heart clicked. There! There it was, what the poets talked about, the headiness of wine, that sweet intoxication. When we wed, the love I had never known sprouted like spring weeds and Fataneh was its earth, its sunshine, its water. I would have been her slave, her dog to kick if it meant I would feel her silk slipper against my skin."

His face collapses. "Then, she, the family I had awaited since boy-hood, for whom I would have given everything, betrayed me. *She* killed the woman who had loved me. When I executed her, I executed my wife's murderer.

"Still, ay Khoda, my heart aches for her. If she only exists in my memory, then there, at least, she still looks at me softly and knows my heart like Surah al-Fatiha. But I know now: everything I love ends in blood."

Twelve

◇◇◇◇◇

We have pushed west past Esfahan, leaving behind the zigzag profile of the Zagros Mountains with their dark roots and snowy peaks. The land is rocky, dry with shadowy scrub. The days have steadily warmed, and I am grateful for the evening coolness. My scalp and mouth are salty with sweat and sand.

Hazy against the orange sky, the Malik's falconers ride ahead, their birds ready to snatch unwary prey flushed out by drummers. Scorpions trundle across the sand like dark shadows, bobbing from side to side, disturbed by the drumbeat. Shahryar and his boon companions, Baba's cat's-paw Faramurz, Dunya, and Mahperi follow close behind. I linger back, but careful to never lose sight of my companions—although I have a companion of my own. I look at my new mamluk, Bahram, a young man with shining Circassian blue eyes and a tight mouth.

"The scrub is as dead as can be. I don't think we'll find anything."

Atsiz, who rides nearby, hears me and smiles crookedly, conspiratorially. For some reason, I find this endearing.

"What is it?"

His green eyes flash mischief. "If we can escape from the drummers, we may be able to find a cheetah. I've heard they can be found here."

Two answers boil up in me at once: no; yes. No, because my husband is Shahryar and Shahryar does not trust women, does not trust his wives, does not trust me. Would not trust me disappearing with anyone, even his most trusted emir, especially him, into the desert. Yes, because Shahryar has hardly spoken to me in the weeks since Atsiz rescued me from death in the habub and he made his confession. Instead, Atsiz has been the one to pass me small courtesies. Yes, because the march has been uncomfortable and long, and suddenly, I want to be alone at dusk with Atsiz, both safe and unsafe. Suddenly, I am tired of walking with care, a step away from terror. Temerity grasps me by the gullet.

"Bahram. Follow me and Emir Atsiz, but remain silent and keep your distance."

We spin our horses from the clatter of the drums and ride until their booms fade and the falcons' shrill cries are no more.

"Who told you about cheetahs in this desert?" I ask softly, watching him as the day's last light catches on his high cheekbones and loses itself in his dark hair that he wears loose around his shoulders.

"My father was an emir in Azerbaijan, and when I was young, he sent me to train with Emir Ildegiz who was serving in Ganja then. Years before, while on a campaign here, Emir Ildegiz found a cheetah cub beside its dead mother. His soldiers told him to kill the cub, that it would be a mercy, but he brought the cub back for his daughter, Nurani, to raise. Nurani leashed it with a red leather collar, and it followed her around, sweet as a kitten.

"But the cub grew older, and in the end, a cheetah, even coddled, is a wild thing. It swiped at the girl's mother and scarred her arm. The cheetah was sold to a menagerie the next day—and only because Nurani pled for it to not become a rug."

"Will you capture a cheetah for me, Emir Atsiz? A good one, that I can keep in my lap?" I do not know where I have found this silver lode of coquetry; I try to tamp it down.

Atsiz looks at me sidelong and then laughs. "So you can train it to attack your enemies?"

"What enemies?"

"You are a Seljuk Khatun. If you do not have enemies, you certainly will."

"Then my request is doubly important."

Glancing at Bahram, Atsiz says, "You are well protected."

"What if I need protection from my protectors?" The joke falls heavily. Still, Atsiz chuckles and Bahram is too far to have heard.

We ride ahead quietly.

"Shaherazade Khatun. Shaherazade."

The way Atsiz says my name, a hiss, a whisper, raises the hair on my neck.

"It's not a common Seljuk name," he continues.

"My mother found it in an old book of Sassanian tales."

"Fitting for a daughter who turned out to be a storybook heroine." His deep voice is like honey, warm with a secret joke.

My cheeks flush red as pomegranate blossoms, and I'm grateful that the sun has almost disappeared. I want Atsiz to think me a grand figure, the heroine he supposes me to be, but I also want him to know that I am just a girl, who has made mistake after mistake. I fear the moment when he—and the rest—will discover that I am nothing special at all.

"Your mother is—?"

"Yes," I reply.

"Mine as well, may Allah have mercy on her. How old were you?"

"Just a child. She died in childbirth," I say softly. "A brother. He died as well."

Atsiz puts his hand over mine, tender and firm. Despite the impropriety, his touch feels like it belongs. I let it remain. "Ay Shaherazade. I am so sorry."

I remember the day. Baba had sent Dunya and me with Gulnar to Ismat's while our mother labored, promising us a baby, for which Dunya and I had begged. When an ashen-faced servant summoned us home, I knew. Baba would not let us see her until she was bathed and shrouded in white, but I imagined it, the bed red with her blood, a blue baby boy in her arms. If Shahryar wants to murder me, perhaps he should get me with child.

I take a deep breath and bring myself back to the warm mulberry twilight, the crackle of shrub beneath us, the companionable silence with Atsiz, who watches me carefully but says nothing.

And there!

A glimmer of golden eyes, glowing like oil lamps, like stars in the night. My hand flies out and squeezes Atsiz's arm. He grins. She slinks through the shrub, her shoulders bobbing like liquid mercury. A night-cool wind blows and Andalib throws her head back, neighing at the cheetah's scent. The cheetah chirps and then springs—

She crumples, mewling as the warm light of her eyes sputters out. An arrow has punched through her belly, blood matting the downy fur. Atsiz's hands are empty. I look back at Bahram, who calmly lowers his bow. In those mean blue eyes, I read a world of disdain for the life he has snuffed.

"What in Allah's name possessed you to kill that creature?" Fingers curl as I strive to master my rippling anger. I cannot look at the poor dead animal, dead because I wanted to see it, dead because I wanted an adventure, dead because I got what I asked for.

"It was a threat to you, Khatun." Dismounting, he swaggers to the cheetah's corpse and examines his handiwork. He leans over, picks up, and then releases a paw. It flops heavily to the earth.

"What are you doing?" I snap.

"I shot the cheetah. It's mine. It will make a fine rug."

"I forbid it."

He scowls, but I am the Khatun. Even if these mamluks are Shahryar's spies, they owe me nominal obedience, in small things at least. I hear Atsiz ride up behind me and see Bahram's gaze twitch between us, calculating.

✳ ✳ ✳

"What do you think the Franks will be like?" Dunya asks, flopped on her stomach, heels kicked up in the air.

"Do you think they'll be handsome?" Mahperi adds, wrapped in a rose-colored robe on the deep blue-and-red rug spread in their tent.

"In his chronicle," I say, "al-Qalinisi writes that when they came to Muslim lands a hundred years ago, the Franks killed thousands of towns-people, that they burned Jews who took sanctuary in a synagogue."

Now, they return to inflict more of the same on people who have done nothing but live in their own homes and tend their own lands.

"I think they will be hard, brutal men. As for their appearance, Mah-peri, I do not recall if the chronicle says anything, but I have it in a trunk. You can read it and we can discuss . . ."

Mahperi and Dunya are giggling. "The one benefit to you becoming Khatun was the end of your 'lessons'!" Dunya says.

I give her a hard look, but Dunya only laughs harder. "Run, Mahperi, before she assigns you more work. Now that she's Khatun, she can make us do it!" Without looking back, Dunya pulls on her slippers and dashes out.

Mahperi shakes her head at Dunya. "I should be happy to read the chronicle, Shaherazade. It would be good to know who we're going against."

Searching through my trunk, I find the book and pass it to Mahperi. After a few moments, I clear my throat and draw a furred mantle over my gown. "I'll go for a walk around the camp. You stay here."

Outside, I pass a dark-eyed mamluk. "Did you see where Dunyazade Khatun went?" He points toward the outskirts of the camp that shines, as far as the eye can see, with torches and campfires. He makes to follow me. "Oh no, Mahperi is inside. Please watch over her. I'll return in a moment."

He hesitates but I regard him sternly, until he steadies himself at his post. Free of him, I walk through the camp. Even without a guardian, the soldiers recognize me and bow their heads, respectfully murmuring, "Good evening, O Khatun." I give them heartening smiles as a Khatun should.

Now at the edge of the camp, I still have not found Dunya, but away from the campfires, the hailstorm of stars glows brighter. How amazing that these stars float above us, surrounded by worlds like our own, with life that I cannot even begin to imagine.

"'Asr bikhair, O Khatun."

I start and glance over my shoulder. Atsiz. He is so close that I can smell his fragrant attar. It makes me feel light-headed. Before I can ask him why he is here, why he keeps finding me; I hear a familiar laugh. Two figures, one curved but willowy, the other broad shouldered, walk together, backs to us.

"There, do you see those stars that create a snaking line?" says Faramurz.

"Yes," Dunya answers breathlessly. The twilit profile of her head turns up toward him.

"That is at-Tineen, the sea serpent. Do you see how those stars form a circle? The Bedouins see it as a ring of mother camels. There below—that is al-Jathi, the kneeling man, who crushes the serpent beneath his feet. An ancient god sent him into a blind frenzy, and he killed his wife and children. For this sin, he atoned by performing twelve tasks. If I had a wife, I would treat her with only the gentlest kindness."

I do not know how Dunya reacts, but I stifle a snort at the last. Atsiz bites his lip and whispers, "He is no Nizami, but perhaps your sister does not mind."

I feel a twinge that Dunya has not confided any of this to me, but maybe it's nothing more than a flirtation born of long, dull travel. "It appears so."

Atsiz looks intently into my eyes, as if searching for something. "I envy him."

The warmth of his breath sets me afire.

Thirteen

ong grass and palm fronds wave languorously along the verdant banks
of the Tigris River, which flows in filigree ripples past mud-brick fishing
villages and farms surrounded by radiant fields. It is more water than I
have seen in my life, the Chelekhoneh a stream beside it.

Shahryar, who has still not summoned me, converses with gray-haired
Emir Ildegiz near the caravan's head. Seeing me looking, he dismisses
Ildegiz and beckons.

I swallow, and let Andalib canter beside him. My rose gauze veil flies
furiously over my face, harried by the breeze sweeping off the river. I try
to bind it back, but it slips from my fingers and flutters away, leaving my
long braids covered only by a diadem. I mutter an oath.

To my surprise, the Malik chuckles. "Let it be." He unwinds the cotton
scarf from his own neck and ties it beneath my braids. Heat pricks where his
fingers brush my neck. "There. Now you look like a desert child, and some
village boy will find your silk veil and gift it to his sweetheart." He smiles,

and it fills his face with all the warmth and lightness that I have missed. That I extinguished. It fades quickly, but my heart drums in my throat.

"Sometimes, I think of you still as a child. Then I remember you are my wife."

I can hear the unspoken question: *How did we come to this?*

I feel myself on the precipice of confessing, the words are on my lips, how *I* discovered Fataneh, how *I* slipped him the note, that *my* hand pushed us to the present with four dead wives behind us. He speaks again, and the madness of confession glimmers away.

"You are still the innocent child you ever were, aren't you, little Sha-herazade?" He tugs a plait as if I were a girl in truth and softens with patronizing kindness.

My skin crawls. Unwillingly, my mind darts to Atsiz, who was never cold, who has never seen me as the child I was long ago. But perhaps it is safer if Shahryar decides to view me as a child. Only a monster would execute a child, even if he had bared his most vulnerable soul to her.

"Will you spin a tale for me?"

I bite my lip. "Would you like me to continue the last one?"

His stallion's snowy head jerks up; Shahryar's knuckles tighten on the reins. He masters himself and says, "Whatever you wish."

The warning is clear.

"It is said, O Malik, that the parrot continued his tale: 'The sorcerer arrived at Aminata's home, an old man, gnarled and beaten with the evils of the magic he wielded. It was forbidden to humans with good reason, for it corrupts the soul, like rot spoiling good meat.

"'Upon entering the house, the sorcerer sensed me. "Ah," he said, "it is good you have summoned me, for this spirit is evil indeed and it desecrates your home." I longed to laugh at the irony. I, a creature of light and goodness, called a spirit of evil by a man whose soul was so corroded.'

"As Jauhara listened, fear darted through her. She had tampered with magic, dabbled with it in ignorance. Was she too so corrupted?

"The parrot said: 'The magician extended his hands, uttering a strange word. His fingers seized me, I, who until then had known no corporeal form nor the touch of this universe. He squeezed until the world went black, squeezed until the blackness was lit by stars, squeezed until the stars turned everything white. When I awoke, I was in the hands of a trader in my present form. I do not know why the magician let me live. Perhaps he tried to kill me and found that angels are made of more everlasting stuff.

"'I have been passed between traders and owners for a century. Aminata is long dead and my lesson learned. Now, I wait to be found.'

"Jauhara started as the old woman serving her tea leaned over her shoulder. Jauhara's hand twitched protectively toward the parrot, but it looked on with an expression so blankly dumb that Jauhara wondered if she had imagined his entire story.

"The old woman turned her eyes, pearled with cataracts, upon Jauhara. 'It is known that all paths lead to the Creator. But a path needs a guide, and perhaps you, my daughter, need one too.' Those rheumy eyes winked ever so slightly at the parrot. 'Some say a wise Sufi resides high in the mountains who can help those who are lost.'

"'How would I find him?' Jauhara asked.

"'Walk north and west for two days until you reach a valley, which opens onto an immense glacier and lake below. In this lake, you will find gold, purple, and red fish. The red fish are the smallest and rarest and cleverest too. You must catch one, eat its flesh, and burn its bones. Only when you have completed this ritual and are pure of heart will the Sufi come.'

"'What do you think?' Jauhara whispered to the parrot as they returned to the troupe's camp. 'Shall we do this?'

"'It is human to seek your destiny. We angels follow the path He sets for us and do not deviate. Forgiveness is not mine to seek. The decision is yours.'

"Jauhara gathered her few things, placed the parrot on her shoulder, and set off toward the Sufi through high mountain passes, where snow and mica cast blinding reflections, where they were as close to the sky as any man had ever been.

"After a day of walking, they reached a glacial lake that curled and coved, the turquoise water reflecting black-and-white mountains, the green grass they stood on, the sliced glacier above. Jauhara peered into the water, seeing her face clearly for the first time in months. Her skin was no longer the polished ivory of a princess, but gleamed bronze, marked by sun and wind. Her cheeks were narrower, her chin more pointed. In that, Jauhara could see more of her mother, Soraya. Her mother's face in her own squeezed her heart.

"'Do you see any fish?' Jauhara asked the parrot.

"The parrot took wing and circled the lake, hovering over thin reeds and pale-blue ice. His russet wings brushed her cheek as he landed on her shoulder. 'There are purple and green fish around the edges, but the red fish swim only beneath the ice.'

"Jauhara squared her shoulders and strode to a glazed corner of the lake. Telltale glimmers of red pulsed beneath the ice. Unfurling her shawl, Jauhara bunched its ends and dipped it into the water. Dozens of fish flickered forth, and with a loud 'Aha!' Jauhara pulled her shawl out. Eagerly, she poured her catch onto the grass: cold water and scraggly weeds. Her face fell. Red fish darted toward the center, impossibly out of reach.

"As Jauhara wrung out her shawl, the parrot flew to the lake's center and dove once, twice, thrice. On the fourth try, something crimson flopped in his beak. He dropped the wriggling fish into her open palms. The girl and the parrot watched with discomfort as the fish writhed and gasped until it stilled.

"Jauhara put the fish to steam on a lit mound of dried reeds. When its scarlet skin began to crack, she picked it off the flame and bit into it. She gagged as the flesh slipped down her throat and its blood dribbled down her chin. Grimacing, she threw the skeleton into the fire, where it smoked in a tall spiral. The fire started to spark: first yellow, and then green, blue, violet.

"Then, a voice echoed in the circle of mountains, shaking against the glacier and sending waves through the water. 'Who seeks my counsel?'"

***

Two rivers cup Baghdad, the City of Peace. We clatter over brick bridges that arch across canals and ride toward immense golden walls topped with towers, their blue tesserate domes extending to the sky. Some domes are striped, others patterned with arabesques that glint with gold. Black 'Abbasid flags wave from their peaks.

"Who seeks entry into the city of Baghdad?" calls a man wearing a crimson turban.

"I am Shahryar, Malik of Kirman, and I have been granted safe conduct by his most esteemed grace, Caliph an-Nasir li-Din Allah, as we journey to battle the Frankish invaders."

The man touches his chest. "It is my pleasure to welcome you, O Malik. Unfortunately, I cannot permit the whole of your army past the second gate. They will have to remain in the outer city."

The Malik's lips thin, and I almost wish to see him turn his anger on someone else, on a man, if only for a moment.

"These men are tired, and the Caliph has promised us entry."

"They will be housed most comfortably—just not within the inner city."

The Malik frowns. "Very well. But I shall check these accommodations to ensure that they are fitting."

The man inclines his head.

The double iron doors groan as they are hauled open by muscled men, revealing a colorful mass of city, squirming with smells—roasting meat, sweet smoke, and donkey shit—and teeming with noise—the greetings of friends, the cries of vendors, and enthusiastic haggling. A double line of armed troops border the road as far as I can see. I have never seen anything so magnificent; even al-Tanukhi's thousand-page account of life in Baghdad could not do it justice. I press Andalib closer to Shahryar as hawkers and urchins bear down on us, presenting their wares for our consumption, their hands for our charity.

The bulk of our army is shepherded away by the Caliph's guards. Shahryar watches them, unable to hide his worry.

Atsiz approaches Shahryar. "Shall I accompany them, O Malik?"

Shahryar nods, relieved. "If something seems suspicious, send word immediately."

Atsiz follows the army, and I ask Shahryar, "Why would anything seem suspicious? The Caliph would not harm an army journeying to defend the ummah."

"Who do you think funds the Khwarezmid attacks against Sultan Toghrul or the Oghuz skirmishes against Kirman? An-Nasir is ambitious, and it rankles him that we Seljuks had the 'Abbasids under our thumb for a century. If it were possible to avoid Baghdad entirely without rousing his ire, I would have done so."

"Surely the Caliph can put aside his scheming for the holy war against the Franks."

The Malik snorts. "As far as he is concerned, by receiving us and letting us pass through Baghdad unmolested, he is doing his duty as a Muslim and the leader of the faithful. It would be unwise to test our luck." Shahryar pulls me close and his lips against the ridges of my ear chill my back. "Trust no one here, little Shaherazade."

A man in striped maroon and pink trousers rides to us on a silver-saddled mare. "Assalamu'alaikum and marhaba unto you all. O Malik, I am Quzman ibn Hudayj, a steward for the Caliph an-Nasir. I welcome you on my master's behalf to Baghdad. I shall take you to August Divan, where the Caliph awaits to receive you."

He falls beside Shahryar, pointing out the sights. "We are now beneath the Bab al-Amma," he says as we pass beneath the peaked arch of a wide stone gate. Ibn Hudayj then gestures toward a large building, built on porticoes of marble columns. "This is the Khan al-Khayl. A riding house."

I gasp. On the right stand at least five hundred mares, saddled in gold or silver. On the left are another five hundred mares, covered with brocade saddlecloths. I shake my head. If the Caliph wishes to vanquish us, he could do it with one swift crunch.

Ibn Hudayj notices my awe with distinct pleasure. I try to match Shahryar's unimpressed mien.

Dunya rides up beside me and whispers, "Seems awful foolishness to waste brocade and gold on creatures that shit in the road."

I snort.

The 'Abbasid steward glares at me. "There have been great palaces in Baghdad—the Firdaus, the Mansuri, the Pleiades—which declined over time. Other palaces were destroyed in war. The Palace of the Golden Gate for one, which Caliph al-Mansur designed as the eye of the Round City of Baghdad four hundred years ago, was destroyed in the war of succession between the sons of the great Caliph Harun ar-Rashid."

Does every guest of the Caliph receive this lecture, or is it specially crafted condescension for the barbaric Seljuks? Although, after seeing the splendor of the dozens of palaces and colleges behind their ornate gates, I think perhaps they do have some right to condescend. Bam suddenly seems closer to the windblown tents of the steppe.

One of these palaces looms before us, with huge half-moon towers and pointed arches carved with leaves and flowers. Supported on ten columns, it rises above the canal like a crown. Intricately tiled domes rear above, blossoms shaded in cobalt and gold with calligraphy rimming the edges.

Ibn Hudayj does not take us through the main gates, but through the side. For a moment, I think he is piling on another insult, but then we enter an immense park shaded by trees of every kind. A roar sounds from deep within, and startled birds erupt from the branches. A chorus of roars and strange trumpetings follows.

The steward, seeing us suitably confounded, smiles. "This is the Park of Wild Beasts. On the other side lies the Palace al-Thurayya. Yalla."

Ibn Hudayj guides us through a maze of gardens, and the roars louden. I yelp and look around in embarrassment as we approach a square teeming with golden lions. One wears a proud mane, while the others slink smaller: a male surrounded by his harem. Their iron collars and chains look inconsequential beside their bulk. Some pad closer, their orange eyes alight with curiosity. What a pity to bind such magnificent creatures to such a small domain.

We follow the steward through more plazas of lions until we have passed hundreds. Ibn Hudayj shows us a vast lake surrounded by elephants swathed in peacock brocade, their jaundiced tusks long and pointed.

"We use their tusks for ivory once they die. The lions and other creatures are skinned as well." As though we are to admire their frugality.

We see creatures I've only read of in books: swan-necked giraffes standing so tall that I wonder how they manage to navigate the earth so far below; leopards draping their muscular bodies on low-hanging branches; sleek, chittering dolphins leaping from the artificial lake.

A marvel, this city is truly a marvel, a small paragon of human achievement, of gross excess, of vanity run amok—and a reminder of just how tempting it all is.

"Now," the steward says with a warm bow, after we have been appropriately awed by the majesty of his sovereign's estate, "allow me the honor of escorting you to the August Divan of Caliph an-Nasir."

✳ ✳ ✳

Caliph an-Nasir li-Din Allah is not the graybeard I had expected. He is a robust man in his prime, only a handful of years older than Shahr-yar. He was likely not much older than I am now when he became Caliph a decade ago. He wears a violet mantle of variegated silk bordered with silver tiraz bands at the collar and sleeves, and red leather boots. A gold scepter of state lolls in his hand. His hair and eyes are dark, his skin golden, his nose long and slightly hooked. With his high cheekbones, Caliph an-Nasir's face is regal, but ruthlessness peeks from his polish of politesse.

Shahryar is right to be wary.

Of the two men, Shahryar is broader and taller, more handsome, but as he sits imperiously in his wood-and-metal throne, there is no doubt that Caliph an-Nasir is master of this realm. Nervously, I finger the carmine robe of Dabiqi linen interwoven with strands of silk and gold that I had stitched for this presentation.

The majordomo announces, "Caliph an-Nasir li-Din Allah, Prince of the Believers, Commander of the Faithful, welcomes you, Shahryar, Seljuk Malik of Kirman, son of Turanshah."

Shahryar steps forward, and his crown of six lily-shaped gold pieces, hammered and etched, glints on his brow. "Peace be upon you, O Commander of the Faithful. My people and I thank you for your hospitality. Please permit me to present to you a few modest gifts so that we might show our most humble appreciation."

Shahryar extends his hand, inviting white-robed slaves bearing chests to process forth. They open the chests one by one, in quick succession, waiting for the Caliph to nod his approval before removing them. Mounds of salt from the Dasht-e-Lut, pyramids of pistachios and oranges from the groves of Kirman, silk and cotton from Bam, enough stuff to swathe the throne room half a dozen times, jeweled chalices imprinted with dragons and double-headed eagles, gold plates stamped with griffins and harpies, and silver mirrors as tall as men that dazzle the court as they are presented. These gifts, lavish in Bam, seem paltry after all we have seen.

Four burly slaves, their muscled arms slick with sweat, bring out two immense *somethings* hidden by black silk. Carefully, they set them before the Caliph. I gasp as the coverings fall away to reveal matching sphinxes, winged and bearded, their faces clay-complected, their tall crowns and bodies painted gold.

An-Nasir leans back, at last impressed. A pair of slaves brings one of the sphinxes closer. An-Nasir runs an appraising hand over the linear curls of the beard and ridged arches of the feathers. He smacks his lips. "Very fine indeed. We thank you, Malik Shahryar and your lovely Shaherazade Khatun. Verily, these are kingly gifts, and we bid you welcome to the joys and comforts of Baghdad." He raises his voice. "We pray for the sake of all believers that you are successful in this holy war against the accursed Franks."

There is a *takbir*, as though the courtiers of the August Divan really give two figs for the outcome. To an-Nasir's court chroniclers, the Frankish incursion will warrant at most a brief sentence in their summation of the 587th year after the Prophet Muhammad's flight from Mecca.

The Caliph raises a hand, and silence descends. "We shall feast you tonight, but until then, if I may, Malik Shahryar, while you refresh in your suite, I would like to show your wife our gardens." He smiles at me too kindly. I shift closer to Shahryar. "I think you shall find the blooms most pleasant."

Shahryar's mouth twitches, and an-Nasir flicks his fingers disinterestedly. "Let her be accompanied by her guards." In a mock-whisper, he hisses, "Propriety," and the court chuckles at our expense, although I doubt the Caliph would have the audacity to make such a public request of one of his own countrywomen, who, unlike Seljuk women, live sequestered in their harems and wield their power like unseen spiders. I do not miss that I am the only woman in the August Divan.

With as much graciousness as I can muster, I nod. We cannot risk the Caliph's ire.

As the courtiers disperse and the Caliph walks me to the gardens, I catch Shahryar's gaze and shake my head, trying to convey my confusion and distaste. His eyes narrow. I cannot read where he directs his malevolence.

With all six of my mamluks at my heels and a dozen of the Caliph's own guards, we are far from alone. The Caliph genially inquires about the journey before asking delicately about the circumstances surrounding my marriage.

Shaking my head, I murmur, "I am very blessed, Alhamdulilah."

"So you have no cause for complaint from your husband?"

His knowing smirk makes my back prickle.

"Of course I do," I rejoin. "What is a marriage without complaints?"

He laughs and turns the conversation to easier topics. "What do you think of our city?"

"Your steward showed us the Park of Wild Beasts and I think nothing more delightful exists in this world."

Caliph an-Nasir smiles at the praise and leads me—and my mamluks—toward the riverbank into a sweet-smelling garden. It is surrounded by the crumbling ruins of a courtyard, where trees bow with the weight of red and yellow fruit; I breathe in the fresh citrus smell of oranges. Time has latticed the branches together, and starry white light peeks through as the leaves sway in the river breeze.

Sheltered from the hustle of Baghdad, I can hear the soft trickle of fountains, the whispering rush of narrow canals, as well as the shy purr of turtledoves and ringdoves, the bold chants of parrots and blackbirds. It is a small taste of paradise, a block of sugar melting in your mouth as your eyes fly open at the sweetness.

"The orange trees were brought, some from Basra, some from Oman, and others from India, hundreds of years ago."

I breathe in the fresh citrus-rose fragrance, again and again. I do not think I can ever have enough of it. "Thank you for sharing it with me, O Caliph."

"The great hall in which I received you, the Bab al-Hujra, do you know who built it originally?"

I shake my head. So many names have been tossed at me today, I can hardly keep a straight record.

"Sultan Sanjar, one of your own Seljuks, last of the great Seljuk protectors of the Caliphate." An-Nasir's mouth curls. "Of course, the Qasr at-Taj has been rebuilt, and after prayer, imams read the khutbah in the name of the 'Abbasids, not the Seljuks, but the memories of Seljuk power linger." He slides a bitter look at me. "Just a few months prior, do you know what I did?"

I shake my head—that news has not reached us.

"I destroyed the final standing walls of the Dar al-Malakat, the Seljuk seat. Oh, it had already fallen into ruin, but it was I who erased it completely." His oryx-dark eyes flash with satisfaction.

"Now, the bones of the once-great Seljuk Empire are being picked by the least of scavengers: the Oghuz, the Khwarezmids. The Seljuks are not long for this world. Another ruin I erase."

A premonitory shiver runs down my back.

Caliph an-Nasir cradles a full-blown rose in his hand, soft except where artfully calloused from sword practice. "Such a tragedy when a gardener snips a rosebud. But a rose has her own vengeance, does she not? Hidden thorns that can draw the blood of the unwary." An-Nasir snaps the stem. "I would look kindly on such a rose."

He proffers the bloom, but I bend to pick a jasmine to hide my shock. Do I understand him?

"But what happens to the rose?" I say carefully. "She angers the gardener, and he plucks her bloom."

An-Nasir's handsome face clouds.

"But let us say there are two gardeners," I say.

"Go on."

Perhaps I am not wrong. I feel as though I have been flung into the Tigris, my arms waving, my legs kicking, spitting out as much water as I swallow.

Think of it as a story.

"If the second gardener's desires begin and end with the first gardener's demise, then by all means, he should let the rose do his work." I lower my voice so my mamluks do not overhear. "If the second gardener, however, covets something more—such as the first's garden—he would be wise to bide, because the first gardener has been summoned to tend another, far-off *hadiqa*. This new task may very well finish the first gardener—or render him unable to resist after he returns home."

"Why should the second gardener trust the rose?" An-Nasir bears down on me, taking full advantage of his height. I see brutality, avarice, and the flash of keen intelligence. And I am trying to outwit him? I hope my consternation does not show.

My pulse races, but the words fall smoothly. "For the same reason he approached her: a rose does not like to grow too near a gardener infamous for cutting blossoms."

Does he hear the lie? Or does he take the waver in my throat as hesitancy over a language not my own, Arabic letters put together in unaccustomed ways arching against my Turkic palate, stumbling on my Persian tongue?

Caliph an-Nasir's laughter booms, startling a flock of ringdoves. "Well met, Shaherazade Khatun, well met."

I sigh, feeling as if I have passed an examination. The Caliph leads me beside the Tigris. Great waterwheels lift the river into cisterns, and in the setting sun the river runs bloodred. The way is largely abandoned, and I would be uneasy if not for my mamluks.

There were once two snakes who had trapped a woman, twining their thick bodies around each arm. Afraid to shake them, she stood still, but they only wrapped more tightly. As the snake on her left opened its bone-white mouth to sink its fangs into her soft breast, the right snake hissed, "By what right do you claim her first blood?"

"My wife was a Seljuk. Like you." Caliph an-Nasir points to a great hexagonal mausoleum of golden brick beside the waterwheel, surrounded by an emerald orchard. A single minaret rises from its center. He softens. "The daughter of Rûm's sultan. She lies there now." Returning to himself, he says, "Come, let me show you one of Baghdad's great wonders."

This close to the Tigris, the air is cool and fresh. A prince's *shabbara* barge twinkles merrily on the Tigris and the high-pitched wail of mosquitoes fills my ears. I slap at my neck. I look across the river, to where the sun dips behind the mud-brick houses of the Al-Kurayyah quarter, and spot a low-lying garden at the mouth of a canal, lush with palms and fruit trees. A small palace peeks from behind an overgrowth of vines. "What is that?"

"The Gardens of Rakkah, pleasure grounds of the Caliph." An-Nasir appraises me. "If you wish to see it, I could summon a boat to row us across . . ."

I can imagine how well Shahryar would like that. I snort.

"Well, perhaps someday, when certain hedges have been trimmed, a time may come . . ."

I move away from an-Nasir and crook a finger. Bahram and Fakhruddin are promptly at my shoulder, their bulk a comforting bulwark against the Caliph.

An-Nasir shrugs with ironic ruefulness. "For all your cleverness, you are still very young in the ways of the world, aren't you? A bona fide innocent. One wonders where Shahryar found you—and how he intends to keep you so." Something cruel bubbles beneath his chuckle.

You are still the innocent child you ever were, aren't you, little Shaherazade?

"Is there anything else you wish to show me, your Illustriousness?"

We pass through a baked-brick gate into a palace courtyard. A line of carved horsemen encircles a pool that reflects branches that stretch and twist like a spinner's fingers. I follow along the shaft of an immense tree, cast in silver. I gasp. The tree towers to the palace's second floor, delicate silver branches blushing pink in the fading sun. Leaves of real silver and gold chime as they flash in the breeze. The beaks of aureate and argentate birds open with mechanical rigidity, piping piercing birdsong.

He sweeps his hands wide. "Ad-Dar ash-Shajarah."

The Abode of the Tree.

It is so strange, so extravagant, that I could not have conceived that something like this could exist in this world, that anyone's mind could have produced something so . . . nonsensical, inessential, but breathtaking and overwhelming because of it. "It is all . . . ?"

"Yes, silver and gold—ah . . ."

A man strides up to the Caliph. Momentarily, I take him for a servant, but no—his linen is too fine, and his turban is tall and held in place by a chicken's-egg ruby. His hair is streaked white, his forehead lined, and he examines me with mild curiosity before whispering to the Caliph. Although I cannot make out what he says, his voice sounds pleading. The Caliph shakes his head firmly and the man slumps away.

"A cousin," an-Nasir explains without prompting. "They are kept here, honorably, with every luxury and comfort they could want." He shakes his head. "Still, someone always wants more."

"Can they leave?" I cannot help but asking. I think I already know the answer.

"It is death for them to leave the confines of Ad-Dar ash-Shajarah."

I feel eyes on me as we walk out.

* * *

In the bedroom, Gulnar helps me out of my embroidered robes and into a plain cotton nightgown. Her fingers, long and light, untie and unbind deftly. "Isn't Baghdad marvelous? All the gardens, the palaces! I could not have imagined anything so grand." Gulnar, usually practical, sighs dreamily.

"That is hard to deny, but the Baghdadis put on such airs."

She chuckles, deepening the lines ridging her mouth. "If you lived here, you would put on airs too."

"Still, they need not make us feel like barbarians at every turn."

"They were under Seljuk control for a very long time. I think they are just trying to make sure that the Seljuks know they are masters here now," she says sagely.

I roll my eyes. "With the Khwarezmids and Oghuz ravaging the Sultanate at the Caliph's behest, that is hard to forget."

The door cracks open and my hands fly to my chest, covered only by a sheer linen chemise. But it is only Shahryar, who carelessly tosses his viridescent turban onto a table and strips off his kaftan. Gulnar finishes undressing me in silence and departs.

Shahryar pours a glass of wine, sniffing deeply before swallowing. "You passed a long while with the Caliph today."

I hope he does not misread the blush on my cheeks. "Yes. He wished to show me some gardens."

Shahryar takes another sip of wine and looks at the goblet distastefully. "It's too warm." He hurls it against the wall, where the chalice rings against the marble and spits grape-red on the wall and carpets. "What did you speak of?"

I shake my head, and he says with silky threat, "What do you hide from me, little Shaherazade?"

I climb into the bed, lay my hand on his shoulder, and whisper in Oghuz, "These walls hear everything." My voice resumes its normal volume. "I should like to see the Bait al-Hikma and the Papersellers' Street tomorrow. Will you accompany me, husband? The House of Wisdom is perhaps one of the few places in the world where every query can find an answer."

His eyes meet mine, alight with understanding, and for once, he seems to perceive me. "Well, give these walls a story to listen to, will you?"

The quiet grumble of his voice sends a jolt through my stomach. Once more, I flush. I move to my customary sitting position, but Shahryar stops me. "Douse the lamps and lie beside me."

I curl on my side and prop my head on my fist. For a moment, I meet his eyes and it is like staring into the sun.

"O Malik, it is said that Jauhara stared dazedly at a swart, snow-bearded Sufi.

"'Who seeks my counsel?' the man repeated, and Jauhara swallowed her surprise.

"'I am Jauhar, a traveler with a troupe of entertainers.'

"The Sufi smiled patiently. 'Child, if I am to help you, you must not lie.'

"Jauhara flushed, but the Sufi did not look irritated. 'Try again,' he suggested.

"Jauhara exchanged a look with the parrot. 'My name is Jauhara bint 'Omar, who is the governor of Egypt, and his wife Soraya, who was the daughter of his predecessor. I *am* a traveler with a troupe of entertainers, but I am not alone.'

"With the same placid smile, the Sufi turned expectantly to the parrot, who puffed his chest and spoke in his melodious voice. 'I was once an angel but was trapped in the form you see.'

"'Follow me,' the Sufi said, setting off toward the shadowed mountain. Sprightly despite his bent back, he led them up the mountain.

"As the cold air burned Jauhara's lungs and her wheezing breath burst into mist, she ascended the glacier valley. After hours of climbing, they stopped before a circular stone stupa nestled in the mountain face.

"'Is it not strange that you, such a wise man of Islam, reside in one of Gautama's temples?' Jauhara asked, as the Sufi led them inside.

"'Do we not all pursue the same truth?' the Sufi said, lighting an oil lamp that dimly illumined a rough pallet, a thin rug, and a simple, low table. 'Our paths deviate, but there is wisdom along each path.'

"Jauhara didn't know what she thought of that argument, but the parrot nodded.

"Shadows pulling long and dark across his face, the Sufi turned his tilted eyes upon Jauhara. 'What do you seek?'

"Jauhara paused, contemplating. 'I left my home in pursuit of adventure.'

"'Did you find it?'

"Jauhara considered. Had she found the heart-pounding adventure she had dreamed of, that she had heard in her parents' tales? She had tasted excitement, fallen into a world of wondrous mountains and markets, spoken to strange creatures and heard strange stories, but was it adventure as she thought she would find, with lands to be rescued and demons to be defeated?

"'No.'

"The Sufi smiled, a little sadly. 'I knew a boy once. His world was different from yours. For one, he was a boy and that tends to make life easier. But he was poor, the son of a peasant, and that tends to make life harder.

"'He lived in a village in Tarim, west of Cathay, where every Friday, he would go to the market and sell his father's crimson cabbages and violet carrots. For some months, a beautiful girl visited his stall. She was the daughter of a wealthy merchant and came with her housekeeper to learn household economies in preparation for marriage. She would smile at Talant, flashing her small white teeth, and ask, "How much for this eggplant? For this cabbage?" and Talant fell more in love with each question. One day, the idea set upon him: Why should he not wed her?

"'He began performing extra tasks in town, weeding gardens, mending nets, saving money and memories of the girl's smile, until he felt he had enough of both to justify a proposal.

"'He went to her father's home, a red-lacquered building with a roof that swooped with a calligraphic flourish. Her father was a large man with thin, drooping mustaches and the same small teeth as his daughter. When Talant spoke his business, the father laughed and laughed.

"'"Presumptuous," he chortled. "I, who keep my daughter in silk and jade, would affiance her to someone with no merit except a plot of land that produces exceptional carrots? Be off boy, before you humiliate yourself further."

"'A red fury seized Talant, but what could he do but kowtow and depart? As his rage stoked like wood cracking in a furnace, he vowed that the merchant would regret his refusal. Talant decided to leave for Qashgar that very day, confident that the city would open to him like an oyster with a pearl.

"'But what talents did Talant possess? None that brought the blue-arched city of Qashgar to its knees. Soon enough, the money he had winkled away for his bride began to drain from his pocket. One of Talant's new-made friends suggested that a gambling den was the remedy.

"'Talant threw himself into gambling, wagering recklessly and crowing when he landed small windfalls. But to be a successful gambler, a man needs a cool disposition. Talant's victories soon waned, rapidly replaced by dinars of debt and knocks about the head from black-eyed thugs demanding repayment, until Talant knew the only disbursement left to him was his life. So he, a free man born and raised, sold himself into slavery.

"'He was bought into the household of a wealthy prince, the son of a sultan, and Talant thought, *If I win his generous favor, perhaps he will grant my freedom and put a little gold in my hand before sending me on my way.*

"'But this prince was not the sort for whom *Mirrors* are written; he was a stupid young man with vain eyes and a cruel red mouth. Talant soon fell into the anonymity of his slave life, rising before dawn, sleeping only after midnight, until even the memory of small pearl teeth patched and faded into an unfamiliar dream.

"'Talant was no stranger to hard work, and if he were not a free man, he still lived in a gilt palace. The scheduled pace of life restored the equilibrium he had lost when he decided to wed the merchant's daughter.

"'One day, Talant was dusting a bronze urn when he heard voices from a spare room. He had learned by this point that a good slave was not heard and a better slave did not hear. He tried to concentrate on his task rather than the conversation that drifted through like smoke.

"'"When we kill the Sultan"—at this, Talant's head jerked up in spite himself—"you shall take your father's place and we shall be your council."

"'Another voice added, "It shall be done tomorrow. Ready your grief, my prince."

"'When the prince emerged with his two companions, one a compactly muscled man and the other rangy and long fingered, none spared a glance at the boy polishing the urn.

"'Talant knew that if the prince succeeded, he would be as unkind a sultan as he was a master. The next morning, he begged time from the steward and went to the Sultan's Divan.

"'A massive line of petitioners snaked around the audience chamber—men dressed as simply as himself, others garbed in magnificent silks. There, behind the Sultan's throne, pouted the prince, and behind the prince, drawn into shadow, stood two men. Unaware, the long-bearded Sultan attended on all with equal consideration.

"'Finally, it was Talant's turn.

"'"Your Highness," he said nervously, "I bring you news of a plot against your person." The prince's face did not pale as Talant had hoped. "I am a slave in your son's household. Last night, I heard him scheming with two men to murder you today and install the prince in your place."

"'The prince sneered at Talant and said sweetly to his father, "This man accuses me falsely. Tell me," he said to Talant, "do you have any evidence? Any witnesses beside yourself?"

"'With great reluctance, Talant shook his head. He could feel himself humming with embarrassment.

"'"You see, father," the prince said. "He is a liar. As he has confessed that he is my slave, I should see him punished for his slander. Call your executioner and let us set an example of what happens to those who seek to divide father and son."

"'Talant prayed that the Sultan would stop his son, would ask, "*Why son, why are you so eager to destroy this man?*"

"'Talant was led to a straw-strewn courtyard, where he was ordered to drop to his knees and bend his neck. *Any moment now*, he hoped, *any moment now, the Sultan will come and stop his son. Any moment now.* The prince stood before him, the broad man behind him, blade in hand. Talant shut his eyes and saw a small-toothed smile and knew no more.'

"Jauhara regarded the Sufi incredulously. 'What sort of story was that?' she demanded.

"'A true one,' he replied, equanimous. 'A lesson, a warning. Sometimes, what you seek is not what will make you happy. I shall perform *istikhara* and tomorrow, insh'Allah, we will know whether the All-Knowing will provide us with guidance.'

"The next morning, under clear mountain light, the Sufi awoke, an answer in his mouth. 'You must return home, Jauhara, and you, Parrot, must accompany her. Follow the river south; if you meet someone heading toward the sea, join him.'

"And so, Jauhara and the parrot descended from the high mountains and followed the foaming green river. But what is this compared to what happens to Jauhara next?"

Fourteen

I squirm as my palanquin lowers. Hundreds of shops and stalls wedged with books crowd both sides of Papersellers' Street, stretching to the New Bridge that arches over the Sarat Canal.

Impatient, I do not wait for Shahryar and sprint to the nearest shop. Dimly lit, it smells of clean paper, bitter ink, and binding leather, and it proffers a selection that rivals all the booksellers in Kirman: a book of poems by the 'Abbasid princess Ulayya bint al-Mahdi, al-Ma'ari's *Epistle of Forgiveness*, the *Diwan* of al-Mutanabbi. They sit on wooden shelves, their gilded spines gleaming, and rise in hillocks from the floor, some small as my hand, others as large as my arm. I shrink to navigate the maze of books as dust motes dance in the soft light.

I gasp.

Debossed in rubbed-away gold is a collection of the ancient poetess al-Khansa's elegies. A book I have longed for, which Baba, despite his efforts, has been unable to procure. I spring for it, a lion pouncing on prey, and clutch it as though someone would snatch it away.

The bookseller, festooned with a grape turban, gapes. The shock turns into obeisance as Shahryar enters with our retinue of mamluks.

"Ya saidi." The shopkeeper bows, drinking in Shahryar's luxurious lapis kaftan, the rubies and sapphires glinting on his fingers.

Seeing me clinging to al-Khansa's chapbook, Shahryar smiles with a fondness that falls just short of his eyes. "Purchase whatever you wish, little Shaherazade."

"Can we bring it all with us?"

"Whatever we cannot carry, we send back to Bam."

Like a child, I dart around the shop. Once finished here, I patronize two dozen more, my arms aching with the weight of my purchases.

At the last bookshop, I spy Rudaki's *Kalila wa Dimna*, his verses based on ancient Indian fables. It looks identical to Mama's copy, which we lost in the maelstrom after her death. I touch the cover and it yields in the same way hers had, the fore edges marbled rose and white just as hers had been.

I open it. *"No ordinary teacher will ever reach, those whom Time has failed to teach,"* and it is not my voice, but hers. My vision blurred, I grip the book to my heart.

✳ ✳ ✳

The House of Wisdom's copper dome gleams like a molten second sun against the kingfisher sky. Tiles, creamy with *thuluth* calligraphy, wind through azure-and-gold blossoms that frame the beaten-brass doors. Within, the walls are tiled with starbursts of sky-blue and gold. Ridged and swirled plaster, in ocher and crimson, crowns the walls. Groups huddle around masters seated in teaching thrones: some are bearded men, others beardless youths, and others still are veiled women, whose demurely arranged hands do not distract from the sharp intelligence in their eyes.

A man strides toward Shahryar and me. His turban is large and white and rises to a frothy peak. It dips with him like an enormous onion bulb as he bows. "Welcome to the Bait al-Hikma. I am called Badiuzzaman. I am a scholar of the House of Wisdom. His Illustriousness the Caliph has requested that I illumine your explorations."

A spy.

Badiuzzaman guides us through various rooms: one full of crumbling Hellenistic manuscripts; another in which said manuscripts are being diligently transcribed by copyists; and yet another where they are being translated from Greek to Arabic, from Arabic to Persian, and some even into the Franks' Latin.

"One is almost surprised they have their own written language," Shahryar comments acidly.

Badiuzzaman shrugs, the burnt orange of his robe crinkling at the shoulders. "They are not huge consumers of Greek knowledge, but we do have a small trade with a few among them."

"Enough to entice them to push east," I say.

Badiuzzaman smiles. "Even the ignorant can differentiate silk from wool and covet the finer."

In an indigo room, we find scholars at tables spread with maps and globes, astrolabes and compasses and measuring sticks. Geographers and geometers, studiers of the world and masters of its forms. They are too engrossed in their discourse to pay mind as I walk to an abandoned globe, its heavy head bobbing precariously on a slim bronze stem. My finger runs over its curved contours, tracing our path from Bam to Kirman, past Esfahan and through the Zagros Mountains. It halts at Baghdad, which lies two-thirds of the way between Bam and Jerusalem.

I spin the globe and face the other end of the world: Europe. Here is al-Andalus, which the Almohads wrested only five years ago from the Almoravids; northwest is the France of Philip; and across a narrow sea is England, home of Malikric the so-called Lionheart. And they have made their long way across the Roman Sea with their sails and their swords, crossing half the world to have at us. And we cross just as vast a distance to stop them.

Shahryar taps the globe, right on Muscovy, to draw my attention. "What did an-Nasir want?" he whispers in Oghuz.

Beneath the blur of the geographers' conversation, I tell Shahryar. His lips whiten. "So he plans to attack Bam," he interrupts. "We must turn back immediately."

I shake my head and point at the globe. "And what? The Caliph will notice that we are heading away from our supposed destination."

"If we do not return, all will say that I hid when my province fell."

"All will say that the Caliph struck like a scorpion, while you were defending the ummah against barbarians."

"Who cares what all will say if Bam falls!" The exclamation attracts the notice of a frowning Badiuzzaman.

"Do you not think I care for Bam as well?" I hiss. "My father lives there, my mother died there; it is my heart's blood. For this reason, I think I managed to convince the Caliph to stay his hand. At least until we return."

Shahryar stares, his incredulity almost an insult. "You? How?"

I relate our conversation of gardens and roses. Shahryar raises an eyebrow. "What makes you think that the Caliph was not twisting you in his own string?"

I think of the eel-smooth an-Nasir and doubt creeps in. I wish I could recapture my earlier confidence.

Badiuzzaman comes closer and Shahryar takes a deep breath. "I shall confer with the emirs." A long pause. "Mutashakaram."

"Ah, I see you are intrigued by the globe," says Badiuzzaman. "It *is* a magnificent piece." Shahryar and I listen as he elucidates the history of globe making in Baghdad, as though nothing heavier weighs on our minds.

***

Letters from home have caught us today: from Baba, Leila, and Hanna. Baba reports, in his precise *naksh*, that the Khwarezmids continue to fight for Khorasan and the Oghuz are quiet; nonetheless, Shahzaman drills with the soldiers daily, our army is strong, our stores deep. I have no doubt that the letter has been thoroughly pawed by 'Abbasid spies. How much of it did Baba write for their benefit?

Leila's letter tells of her preparation to depart to Esfahan to visit her husband's parents. Hanna's note is light and equally inconsequential, but I notice stray words, placed here and there: *no* and *burns* in Leila's and *longer* and *city* in Hanna's. It takes a moment for the sentence to rearrange itself: *City no longer burns.* Warmth swells in my heart for them and their precautions, the homespun cipher that seems so simple in light of the Caliph's intrigues. I wonder if the Caliph realizes just how close Bam had come to swallowing itself, leaving Kirman ripe for him.

At a knock on the door, I fold the letters into an Arabic translation of *The Metamorphoses of Apuleius* purchased at the Papersellers' Street. Dunya pushes through. Although her face is freshly washed, it shines with exertion.

"Where have you been?"

Is it my imagination or do her cheeks redden?

"In my room with Mahperi."

The hem of her pistachio-green farajiyya is stiff with mud. "You should ask the steward to send a maid to clean your room; it seems as muddy as the banks of the Tigris."

She glances at her dirtied clothes and her blush deepens.

"Tell me true, Dunya. Where were you?" I try to say it as lightly as possible, but concern leadens the question.

She smiles easily. "I went for a stroll by the river."

"Alone?"

Her dark eyes flash upward, honest and sincere. "Yes. How else, what with you always occupied with something or other and Mahperi too mousy to leave the palace?"

"Do you know how dangerous that could be, Dunya? We are not in Bam where you are well known and know everyone well. Baghdad is immense and full of dangers. Take a mamluk with you, please, use your head!"

She pouts, but I say what must be said, what it is my duty as her older sister—and Khatun—to say.

"Fine! I was not alone," she exclaims in a rush. "I am not such a fool as to wander a strange place alone."

"Who were you with then?"

"Faramurz." Even as she squares her shoulders defiantly, her mouth softens as she speaks his name.

I try to conceal my shock at my little sister's impropriety. I should have reined her in when I spied her with Faramurz. I reach to pat her hand, but she snatches it away.

I attempt to emulate Mama's no-nonsense calm, Baba's kind patience, but my response emerges with a harshness that is only mine. "Dunya, this is foolish. You must know it. You will spark rumors, damage your prospects, *his* prospects. This is a place full of strangers who would have no compunction in destroying your reputation—especially when they could harm the Seljuks with it."

"What of you and the Caliph?"

My face burns. "Entirely different. We are two sovereigns."

"By my eyes!" Dunya slaps her hand against her thigh. "I am old enough to choose my own steps. I do not need my older sister puffing her feathers at me whenever I brush a direction she does not approve of."

"It's not the direction I'm afraid of you brushing!"

Her forehead reddens and she starts toward the door. I regret the retort. With her eyes wide with frustration, I wonder if she realizes just how young she looks. I lower my voice. "Listen, jaan, I *am* the Khatun, and you are one of my damsels. Even if you were not my sister, I would counsel you to temper your behavior." I hesitate before adding, "If need be, I would forbid you."

"*Khatun!* We all know how quickly you jumped to wed the Malik. For all everyone saw you as a great heroine, I know you better. Have you made the Malik love you yet, Shaherazade?"

Sudden, viscous tears heat my throat, but Dunya shoves forward.

"No, and you won't! This is not one of your stories. If you ever wake from your dreamworld, you will realize how deeply you have knotted yourself into unhappiness."

I am speechless, watching my sister, spent of her savagery, sob in squeaking hiccups. I try to remember how the fight arrived at this thunderclap of furious words, but the chain of transmission is foggy. She opens her mouth—*to apologize?*—but it snaps shut as a throat clears behind us.

Shahryar.

I hastily wipe my cheeks, smearing kohl on midnight silk. Did he hear? I want to melt into the tiles and run in rivulets down the joints until I flow into the Tigris or the Euphrates; either river will suffice.

"I would speak to Shaherazade alone."

Dunya does not look up, does not look at me as she crosses her arms and departs.

After the door closes, Shahryar says, "Her marriage should be seen to. She could prove useful."

My face burns. "As you say, O Malik."

He begins to polish the swirled damascene dagger he wears at his waist with quick, precise motions. An image: Shahryar's arm rising and falling as he steadily hacks my neck from my torso, my warm blood drenching his hands and crusting the moons of his fingernails. All I have within reach is *The Metamorphoses of Apuleius*—but what defense is an ancient story against a blade?

"Acre has fallen."

My mind clears of its bloody mist. "Che?"

"It fell some weeks ago. Sultan Saladin's garrison was imprisoned and Conrad of Montferrat raised the banners of the Kingdoms of Jerusalem, France, England, and Austria over the city."

I am as astounded by the news of the great city's titanic fall as I am by Shahryar's decision to confide in me. "What will happen now?"

"It's a tremendous victory for the Franks. So tremendous that the

Caliph has promised to dispatch a battalion to accompany us to join the fight to redress the balance."

I imagine an-Nasir's battalion, a flock of crows with glinting eyes trained on us. "What does that mean for us?"

Shahryar lowers his voice. "That if I had planned to return to defend Bam, it would be impossible." He looks up at me. "We'd better hope that you were as successful in persuading the Caliph to stay his hand as you believe yourself to be."

* * *

Candles flicker-flicker-flicker as the Tigris breathes through the bedchamber's open windows. A silver mirror, edged with clawing, vine-twisted griffins, reflects my face in its foggy glass, illumined gold one instant, ghoulishly shadowed the next. I twist my mouth. Smile seductively. Smile sincerely. Pout as if I were a woman beautiful enough to cradle a man's heart in her hand.

I am left alone while Shahryar feasts and enjoys the company of dancing girls with the Caliph and their favorites. Friends for now, enemies when chance wavers, a knife balanced on a fingertip.

My breath catches as I remember Dunya's bone-cutting words. I look at my face again. Eyes, slanted and long, even. I peer closer. Deep mahogany irises that refract umber in the light. One eyebrow arching slightly higher than the other. Pointed chin, broad forehead, full lips. High Turkic cheekbones. Long hair, black and braided, skin the color of almond flesh.

I look away, unhappy, embarrassed. Beneath my hopes of saving other girls, of quelling revolt, my intention was impure. I hid it mostly from myself, entirely from Baba and my friends, but my little sister, with her canny eyes, saw all. I thought I could make Shahryar love me for myself and forget Fataneh. But how could he? Fataneh was a beauty, a *houri* who would have been as beautiful if she had been born a farmer's daughter.

What am I beside her?

Perhaps I am being unfair to Dunya. She sees something in Faramurz and I should trust her decisions as I trust her with my life. Try as I might, I cannot force my will down her throat, down anyone's throat. I try and try to be Fataneh, the woman Shahryar loved. Not Fataneh as she was, but Fataneh as he thought her to be. But I am not her: neither the good nor the bad, neither the beloved wife nor the beheaded betrayer.

I blow out the candles one by one, watch the gray smoke curl and stretch, briefly sweetening the air until the room is dark.

A tap whispers on the door. Perhaps Dunya has come to apologize. I push the door ajar and blink against the torchlight. It is a man, his back to me.

"Yes?"

He turns.

Atsiz.

Somehow, I am unsurprised. He smiles warmly, but his eyes flick to his left, to his right, examining the mamluk guards that Fakhruddin set on my door. I do not open the door wider.

"I hope I have not awakened you." He glances at the guards. "Is the Malik here?"

"No. He is with the Caliph."

Surely he knows this. Surely he is among the close companions invited to carouse tonight. "How is the outer city?"

"Just as the Caliph promised, our troops have been hospitably housed. Not for long, though: we march the day after tomorrow." He pauses. "One almost wishes we did not have to move. Baghdad has just begun to open herself to me again."

I think of the globe my fingers had run over. "But so much of the world lies ahead. Have you been to Baghdad before?"

He grins. "As a traveling emir, I have made the rounds: from Ghazni to Ghor, Delhi to Damascus, Aleppo to Antioch, from Chang'an to . . ."

He is at a loss.

"Chak Chak," I supply, naming a small Zoroastrian pilgrimage site.

"Perfect—though I have never been to Chak Chak."

"You should have thought of that before you named Chang'an." Amusement fades into self-consciousness. I glance at my mamluks, who stare ahead but register all. "If this is all, Emir Atsiz, I bid you goodnight. I will tell the Malik that you asked for him."

I move to close the door, but he fishes in his melon-striped trousers and extracts something. For a moment, I think it is jewelry, but no, it is better. A book.

"So long as I am here, I saw this in a bookshop." He slips it into my hands before I can refuse him. "*The Book of Fixed Stars* by Abdurrahman as-Sufi. I must confess: I first thought of Faramurz when I saw it."

His mouth quirks into a smile and my vision spins.

"Is something amiss? It is a trifle. I hope it does not offend."

How can he gaze at me owlishly, seemingly blind to the danger? How can he come to my door at night bearing a gift? I try to quell the rising panic even as something else, sweet and golden as honey, bubbles close behind. "Of course not. I will inform the Malik you were looking for him and that you brought him this gift."

Atsiz appears startled and then, finally, understands. He steps back and bows formally, clasping his fist to his heart. "I am obliged. Shab bikhair, Shaherazade Khatun."

And I see it, the softness at his mouth as he says my name, the same as when Dunya spoke Faramurz's. How can I scold my sister when I am wading through an even more dangerous marsh? My throat tightens.

"*Shab bikhair,*" I whisper as he strides away, perhaps joining the fête, to drink and feast on the great sweetnesses offered by the greatest city of the world. "Shab bikhair," I say to the mamluks. I wonder if they are as bewildered as I am, if they gossip, if they will make the worst of this exchange—or make what they should.

I open the book, and a paper slip flutters to the mosaic floor. I catch it. It is headed: *To Faramurz.* I smirk.

Let my eyes feast upon
your beauty,
your rose mouth, your nightingale eyes
For you are like a dawn,
a dream
of the rising moon.

The smirk crumples. My pulse quivers, from my lips to fingertips. Unsteadily, I slide the verse back into *The Book of Fixed Stars* and will myself to forget its existence, to forget this midnight meeting and the rush of gold that rose within me.

Fifteen

ireflies wink on the Euphrates like low-settled stars. Because of the high summer heat, we travel by night, the sareban at our head guiding us by stars and brass astrolabe. Despite the caravan's chorus—the pound of hooves, the clatter of spears, the hum of conversation—the world feels quiet after Baghdad. This is our last day near its twin rivers; beyond this, al-Anbar is dust and stone.

Next month, we will be in Palestine.

In a large tent, the Malik hosts a grand supper for the nobles before we start the night's march. We mix uncomfortably with the few 'Abbasid aristocrats an-Nasir sent with his force of three hundred, a number so obviously stingy that I wonder that the Caliph does not feel a prick of shame.

Perhaps inspired by Baghdad's decadence, or to impress the sophisticated palates of our 'Abbasid companions, or simply to make use of the foodstuffs gifted by Caliph an-Nasir, our cooks have delivered an elaborate repast. Chicken rubbed with saffron and pepper and buried in hot sand and embers until the meat is roasted off the bone; small river fish fried with onion and flour, and carp stuffed with chopped citron leaves, apple peel, and rue; gazelle packed with almonds and pistachios, sprinkled with mint and parsley; pigeons stewed with chickpeas and dumplings; sour pomegranate soup with pullets. To drink, there is sekanjabin and ice milk sweetened with syrups. Even the 'Abbasid party looks impressed.

My muscles, thawed from a week of rest in Baghdad, squawk as I cross my legs on a pliant cushion at the low table beside Shahryar. This close to the river, the whine of mosquitoes is a persistent ear throb.

Dunya, who usually sits to my right, has settled herself closer to Faramurz, her face set with uncertain stubbornness, as though she anticipates a reprimand. Mahperi is at my elbow instead, smiling with tentative empathy. "It's hard not to miss Baghdad," she sighs. "Or Bam."

I think of an-Nasir. "Baghdad not so much."

"When I was in one of the gardens, I noticed a nobleman watching me," she says, giddy. "I was hoping he would accompany us."

Sidewise, I watch Atsiz speak to a sloe-eyed woman with thinly plucked eyebrows. Her voice is low, modulated, and Atsiz leans in to listen. She is familiar, Seljuk, although I do not know her name. I feel foolish that I thought, even for an instant, that *The Book of Fixed Stars* was anything more than a joke.

"If he had proposed marriage, and I had remained behind in Baghdad, you would not have minded, would you, Shaherazade?"

Returning my attention to Mahperi, I do not know which pricks my heart harder: her simple excitement or the intimation that I do not care either way for her presence. "Oh, Mahperi." I pat her hand. "Of course I would miss you, but if he proposed marriage and were the kind of man to whom I could entrust you, then how could I not release you?"

"Oh!" she hugs herself excitedly. I think of Shahryar's counsel of finding Dunya a husband, and I wonder if Mahperi would not be better served. Uncomfortable, I change the subject. "Did you hear from your parents?"

Her smile wavers, but some of the frenetic light falls away. "Yes, Pader and Mader are well. I received small notes from Leila and Hanna too—although I am sure you received much longer letters."

"Not so much," I say around a mouthful of pigeon, guiltily feeling more than ever how Mahperi has always been on the outskirts of our group, a robin pecking at a window hoping to be let in.

***

In Shahryar's stuffy tent, I sit on a feather-filled pallet, sore from the night's ride. I lower my eyes as Shahryar strips to his undergarments. I too am dressed only in my translucent cotton chemise. It is too warm to be bearable otherwise. He reclines on the mattress beside me, stretching his muscled legs. His skin sticks to mine but despite the heat he does not move.

"Continue the tale, little Shaherazade."

I strain for some hint of change since Baghdad, any recognition of my cleverness, my usefulness. But if anything is new, it is interred beneath his studied indifference, the only grain of familiarity the easy touch of his leg.

As I obey, nostalgia flashes for that terrifying first night when Dunya sat close.

"O Malik, it is said that as the Sufi had instructed, Jauhara and the parrot followed the river south until it converged with the River Sindh and mountains gave way to fertile fields and marshy rice paddies.

"At the end of their second day, they saw a man sailing down the Sindh in a wooden skiff. Spotting Jauhara, he rowed to the bank and cried, 'Salaam! Where are you heading, aqa?' The man was a few years older than Jauhara and more handsome than a man had a right to be, with flopping black hair, saturnine eyes, and a burnished bronze complexion.

"'Down to the sea!' she called back.

"'What, by walking?' He flashed a white grin. 'I too am heading for the sea. Let us journey together!'

"Jauhara traded a furtive glance with the parrot, who rolled his yellow-crested head.

"'*Shukraan*, kind saidi,' Jauhara said in a false baritone as she swung into the boat. 'What is your name?'

"'Kushyar. Yours?' he asked, straining to adjust the swollen sail.

"'Jauhar,' Jauhara said. 'What's your business in the south?'

"'I head to Debal to take a ship westward, to 'Aydhab in Egypt or across the Red Sea to Jiddah on the Jezira,' he said. 'My only business is fleeing the she-demon who almost ruined me.'

"Jauhara's impression of him soured. 'What do you mean?'

"'I was not always as you see me now—a penniless vagrant with only a shoddy raft to his name. Nay, I was prince and heir to a great kingdom, the son of my father's favorite wife. I was raised in splendor, educated in verse and horse and polo and all noble pursuits. My father died, not one year ago. On the night of his death, while my mother and I mourned, his most-favored concubine bought the palace guards and placed her son, my half brother and a dullard, on the throne.

"'She imprisoned me, intending to execute me, but my brother, maybe thinking to mimic the mercy of kings, decreed that instead of death, my eyes would be burned out. Before he could, my mother bribed the men guarding my cell. She gave me this"—he tapped the whorled damascene shamshir at his waist—"my father's sword, and a sack of gold, and bade me to flee to Kandahar, where, she promised, she would find me.

"'Like a child, like a fool, I fled, never thinking my gentle mother would be unable to fulfill her promise. I waited eleven months in Kandahar. During those months, I rented a small house in a wealthy neighborhood. When I arrived, I told the guards at each city gate that my mother would be coming. For weeks, every morning and evening, I circled each gate, praying she had come.

"'She never did.'

"'But why,' Jauhara interposed, 'did you not return to save her?'

"Kushyar shook his head. 'Did I not say she-demon? You see, in the home beside mine lived a beautiful woman, quite alone. A widow, the neighbors understood. *Young and very, very rich*, the youths whispered when I inquired. *A beauty of stars and diamonds.*

"'So she was. Slender as the willow, cheeks pink as myrtle, breasts like pomegranates, and a face like the moon. As I returned from the gates one morn, she opened her door and called, "Day and night I see you leave your home hopeful and return dejected. What ails such a handsome man? Come, confide your ills."

"'In her home, she pressed goblets of wine upon me, never drinking herself. When I was in my cups, I pressed myself upon her.

"'Her carnelian lips stretched into a smile, and with ease, she pushed me back. Other than her hands, her high-necked crimson robe left only her face bare.

"'She said, "No, you will not, but you are a sad boy. Perhaps I may lessen your grief." She raised her skirt, revealing a pale ankle and hinting at the smooth expanse of leg above. Seeing desire kindle in my eye, she laughed, "Now, good neighbor, go home."

"'That evening, still drunk, and now frustrated as well as morose, I made my rounds to the gates. As usual, my mother was not there. When I returned, my neighbor stood in her doorway, smiling like a jackal. "Come in for a glass of wine," she invited. Although I intended to refuse, my feet followed her. Again, the same dance, the chalices of wine, while she sat sober and I grew drunker. At the night's end, before she bade me farewell, she refused my second proposition. Instead, she pulled down her collar to display a swan's length of neck. "Shab bikhair, neighbor. Sleep well. Perhaps I shall see you tomorrow."

"'So it went. Every morning and evening, she invited me inside, revealing her body inch by inch: a slim wrist, a delicate collarbone, a flat navel, a well-shaped leg, until my daily walks went no farther than my neighbor's door. Until I forgot my mother. My princely birthright. My noble duties.

"'Then, a few weeks ago, she said to me, "I have seen your mother—"'

"Abruptly, Kushyar fell silent, and Jauhara asked, 'What happened then?'

"He pointed to the colloid twilight and said, 'Not now, while light surrenders to darkness.'

"Making a last adjustment to the sail, he spread gray wool blankets across the sole. 'There's little room, so we shall be snugger than two strangers might like.'

"Jauhara's head snapped up in alarm. 'Can we not sleep on land?' she ventured.

"'I would be in Debal as soon as possible.'

"'Oh, of course,' Jauhara answered in a small voice, forgetting her assumed baritone.

"Kushyar clapped Jauhara's thin shoulder and stretched out comfortably on the blankets. 'Nothing to fear about sleeping on a boat. Let the river rock you to sleep, like your mother's own arms.'

"Jauhara kept first watch and when Kushyar was sleeping soundly she pulled her magic book from her satchel. Despite the Sufi's warning in her ears, she spoke soft words and a breeze filled the sails, hastening their journey south."

Sixteen

It is said that among the golden dunes of Arabia, a Bedouin woman danced through sandstorms, tore her robes, and abandoned her children for love of a djinn, who brought droplets of honeyed poetry, sweet as nectar, to her tongue . . .

I blink and the scene dissolves, replaced by bobbing torches, the silhouettes of camels and mules and soldiers on horseback riding through the dark of al-Anbar.

"Did you read it yet?"

I recognize that baritone, that slow drip of words.

"Read what?" I hide a smile.

His face, beneath a conical green kuleh, drops comically. *"The Book of Fixed Stars."*

Yes. I do not tell him how I palmed the cover, imagining where his hand had touched the book, feeding him thoughts, rose water sweet, that he might have had as he purchased it for me.

Atsiz watches me, waiting. I tip my chin toward the milky swirl of stars, the moon that winks like half a silver dirham. "The illustrations are beautiful, but I confess, I cannot pin as-Sufi's drawings to the stars above."

"If you were lost again, you wouldn't be able to find your way back?"

I laugh. "I'm afraid not."

He runs a hand through his spiraling hair. "I would find you. Again and again."

The air tightens, a rope coiled around my chest.

Atsiz jabs his thumb behind us toward my flock of mamluks. "And if I couldn't, your crows certainly would."

I snort.

"Come and proceed with your tale, little Shaherazade." Shahryar's order cuts through the caravan's hubbub. I suppress a wince at the diminutive, the disappointed furrow in Atsiz's brow. Rising like a mercurial mirage, Fataneh's specter smirks.

Atsiz tilts his head as if to say, *Go to your husband, Shaherazade Khatun.*

And I go.

"O Malik, it is said that Jauhara awoke to a glaring sun and a fusty mouth. Kushyar sat by the sail, bathed in light like a golden god. When he saw her, he tossed her a dried apple and a *good morning*. After she had washed her face and drunk of the still night-cool river, Kushyar resumed his tale.

"'My neighbor claimed she had seen my mother. This I found incredible, for merely traveling to my kingdom is a week's journey and I had visited my neighbor's home only that morning. I told her so, and she laughed deep in her throat, a diabolical sound. At last, I sensed something unnatural, but she smiled, halva-sweet.

"'"Your mother is dead," she said. "Perished of a failed heart the night you fled, Sudun Abdullah reported. I saw her grave."

"'Again, I was astounded, for that was the name of my father's physician. Seeing my astonishment, she cackled.

""""Your mother left a token for you, a final bequest for the son who abandoned her to die. The physician entrusted it to me to impart to you. Closer now, if you want it." She held a gold ring, set with jasper, an ibex carved into it. It had been my mother's seal ring and her father's before that. If knowledge of the physician's name had not confirmed my neighbor's story, then the ring certainly did.

""""You grieve, my dove," she said. Tenderly, she slipped the ring onto my smallest finger. "And rightfully, for the loss of a mother is a dreadful thing. Come, we have been friends for very long, and I have revealed myself to you measure by measure. Let me show myself to you wholly."

"'Her robe puddled around her feet and she glowed with an unearthly beauty. Then, her flesh began to slide on her bones, to melt and reform. When her shape firmed, her skin was red and cracked, her hair brittle and black.

"'Screeching, she lunged at me, claws outstretched.

"'Perhaps because of her excitement, the *qarina* had not given me wine, so for once my mind was clear. I brandished my father's shamshir and struck the qarina across her face so she bellowed in agony. Pushing the door open, I fell into the sunlit street. But the bloodsucking she-demon slammed the door with a furious roar. "When the sun sets, I will claim you!"

"'I packed my spare belongings and fled Kandahar. Not even a qarina can follow me across the sea,' Kushyar finished.

"'But will you not fight her? Will you not return to your father's seat and claim your birthright?' Jauhara asked.

"Kushyar chuckled dryly. 'I have no desire to test my strength against a qarina. What man can?'

"Jauhara almost protested that *her father* had done just that and, in doing so, had won renown and respect. Reading her mind, the parrot dug warning talons into Jauhara's shoulder.

"'As for my father's kingdom . . .' Kushyar sighed bitterly. 'By abdicating, I do not tear the world apart. Whereas if I tried to stake my claim, I would rip my land into bloodshed. And for what? My vanity?'

"'But the concubine . . .' Jauhara said weakly.

"'Her son is a dullard, but she is no fool,' Kushyar said. 'She had been advising my father long before his death; we all knew that. No, that is a world I am eager to forget. I have put my trust in Allah and the path He has laid for me.'

"Jauhara, who had been weaned on stories of heroes, found this prince's pragmatism most unappealing and they traveled some days in silence. In Debal, they found a spice-laden dhow headed to 'Aydhab, desperate enough for crew to hire their inexperienced hands. Once their ship set sail, their adventures began."

––––––––––––

An audience has gathered. First, it was only Dunya, who pressed a garnet pendant that had once belonged to our mother into my hand by way of apology. Then, like moths to a candle, followed Faramurz, then Mahperi and Gulnar, and a coterie of 'Abbasids and Seljuk nobles, including the sloe-eyed woman from the dinner, with Atsiz beside her. I have learned from Dunya that she is Nurani, daughter of Emir Ildegiz, she of the cheetah cub. She murmurs something to Atsiz and his mouth quirks in amusement. My hands tighten around Andalib's reins.

And of course, my mamluks, not quite out of sight. A not-so-distant Shaherazade would have stumbled over her words, lost the thread of her tale, wanted to hide her face in her hands before a vast, stranger-filled audience. But that girl has no place in this world.

The cloud of my audience condenses eagerly, but as I continue the story, I feel only two pairs of eyes, straight to my marrow.

––––––––––––

"O Malik, it is said that a rough boot in Jauhara's back woke her late on their third morning on the dhow. 'Up! A storm is coming.'

"On deck, the crew frantically tightened the rigging as the first raindrops spattered onto the heaving hull, soaking the hemp cords that bound the floorboards.

"The smallest and sprightliest of the crew, Jauhara was sent climbing up the swinging teak mast to survey the storm. She clung tightly as the lateen sails bellowed like cotton clouds. Whorls of pricking rain blinded her, and her voice, high with fright, was lost in the crashing storm. Jauhara hugged the mast more tightly, praying furiously as the deck rolled and the dark sea foamed. She felt something slip from her pocket, and her magic book twisted into the darkness below.

"Lightning snapped through the black sky and illuminated the dhow in bone-brittle white. Rolls of thunder, an all-encompassing parade of tablas, rattled the mast and drowned out the shouting men and pounding sea. A frozen blaze of lightning inverted Jauhara's vision, but when it faded, she knew what she had seen.

"'Land!' she cried to the men. 'Land!' But they could not hear, not with the shrieking gale and bludgeoning waves.

"She screamed as something soft and warm collided with her face.

"'Jauhara!' the parrot squawked.

"Blindly, she grabbed hold of the windswept parrot. 'I see land!' she cried.

"'You must tell them,' the parrot responded, but Jauhara closed her eyes and shook her head.

"Only with a stream of gentle encouragement from the parrot could Jauhara climb down the shuddering mast, but by the time her bare feet slapped the wet deck, the gale was whisking the dhow toward a mangrove forest.

"Horrified, Jauhara and the crew watched as the dhow cracked against the shallow coral reefs and skidded across storm-packed sand, narrowly missing the mangroves. Jauhara lurched against Kushyar as the ship shook and waves heaved the vessel up the beach.

"When the storm finally ceased, the sun shone with cheery heat and mist steamed from a jewel-like jungle. As Jauhara stepped into moist, white sand, the dhow's hull cracked open, revealing its dark berth, the binding cords having disintegrated. The crew groaned in despair.

"Ever levelheaded, the captain said, 'Perhaps the inhabitants of this isle will know how to make these small repairs. For be assured, these are small repairs that we could make ourselves, but if expert hands are available, I have no doubt they would be grateful to exchange their skills for some cinnamon or turmeric.' His eyes scanned the sailors and landed on Jauhara and Kushyar. 'You two—if there is a shipwright on this island, bring him here!'

"Without delay, Jauhara and Kushyar stumbled against the sand until they sank into the loamy jungle trail. Fat drops of cold water spilled from green leaves, skating across their scalps and down their necks. The jungle vibrated with animal noise: the high-pitched chitter of birds, the winged whirr of insects, the hiss of snakes, and soft padded footsteps, shadowing close and then sprinting away.

"Jauhara, Kushyar, and the parrot drank from a silver stream and then followed it for hours, until the jungle dimness vanished into the blinding zeal of a tropical sun at its zenith. A white marble medina wound up a hill to a vast palace surrounded by white walls. Despite the sloping cupolas of houses and the minarets of mosques, the city was unnaturally still, supernaturally silent.

"Jauhara's skin prickled.

"'Perhaps the townsfolk are napping?' Kushyar said, twisting his mother's jasper ring.

"'Perhaps,' Jauhara agreed, although she did not quite believe an inhabited city could be so lifeless.

"Their steps clapped through the medina as they curved up the hill, and still, no one appeared. The feeling of watching eyes grew stronger.

"Finally, they approached an immense marble archway, which opened onto a glistening palace courtyard. Like the medina, it was empty, but freshly swept and scrubbed.

"'We are not alone,' the parrot whispered. Jauhara hesitated beneath the epistyle, but Kushyar strode boldly as if, as a prince of one kingdom, he had the right to enter all the palaces in all the world.

"As Jauhara rushed after him, the walls began to shake, and a voice like a landslide reverberated through the courtyard, throbbing into Jauhara: *'Who dares enter the Palace of the Queen of Djinns?'*"

Seventeen

$\diamond\diamond\diamond\diamond\diamond\diamond$

Dunya furls beside me on the mattress like a little cat, turning my garnet pendant between her fingers. It refracts red freckles across her nose and cheeks. I remember it swinging from my mother's neck and catching the firelight.

Dunya takes a deep breath. "Shahera, in Baghdad, I wrote to Baba, seeking his permission to wed Faramurz. Faramurz plans to speak to Shahryar soon."

Although the pendant was her apology, we have not spoken of Faramurz since our fight. "Are you asking my permission, Dunya?" I ask carefully.

"I seek your blessing."

"I think he is too . . . immature . . . to wed." I remind Dunya of Faramurz's hotheaded zeal at the dinner at Leila's home. Even as I say it, it seems small in the face of his sobriety when the Malik's idiot boon companions goaded him to raid Oghuz encampments. And did Baba not work with Faramurz to persuade the Malik to eschew raiding and go to Palestine? Why am I so insistent on not allowing Dunyazade to chart her own path?

"Wasn't he right?" Dunya says, echoing my thoughts. "Did we not leave Bam to march for Palestine?"

"We are not commoners who might marry for love. You are a Khatun's sister, and there is political advantage in your marriage."

Shahryar himself had intimated as much, but even as I say it, I think of Altunjan, Shideh, and Inanj—and even Fataneh—wed to Shahryar because their fathers saw an advantage. Where could Shahryar find advantage in bartering Dunya? I flinch, thinking of Dunya wed to a barbarous Khwarezmid commander or uncivilized Oghuz chieftain.

"I want it," Dunya pleads. The garnet pendant shakes, spraying red, like drops of blood, across her hands. "It is a good match. He is of a good family, rising in Shahryar's esteem. We would be happy."

Why should Dunya not have what she wants? I think of the Khwarezmid Shah Tekish swiping Persia, the Oghuz Malik Dinar worrying at Kirman's villages, Caliph an-Nasir inviting me to his pleasure palace and threatening to conquer Kirman, Malikric savaging Palestine, Shahryar murdering wife after wife. Their desires rule this world, and we always assent, yielding ourselves little by little.

***

Faramurz must have pled his case well before Shahryar, for my sister rides beside him, beaming. They must still await Baba's permission before officially announcing their betrothal, but Baba likes Faramurz, and if Shahryar has blessed their engagement and Dunya wants it, then no force in this world can stop them. I feel a flash of envy that Dunya has found that rare privilege—choosing whom she wants to marry and having his love in return. I feel a burst of shame for envying my sister, she who left her home and father to keep me safe.

Faramurz catches me watching. I look away, toward the low-ridged mountains greening with grass and the patchwork farmlands lit darkly by a crescent moon.

Approaching me, he performs a half obeisance from horseback. "Mutashakaram for supporting Dunyazade, Shaherazade Khatun. I want to assure you that I vow I shall bring happiness to your sister and honor to our families." A boyish grin cracks through and I cannot help but smile back.

"I hope you make Dunya happy. It is on that dower I gave my blessing."

He clasps a fist against his woven leather cuirass, above his heart. "As you say. Insh'Allah."

I watch him rejoin my sister and feel unexpectedly melancholy. When I hear Atsiz's voice in my ear, I start, Andalib swerving beneath me.

"So, Faramurz shall wed your sister? Perhaps he should become my *ostaadh* and I learn at his feet."

Shahryar is somewhere, lost in the labyrinth of the caravan. Atsiz has a knack for finding me away from him—or perhaps, he is simply being gallant. The thought is sour.

"If you had half a mind, I am sure you could fill all four wifely spots." I bite back a mention of Nurani, for then he would know how closely I have been watching him.

He grins mischievously, like a little boy with a sweet melting in his hand. "Perhaps you are right, but I could not surrender wandering to hearth and home. Nor could I ask a wife to forgo those securities—nor abandon her for years at a time."

"That's foolish." My words snap more than I had intended. "Look at this caravan and the Seljuk women who have chosen to leave hearth and home. You would not have to search far to find a woman who wishes to see the world as you do."

I fear I have said too much in my haste. I urge Andalib away, twist her through the caravan of horses and camels and donkeys, until I find Shahryar, a solitary figure near the caravan's head.

"Are you happy with the match?" Shahryar says, without turning.

"If my sister is happy then so am I."

"Women make fools of themselves in pursuit of small happinesses."

"The world would be a better place if it were ruled in the pursuit of happiness and not glory and gold," I say sharply.

Shahryar's taut silence clangs in my head. Before he can dwell too long on my insolence, I leap back into Jauhara's world.

"O Malik, it is said that as he walked into the marble palace, Kushyar cried, 'I dare enter! I, who was born of a king and queen, entreat to speak to *your* Queen.'

"Wind funneled between Jauhara and Kushyar, lifting the parrot from her shoulder and howling with the force of a habub. Jauhara's eyes shut against black heat as she floated toward the sky. Then the wind dropped her, and she crumpled to the floor.

"A silver-robed woman sat on a silver throne, a tall silver crown rising from her long black hair, a peacock-feather scepter in her hand. At the throne's base, half a dozen peahens pecked at invisible grains. Jauhara's skin prickled as a dry heat brushed her neck.

"'A prince, you said?' the Queen chimed. 'What are you then?' she asked Jauhara. 'A princess?'

"Kushyar looked in bewilderment at Jauhara, who puffed her chest and proclaimed, 'A princess? Your Majesty, I am no girl, but a man of Egypt!'

"The Queen concealed a smile behind a long dark hand. A man's signet ring gleamed on her longest finger. Hot air scraped Jauhara's skin and to her horror the bandage that bound her breast unwound, revealing two slight peaks beneath her tunic. Kushyar gawped in unabashed shock. Jauhara resisted the urge to bring her hands to her chest.

"'It is all right, ya Sitti,' the parrot whispered as he hovered and glowed. A light flashed, and the parrot flew back to Jauhara's shoulder. 'You are ether and fire,' he called to something unseen, 'but I am the will of the Creator made light and your power is not greater than His.'

"The Queen nodded graciously at Jauhara. 'A *man* of Egypt, you say?'

"Mustering all her bravado, Jauhara threw out, 'I am Jauhara bint 'Omar al-Hakim, governor of Egypt, slayer of djinn and freer of souls.'

"'Oh,' the Queen said in faint surprise. 'I was not aware we were listing the glory of our ancestors. I am Shirin, Queen of the Djinn, as my mother was before me and her mother before her, our line extending to Bilquis, Queen of Sheba, and her husband, King Suleiman, may peace be upon him, the Prophet of Allah, son of King Dawud.

"'Now, what brings a prince, a governor's daughter, and an angelic parrot into my abode?' She leaned forward, chin on her fist, rapt with attention.

"Since Kushyar was too awed to speak, Jauhara said, 'O Queen, we have a simple purpose. We are sailors. A storm ran our ship onto your shores. We search for a shipwright, who might mend our vessel and allow us to continue our journey without further disturbance to you.'

"Tapping her full lips, the Queen said: 'I can send a djinn with you who will repair your craft, but in return I require . . .' She eyed Kushyar with clear appreciation, and Jauhara felt an uncomfortable twitch between her shoulder blades.

"'Your Majesty?' Kushyar said, not grasping what Jauhara had.

"'An heir,' the Queen said bluntly. 'Tell me, Prince Kushyar, would you like to be King of the Unseen Realms?'

"Entrancement lit Kushyar's handsome face and a discomfited Jauhara cried out, 'Your Majesty, we have seen no living creatures here except yourself and the peafowl at your feet. Who are they?'

"The Queen chortled. 'There can only be one Queen, and rivals . . . complicate matters. Permit me to introduce my sisters.'"

✳ ✳ ✳

Despite the long journey, Dunya is animated, flying on the wings of her hopes, as she sits beside me in the Malik's tent. Even as my eyes flutter drowsily, she chatters: "A wedding in Jerusalem would be splendid. Why, even Sultan Saladin might attend, and *that* would be a tale for our children and grandchildren."

"What about Baba, you heartless fiend?" But there's no sting in my remark.

I see my own wedding, but reconstituted with a groom whose grass-green eyes pool with adoration. I pummel the traitorous thought into a bloody mass.

"Of course, Baba would have to permit it and I want Baba at my wedding, but he may forgive our rush if I can serve him a grandchild on our return!" She blushes impishly at her audacity.

I jerk up from al-Khansa's *diwan* of poems. "Dunya!" Shahryar is here, reviewing accounts, but he does not appear to have heard.

Irrepressible, Dunya turns to him, twisting a braid around a finger. "Brother Shahryar, would you act as my wali, my guardian, for the marriage contract, should Baba permit us to wed here?" she asks with artless charm. Shahryar looks up from his papers and his handsome face softens, pulled in, despite himself, by my little sister's glamour. I feel another prick of jealousy.

"It would be my honor."

"*Mamnoon,*" Dunya murmurs.

The easy silence is broken by Shahryar's chuckle.

My eyebrows jump; hearing his amusement is like sighting a rainbow-winged simurgh overhead. Tentatively, I ask, "What is it?"

He holds a letter covered in a familiar scrawl. "A letter from your father. Your cart of books has arrived from Papersellers' Street. He chides me." Shahryar clears his throat, softens his voice. "'*Shahryar,*'" he mimics Baba, "'*the treasury is strained, the library already full. You should have curtailed my daughter's profligate ways!*' Vizier Muhammad seems pleased." Shahryar grins. It is a lance through my heart.

"It wasn't a *cart,*" I mutter from the pallet, which only elicits laughter from Shahryar and Dunya. I smile too. I wish I could decant this moment into a crystal vial, releasing the stopper only now and again to inhale. Here he is, the Shahryar of old, a creature of myth like the simurgh itself.

The creases around his mouth deepening, Shahryar begins flipping through one of my books. The cover flashes: *The Book of Fixed Stars*.

And I remember leaving it on top of my trunk while searching for my trousers this morning. Why did I not bury it again? What unhappy chance deposited it among the Malik's documents and cahiers? A squawk of alarm dies in my mouth as the Malik extracts a leaf-thin paper from between the pages. My head feels cold, my cheeks hot. His eyes run over the note, his countenance clouds, and the paper shakes in his hand.

Oh, why didn't I burn it? Did I keep it purposefully or did I absent-mindedly slip it into Atsiz's gift? I cannot remember. All I can remember is the flame of the lamp flickering, and instead of allowing it to consume the verse, I tucked the note away.

"What is this?" His voice cracks like a whip, strikes me across the face.

As Dunya shifts uncomfortably, he snaps, "No, you should stay for this." Shahryar recites the poem, dedication to Faramurz and all.

Dunya's face whitens.

Shahryar walks to me, squeezes my chin, pulls me close until our noses touch and his face blurs. His breath is hot and I taste it in my mouth. If he wanted, he could snap my neck with a flick of his wrist, a rose bloom broken at the stem. My body shakes.

"Why do you have a love poem for Faramurz among your things, little Shaherazade?"

I have no story at the tip of my tongue. I can only look at him dumbly. His gaze holds none of his usual distance. No, his dark eyes shine hot as coal, probing and burning, a torch that would sear every shadow from my soul.

"The poem is mine, Brother."

Shahryar releases me, and I stumble back, catching myself on Dunya's shoulder. I rub my smarting jaw.

"Is that so?" he whispers, and Dunya meets his eyes boldly. Two red spots that Shahryar might mistake for embarrassment pop on her cheeks.

"It is humiliating, oh, do not read it again! I gave it to Shaherazade to pass judgment." A wave of gratefulness for Dunyazade, loyal and brave Dunyazade, rushes over me.

He turns to me. "Does your sister tell true, little Shaherazade?"

Four beats of fear vibrate through me. "Yes, O Malik." I try to infuse my words with that honest innocence Dunya manifests so easily, but I cannot meet his eye.

"What do you think of it?" Dunya inquires with a smile.

He regards the poem like a cobra in his hand. "Charming verse," he finally says. "It appears your sister is not the only literary one in the family." Shahryar crumples the paper, the verse Atsiz wrote with me in mind.

Perhaps sensing his looming darkness, Dunya prompts, "Dear sister, while we have some time, will you not continue your wondrous tale?"

I do not want to sit in this tent with him, but Dunya is right. I cannot leave him to dwell. Dunya squeezes my hand, perhaps a little harder than necessary. As I begin to speak, she pours wine from a clay jug and presses the iridescent goblet upon Shahryar. Without comment, he swigs it down.

"O Malik, it is said that to Jauhara's surprise, Kushyar accepted the Djinn Queen's terms.

"'You must not!' Jauhara found herself exclaiming. 'Kushyar do not forget . . .' She trailed off as his eyes narrowed with warning. She could not understand how Kushyar could let himself be entrapped by beauty once more. The place of her soul, behind her breastbone, squeezed with disappointment.

"The Queen watched, amused, but Kushyar said, 'You vow, Your Majesty, that if I give you a child that Jauhar . . . will reach the ship and deliver the aid promised?'

"'I swear to you by my forebears, the Queen of Sheba and the King of the Israelites. I swear to you in the name of our Lord that she will reach her ship safely and will sail away just so.'

"'Very well.' Kushyar took his place beside the Queen on the high dais, looking down upon Jauhara.

"The Queen clapped and hot air skimmed Jauhara. 'Go with the girl and repair the ship.'

"Jauhara avoided Kushyar's eyes as the wind blew her into the glaring medina and down its marble steps. Only when she was in the glossy-leafed jungle did she realize her shoulder felt light.

"The parrot was gone.

"Her heart clenched, but then relief flooded her like cold water: the parrot, the parrot whom the Queen's power could not touch, was with Kushyar.

"When they broke onto the beach again, the shipwrecked sailors, their faces crisped red, gazed upon Jauhara as though she were an apparition. The hot breeze whooshed past her, and the water rippled as though someone were skimming atop it. The dhow's sails fluttered.

"'Jauhar, lad!' cried the captain, staggering to her. 'We thought the jungle had taken you and Kushyar. Where have you been? Where is Kushyar?' The captain looked at Jauhara's shoulder. 'Where's your bird?'

"Before she could answer, the captain turned at the men's gasps. The dhow was righting itself, the hull's torn wood patched, the ship's deck solidified. The captain began a soft prayer, but Jauhara stopped him with a stern hand. 'Unless you wish to drive our helper away.'

"With a few significant omissions, she recounted what had passed. She eyed the sailors' bedraggled beards.

"'If I were not watching this myself, I would call you a liar.' The captain's steeled mouth could not entirely conceal his discomfort, but like the sailors he was transfixed.

"'How long have we been gone?' Jauhara asked.

"'Two weeks. We had despaired of you returning or us ever leaving this isle.'

"Jauhara glanced into the jungle's dark recesses. The captain clapped her shoulder. 'Keep your eyes forward, lad. Your friend did a brave thing. We would have died without ever seeing our families again. Besides,' he winked, 'most men wouldn't complain about a life with the Queen of the Djinn.'

"But thinking of the peahens, Jauhara was not so sure.

"Finally, the ship stilled. A sailor waded into the sea and nervously knocked on the dhow's hull. A hollow, whole sound rang out and the crew cheered. The hot breeze fluttered through Jauhara's shorn hair before disappearing.

"Eagerly, the crew loaded the dhow with fruits scavenged from the jungle's edges and rainwater gathered in barrels.

"Jauhara wished they would not rush. She stifled tears at the lightness of her shoulder and hung back even as the last barrel was rolled onto the ship. Her feet dragged on the dhow. She leaned against its railing, her hands cupping her trembling chin. The ship shuddered as it began to drift. As she wiped a tear, something soft collided with her face. Her shriek of fear became one of delight when she recognized those black eyes, the red-and-green plumage.

"'Oh Parrot! Oh Parrot!' she cried, ignoring the crew's stares.

"'Kushyar comes,' the parrot whispered. Jauhara called out as a figure emerged from the jungle. The dhow shivered to a stop. His strides long, Kushyar traversed the beach and launched himself into the cerulean sea, swimming with broad-stroked swiftness. Nimbly, he scaled the rope thrown to him and landed on the deck. He embraced Jauhara in a hearty, wet hug as though she were still just Jauhar.

"To the shocked captain, Kushyar said, 'Make this ship fly. The Djinn Queen does not take well to broken bargains.' To Jauhara, he whispered, 'My dear friend, little sister, governor's daughter, have I a tale for you.'"

———

Dunya stretches her arms, the blue sleeves of her robe falling past her elbows, and yawns dramatically. "Oh, I am tired. Walk with me to our tent, Sister?"

Dunya has plied Shahryar with wine throughout the tale, and his head bobs sleepily. If the wine has not made him jolly, it has buffed him soft. He pays no mind as we steal out.

As soon as we are outside and away from Shahryar's ears, Dunya touches my arm. "Did he hurt you?"

Other than a scattering of sentinels, the dusty path between our tents stands empty. My jaw throbs where he squeezed it. "I'm fine."

"I cannot believe he would do that. If I'd had a scimitar in my hand, I would have run him through." Her shoulders quaver.

"I'm lucky he only pulled *at* my neck and didn't pull it off." We slip into the hot tent, where Mahperi sleeps, her hair fanned out in dark waves over her pillow. Although Dunya does not ask, I know she wonders.

"The poem was from Atsiz," I say in a whisper so soft I can hardly hear it, but Dunya understands perfectly. Her thick, curved eyebrows rise toward her hair, like twin ravens in flight. "The dedication was a joke, as was the poem, I'm sure. But thank you for your quick thinking, Dunya." I rub at my neck.

"Joke or not, this is dangerous, Shahera. I can save you once, but for a man as suspicious as the Malik, you must be above suspicion!" Wrapping her arms around me, she buries her face in my shoulder. "I don't mean to scold, but I fear for you. How can you bear to be married to him?" Her frightened tears, like warm, summer rain, wet my tunic.

"Because I must," I say faintly, even as I imagine saddling Andalib and racing until I disappear into the horizon.

***

Shahryar rides with Atsiz and an intermix of 'Abbasid and Seljuk nobles beneath an aureole of moonlight. Dunya looks over at me and draws her shoulders back. "Faramurz, I have written a poem for you," she announces after a breath. Loudly, she declaims Atsiz's poem before the company, each verse punctuated with approving exclamations of "*Bah, bah!*"

Shahryar watches the performance, his face granite-cut. My eyes flicker to Atsiz, catching his visage crumple like paper, before smoothing again. Perhaps he thinks that I read the poem to Dunya and we laughed, and she said, *Let me read that aloud to Faramurz while Atsiz listens. What a joke that would be!*

At the end of the recitation, Faramurz stretches his hand as though he would touch Dunya's chin. "Mutashakaram jaanem, that was lovely." He murmurs something else, just for her ears, and she ducks her head with a small smile.

I wish Atsiz would understand the nature of this recital, that it would not mar our friendship. I wish that Shahryar will accept it for what it seems and forget this matter.

Dust flies in my face as a pair of russet-robed men rush to Shahryar, who waves the nobles away when the physician indicates a desire for privacy. The physician's long face is grim. Passing a hand over his eyes, Shahryar nods tiredly. Together, physician, orderly, and Shahryar ride toward the caravan's rear. Whispers lift from the sand like wind.

A Seljuk nobleman proclaims, "It is camp fever. A physician from my father's holdings told me earlier. They have a whole cartful of dead and dying men in the back."

***

lowing orange embers illuminate Gulnar's cheekbones and weary brown eyes as she stokes the brazier burning medicinal sulfur to keep plague vapors at bay. The heaviness of the smoke, the warmth in the closed tent, the unpleasantness of the smell make my head spin. As camp fever has ravaged the caravan, Mahperi, Dunya, and I have spent a week sequestered at Shahryar's orders. Confined, the days have begun to run together, sunrise bleeding seamlessly into sunrise, the hours punctuated only by the azaan, as we hear the moans of ill soldiers, the steady scrape of shovels.

The burdens of managing this epidemic have kept Shahryar away from me. I have not missed him, the near disaster in the tent too raw. Atsiz has not visited either, although I hope to catch a glimpse of him or hear his footfall outside our tent. Perhaps he avoids me because the incident of the poem still tastes bitter as lemon rind. Maybe that is why Shahryar keeps away too. Instead, Faramurz, who crosses his lanky legs on a stack of cushions, has been one of our few windows into the world. His aquiline nose twitches at the yellow malodor of sulfur, his cheeks suffused with color in the warmth. "Four more men have died in the last hour. To Allah we belong and unto him we return."

Dutifully, we echo him as we have dozens of times. Hundreds of men have died already—of a cough, which becomes a fever, which becomes breathlessness, which finally becomes death. Yet, the disease continues to gnaw, insatiable.

"Do they know yet what causes it?" Mahperi asks.

"The physicians speak of humoral imbalance and astral influence. Others say it is the work of a malevolent djinn. I'm not a learned man and it makes little sense to me."

"Is the illness abating?" I ask Faramurz this question each time I see him, each time hoping he says yes, yes, it is over, yes, it was not as disastrous as they had feared, yes, the men are healing, yes, all will return to be as it was before.

Faramurz tugs at the green brocade kaftan that Dunya and I have stitched for him this past week, seeking some task for our idle hands. The yellow-banded sleeves slipping around his wrists reveal that our measurements were incorrect, but he wears it proudly and without complaint. I feel a surge of fondness for him.

"The physicians say hundreds more will perish before the disease runs it course."

We are an army of just four thousand, and the recitation of funerary prayers has been constant. These men die in the heat to be buried in faraway desert graves only because they marched to war at Shahryar's orders, orders that came because Baba had to maneuver Shahryar's departure from Bam, because one sun-filled afternoon I stumbled upon the Khatun, compromised, and forced the Malik to look askance at her.

"But the Malik will keep you all safe—" Before he can finish the sentence, Faramurz begins coughing, bent over as though some great hand pushes him to the ground. I exchange a frightened look with Gulnar.

Dunya touches his chest protectively. "Are you well?" she demands.

Faramurz holds Dunya's hand to his heart. "With you beside me, always, jaanem," he says roughly.

Dunya frowns and places the back of her hand against his forehead and then his flushed neck. "You're hot," she says. "Gulnar, will you fetch a physician?"

Drawing her veil, Gulnar hurries out. Mahperi brings the plate of burning sulfur close to Faramurz and conscientiously wafts its fumes in his direction. He coughs harder, but then laughs. "You look at me like hens worried over a chick."

Faramurz smiles sheepishly as Dunya watches him with hawk-eyed concern. "Trust me, Dunya," he says. "I will not perish before setting foot in Palestine and fighting beside Sultan Saladin. I will not perish before I become your husband."

"Insh'Allah," Dunya murmurs.

I imagine Faramurz's handsome face, his sparkling eyes dulled and glassy with fever. *"Astaghfirallah,"* I murmur to myself, trying to dispel the evil thoughts before, caught by some stray wind, they catch fire.

After some time, Gulnar reenters with a physician, an older man with curly white hair that springs above his ears like gull's wings. The physician genuflects before me before turning to examine Faramurz. I draw comfort in the confident deftness of his hands as he touches Faramurz's forehead and throat, feels his pulse at his wrist, smells his breath. The physician frowns. "How do you feel?"

"A little faint, but it's been warm."

The physician purses his lips and folds his hands into his wide sleeves.

"You have a fever. Likely the camp fever, but early. You should not stay here. We will take you to your tent, bleed you to rebalance your humors, and dose you with tinctures. You are strong; there is little to worry about." He says the last to Dunyazade, whose eyes shine with unspilled tears.

Despite the physician's assurances, Dunya reaches for me. I hold her steady even though my own hand shakes. I pray for Faramurz's health, try not to think of the hundreds of other soldiers, as hale and young as Faramurz, who have been felled.

***

Two weeks later, the illness has run its course, the stars have changed, or the wicked djinn has gone, taking with it the breath of a thousand martyrs. We leave behind as many patches of dark, upturned earth, unmarked, with nowhere for families to come read al-Fatihah to give their child succor in the grave. Among them lies Faramurz. Although Dunya wore herself wan nursing him, despite the nights we spent prostrate in prayer, he passed a week after he laughed away Dunya's concern, a week after the physician told Dunya that he was strong and healthy and had nothing to worry about. A week after Faramurz had reassured Dunya he would marry her.

We are a thousand men lighter, but I feel heavy, oh so heavy, as we resume the march to Palestine.

PART THREE

Eighteen

F inally, Palestine.

A few parasangs before al-Kharruba, the small town where Sultan Saladin has situated the Muslim forces, a pair of his scouts ride to meet us. They lead us through a landscape dotted with olive trees like drops of dark, fresh henna. Tents upon tents unfold on the hills, white as the crest of a wave, ringing a brick-and-rubble castle. Yellow Ayyubid flags fly proudly overhead, shining like small suns.

Although I tried to persuade Dunya to ride with us to meet Sultan Saladin's army, she did not stir, prone for all the nights and days since Faramurz died. I never thought to see her laid so low. For all my efforts, I cannot lessen her grief.

Troops in battle lines march to greet us, led by a young man in gold-washed armor. "Well met, Malik Shahryar!" he calls.

Shahryar looks at the man questioningly, and he eases into a gracious smile. "I am al-Afdal, son of Sultan Saladin. He eagerly awaits your arrival, Malik Shahryar."

"We are honored to join this jihad," Shahryar answers.

"How many soldiers are with Sultan Saladin?" Atsiz asks quietly.

The man, the nasal plate of his peaked helmet dividing his face, says, "Right under twenty-five thousand." His black eyes tighten. "That Inkitar swine, Malikric, holds three thousand of our men, with their wives and children, hostage in Acre. There's more to it, but Sultan Saladin shall apprise you."

A small, excited smile pulls at Shahryar's mouth as he urges his horse to speed. It's hard not to share his anticipation. We have survived mountain and desert, caliphal courts, and camp fever to join Saladin, a man marked by destiny and respected by all—from Caliph an-Nasir, who is hard-pressed to respect anyone, let alone a Kurdish upstart, to the Frankish barbarians, who see in Sultan Saladin's storied courtliness a glimmer of their own chivalric codes.

Guided by al-Afdal, Shahryar, and Atsiz, I, and a representative of the Caliph called Marwan ibn Hatim, enter Sultan Saladin's tent. Because I stick like a burr to Shahryar, I am enfolded into this assembly.

Carefully, I navigate around maps that clutter the ground and gleam with freshly inked hills and streams. Blocky Arabic blackens their edges, the notes too dense for me to make out more than the occasional word: flank, arrows, dirhams. Scribbling clerks glance up with brief interest before returning to their work.

"Assalamu'alaikum, Father," intones al-Afdal. "I present Malik Shahryar of Kirman, leader of the Seljuk Turks, victorious in this world in faith. I present Marwan ibn Hatim, emissary of Caliph an-Nasir li-Din Allah, the Victor for God's Religion. I present Emir Atsiz ad-Dawla, Emir Ildegiz Razi, Emir Savtegin ibn Shavur, and Her Grace, Shaherazade Khatun, wife of Malik Shahryar."

Sultan Salahuddin Abu al-Mozaffar Yusuf bin Ayyub bin Shadi strides forth. Although Shahryar, Marwan, and the emirs stand respectfully, Saladin clasps their arms and pulls them into brotherly embraces. Seeing me, he inclines his head magnificently. "You are most welcome." His mouth twists ruefully. "*Most* welcome."

Sultan Saladin's skin is the color and texture of parchment, with fine, sun-tarnished wrinkles. Beneath his wine-colored turban, his eyes are small, slanted. His gray-streaked beard has been oiled into two forks. He is not as I imagined, both larger and smaller at once. While he wears a crimson kaftan of Dimyati brocade, I spy his hauberk and scaled lamellar cuirass writ with gold-washed Qur'anic verse propped in a corner. For all that Saladin is a hero, and we think of heroes as vibrant youths, he is past fifty, but before Atsiz and Shahryar he is no less vital.

A younger man, with Saladin's eyes and an undeviated beard, approaches.

"This is my brother, Saifuddin." Saladin smiles. "He is my right hand, my sword of faith indeed."

Saifuddin bears the same deep nobility as his brother, but it sits a little lighter on him. He embraces Marwan, Shahryar, and the emirs and welcomes me with a flourish.

Another man, short and thin with a clever face, waves ink-stained fingers from a corner.

"That is Yusuf ibn Shaddad," Saladin says fondly. "A judge of the army and a chronicler, recording our great deeds for posterity."

Saladin gestures for us to sit. I watch ibn Shaddad furiously scratch notes into his ledger. A tale-teller too, but his tales are given the weight of history and truth, the chance to live for centuries. Envy pricks me.

Gingerly shuffling papers aside, I perch on a cushion. A quick, apologetic flash as Saifuddin leans over and whisks the papers from my hands.

"Your arrival gladdens all our hearts. You will meet the host of my commanders and generals—Gokbori, Abu al-Heija, Behaddin Kara-kush . . . we are blessed by many honorable leaders—but that is for after you have rested. For now, tell me," Saladin turns to Marwan, "how fares our brother and benefactor Caliph an-Nasir?"

A wide gap between his two front teeth, Marwan spouts some drivel about the Caliph an-Nasir's well-being. He then says, "As a mark of his everlasting support and hopes for the advancement of the Muslim cause, the Caliph an-Nasir, blessed be his generosity, has sent you three hundred soldiers."

I have waited for this figure, and I'm rewarded by the sarcastic pull in Saifuddin's expression, the hollow pleasantries from his courteous mouth. "Only Allah knows the grain of sand that will tip the scale. May your master meet Paradise for his munificence."

Saifuddin's eyes flicker to his brother. I can guess his thoughts—*Three hundred men from the Prince of the Believers, who bathes in gold, sleeps in silk, and has enough men in his personal army to kick the unwashed defilers back to their flea-bitten pope.*

"This is in addition to last year's naphtha experts," Marwan puffs, "and the warrant from Caliph an-Nasir permitting the loan of up to twenty thousand dinars from merchants."

Saladin inclines his head with good grace. "And although we did not draw on that generous sum lest it oppress the people of the provinces, we have made good use of the naphtha hurlers. As always, Caliph an-Nasir is in our prayers.

"And you, Malik Shahryar," Saladin turns his gaze on Shahryar, sharp as a raven. "*Mabrook* on your recent nuptials."

I wonder if Saladin, the greatest hero of his age, second in valor only to the Prophet Muhammad, knows the provenance of those nuptials.

"But war is a dangerous business to carry an innocent bride into. Have you heard what befell those besieged at Acre?"

Shahryar shakes his head, accepting a warm glass of mint tea from a servant. "Only the little your son told us, O Sultan."

"You have your teas? And are none too tired? Shaherazade Khatun, I daresay, you seem a little wan. Please, take my seat. It is the most comfortable. No, no, I insist. I am not such an old man that a woman need sit in discomfort at my expense."

Reclining on a silk cushion, Sultan Saladin takes a deep breath. "Five years ago, at the Battle of Hattin, my army reconquered a portion of what the Franks call their Kingdom of Jerusalem, and what we, for centuries, have called home. On the anniversary of the Prophet's Night Journey, I entered Jerusalem. In doing so, I righted some of the wrongs against us that began after their first incursion into Jerusalem, nearly a century ago, when the Franks drowned Muslims and Jews alike in their own blood.

"You know this: it is old history, well trodden by chroniclers. Two years ago, however, the Franks came again, besieging the coast with boulder-hurling mangonels. Many battles were fought, but there was no decisive victor.

"However, in the summer, the balance shifted in our favor. Fifty of our galleys broke through the Franks' sea blockade and supplied Acre with food, while the Franks were reduced to eating horses and vermin. Great men among them, Frederick, Malik of Swabia, and Theobold of Blois, perished of sickness. If, in their misery, they had sought surrender, I would have released them with full mercy.

"This winter, Acre's garrison walls fell to the Franks. In turn, we attacked and broke the Frankish lines. I regret, now, that we did not break their whole force, for by spring, two new kings joined: the Malik al-Inkitar, Richard, and the Raidefrans, Philip.

"We attacked, we distracted, we gave the Muslim fighters in Acre's garrison the chance to rebuild their walls."

Ibn Shaddad looks up. "Come now, they shall think this war business all very serious. What of the dancing and the boys' battle?"

Saladin grins wolfishly. "You tell them, old friend." Turning to us, he adds, "It's his favorite tale."

"This siege was long," ibn Shaddad intoned, the tale's melody familiar to him. "The soldiers of both sides grew so accustomed to meeting that sometimes a Muslim and a Frank would leave off fighting to converse. Sometimes the two parties would mingle, singing and dancing, so intimate they had become. Afterward, they would resume fighting.

"One day, wearying of the warfare, soldiers of both sides said, 'How long are the men to fight without allowing the boys their share in the pleasure? Let us arrange a fight between young fellows from each side.'

Muslim boys were fetched from Acre to contest with Frankish youths, with soldiers cheering as the boys laughed and fought." Seeing our incredulous expressions, ibn Shaddad swears, "By Allah, it is all true. War is a queer thing."

"Be that as it may . . . the garrison at Acre, besieged for two years, with their wives and children, could withstand the assault no longer. After two years of my failures," Sultan Saladin says, "they lost hope. Two weeks ago, they surrendered to Malikric, who promised to spare their lives if they ceded Acre.

"In exchange for the men, women, and children he holds prisoner, the Lionheart demands a relic of what those kuffar"—for the briefest moment, moved by the hostages' plight, Saladin's balanced politeness cracks—"think to be the True Cross, sixteen hundred of our Frankish prisoners, and two hundred thousand dinars." Saladin slaps his knees in frustration. "Their splinter I can return, their men as well; it is the gold I do not have . . . but Richard is an honorable man. I pray Allah will guide his heart to an amicable solution."

"Sultan . . ." Shahryar begins tentatively. Just as it was strange to see him defer to Caliph an-Nasir, it is unsettling to watch him submit to Saladin. "We have specie we could contribute. Not two hundred thousand dinars, but something to help."

"That is good to hear. And how many men have you brought?"

"Three thousand, O Sultan. Some foot soldiers, but the rest are cavalry and archers. There would have been a thousand more, but we were hard hit by camp fever." Shahryar's mouth twitches with still-fresh grief.

"To Allah we belong and unto him we return," Saladin and Saifuddin murmur.

"But the remaining men are the strongest, their swords the surest, their shots the truest," Shahryar adds. "We also have hundreds of well-trained riderless warhorses."

Saifuddin beams in approval. "Turkmen archers—not to be scoffed at. Well met, Malik Shahryar, well met indeed."

A curly-haired officer ducks into the tent. His brow wrinkles in surprise at seeing me in the Sultan's seat. "Crusader envoys await, O Sultan, five miles toward Acre. To discuss, ah, the prisoner exchange."

"Organize a contingent of archers," Saladin says to Saifuddin in a low voice. He turns to us. "If you wish to join, you are welcome."

Marwan slinks away, muttering, "I should see to the caravan . . ."

Outside, Atsiz and Shahryar swing onto their horses, excited as boys. When I move to follow, Shahryar extends a warning hand. "Not you, Shaherazade."

"Sultan Saladin did not exclude me from the invitation!" The anticipation of seeing an accursed Frank with my own eyes moves me to boldness.

"This is not a feast, Shaherazade Khatun," Emir Ildegiz drawls. Shahryar shoots him an irritated look.

Taking that as my signal, I reply, "I am your commander's wife, Emir Ildegiz."

"Not every wife," Shahryar says slowly, as though unwinding a theorem, "would be brave enough to meet the unclean ones herself."

"I am but your mirror, O Malik," I say with a ready slickness that surprises me, recalling, with sharp physicality, his hands gripping my chin.

✳ ✳ ✳

A light *khatti* hangs from Andalib's saddle; a spear, unlike a bow or blade, can be useful only with primal instinct. The leather cuirass Yaghmur procured for me is a little too large and slides from one shoulder to the other with each step, but with my braids bound in a cap, I could be taken for a mamluk-in-training. Atsiz rides near, but his gaze slides past me, cold and unseeing, as though I were an invisible djinn.

With only a small, mounted group, their armor shining in the midday sun, Sultan Saladin's party reaches the appointed spot in little over an hour. Two armored men astride their horses straddle the road. Their square helmets leave only slits for eyes, and they look like monsters from an alien world. Sultan Saladin stretches his hand and we fall back, save for Saifuddin and a small translator.

"Frankish crossbowmen in the woods," one of the archers murmurs, nodding toward the thin copse.

Sultan Saladin says something, laughs, and the envoys doff their helmets.

Malikric's emissaries are garbed in lambent surcoats, one red, the other yellow. Matching shields and broadswords, so long they threaten to scrape the earth, swing from their saddles. Their legs, swathed in mail leggings, cannot be comfortable in the summer heat. Even from this distance, I can spot unwashed faces, and although I had read that the Franks were so pale as to look sickly, these men are as red as this one's surcoat, their stringy hair as yellow as that one's.

Heated Frankish voices fracture the silence. Their Arabic is unsubtle, clunky, and almost indecipherable, each word forced out of their unaccustomed mouths like a hammer stroke. A few phrases—curses, I assume, by their delivery—spoken in the rough Inkitar language conjure wet wool scrubbing miserably along the tongue. The hand of the sulfur surcoat drifts to his blade in frustration. Twangs of bowstrings reverberate. His head jerks up and his fingers fall away.

Through it all, Sultan Saladin remains unruffled. Seeing the uncouth Frankish emissaries, I am startled: How did *he* lose Acre to *them*?

Sultan Saladin nods his noble head, and only when the envoys bend in answer does Saifuddin bow as well. When the brothers turn back, their faces are so identically grim that the expression seems ancestral.

"The wingless grasshoppers are unyielding," Saifuddin reports. "We shall see what the Lionheart says. I offered them the money we have now, in exchange for the prisoners, with the remainder to be paid later and guaranteed by Muslim hostages." Sultan Saladin stares somberly at the envoys' backs. "But I fear he will not be favorably inclined."

Nineteen

◇◇◇◇◇◇

At Sultan Saladin's command, Shahryar and the Seljuks train with the Muslim army, thick in the great affairs of the world. Meanwhile, at the ramshackle castle of al-Kharruba, I punch a thick needle through hard boot leather, stitching raiments for soldiers with a few noblewomen in a bare garden, deserving of the name only by virtue of a single shivering olive tree and a few dry rosebushes. Among the women are some who accompanied us from Kirman, including Atsiz's dark-eyed friend Nurani and a few wives of Saladin's commanders. Chief is al-Afdal's wife, Sitt Jalaliyya, who is perhaps thirty and serious-faced, a beaten gold tiara gleaming at her brow.

"Malikric executed the garrison at Acre, the men, the women, the children, all three thousand souls," Sitt Jalaliyya informs us. "All because Malikric was enraged that my father-in-law could not pay their exorbitant ransom quickly enough."

My needle slides past the leather and stabs my thumb. Murmurs of shock stir like blown leaves as Sitt Jalaliyya continues. "Malikric herded the women and children before our vanguard stationed outside Acre so that they could watch them bleed. He slaughtered any soldiers who tried to help—so that they would know they were powerless."

"What happens now?" asks Nurani after a heavy pause.

Sitt Jalaliyya's voice could cut iron. "We will avenge the martyrs. We will rake the Franks, those dishonorers of the name of men, across the fiery coals of hell."

Wiping tears, I consider the loss, how women like us were dragged outside by Frankish soldiers, how they watched their husbands die, and then their children. Perhaps they were grateful for death in the end.

I cannot fathom the barbarity, the cruelty required to think up Malikric's slaughter of innocents. But then I imagine Altunjan and Shideh and Inanj, their knees in the sand, great Frankish broadswords striking their necks, blood drenching their gowns. Three thousand lives or three, to take even a single life unjustly is to murder all of mankind. Can a soul stained so dark be redeemed?

Breaking the long quiet, Sitt Jalaliyya asks sharply, like a coiled spring, "We have heard of the most—forgive my forthrightness—upsetting nature of your wedding, Shaherazade Khatun. Is it true? Was the Malik murdering his wives?"

The directness of her question catches me off guard. "What do you mean?"

"Did he begin marrying and murdering girls after he killed his first wife for philandering?"

What can I say? "Rumors have fast feet."

Sitt Jalaliyya's mouth turns up in disgust. A sapphire the size of my eye swinging from her circlet catches fire in the late sun. "I cannot believe my father-in-law would accept aid from someone like that."

If I were in her place, would I not think the same?

Before I can reply, a commander's wife, an older woman, gently pushes back. "Ya Sitti, the Malik has traveled far to offer his assistance in desperate times. The Sultan would not be pleased by discourtesy to the Malik's wife."

"If you have so many questions, you should ask Malik Shahryar himself," Nurani adds. Something in her sharpness evokes Fataneh.

"You are right, Sitt Jalaliyya," I finally say evenly. The needle and thread are slick in my hand. "My husband has committed shocking acts. But your companion is right—Sultan Saladin has accepted Malik Shahryar's assistance. Maybe in this way, Malik Shahryar can begin clearing the balance of his deeds."

Sitt Jalaliyya gazes at the dry, golden rosebushes. "I urged Sultan Saladin to refuse your husband's assistance, but he spoke as you spoke."

"Khoda knows best," I reply equably, trying to close the conversation, fearing I have already said too much.

As I finish patching the boot, al-Afdal strides in. He has the Sultan's small, pointed eyes, a wide mouth like Sitt Jalaliyya's, and a close-trimmed beard. He bows to the women. "May peace be upon you all," he intones. I do not miss how his gaze catches on Nurani's fine eyes or Dunya's lovely face; Sitt Jalaliyya does not miss it either.

He kneels before me. My heart drops. Why would the son of the Sultan kneel before me?

"O Shaherazade Khatun, I bear news. My father sent Malik Shahryar and me to look for weaknesses in the Crusaders' line of march—"

"Where do they go?" Sitt Jalaliyya interrupts.

"To Jerusalem."

Something nags in her voice; something snaps in his.

"What has happened to my husband?"

Al-Afdal smiles reassuringly. "Be easy, Shaherazade Khatun. Your husband is well. A remarkably courageous fighter, but a Frankish scout's arrow clipped his shoulder. A physician attends him, but I thought the wounded warrior would appreciate tea from his wife's hands."

Sitt Jalaliyya makes a choked noise.

"Alhamdulilah," I murmur, wiping my clammy hands against my tunic.

"What did you see of their army?" Sitt Jalaliyya insists.

Al-Afdal rattles his report impersonally like a soldier reporting to a captain. "The Frankish knights are separated into three columns, with foot soldiers screening the left flank, their supply galleys in the sea on the right."

"Where will you attack, then?" Nurani asks.

"Ah, ah, ah," al-Afdal reprimands with a flirtatious wink. Sitt Jalaliyya's lips disappear. "We cannot tell you all our secrets. Now, Shaherazade Khatun, permit me to rescue you from this hotbed of deceit and return you safely to your husband."

***

Shahryar's tent smells of healing cinnamon. The dark-haired physician hums an Andalusian air as he firmly knots a white bandage around Shahryar's shoulder. It rapidly stains red. I am reminded of months ago, when Shahryar returned to the Arg-e-Bam wounded from his follies against the Oghuz and how Faramurz, Atsiz, and I carried him to his room.

The physician hands me a bitter-smelling clay cup as he exits. "Help him drink this to stave off infection."

I kneel beside the mattress and whisper, "Salaam."

Shahryar seems faintly embarrassed by the attention. "It is not so bad." The cot creaks in protest as he struggles to rise. Taking the cup, he raises it in ironic salute.

Wounded, he seems so fragile, like a day-old kitten. Settling on the corner of the mattress, I resist the urge to pass a gentle hand over his sable hair. "Did you see the arrow fly toward you?"

"Not until it was in my shoulder, but by Allah, my arrow struck that archer's eye." Beneath his bravado, I hear a current of vulnerability, of fear.

I blanch, but is that not war? A fine line of chance dividing the living from the dead, men who draw breath in the morning suffocated beneath the earth by night?

Shahryar knuckles the bandage. "The physician's herbs already begin to itch. I beg you, O Shaherazade: distract me with your tale."

Pleasure prickles at the sound of my name in his mouth.

"O Malik, it is said that Kushyar leaned against the ship's railing, the sun's luster gilding his dark skin like an idol of yore, and told the rapt sailors: 'I knew that for there to be any hope of your escape from this isle, I had to remain with the Djinn Queen.'

"'She took me to her bedroom . . . and by Allah, if she does not carry an heir in her belly it is not for lack of effort!'

"The men hooted. Although she tried to join their ribaldry, Jauhara could hear the lie in her cheers.

"'Afterward,' Kushyar continued, 'she fell asleep. I couldn't decide whether to try to escape or accept my fate. Not knowing who might be watching, I walked around the palace, pretending to explore. I entered the courtyard, where the Queen had greeted Jauhar and me. Past its blinding whiteness, I could see the dark jungle. The gate was open. And I thought, *What could be simpler?*

"'Without looking left or right, I ran to the open gate, but before I could reach it, it slammed shut. The courtyard darkened. A black storm opened and the Queen of the Djinn, her hair and face wild in the gale, found me.

"'"What is the meaning of this?" she howled like a she-wolf.

"'I did not know what to do. I considered scaling the walls, or flying at her, but she was an otherworldly creature of great power and I only a mortal.

"'"You gave me your word," she said sadly. I screamed as hot, invisible bonds crisscrossed my arms and legs.' Rolling up his sleeves, Kushyar revealed the crimson weals on his forearms.

"'Over my screams, I heard a cacophony of squawks. The flock of pea-fowl rushed the Queen and as they ran, they each were trapped in amber light. Their feathers fell, wings became arms, their torsos stretched, and where there had been six fowl now stood six women, each as beautiful and terrible as her sister, with murder in her eyes. In the Queen's shock, my bonds dissipated and the gate swung open. I did not look back. I sprinted into the jungle and did not stop until I found you.'

"And so, with fair winds at their back, the ship sailed through a dozen sunsets. The captain reckoned that after a dozen more, they would reach the Hijaz. From there, Jauhara would sail up the Red Sea to the Egyptian coast. Once in Egypt, al-Askar—and her parents—would only be a few days' journey. She was that close. She could taste the Delta's salt, smell the roses of her mother's garden, the attar she dabbed behind her ears.

"On the dhow's deck, Jauhara stood beneath a moon as large as she had ever seen, a white pearl that shone as luminously as the sun. Suddenly, the moon winked out and a dark wall of water undulated in its place, unrolling from horizon to horizon. The ship shuddered to a halt.

"'What is that?' Jauhara whispered to the parrot.

"'Another world.'

"'Another world?'

"'You thought yours was the only one? Allah created seven heavens and earths like them. In our own universe are millions of worlds and millions of universes lie beyond ours, and in those universes, millions of worlds—and Allah is master of them all.'

"Jauhara deliberated for a moment. 'Are there any universes of which Allah is not the master?'

"Although Jauhara's question was heresy, the parrot answered equably. 'In this universe and those infinite universes that this universe touches, Allah is master. Are there unfathomable universes, unreachable to us, where someone else reigns? That is not knowledge Allah has seen fit to bestow upon me.'

"'Wonder of wonders,' murmured Jauhara. She could not wrest her eyes from the rippling wall.

"The captain stormed to the prow. 'Ya Allah, what is this! Can we go through it?'

"'No,' the parrot whispered in Jauhara's ear. 'They must wait for the universe to unpinch herself—or go overland. If they try to pass through, they will enter this new world, and the way back is never so easy as the way forward.'

"'Is there a way back?' Jauhara asked.

"'There is always a way back,' the parrot responded.

"And Jauhara, who had been so close to home, found herself tempted once more by adventure.

"'Someone should be sent to check whether the wave is passable,' Jauhara found herself saying.

"'I have heard of these walls,' an onyx-eyed sailor whispered fearfully. 'Those who pass never return.'

"'If we cannot pass through the wall, then we will have to return to Debal,' Jauhara pointed out. 'We have already lost weeks. Send me. I will test it.'

"Jauhara ignored the small voice in her head that sounded like the Sufi telling her that adventure was not worth this foolhardiness. Then the voice she had been hoping for, resonant and smooth, announced, 'Jauhar should not go alone—I will go too.'

"Jauhara and Kushyar were lowered in a rowboat into the wine-dark sea. As the boat rocked in the air, Jauhara stole a glance at Kushyar. He was watching her. She looked down. She could hear the smile in his voice. 'How could I have missed that you were a girl?'

"Jauhara's ears went hot.

"'And you, Parrot, I did not imagine you either?'

"'Your memory serves you well,' the parrot said.

"Icy water splashed Jauhara as the boat bounced against the ocean. Jauhara took one oar and Kushyar the other. Together, they rowed toward the petrified wave and stopped before the inky, light-swallowing wall. Jauhara's pulse stomped in her throat. With a trembling hand, she touched the wave. It was wet, but her hand came away dry.

"'Do you still wish to do this?' Jauhara asked Kushyar.

"'What lies beyond?'

"'Another world.'

"'Allah protect us.'

"'Shall we return to the ship?'

"'Another world hovers within our grasp and you would return?'

"Jauhara laughed. She was giddy. Nervous. Scared. And she was beginning to think she was in love. 'No!'

"'Well then, Jauhara bint Omar al-Hakim, slayer of demons, freer of souls, let us go forth.'

"With Allah's name on their lips, they rowed into the wall, and although they remained dry, suddenly they became very, very cold."

*** ***

Now that the Crusader army fully occupies coastal Acre after massacring the garrison, al-Kharruba is too close for safety. Sultan Saladin has ordered the women to travel with the baggage train to Caimun, a fortified tel to the southwest. While the other tents have been disassembled and packed onto donkeys, Sultan Saladin's striped tent still stands, flanked by sharp-eyed mamluk guards. Recognizing me, they let me sidle in.

Only the chronicler, ibn Shaddad, notices me enter, and he lifts his reed pen in salutation. The other commanders, including Shahryar and Atsiz, crowd around a flush-faced messenger.

"—If al-Afdal had had a full force," the messenger declares, "we could have taken every Frankish swine prisoner!"

There are some indiscernible murmurs and Saladin says, "I shall lead Kurdish and Bedouin contingents to al-Afdal myself. Malik Shahryar, you will join with a party of Seljuks."

Shahryar raises his head, proud at the distinction.

Ibn Shaddad beckons to me. "This council is for commanders."

Although there is no real bite in his reprimand, I cannot suppress a trickle of embarrassment, even as I thrill at being near the ummah's greatest commanders as they plot against the Franks. "I . . . was . . . looking for my husband."

"It must be hard," ibn Shaddad says sympathetically, "to have passion for the glorious cause and be kept away from its core."

"You do not fight."

"No, but I write," he says serenely, as sure of himself, armed with his qalam, as any saber-shaking soldier. "Without me, who will know of the warrior's deeds?"

Finally sighting me lurking with ibn Shaddad, Shahryar narrows his eyes and looks over his shoulder to check whether Sultan Saladin has seen me. He jerks his chin toward the exit. I hurry out.

Shading his eyes against the blitz of the unadulterated midday sun, Shahryar emerges from the tent. "You should be with the women."

I fiddle with a plait and then lower my nervous hands. "O Malik, I have been thinking. Ibn Shaddad is the Sultan's chronicler, but should you not have your own to tell what you and the Seljuks do for the generations to come?"

He regards me flatly.

"Might . . . I not do that?"

Shahryar frowns, a schoolboy furrow in his brow. My ears pound.

"Perhaps . . . the heroism of the Seljuks should be recorded somewhere to be remembered. I will consider it."

"As you say, O Malik." Ignoring the quicksilver shimmying over my skin, I grasp his large hands, hardened at the fingertips by bowstrings, at the base of his fingers by sword hilts. "May Allah guard you against the Franks."

"Mutashakaram." He speaks so lightly that the words could have been borne on the backs of butterfly wings.

＊＊＊

As the baggage train travels toward Caimun, I pull Andalib up to Atsiz's charger. The dying sun sharpens the angles of his face, shadows the forest-green of his eyes. His handsomeness snatches my breath. This close, I am hammered by the void he has left, the tide of our easy rapport having ebbed away since Dunya recited his poem.

I roll the question in my mouth, letting my courage condense. "Will you not speak to me?"

He focuses on Nurani, who rides beside Dunya, their heads bent like heavy tulip blooms in conference. Sharpness cuts my belly.

"Do you toy with me and the Malik both?" Atsiz demands. He spurs his stallion away.

I cannot race after him, not before the whole caravan. Rejection burning my stomach, I let Andalib trail him. "Please, let me explain." The wind whipping between the olive-silvered hills buffets my veil and braids. "He found *The Book of Fixed Stars*. And your poem. He became angry, so Dunya claimed to have written it for Faramurz. Her declamation was not meant as a mockery, but to save me." I struggle before I speak. "I will always bear your words in my heart."

There is so much more I want to say, but his face is a stranger's, varnished hard and devoid of tenderness. Then it shatters, a lusterware vase plunging to the floor.

"I cannot do this, Shaherazade."

His mouth crumples, and I wish I could envelop him in my arms.

"I cannot," he repeats. "We cannot. Let this be. We must."

The dismissal is clear. I bite my shaking lip and let Andalib fall back. It is natural that whatever germinated between us ends thus, abruptly and uneasily. It's a strange loss, that of something that had never been mine. I push my palm against my breastbone, trying to ease the blossoming pain, the cracking of my glass heart.

Atsiz draws Nurani from Dunya. I imagine her hooded eyes lingering on him, watch her curved body lean toward him as though she were a plant growing toward his sun. My nails dig hard into my hand.

Dunya approaches on Shaheen. "What were you and Atsiz speaking about?" She cocks her head like a serious-eyed bird.

I lower my voice. "I told him the truth about your recitation of his poem, but whatever there was . . . it is done."

"And rightfully so," Dunya says with unsympathetic hardness, the ribbons tying her braids fluttering like flags.

"What were you and Nurani talking about?" I ask after a pause, trying to keep my tone neutral to mask the sting of Dunya's answer.

"She was offering her condolences—she was widowed recently."

"I suppose then . . . that she understands your grief." *And you think I do not understand it at all.* But what can I say? She does not wish to hear platitudes of trials and martyrdom, but when I try to comfort her, my tongue finds only aphorisms. "How did you first come to love Faramurz?"

The happy force of memory elicits a smile, and I am glad to have brought it to her face. "I first noticed him at Ismat's banquet. He was so brilliant and passionate, I could not wrest my eyes from him. It was as if I knew him, as though our souls had stood together before Allah at the beginning of time."

What had Shahryar said at his wedding to Fataneh, eons before? *I fell in love, as though we had been made from one soul cloven in half in the Therebefore.*

"You never told me this."

"I did not want to draw the evil eye upon it. Was I not right? No sooner did we receive the Malik's approval than Faramurz died." Her speech is calm until she chokes at the end. "He died."

Twenty

◇◇◇◇◇

ach night, we pitch our tents on new earth. After a day in Caimun, we were sent into the shelter of a nearby pass, then onward to Majdal Yaba, then back to the coast to supply the troops camping in the seaside village of Qasarea, where a pound of biscuit costs two silver dinars.

Away from the camp, mamluks at my back, I walk along hills high above the White Sea, which stretches wider than a thousand Euphrates. The air is salty, reminding me of the breeze off the Dasht-e-Lut. The water sparkles like tumbling gemstones: diamonds, sapphires, emeralds, what is their lauded luster before this splendor? I watch, mesmerized, as a ripple emerges into a white crest that swells into an explosive slap against the cliff. I could stand here forever enraptured. How could I have thought to tell a story of Jauhara and the sea when all I knew were rivers and fountains?

"Salaam, Shaherazade."

I stumble, sending my diadem's emerald beads clicking.

Shahryar lopes up the hill past my mamluks. Each step lifts his crocus tunic, revealing saffron trousers that clash merrily with green embroidery. He loses his breath at the sight of the sea.

I feel a prickle of foreboding and sidle away from the cliff's edge.

It is said that beneath the sea, a great fish called the bahamut *holds the world aloft on its silver-green scales and when it moves, the earth quakes . . .*

Shahryar folds his arms across his chest, wavers, returns them to his sides. His wounded arm hangs stiffly. "I came to speak to you of recent events with the army. For the chronicle. I see you do not have pen and paper."

I cannot suppress my spreading smile. Do I imagine it or does something warm flicker behind the Malik's eyes?

"I will be able to remember." But as he speaks, I wish I had a qalam and paper. His narration is a loop of arrivals of this rearguard, crossings of that vanguard, this emir spying on the Crusaders, that tactical move by Malikric.

"I spoke to Sultan Saladin," he adds, "who says you may attend some councils for your chronicle." I spot a brief flash of expectation at the gift, the wink of a younger Shahryar.

"Mutashakaram." I clasp a fist to my chest. "I am your servant."

His mouth twitches and my heart jumps. "Or my chronicler, at least." He pauses. "I had a letter from your father."

"Oh!" This means that there will be a letter for me too and another for Dunya. A poor imitation for curling up beside Baba's warmth, but reading his whispered words closes the parasangs dividing us. "Is all well?"

Gazing into the distance, Shahryar frowns. "More Oghuz raids. Vizier Muhammad thinks Caliph an-Nasir has increased his support."

Recalling my conversation with the Caliph and Shahryar's drunken raids on the Oghuz just months past, I feel a burst of misgiving. Oghuz raids are not uncommon, but with the Seljuk Empire in disarray, I fear what this could mean. "Is Kirman still safe?"

Surprisingly gentle, he answers, "While Vizier Muhammad safeguards it, always."

Our robes flap like great, colorful wings against the rising wind as we stare into the sea. To think, I have traveled from Bam, but more of the world still stretches beyond. Is it greedy to want more? Baba's voice tickles my ear: *There is always more, Shaherazade, but a wise man knows when to be content.*

*** *** ***

At Qasarea, Sultan Saladin holds court. People throng Saladin's tent, which, while expanded by several other tents, is crowded, stuffy, and oversweet with sweat and spice and perfume. Even slaves diligently waving fans of fronds and feathers cannot relieve the oppressiveness.

On the platform, al-Afdal sits to Saladin's left, Saifuddin to his right. Qazis and jurists huddle close, ready to advise the Sultan on matters of shari'ah. Dunya and I sit with Sitt Jalaliyya behind the Sultan, concealed by a nacre-inlaid cedar divider.

I press my eye to the spaces between the wooden blossoms and leaves nicked into the screen. At Qadi al-Fadel's direction, supplicants enter one by one to press claims for perished horses, broken blades, lost livestock. In response, Sultan Saladin bestows hundreds of gold pieces. Al-Afdal's mouth narrows. Even Saifuddin eyes his brother at some of the more generous benefactions.

The next pensioner is a woman clad in a bedraggled brown robe. Her red-white Crusader skin is gritty, her eyes swollen with tears. One of Saladin's soldiers follows her. Her eyes dart fearfully as if she expects us to lash her with scimitars, ululations on our lips.

Folding to her knees before Sultan Saladin in a *sajda*, she presses her forehead and nose to the ground. The supplication is sacrilegious. I wonder where she saw the gesture, who told her that bowing thusly would curry favor.

"Rise." Sultan Saladin extends his arm. "There is no need to bow before me as though I were a deity. What brings you here?"

The soldier explains, "O Sultan, I found this woman wandering near our lines. I could not understand her, but she said your name so I brought her here."

A plump translator is ushered forth. The woman's weeping warps her words, but the translator listens, his head tilted, face placid. When she pauses for breath, the translator says: "Thieves in our employ entered the Frankish camp last night. Instead of stealing soldiers for ransom, they stole her child, a girl of four called Alys. The mother, this woman called Margaret, went to the Frankish lords. They said they could not help her but told her you were a merciful man and advised her to beseech you."

"They advised well then," Saladin says, but I feel annoyed that these infidel princes have the audacity to shunt their countrywoman to the Sultan days after massacring three thousand of our men, women, and children. While showing our children no mercy, they expect to receive it from us. And this woman is no innocent. She came to our lands buoyed by the same hatred as the men who swing their broadswords, by the same greed and zealotry against which we fight.

As I convince myself of the rightness of turning her away, the Sultan's eyes brighten with sympathetic tears. He says to a messenger, "Go into the bazaar and find her little one. Pay the price and bring her back—with the thieves."

The translator interprets Sultan Saladin's order. The woman lurches forward, kissing the hem of Saladin's azure-and-red-patterned robe. Saifuddin raises her and gently hands her to the soldier.

Even as other petitioners file through, she cannot stop watching the white light of the tent's opening and I cannot stop watching her. Each time someone enters, she starts to her toes and then, disappointed, falls back on her heels. On her toes, her cheeks glow pink and light catches in her eye. On her heels, her mouth crumples and her face creases. She touches the pewter crucifix at her neck. She jumps up again, her face haloed. She does not fall back.

"Alys!"

Skirting around the latest petitioner, she gathers her tangle-haired daughter from the messenger. Cradling the girl, she weeps into her neck as Alys's small hands clutch her. I wonder at the strength of her hatred that led her to carry this little girl to Palestine, and at the smallness of my heart that would have turned away this reunion.

***

Amber lamplight waxes and wanes in Shahryar's tent as I await him, ready to record events in my budding chronicle. The lamp flashes, dispelling all shadow, and then wavers, felling the tent into dusk.

Shahryar barges in; his steward, Yaghmur, follows. He says to Yaghmur, "Two weeks' clothing should be enough."

I hesitate and then ask, "Where are you going?"

"I am to lead a riding to bring Turkmen reinforcements from Sham." He buzzes around the tent, tossing trousers and tunics and robes for his steward to fold.

"Sham! But when will you return?"

"Within the fortnight, insh'Allah."

I do not know if I feel liberated or abandoned by the Shahryar I am beginning to see again. "What if . . . ?" I cannot speak the inauspicious words aloud, lest they be transformed from breath to truth.

His eyes on me are dark and soft as a gazelle's. I wait for that fleeting sun to be clouded again. It remains. He reaches toward me. I step forward. Dismissing Yaghmur, he embraces me gently, as if I am a hollow-boned bird fallen from its nest. His heart gallops against my ear, his lips press my forehead.

Quietly, we watch each other. My nerves are on fire; my stomach turns in anticipation. I tilt my chin forward. A prompt, but not a demand. Slowly, slowly, he leans forward. His nose brushes mine, and giddiness flushes through me. My fingers curl around his neck, my lips meet his, and slowly, slowly, I pull him to bed.

After, my head rests on Shahryar's chest; he traces the ridge of my bare hip. My skin is perfumed with Shahryar's leather and verbena smell. Atsiz's face flashes before me. My heart constricts, and I banish him. I squeeze my eyes. My husband deserves better than this, two wives who refuse to love him, even as he reveals himself.

But does he?

I huddle closer to Shahryar. Try to drive the *waswasa* of Atsiz away.

"Tell me what happens to Jauhara next, so I can imagine the possibilities as I ride to Sham," he whispers sleepily.

"As you wish."

"Jauhara, Kushyar, and the parrot slid into the new world on their backs, headfirst. The boat had disappeared somewhere in between. The first thing Jauhara noticed was the grass she was lying on, plush and verdant. She curled her fingers through the supple blades. The second thing she noticed was the snowcapped mountains arching so high that they covered the whole sky in stark white. No, the mountains *were* the sky. Red-roofed houses and cows and goats and asses hung upside down, dotting the snow above. A flurry fell on her nose. Jauhara could not tell who was above and who below.

"Then, the world at her back started to skew.

"Jauhara thumped into a pile of marvelous snow, cold and fluffy, sparkling like crushed glass. Here, the sky was not green grass but an inky black studded with a blizzard of stars. Two moons hung in the sky: one a large orange crescent and the other a small blue ball.

"Jauhara pulled herself up and dug the parrot out to warm him, but found him much warmer than she was—she and Kushyar wore cotton pants and tunics and leather sandals, all perfectly wrong for the weather.

"Far and away, she could make out the red-roofed houses, gleaming in the snow's crystalline light. They stood in a flat valley, jagged mountains protruding around them. Much closer stood an immense building. A palace? A mosque? It was like and unlike anything Jauhara had seen, with immense green-and-white stone walls and windows lit in gold. Most arresting were the dozens of turban-shaped domes. Some were striped red and gold, others crosshatched silver and orange, and yet others bore yellow quatrefoils and blue arabesques.

"By now, Jauhara was shivering. Tucking the warm parrot into her shirt, she looped an arm around Kushyar's waist. Together, they began walking toward the palace.

"The knee-high snow made for slow going, each step requiring them to sink waist deep into the snow and then climb out again. The snow melted into their clothes, and Jauhara's legs began to cut so deeply with cold they felt hot.

"They heard jingling.

"It was faint at first, but soon it loudened. Jauhara and Kushyar exchanged looks—fear and hope.

"A malachite sleigh, pulled by four wolves, matched and sized like horses, erupted before them. The wolves' amber eyes glowed like fireflies, and Jauhara wondered if the cold had driven her mad.

"A man drove the carriage, dressed in a greatcoat of gray-and-white furs. He was a tall black man with a long black beard, eyes the color of walnuts, and teeth snow white.

"He laughed, and Jauhara could not tell if he was pleased or angry. 'Who are you?' he asked. 'And what brings you to my kingdom?'"

Twenty-One

◇◇◇◇◇◇

Sitt Jalaliyya's tent is overripe with the smell of women's sweat and aloe-wood incense. I try to breathe through my mouth, try to not imagine sweat droplets condensing on my tongue. In the corner, a fair-haired slave girl sings in a mountain language, eyes closed, as if the song carries her home. I kneel on the thick silk carpets, surrounded by other noble-women, sewing a sturdy cotton tunic for some soldier to bleed into; I knot the thread with a prayer for protection.

The warbling ceases as the 'Asr azaan curls through the tent. It stitches together time and space, closing the distance between here and Bam. It reminds me of pink sunsets, of warm desert wind grazing my cheeks, of Baba nudging me to pray if I dawdled too long over a book.

"The Sultan has decreed a day of prayer today," Jalaliyya says once the muezzin's echo fades. "I gather he plans to make battle at Arsuf soon."

Before the murmur of interest can become questions, fresh air stirs the stuffy tent.

"Shaherazade Khatun, a letter came by pigeon for you."

I start, and my carob juice splashes thickly over my hand. It will dry sticky in the heat.

Atsiz pulls off his leather boots before entering. He presents me with a packet. Our fingers do not touch. I peel away the seal; it is not my father's but Ishaq's six-pointed star carried on the back of a marching Seljuk lion. Missives from Hanna? I unfold the letter: the script isn't Hanna's; these letters swoop confidently, save for where they break as though the hand was trembling. I recognize Ishaq's writing. My stomach turns.

In the name of Allah, the Most Gracious, the Most Merciful

O my dear daughter Shaherazade,

May Allah bestow you with all His blessings. It is with a heart that breaks anew every hour that I must inform you that your father fell ill two weeks ago and—

I cannot read any more. I know what is coming. I do not want to know. My hand shakes. My breath rattles. I stand, although my legs threaten to break apart like straw. I feel the despair writ on my face. I sense everyone's eyes upon me. "I need to go." My voice does not sound like my own.

Protests, inquiries, but I cannot make them out. The world is dull and I feel light and hollow. A shell. I leave Sitt Jalaliyya's tent. I tumble into Shahryar's tent, fall onto the mattress. My legs can't bear to hold me up.

Perhaps Baba is gravely ill. Ill, but alive. Perhaps he is held captive by the Khwarezmids. Perhaps he is an Oghuz hostage. Perhaps he took ill and is now better. Perhaps he took ill and lost his sight or hearing. Perhaps he fell ill and was nursed to health by an industrious noblewoman whom he married and Ishaq, as his oldest friend, does not approve. Perhaps Ishaq wishes me to write sternly to Baba and tell him he cannot wed without consulting his daughters or his Malik.

I take heart from the sea of possibilities, laugh at myself for always dreaming the worst.

—and on the 19th night of Mordad passed from this world into the next.

Here, Ishaq's writing is unsteady. Or is it my own trembling, my eyes blurring? The nineteenth of Mordad. My father has been dead almost a month. A splash on the paper, and the ink bubbles and fans.

What can I say to you of your father that you do not already know? That a gentler, kinder, cleverer man than he did not exist? That he was a father who did not shy from mothering his daughters?—

I curl tightly around myself, feel his fingers braiding my hair, remember the golden glow of lamps as he tried to tell my mother's stories to Dunya and me before bed, his shaking sobs after her death.

—That he was a true friend to me even when it was dangerous? That as a vizier he was honest and good and brilliant, a solitaire pearl who did honor to his post as no one has since the great Nizam al-Mulk? That he loved you and Dunya more than anything in this world, that he carried your mother in his heart until his last breath?

I will spare you the details of his illness, but my wife and Hanna attended him as you and Dunyazade would have. And I sat beside my old friend through his nights. It will not decrease your pain, but know that his departure was painless. He slipped away with the ease of an unblemished soul. Shahzaman will see to his burial and *janaza*, and all of Bam weeps, rubs ash into the archways, and festoons itself with black in mourning.

Enclosed are missives from Hanna, Leila, and Shahzaman. There are also final letters to you and Dunyazade from your father that he was writing.

May all of Allah's blessings be upon you,

Ishaq

Ishaq's letter falls onto the bed, and I scrabble through the other letters looking for Baba's. But I cannot open his letter and know that these are his last words to me, that after this nothing more will pass between us. That he will be dead. That he has been dead for the month since these letters were written.

My legs fold to my chest and I hold myself tight. I wish someone would hold me through the grief. But I cannot tell Dunya, not yet, not so soon after Faramurz, when I can barely hold myself up let alone her. And Shahryar, who so honored Baba, is in Sham.

Closing my eyes, I feel Baba's thin chest against my head, his arms tenderly enfolding my shoulders. *Give me your weight, jaanem, and I will make you light.* I feel him, hear him, and I cannot reconcile that I will never see him again, pray behind him as he lilts Qur'anic verses, debate with him the latest poem or treatise. See him shine when I bring him pride.

My fingers bite into my palms and keening fills the room. The noise is mine, and I swallow it down.

A hand on my shoulder. I jerk up, wiping my eyes.

"I heard . . . heard you crying," Atsiz says.

I throw my arms around his neck, knocking the cap from his head, and his hands tighten at my waist. I sob into his shoulder, his neck warm against my cheek, his beard soft against my temple. My tears dry stickily against his skin.

"What happened?"

"Baba—" A sob strangles the rest.

"Shaherazade jaan," he murmurs, caressing my braids. I collapse into the comfort of his arms, breathe in his attar of agarwood and ambergris. "Whatever it is, it will be fine."

"It won't. Baba's dea—" I can't finish the sentence.

"Ay, azizem." His voice thickens with sympathy. Something in my chest crumbles at his kindness.

"What is this?"

I leap away from Atsiz.

Bahram's slanted eyes narrow needle thin. Behind him stands a panting Fakhruddin. Bahram's gaze shifts between Atsiz and me, the mattress below us, our matted tunics and tangled hair.

My words are dammed in my mouth.

"O, Khatun," says Fakhruddin, "I tried to stop him but he pushed through." His jaw is tight.

Atsiz is irreproachable as he answers, "The Khatun has received word that her father has passed away."

I wish he hadn't said it. I wish he hadn't taken my father's death and flung it as a cheap shield. It is mine, his death is mine, how dare Atsiz take it. I shift away from him and then back.

"Inna lil-lahi wa inna lahi rajioon," the mamluks dutifully murmur.

While Fakhruddin offers condolences, Bahram drinks in the view, squirreling away tidbits: Atsiz's fallen kuleh, the kohl from my tears staining Atsiz's cheek.

"You may return to your posts. Do not speak to anyone of my father's . . . I wish to tell the Malik and Dunyazade Khatun myself before the news spreads."

My mamluks bow in agreement, but I do not miss the last avaricious sweep of Bahram's eyes before he departs.

I press the heels of my palms against my eyes until radiant patterns explode in the blackness. It all speeds before me, the glances, the whispers, everyone who has seen everything, who can bear witness against us, against me, all the servants and slaves and courtiers who can say, "I saw the looks that passed between them," and Bahram with his damning evidence, "I saw him take her in his arms, in your very tent, Malik, while you were away in Sham," and Baba dead, dead for a month, bound in a white shroud and smothered beneath Bam's clay.

I cannot bear this. Not today.

* * *

"A rout." Atsiz winces as a medic binds his shoulder with linen. A broken and bloody lance, still strung with gore, lies beside him, remnants of the battle hard fought at the coastal thicket of Arsuf. Now that the battle is done—lost—I have emerged from the camp's safety, surrounded by my mamluk guard. I stand with my arms folded, the Malik's representative while he is away, observing the scene—observing Atsiz—from an aloof distance. But seeing him wounded, I am hard-pressed to resist the impulse to touch him. He moves his arm and winces; I wince alongside him. "Sultan Saladin was fantastic. A hero. But he is not invincible."

The Franks have taken to the tops of the tels, pitching their tents at Arsuf's walls, while we make do with the edge of its forest. We have no tents, only pieces of cloth erected to shade the wounded and the Sultan.

Another medic packs al-Afdal's wound with *sultani* herbs and neatly stitches his cheek with catgut. The medic's fingers are red-tipped with blood, vivid as a bride's henna-stained hands. The left side of al-Afdal's face is drenched with blood from a wound that reopened during a charge, painting half his face scarlet as though he were a Frankish minstrel.

"He cannot bear it," al-Afdal snorts, "being proven as fallible as we. He does not lose, and now that he has, he sits awash in his guilt, refusing food or drink, offering his own horses to those who have lost their mounts to assuage his grief."

The medic hushes him; the careful stitching has come undone.

The miasma of rotting meat, sweet and sour, clouds the air. I swallow. If I look north, I can see the littered corpses, of mamluks and *ghulams*, of Bedouins and Seljuks and Kurds and Nubians, all those who came to fight under Saladin's Ayyubid yellow.

I try not to let the overwhelming death remind me of Baba, try not to let death be how I remember him.

Soldiers move heavily among the dismembered heads and crushed bodies, searching for the wounded and hauling to graves as many of the dead as they can. More will be left to be picked over by the Franks and to rot in tomorrow's hot sun. I watch two medics, small brown figures at this distance, heave up a convulsing man. Even from here, his shrieks scrape like iron fingernails down my neck.

I raise my voice above the sound. "How many men did we lose?"

"More than six thousand martyred." Al-Afdal hisses as the medic daubs his cheek with vinegar.

"Six thousand!" More than the entire Seljuk force, almost a quarter of Saladin's army.

"How many Seljuks?"

"We do not know. Maybe five hundred. Maybe more," Atsiz says.

I clutch my heart, realizing how blessed I am that Atsiz was not among that vast number. Our men keep dying. And for what? Is it glorious or is it tearing fathers from daughters, husbands from wives, the living from life?

"It is a huge loss," Atsiz says reluctantly.

I feel it too, betrayal at the recognition that the great Saladin, unconquerable and chivalrous, has led us to such a degrading defeat.

"The Franks made their own errors, or it would have been worse," Atsiz adds.

"What was the Frankish loss?"

"Of their twenty thousand, we took less than a thousand lives."

I cringe.

"We captured five prisoners, including a woman. And four horses." Al-Afdal spits. "A shameful day."

"It was not all shameful." Sultan Saladin moves among us tiredly. For the first time, he looks his age, older. The greased forks in his beard droop and his tilted eyes are bruised with shadow. I wish it were proper for me to embrace him as I would Baba after a tiring day.

"Many of our soldiers fought bravely. They dropped from their horses to fight the Franks on foot; they took to the trees to shoot at them. Emir Taqiaddin led seven hundred of my own household guard under his banner to great valor."

"And the fugitives who fled the battlefield, Abbi?" al-Afdal interjects.

Sultan Saladin sighs. "They returned when I called. A man whose courage breaks is not faultless, but only the bravest mend their courage and return. And they returned and may Allah bless them, many of them shed their blood, martyrs at the end." Saladin pauses. "You too, my son, have brought me great pride on this most grievous of days." He runs a gentle thumb below the medic's stitch on al-Afdal's cheek.

Al-Afdal flushes and lowers his head, but he cannot hide the gratification pulling at his mouth.

Sultan Saladin turns, and once more he stands tall, his dusty green robes, frayed and bloodied, kingly trappings once more. "This is not the end. We shall move our troops to the river and strike the Franks again. Their word will not be the last."

Twenty-Two

◇◇◇◇◇

Eyes shut, I walk through the camp with Mahperi. In the still heat and white-bright sun, I could be at the Arg-e-Bam, the Dasht-e-Lut stretching endlessly barren to the north, snow-topped mountains rising to the west and south, my father toiling somewhere in the citadel's depths.

A week has passed since the Battle of Arsuf, and we camp near the city of Ascalon. Its ramparts glitter iron-gray against the turquoise sea. Whitewashed homes with gardens of bursting red-and-pink blooms twine around the city's flush fountains and bazaars. Something about how Ascalon wraps around the hill reminds me of home.

I still have not told Dunya about Baba. Sometimes, I convince myself that I too have forgotten. How much longer can I hide this from my sister? How much longer before protection becomes betrayal? I try not to think of what will happen when Shahryar—a man who, when he last heard bad news, murdered four women—learns of Baba's death.

I collide with a warm block. Startled, I look down. A shackled man with golden hair cropped at his ears, face shaven in the Frankish way, crouches on the path. His jawline is strong, shoulders broad. Mahperi's eyes are moon wide. I elbow her side.

"Who is this?" I ask Atsiz, who emerges from a nearby tent.

"A prisoner from Arsuf. His Arabic is as good as yours or mine, so be careful what you say."

"How does he know Arabic?" Mahperi asks.

"His father is a lord of the Kingdom of Jerusalem. Both the father and son are called Humphrey of Toron."

Humphrey, who had been staring blankly, looks up at the sound of his name. "How are you called, ya Sheikha?" the Crusader asks Mahperi. His voice is low and raspy, his Arabic almost unaccented. If I closed my eyes, he could be one of us.

Mahperi reddens like a poppy, but before she can answer, Atsiz cuffs the Frank and pulls him away. Once they are gone, Mahperi whips toward me and there is an iridescence to her, as if she were awash in moonlight.

"Let me learn Frankish from the prisoner. Let me be useful to you and the Sultan." At my hesitation, she protests, "I never ask for anything! I serve you faithfully and accept that you will never love me as much as Dunya or even Hanna or Leila. I wept for you when you wed the Malik and now that you are the Khatun, I pray that Allah preserve you. You may sit in war councils, but I may not learn a language for Shahryar to have his own translator?" Hot pink spots her cheeks.

My eyes widen at her breathless declaration. "Even if it were not wholly indecent, he is a Frank." I touch her shoulder. "You have a soft heart. He will use it against you."

Her lips compress in anger; tears dazzle like diamonds on her lashes. "You act as though it is not my heart that is soft, but my head. That simply because I am not a Khatun or a great storyteller I cannot be helpful—that I sought the opportunity to learn Frankish simply to be closer to a man. You insult me, Shaherazade Khatun." She whirls away, her sage farajiyya blowing behind her like windswept leaves.

Warning thunders in my head, but maybe Mahperi is right. Perhaps I am selfish with glory, choked with ambition.

* * *

Dunya whirls into my tent, her arms full of yellow and orange wildflowers gathered from behind the camp, their long leaves dangling limp. Her braids are mussed, mud streaks her cheek, and she smiles wide seeing me. "I was going to leave these as a surprise." She drops the sunny bouquet on my lap.

My throat constricts. "Mutashakaram, jaanem."

Dunya pokes Shahryar's papers. "Have you heard from Baba? We should have received letters weeks ago."

The tranquil face donned for Dunya's benefit contorts. The break is brief, but she does not miss it.

"What is it, Shaherazade? What's happened?"

I cannot hide the truth any longer. I try to tuck away my grief and tug an unresisting Dunya beside me. We crush her flowers, the broken petals sweetening the air. "Dunya jaan, I've had a letter from Ishaq."

"From Ishaq?" Her expression wars between fear and calm.

"Dunya, the news . . . it is not good." Why did I not slowly prepare her? I should have hinted at Baba's illness, its severity, allowed her time to adjust to the possibility of calamity.

"What is it?" Her nails nip into my palm.

I cannot look at her. My gaze drifts to her flowers. A small insect crawls from the petals. Instinctively, I crush it between my fingertips, feeling the slight crack of its fracturing shell. "Dunya, Baba took ill. Grievously so. He . . . did not survive it."

"How long ago?" The question is clipped, a malik eliciting a clerk's report.

I bite my lip. "Baba passed on the nineteenth of Mordad. I received a letter from Ishaq three weeks ago."

"Three weeks!" Dunya leaps up. In her fury, she grows tall and her braids whip like a sandstorm. "You concealed Baba's—this—from me for three weeks?" She strikes Shahryar's ledgers, and the papers fly. "How could you?"

I flinch.

Crumpling the documents beneath her feet, she yanks the bedding and the heavy wool blankets tumble to the floor. She turns over stools and trunks and hurls whatever small things—inkwell, cup, book—she can reach, and shards of porcelain gleam like eggshells. I do not stop her.

She collapses in the heap's heart. Sobs rack her body, a gale uprooting a tree. I weep too, for she is the tenderest part of my heart.

"First Faramurz and now Baba." Her voice is waterlogged. "How have I sinned, Shaherazade, that I deserve this punishment?"

How can she think that, this girl who is all that is brave and good? "No, no, no, no." Kneeling, I rub her shivering shoulder. When she does not push me away, I enfold her. "Did Allah not test the Prophet the same way? It is not punishment, azizem."

Dunya's eyes shine pink, the tip of her nose flushed. She folds forward to the floor and lies prostrate for minutes, for hours. I crumple alongside her, and the shattered porcelain digs into my scalp. The pain is bright. It feels like a kiss; it feels like nothing.

When Dunya rises again, she asks, "Why didn't you tell me?"

"Ay little dove," I whisper. "I said nothing so that he would still live for you, and so, selfishly, he would live for me too. Forgive me."

She disintegrates into my arms. I remember holding her just so after Mama's death, as the household whirled around us, sweeping away bloody sheets, washing her dead body and our brother's while Baba keened. Dunya was so small then, how could she have understood death? But in her leaden grief, then as now, she sank against me. At least then, I had Baba to hold me upright. Now, I am alone.

***

Ah, Baba. Babababababababa.

I think the word again and again and again until a word that no longer has any meaning for me loses all meaning. I wish I knew what would heal my gaping heart. Would screaming? Weeping? Tearing the fabric of my dark tent? Stamping the earth with my feet?

I do not know. While I maintain my composure during the day, at night, the loss of Baba fills the dark. I wish to be alone. I banish Dunya. I cannot bear to be alone. But the only one I wish to see, the only one who can fill the chasm rent through me, is dead.

I should be grateful, for my health and Dunya's.

But I am not.

What if we had stayed? The thought twists through the maze of my day, facing me in the polished mirror as Gulnar braids my hair, reproaching me in the shimmer of the sea. I left Bam, took my grieving, bedeviled husband to the end of our world to save my father and my city—only to leave him to die alone, his hand clutched by a friend's, not his daughters' for whom he gave everything.

I weep and I weep, but the tears never run dry. My thoughts are a web, and each dew-laced strand leads to Baba. My eye catches on Sanai's *Walled Garden of Truth* in my open trunk and I remember Baba purchasing it for me, because it had illumined his mind and faith at my age and he had hoped it would do the same for me. The shade of a date palm flickers against my tent and reminds me of Baba selecting the softest dates for Dunya, Mama, and me every *iftaar* during Ramadan.

I find some peace in prayer, but it is not enough, for that too reminds me of him.

"Come with me."

I start. Atsiz's *hatif* voice hovers in the air, a lure, an illusion, but the sound of his breath, the scrape of his boots against the earth, tell me this is no apparition. He says it again.

Hurriedly, I wipe my tears. "Where are you?" I whisper. "Where is my guard?"

Torchlight splays his shadow on the back of the tent: long legs, strong chest, arms muscled from years of swordsmanship. "He had to answer a call of nature, but will return soon. How can you weep alone, night after night? Come with me."

Come with him.

I can feel his arms warm around me again, his heart vibrate through my chest, my worry and weight slip into his body and become air.

Shahera—Dunya's voice shakes me from my dream and there is Baba, disappointed; there is sin, staining my soul.

"I cannot."

I think of how it might feel, his skin warm against mine.

"Take my arms, Shaherazade. Let me bear your burden."

Just for a moment, the urge to join him is overwhelming. It presses my shoulders, cuts open my heart: I do not want to be alone anymore.

I step forward.

But I hear armor clink, my mamluk returning to his post, and with him, my good sense. I hold my breath.

Atsiz's footsteps whisper against the ground, growing softer and softer until at last there is only silence.

***

The following night, Baba's face appears before me—I fear the day it will fade, when I will be able to recall only pieces—his upturned eyes, aged ivory skin softened with time, dry curly hair—but not to stitch them together with his gentle humor and kindness and wisdom. When he will remain in my mind only from retellings, not from himself.

By lamplight, long after the camp is silent in sleep, I write my recollections, my fingers sliding on my wet qalam: when he showed me a newborn Dunya and when I asked him if he loved her more, he told me I would always be his first love; the stories of his boyhood exploits, the fruits stolen from neighboring gardens and the weddings sneaked into with friends; his favorite poems, from Nizami, from Gorgani . . . but I didn't hoard my memories of Baba as carefully as I should have, and they're faded and rumpled and, sometimes, completely dark.

I jump at a rustle against the tent. I glance at Dunya, who does not stir from her sleep.

I have made my decision.

I wait for Atsiz's voice. But there is only the night breeze that runs from the White Sea over hills and through olive trees, salty and sweet.

I once thought opportunities were ever arising, but now, older, I realize how thinly the door to destiny opens, how quickly it shuts.

Twenty-Three

◇◇◇◇◇

At Sultan Saladin's orders, Ascalon, Bam's curving sister city, where the Franks met their final defeat during their First Crusade, disintegrates to prevent the Franks from using it after we leave. I have acclimated to dust-choked air, sweet with smoke, that rolls in great waves. I cannot wash its stink from my hair, its gray from my skin. If I were cut open, my insides would be black as marsh earth.

As I walk through the encampment to Sitt Jalaliyya's tent, fiery air billows from cooking pits and boys sit cross-legged beneath canopies chopping vegetables while cooks labor over iron pots of rice and stew large enough to bathe in in preparation for iftaar—it is the first day of Ramadan. Food is abundant. Since the Sultan announced Ascalon's destruction, its residents have been rapidly selling goods they cannot take. Ten hens for a dirham; once a rich man, now a beggar.

I enter the tent and there, between emirs and generals, 'Abbasids, Kurds, and Seljuks, I see him.

His hair is slick with bathwater and longer than I remember. He wears a crossover coat with a sky-blue body and printed moss-green sleeves. His face is darker, almost teak, from his weeks of riding around Sham, gathering Turkmen reinforcements. He sits to the Sultan's right at a low, long table, on one of the many mismatched cushions. My stomach fluttering, I sit beside him. I can smell his attar of sandalwood above the aroma of roast lamb.

Shahryar smiles.

My eyes widen. I forget to return the smile.

"Durood, Shaherazade Khatun." His greeting mutes the surrounding conversations recounting battles fought and parasangs trekked.

"Durood."

He flicks an ornament at the end of my braid. It tinkles in response. In any other man, I would call the gesture affectionate.

The Maghrib azaan rings out, heralding sundown and the end of the fast. Once the azaan concludes, Sultan Saladin recites the brief, fast-breaking prayer, and the hungry hands of the assemblage reach for sweet, plump dates and cool water.

After spitting out a date pit, I ask Shahryar, "How was your journey?"

"Hard. Good. Near a month of travel when we expected a fortnight. But fruitful." He reaches for a platter of rice and grasps a morsel with his fingertips. The tiraz bands at his sleeves, embroidered in naksh calligraphy, glide against the table.

"Good."

He nudges me. "How is my chronicle?"

I try not to let his playfulness push me off-kilter, try to bury the memory of Atsiz's nocturnal visit so it doesn't taint my speech. "I could not attend the councils after you left, but I wrote of Ascalon's destruction. And the Battle of Arsuf. I was there after."

He smiles. "Yes, Sultan Saladin commended your bravery." He grazes my hand, his fingers rough from weeks on horseback.

Suddenly, I remember. Remember that Shahryar does not know of

Baba's death. He would not have had time to read the letters awaiting him. And so he sits in a world where Baba still lives and cares for Bam in his name. I look at his unburdened face and envy him.

"What has happened?"

My head tilts toward the assemblage. "I will tell you after iftaar."

"Is everything well?"

Swallowing, I shake my head.

His eyes narrow, and I feel the familiar prick of fear. It is almost comforting, like standing on land after a long time on horseback. "But it must wait?"

"Unless you wish to leave now."

Drumming his fingers against the table, he glances at the assemblage: Saladin, Saifuddin, al-Afdal, Sitt Jalaliyya. "If I must wait, then distract me."

"O Malik, Jauhara answered the man's question. 'I am Jauhar,' she said. 'This is Kushyar. We come from . . .' But she did not know what to call her world. It was just that, *the world*. 'Elsewhere,' she finished.

"Unperturbed by her incomplete explanation, the man invited them into his sleigh. Too exhausted to be suspicious, they clambered in. Graciously, he offered them fur blankets. Jauhara dug her fingers into their thick heat and warmth began to pulse back into her.

"The man shook the reins and the giant wolves leapt, sending snow shivering in the air. Ears flat, they sliced through the snow toward the swirled confection of domes.

"'Who are you?' asked Kushyar, clenching his shivering jaw.

"The man's eyes slid toward them. 'I? I am the King.'

"'The King of what?' Kushyar pressed.

"'The King of Here.'

"There they were: Here and Elsewhere, the two geographic points into which Jauhara had to map herself.

"Quicker than they should have, they arrived at the palace. Silent, pale-faced servants wrapped them in furs, took their wet leather sandals, and sat them on plush cushions by a hot fire. The wood crackled as it burned, sweet and evergreen. Jauhara looked around the airy room: the ceiling arced high and intricate mosaics showed scenes of men and women and animals, but derived from no religion or mythology that Jauhara recognized.

"'Where do you come from?'

"Doing their best to explain, Jauhara spoke of Egypt and Kushyar of Kandahar.

"The King clapped his hands. 'But I know those places! You see, I am from There too!'

"'From . . . where we are?' Jauhara asked.

"'From your world, yes,' the King said. 'I was a trader in Baghdad before I was King. I am from Gao, on the eastern bank of the Niger River, where the buildings are made of mud baked hot and hard in the sun to withstand monsoons.'

"'How did you come here?' Kushyar asked.

"'I was one of nine brothers. Our father was a miller and my brothers were barbers and carpenters, butchers and fishers. When my grandfather died, he left me a plot of land. The land was fertile and when I sold it, I bought ten *mithqal* of gold. Have you heard of our gold? It is the finest in our world, pure and yellow, soft enough for the most delicate work.

"'I took my gold to Baghdad and sold five *mithqal* to Baghdad's most famous goldsmith, who created a headdress, a masterwork he called it, for the Caliph's beloved sister. That headdress made my reputation. Within months, I bought a store on Bain al-Qasarain Street, and for many years, business was steady.

"'I thought I was blessed and did what I could to maintain the blessing. I prayed five times a day, paid my zakat, and sent money to my family and to the poor.

"'One Friday, I locked my shop and walked to the masjid. An old man, dressed in only a loincloth, gasped for aid. I told him, anything I could do. He grabbed my hand, and his eyes began to glow, green and red and black and gold, like hellfire, and my skin burned hot. When I looked down, my arms were little but bone, the skin fragile and sagging. Where the man had stood, only a mirage shimmered.

"'Two well-dressed young men fell upon me. I could smell the bitter ink on their fingers. Perhaps I protested that I was not the man they wanted, perhaps I did not. But they took me to the chief of Baghdad's police and reported that I had murdered a *qadi*. Without questioning, the chief threw me in prison where I was to wait until the Caliph Harun ar-Rashid determined my sentence. "Death, most likely," the police chief whispered as he locked me in the cell.

"'The next morning, I awoke in the cell. I had so hoped it had been a dream. For hours, I stared into the dark, until from the corner of my eye, I saw a mirage. It rasped, *"Shukraan,"* but I cursed him, sure I would die.

"'"I understand," he sighed, and the air became thick and hot. "Trust me. I will save you as you saved me. But I must gather my strength."

"'He sounded so sincerely grieved that my anger cooled. "Is it true you killed the qadi?" I asked.

"'"I did."

"'"Then you deserve to sit here, not me," I said.

"'"But the qadi was not a good man," the djinn said. "Or perhaps he had been a good man and did an evil thing."

"'The djinn continued: "One evening, many years ago, I found him weeping under a tree. I revealed myself to him and asked why he wept. He told me that he had recently been appointed qadi. I congratulated him. 'But you do not understand,' he said. 'I do not know the shari'ah. I have not studied it. My father bought the position for me, and he will not let me decline it. Now, I am supposed to render decisions on people's lives that will forever change them.

"'"'Today was my first day, and I was asked to judge a matter of inheritance. A woman said that her brother had hidden her father's will that bequeathed her more than the Qur'anic intestate share. The brother claimed that there was no will, but the mother supported the sister's testimony.'

""""'The greatest magic of the law,' I said, 'is that most of the time, you can mold it to your preferred outcome.'

""""'What should I do?' he asked.

""""'There are two witnesses to the brother's one. The evidence weighs in the sister's favor. Do you have reason to doubt her or her mother's characters?'

""""'N—no,' he said.

""""'Then the answer is easy.'

""""So it went. He would hear cases in the morning, consult with me in the evening, and give his decisions the next day. I thought it would be a good deed and no more than that.

""""After a long absence, the qadi hurried to me in the pink twilight, his shoulders hunched, his fingers entwined. He said, 'You have done so much for me—but what if I come and you are not there?' Before I could answer, he withdrew a strange square box, smaller than his palm, of red cedar and mother-of-pearl.

""""Opening it, he spoke a spell in an ancient tongue. His enchantment pulled me inside and bound me, and although I struggled, the box shut and I was left in the dark.

""""That first night, I expended all my power trying to break the box, to burn it, to freeze it, but the enchantment proved impenetrable.

""""Now, the qadi would command me to advise him many times a day. I tried to withhold my speech, but I could no more resist his orders than I could escape. No matter how I pled, he kept me imprisoned, deprived of light and air.

""""Twenty years passed. The qadi grew fat on stolen wisdom while I diminished. Some days ago, however, I found the enchantment weakening. An attempt to burn the box made it hot. I tried to grow, and the box creaked against my mass. Today, the qadi came to demand guidance and I—I snapped. I channeled my remaining power into breaking the box.

That force killed the qadi. I had not meant to. I had meant to. I was not sorry. He turned into a cruel man.

""""That is all of the truth."

"'Before I could respond, a prison guard announced, "Caliph Harun ar-Rashid will judge you now.""""

✳ ✳ ✳

I tell Shahryar, as I did Dunya, of Baba's passing. It does not get easier delivering this news, watching a glimmer extinguish from the Malik's eyes. My voice cracks, his body quivers, and for a moment I think he will weep. But he only buries his head in his hands. I do not know how long he sits like this, but I remain beside him. When he lost Fataneh, he burned Bam. What will Baba's loss spark?

When he looks back at me, his eyes are red. A muscle in his jaw jumps, catching lamplight and shadow. He opens his mouth and then clicks it closed.

"Che?" I prompt.

"Vizier Muhammad was all I had after my father killed himself." He falls silent, the admission heavy between us.

Hesitantly, I squeeze his sword-calloused hand. I count our breaths, a hundred each, before he speaks again.

"He avenged my father and saved Kirman for me. Refused to control me and the province when he could have, but guided me and protected me in all things." He chokes. "The father I wish mine had been."

Now we both weep and I interlace my fingers tightly in his, as though I can keep us from drowning in the quicksand of sorrow through the force of my grip alone.

Having begun speaking, Shahryar cannot halt, a storm-swollen river overrunning its banks.

"The night my father threw his atabeg, the man who had ruled him for the whole of his reign, out of the Arg-e-Bam, the atabag returned with an army at dawn. I sat with Shahzaman in my parents' chamber, my arms around him, vowing to guard him through whatever passed. Once, we were once as close as you and Dunya.

"My father knew there was no return. My mother—she was an iron rod and she drove my father to break with the atabeg, always excoriating him to be a man, *mard bash, mard bash.*" His voice cracks.

I have heard the story of the revolt before—from Baba, from Ishaq, from whispers in the harem among the concubines—but never before from Shahryar. My breath sticks between my ribs.

"A knock on the door and my blood went cold, like the snow atop the Jebal Barez. I thought that the atabeg had come to murder us all, make himself malik, as my mother had warned.

"But it was Vizier Muhammad. He told my father that the choice to remain or flee was his, but that we would be coming with him. My mother decided they would remain in the Arg-e-Bam and kissed our foreheads. My father kissed us too, clasped our hands, and told us mard bash.

"I did not know that would be the last time I would see him. I would have thought that a last time would signal itself, that I would know: this is the last time I will see my father, this is the last time I will love my wife—"

After a heavy quiet, Shahryar continues. "Your father hid me and told me to be brave, to trust him, and that he would care for me for all his days.

"And so he did."

Can Shahryar fathom how much Baba loved him? Such love for a lost boy that Baba allowed his eldest daughter to wed him in a desperate bid to salvage Shahryar's legacy.

"What should I do?" Shahryar asks the daughter of Vizier Muhammad.

Untwining my fingers from his, I hand him the letters from Shahzaman and Ishaq, the paper's thin edges catching the candlelight's glow. "Read what Ishaq and Shahzaman have written. Then decide."

He reads quickly. His eyebrows lift, he frowns, then his face stills. The tent is silent but for the hiss of paper against paper, the faint crack of a letter being opened. "They write that Kirman is stable, that Bam is calm. That the Oghuz chieftain, Malik Dinar, ordered a few small raids in Kirman, easily squashed. The Khwarezmids continue to destroy Seljuk forces, and the Seljuk armies grow weaker each day. Do you recall that Sultan Toghrul's atabeg, Qizil Arsalan, imprisoned him? Shahzaman writes that Qizil Arsalan's wife incited her mamluks to slay him as he lay drunk in bed."

I try to elbow Shahryar from the thought. "Is Sultan Toghrul then free?"

"No. Qizil Arsalan's nephews now quarrel to decide who is ascendent, and Sultan Toghrul remains imprisoned."

"Ripe for the Khwarezmids then."

I imagine the Seljuk Empire falling apart, cliff crags crashing into a churning, ravenous sea.

"Ishaq writes that the Oghuz may turn to Kirman once they hear of Vizier Muhammad's death."

Baba, who defeated Shahryar's father's atabeg and secured Kirman for his son, who kept Kirman afloat even as Seljuk malik after malik was toppled, Baba, who even the most canny commanders respected.

"A danger not to be underestimated. What will you do?"

Is this how Baba paved Shahryar's path, with a nudge and a nod? I wish I had asked him. But then, I had never truly believed he would abandon me so.

Shahryar folds the letters and stacks them on the bed. "The tide is turning against the Seljuks, and if we are not careful, the current will catch Kirman. The time is coming when we will have to return to ensure that it does not."

Twenty-Four

◇◇◇◇◇◇

Hands trembling, I open Baba's final letter. My heart catches at his swirling script. As I read, I hear his voice. It fills the tent with his smell and
warmth. It is almost taunting, this *hatif* of memory. Even holding the
letter is painful, a reminder that the man who wrote it will never write
again. I fold the letter away. The sensation of Baba fades, and I cannot
bear that loss either.

I open the letter.

Shaherazade jaan,

I pray this letter reaches you in good health and good faith. You
and Dunyazade are ever in my prayers, and your letters bring me
such joy. Sultan Saladin sounds like a great man: you are lucky to
know him.

Your success with the Malik is my continued pride—people
know me now as the father of the Storyteller Khatun.

I have been moved to Ishaq's palace. The physician (your Hanna's husband) tells me I am ill—a tumor in my stomach for which I drink *bindiba* tea. Ishaq fears I will die, but he is pessimistic—that has always been his talent as a councillor.

Still, Yunus does not dispute Ishaq's predictions, although he tells me to drink my tea and eat whatever food I can. Hanna and Sara are wonderful cooks and gracious hosts. The little ones in the house bring me such joy, as you and Dunya did at that age, but I fear my appetite is much diminished.

Perhaps it is true. Perhaps I am indeed ill. Perhaps I—

Perhaps I will die. Perhaps I will not see you two again in this life.

I fear death and I fear judgment—who among us does not?—but I beg that you and your sister do not fear for me. I have done what I can to be a dutiful Muslim and work honestly and harm no one. I hope you will apply these tenets to your lives once I am—

Do not weep, azizem. You are my life and so long as you live, I am not gone. Be a good sister to Dunyazade, a good wife to Shahryar, a good servant of Allah. Forgive your old Baba his foolishness—you are already all of these things. I know I need not remind you, but it is a father's lot to worry.

When you were in your mother's lap, she would recite poems to lull you to sleep. Gorgani was your favorite, Vis and Ramin. By the time you learned to speak, you could parrot the verses back at your mother, each word perfect. My brilliant parrot, my bright girl, with a memory like a trap and poetry in your heart.

Perhaps Ishaq is wrong. Perhaps I will see you and Dunya when you return, my daughters, the terrors of the Franks.

As long as you live, I am with you. As long as you are with Dunyazade, you are never alone. Care for your sister and guard her close.

I am tiring and must write to Dunya and Shahryar. I hope to write to you again but if I do not—

Shaherazade, you are my life, my liver, the light of my eyes, my firstborn, my Khatun—I want to press all these endearments to you to hold in the years that come.

Please pray for me, that I might see you again. Please pray for me, that my stay in the grave is easy and at its end, I ascend to Paradise.

Shahryar finds me in bed, clutching Baba's letter to my chest. *There is no more Baba.* That is all I can think. One day, I will die and Dunya will die and there will be no one who knew Baba and he will disappear from the world's memory like so many men before him, even men who were good and great, like him. It does not seem fair for Baba to be treated thus, to become dust, and then, nothing at all.

"When we return to Bam," I say to Shahryar, my voice wet as the monsoon, "I will build Baba a great mausoleum so that for a thousand years men and women will see his grave and read his name and remember his deeds. A tomb as grand as any in Baghdad."

A strange expression crosses Shahryar's face. I cannot name it, but it girds his eyes. He softly touches one of my braids. "It will be done."

To my surprise, he lies down beside me and curls his body around mine. He cradles me until my sobs cease, his arm anchoring my waist, and I wonder, *Is this what it is like to be loved?*

I roll to face him and his eyes shine with their own grief. I touch his cheek, unsure of how to express my gratitude. But then masks interpose in a series over his face: Shahryar ordering Fataneh's beheading, Shahryar murdering bride after bride, Shahryar, frenetic, setting Oghuz encampments aflame. Confusion throttles me, and I stiffen. Before he can sense the change, I say:

––––––––––––––

"O Malik, the gold merchant who was now a king said: 'I was brought before the Caliph Harun ar-Rashid. The vaulted blue-and-gold honeycomb ceiling, whose small stacked domes extended celestially, glimmered above. The caliphal court's walls of beveled stucco were molded with leaves and acorns, painted with murals of wild animals, nude women, and men on the hunt. I could smell my stale-sweet sweat mix with the court's musk and myrrh.

"'Colorfully robed men with fulgent turbans gilded my path to the Caliph. My heart beat hard. The courtiers eyed me with disdain, a fakir, the murderer of a learned man of a good family. I gathered courage to look at the Caliph, who sat in the center of a gold throne formed of four gold arches shaped in a cube. He was younger than I had imagined, his beard still night-black and his face smooth except for grooves at the corners of his mouth. His attire was grand: a bulbed emerald turban, a tunic of sumptuous ivory silk, a sleeveless robe of rosy velvet.

"'A brown-skinned vizier announced in a reed-thin voice, "Moussa Abbas ibn Idris was found fleeing from the corpse of the esteemed qadi Rafiq bin Assad. The qadi's clerks bear witness that he was the murderer, and the police chief reports that the man was found covered in blood. O Caliph, this man has murdered a learned man, a good judge, a man of a good family. The family refuses blood money: they wish his death."

"'The Caliph said to me, "You may speak."

"'Before the assembly of fine people, and myself disguised as a fakir, I said to Caliph Harun ar-Rashid, "I am not who I appear. My name, as the vizier tells you, is Moussa Abbas ibn Idris, but Moussa Abbas ibn Idris is no fakir. I am a gold merchant from Gao, a respectable man of Baghdad. A man asked for aid and I foolishly offered it. He was a djinn, the qadi's true murderer. He gave me his shape, but I am innocent of his crimes."

"'Harun ar-Rashid's eyebrows disappeared into his turban. "Do you truly believe what you are saying?" he asked.

"'I answered, "It is the truth."

"'"This sounds like madness," the Caliph said.

"'"I am not mad," I replied. "I am in my right mind, just not my right body. Any who know me will attest to it." I peered around, hoping to spot the telltale shimmer, but the caliphal *darbar* held steady.

"'Fingers steepled beneath his chin, Harun ar-Rashid contemplated me. He curled a finger and the guards pushed me forward. I fell to the ground, the old man's knees creaking as they bent in supplication. And still, the djinn did not reappear.

""'Can you see this man is not well?" the Caliph said to his vizier and courtiers. "To execute him would be a crime."

""'You cannot release him," the portly vizier counseled. "He has killed. Even if he tells true, he remains a danger to others."

"'The Caliph closed his eyes in thought. "*Sahib,*" he sighed. "We will send him to a hospital where he will be cared for and others will be protected from him."

"'With a snap, the world I had built, my success as a businessman, the pride of my family, collapsed. Although the Caliph meant his sentence as a kindness, at that moment, I wished for death.

"'The black-robed guard gripped my arm to escort me out. Suddenly, the air began to glitter, growing so hot that the guard dropped my arm to shield his face. Even as I sighed in relief, the courtiers gasped, and the Caliph exclaimed, "Ya Allah!"

"'This time, the djinn did not appear. Instead, a slit opened in the air, like a cut in fabric, and a cold wind blew carrying wet, white dust. Snow, I later learned. Without a backward look, I entered this strange cold world.'"

Shahryar has fallen asleep, tired from his fast. Sleeping, he seems whole. A sweet happy man wrapped in sweet happy dreams. I scrutinize him but no more masks appear.

It is said that there was once a mirror maker of spiral-towered Samarra who, quite accidentally, trapped a djinn in one of his creations . . .

Have I almost broken through?

At the thought, a firework of tenderness bursts in my chest. I lie down beside him and, mustering my courage, press a kiss onto his velvety beard. He does not stir.

Twenty-Five

I n the hour between Maghrib and Isha, the hour of the djinn, I slip into the queerly shimmering twilight, dusk turning the walls between worlds into windows. The Templar castle of an-Natrun, around which the army has set up camp, stands grim and gray on its hilltop. I do not have a destination in mind. When I raise my eyes, I see Atsiz, on a crimson rug stamped with black stars and perforated squares spread outside his tent, drinking tea with the Ayyubid general Behaddin Karakush. Our gazes lock, sending my heart deep into my belly, sending this world flying away.

They rise, Behaddin dipping his red turban and withdrawing.

Atsiz gestures for me to sit. Removing my slippers, I perch at the rug's edge, curling my bare toes under me. As my mamluks watch, I resist the urge to shift closer to him, so close that our knees would be a hairsbreadth from knocking. I tell myself that there is nothing amiss here, that I am merely a Khatun publicly conferring with her husband's emir.

He leans on one elbow, a handsome portrait of ease. The firelight caresses his high cheekbones, his firm jaw. He offers me a steaming glass of tea. I dare allow my hand to touch his as I take it. Does he feel the same spark shake across his fingertips?

"This is a surprise. I have not had the pleasure of your company since your husband returned."

A bite. "That's untrue. We all had iftaar together only a few nights ago."

"You avoid me."

What does he expect when he invites me to his tent when my husband is away? Or perhaps I am the fool to read anything more than an emir offering chaste comfort to his liege's despairing wife. I incline my head serenely. "You know you are ever welcome, Emir Atsiz."

His face closes, and only when it does do I realize how open it had been.

"Perhaps you have heard I am courting Nurani."

I had not, and it hits me in my gut like a sack of rocks.

"I trained under her father, Emir Ildegiz. I have known her a long time."

Perhaps, when they were very young, he and Nurani had loved each other and vowed to marry when they grew up. Maybe she joined the caravan to remind him of the weight of that childish vow.

"Does she return the favor?" I ask lightly.

"I would not have shared if she didn't."

Bitter bile floods my mouth. I know this is best. Yet, even as my mind knows, my heart does not feel it. I remember the radiating love I felt for Shahryar as he slept, but all I feel now is a slice through my breastbone, as though something full has been emptied.

"What other choice do I have?" His eyes, desperate and earnest, meet mine, and I think I read: *Offer me another choice. Run away with me. Take me to the Bulgars on the Volga River, hide with me in the soaring mountains of Hindustan, flee with me to the farthest east, the jungle heat of Champa.*

The proposal is bottlenecked in my mouth, stoppered by Shahryar, Dunya, Bam, Baba. By my faith. By the woman Baba raised me to be.

I answer in my most stately tones, "Nurani is a fine choice. May you both make a success of it."

This is a good thing. It makes my choice easier.

For it leaves me with none.

The Isha azaan's first melodic strains ring out as I dazedly walk away. Soldiers trickle from their tents to gather for prayer, stepping off the path to make way for me.

I stop. A woman's voice sings softly, *"My love, my love, where have you gone . . ."*

A dozy guard, one of her father's soldiers, stands outside but does not stop me. "Nurani?"

The singing stops.

"It's Shaherazade Khatun."

A pause. "Enter."

The guard opens the tent flap, and I am assaulted by mess. Ciclatoun and linens spill over the unmade bed, stained carpet, and strewn cushions. A bronze lamp, with a quail as its handle, perches precariously on the edge of a flung-open rosewood trunk.

Unconcerned, Nurani pats the bed, a thick mattress propped on a fragrant sandalwood frame. Her lips are stained Tyre purple, a half-drained goblet of red wine beside her.

I am taken aback. Even those who imbibe avoid it during Ramadan. I cannot suppress the ugly iron serpent that coils through me and hisses, *This? This is who Atsiz chooses over you?*

"My condolences for the loss of your father. A great man." She drains the goblet. Unbound, her night-dark hair shimmers past her hips and frames a sweet face.

There is no reason for me to be here, and now, what can I say?

"Your earrings are lovely." Gold filigree hoops stretch her lobes. Alighted on the inner rim of the hoops are two birds, beaks kissing, emeralds blinking in their eyes.

Tilting her head, she touches an earring. "They were a birthday gift from a friend, long ago. Someone you know."

And I had been so happy with a poem. "Who?" I ask steadily.

"Your predecessor."

My forehead pinches.

"Fataneh Khatun." Her tilted antelope eyes watch for my reaction.

My eyebrows rise despite myself. "I did not know you were acquainted."

"Oh yes. We were girls together. I was a few years younger, but she was lonely and did not mind."

Courteously, she offers me a painted-glass chalice, her sharp finger-nails glinting at the stem. I shake my head.

"You grew up at her father's court in Ganja?" Atsiz's comments about training with Nurani's father come together.

"My father was under commission to hers when we were young. My mother was her mother's cousin." She drains her goblet and lets it softly roll into the pile on the floor, dregs of wine dribbling from its rim onto her fine robes.

I sense danger. "You must have been devastated after her death."

She looks up to the tent's peaked ceiling. "I was there when Shahryar saw her, you know."

"When they fell in love."

"When *he* fell in love," she corrected, her words round, her breath smelling like fruit.

"I was there when they wed. They were both very much in love."

"You did not know her as I did." The reproach in her voice is sharp. "When Shahryar first brought his proposal to her father, even then, it was obvious he worshipped her like a Sassanian goddess. Fataneh feared she could not match his ardor. Her mother told her that love would grow, and her father was swayed by the match's prestige."

"What did you think?" I ask, curious even as I feel like a grave robber, rifling through a dead woman's fears and wants.

"Me? I told her it is better to be the beloved than the lover. But what did I know? I was thirteen and all I knew of love came from the poetry of Khayyam and Nizami."

I feel a surprising spark of kinship for Nurani and glimpse, perhaps, what draws Atsiz to her. The realization puckers my mouth.

"In the end, how could Fataneh resist?" she continues. "Her father had decided and the Malik had demanded. Her fate was made."

I recall the glow bathing the Malik and Khatun when they were newly-weds. "She could not have feigned that happiness," I say softly.

"In the first few years of their marriage, she was happy—when she thought her love would blossom to match his, but then it did not, and his love became a burden." Nurani shrugs. "After that, people saw what they wanted to see."

She pours another goblet from a stained-glass jug. The wine laps against the goblet's silver rim as she sips. "She began to take risks in her last years. She knew she should not, but she did not control who owned her heart, and these choices, at least, were hers."

"How do you know this?"

"She wrote that in her last letter to me, after Shahryar had imprisoned her: *'Maybe I am broken and this will be what cleaves me in two.'*"

Fataneh walks through my memory to the executioner's block, and I lead her.

"He never noticed that anything was amiss." Nurani stares, unfocused. "How much did he love her, if he could not see her unhappiness?"

Shahryar did not see—nor did anyone else, so bewitched were we by the tale of their great love.

"I received one letter before her last." Nurani holds up a finger. Despite her wine haze, Nurani's eyes train on me. "She wrote that she had had *'a strange interaction with the vizier's odd eldest daughter.'* Do you remember it?"

A sun-dappled courtyard. A man groaning into a woman's breaths.

"No, I can't think of anything," I say slowly, trying to mimic true thought.

"She had never written of you before. Yet, after she did, she was killed."

Panic seizes me. I want to meet Nurani's gaze, to prove that I am trustworthy, but I fear she will peer into my eyes and see straight to my smirched soul. I clench my fingers until pain jars me to my senses. I look up. "What do you suppose happened to her lovers?"

Nurani breaks her stare and shrugs. "How do you relieve yourself of someone?"

"Pay them off." I bite my lip. "Or kill them." The words fall like iron as I recall the servant in the courtyard, the poet in the shadows. "Which do you think she did?"

"It depends on the kind of woman you believe she was."

* * *

I dream that I stand in a sea of bodies. We face a wide wooden stage, its planks extending into the horizon. The sky is white with clouds. We watch a woman, with spring-green eyes and hair to her knees, walk forward. The people around me—tall, broad men—press against me until I cannot breathe. They all wear Baba's face.

I close my eyes, and I am on the stage. My hair tickles the backs of my thighs. I cough, and bloody globs fall into my hand. I squeeze the globules and they burst through the spaces between my fingers. I look up. My hands are clean, but there I stand across from me, blood on my hands, blood on my robes. I stand across from a headless Fataneh Khatun, her head in her arms, while blood pours over me. It warms my head, clots in my hair, drips down my neck, blinds my eyes, and my hands, hands, hands are red as betel.

My head is on my neck and I hold my head in my arms and Shaherazade stands in front of me, drenched in my blood. The crowd has disappeared.

We are in the Arg-e-Bam. I am rising from a deep sleep, and sunshine, thick and oily, pours through the windows. Shaherazade walks in, her plaits trailing long.

"I was sleeping," I say. "I dreamt that I held my head in my hands and you were covered in my blood."

Shaherazade smiles. "How strange."

Does she know something? Then I remember: she saw me with the man, she stumbled upon me, this dumb kitten caught me, compromised my life, held my head in her hands.

"Don't say anything," I plead. "Can't you see? I had no escape. It was nothing. A mistake. I won't do it again." A viscous guilt wells through me, the inevitability of reprisal.

"I won't." I smile, and Fataneh's blood dribbles from my hands.

* * *

It is the last day of Ramadan. After attending a council meeting with the Sultan and his commanders, I ride with Dunya through a green valley beneath a sky hazy with dust. As with the fortresses of Ascalon and Ramla, Sultan Saladin has begun demolishing an-Natrun to prevent its seizure by the Franks—even as Saifuddin corresponds with Malikric's ambassadors to treat for peace. I do not envy the workmen who burn towers and break walls, their dry, fasting mouths caked with grit.

I kick Andalib and she breaks into a gallop. The wind cuffs my face until I slow her near a herd of bleating sheep surrounded by dirham-silver olive trees.

I hear Dunya ride up behind me. "Do you think, now that we have seen so much of the world, that Fataneh was truly a bad woman?" I ask.

Did she really deserve to die?

Do I deserve to die?

"She was an adulteress," Dunya replies with stunning, decided swiftness.

"Yes, but—it is hard to be Khatun. Lonely. She had few true friends in the citadel—none, that I can remember."

"Only because she held her nose too high."

But I remember Fataneh the bride, tentative eyes and a luminous smile; I think of the Fataneh Nurani knew. "She was lonely," I say quietly. "Lonely and foolish. The Malik . . . can be a hard man to love."

Dunya looks at me sharply. I fear she detects my secret, magnifies it with refracting insect eyes.

"He was not a hard man to love before."

Before she betrayed him. Before I betrayed her.

Guilt engorges my throat. My palms feel cold, my fingers feel nothing. I bury my hands in Andalib's coarse mane.

Dunya comes close. Her black mare, Shaheen, nuzzles Andalib's long nose. "Shahera." Her voice is low. "What have you done?"

I hesitate, and hate myself for it. How can I not trust Dunyazade, the light of my eyes, my mouse, my protector? *She was an adulteress*—and my sister's Manichaeism, a soldier's sense of right and wrong, no patience for others' sinful falterings, stifles my answer.

But worry—not judgment—clouds her question. "Is it Atsiz?"

My confession bursts like a blister. "O Dunya, I have never been unfaithful to the Malik. But he, Atsiz, found me after I heard of Baba's death and held me when I was most alone."

"Held you?" Dunya sounds distant, and I want to bring her back to me, to see me again as she always has.

"Perhaps I felt for Atsiz as I shouldn't have but I have *not* betrayed the Malik. I have not sinned."

I know I am not being perfectly honest. Yet, as my sister watches me, I cannot bring myself to say more.

***

I bite into a soft cookie with an anise-flavored date center as Gulnar braids my hair. She is dressed in new finery I have gifted her for Eid al-Fitr, which marks Ramadan's close: a silver brocade gown paired with a farajiyya of sheer vermilion ciclatoun and striped cerulean-and-white trousers. Her veil is an opalescent mulberry and affixed with a flat-topped conical cap. She looks ten years younger.

"You look lovely, Gulnar." She chuckles, and coquettishly, although I do not think she realizes that the gesture could be described so, sweeps her braids over her shoulders. The silver bells at the ends chime.

Gulnar hands me a slim, linen-wrapped package. A strip of paper with one word is pinned to it: *Shaherazade*. My stomach swoops. I recognize that tight scrawl. *Your nightingale eyes.*

"Who is it from?"

Gulnar shrugs. "It was left with the mamluk by a servant. An Eid gift."

"Someone seeking to curry the Khatun's favor," Mahperi says, amused.

I unknot the fabric. It is ibn Hazam's *The Ring of the Dove*. There is no inscription on the endpaper; no note flitters out like a gray-winged moth. The book falls open to a page, as though the binding had been bent there again and again.

If thou ever would deign
To visit me one night
Darkness could not remain
For 'twould be forever light.

The verse is his breath on my cheek, his hand at my waist. Head spinning, I tuck the book deep into my trunk, camouflaging it among its fellows. Balling the linen wrapping, I glance up, but no one has noticed the cherry stain suffusing my face.

Indeed, Dunya still snoozes. Eid prayer, for which Saladin's army, his mamluks, emirs, and soldiers—Kurds, Africans, Arabs, Turks, and Persians—as well as villagers from around an-Natrun, will gather to pray in neat rows, is early but not quite so early as all that.

Mahperi, dressed in a shell-pink robe and dark-blue tunic that brings out the rosiness in her cheeks and the darkness of her eyes, pokes my sister. "We'll be late." Dunya slaps Mahperi's hand and remains folded into herself, eyes staunchly closed.

"Mahperi's right, Dunya. I'm ready, so now it's your turn." Gulnar brushes kohl onto my eyelids and my toilette is complete. In the smoky mirror, my face is polished beneath a sapphire diadem. My gown is a matching spangled blue under a persimmon farajiyya with sleeves so wide they drag on the rugs.

I whip the covers off Dunya, shove a cookie in her hand. Mahperi drags her to the steaming copper tub, concealed behind a wooden lattice screen of hexagons and stars notched together. The tent fills with the sweetness of rose oil.

"That girl," Gulnar says with a fond smile. "The same at sixteen as she was at six."

"A miscreant!" I call out, but Dunya does not respond. Her silence continues and I peek around the screen. Her hair sticks wetly to her scalp and her skin is flush with the bath's heat. The steam breathes on my face.

"Jaanem?"

She looks up, and her cheeks are glazed with tears. "Ay, Shahera," she mumbles thickly.

"What is it, azizem?" I kneel beside the tub.

"Our first Eid without Baba . . ."

I press my hand to my heart, which suddenly feels hollow. I have been trying to forget all morning. After prayer, Baba would embrace us thrice and present us with carefully selected gifts. On my wrist, I wear a hammered gold torque set with a large lapis lazuli that he gave me, along with al-Masudi's *Meadows of Gold and Mines of Gems*, last Eid. "Something pretty for your arm, something prettier for your mind," he had said, softly kissing my forehead.

"And . . . this would have been my first Eid with Faramurz."

I bite my quivering lip. "Neither Baba nor Faramurz would want you to grieve on this happy day, mouse. Now, wash your face and dry yourself. We will be late for prayer and the khutbah." I kiss the top of her hot, wet head, and my lips taste like roses and Dunya, but it cannot mask the bitter grief in my mouth.

Twenty-Six

⬦⬦⬦⬦⬦

"I received a letter from Leila." I pull Andalib beside Shahryar as the army and baggage train wind northwest from an-Natrun to Ramla through silver-green hills. The breeze catches in the leaves, rustling them as if shuffling playing cards. A heavy necklace of rubies and pearls cinches my throat—Shahryar's Eid bequest. "There was another Oghuz attack. The eighth since Baba died. This one so close, she could see the fires burning from her home."

Shahryar pulls the reins tighter, but doesn't respond.

A rising wind wafts the stench of horses and soldiers, turning my stomach even after seven months on the road.

"We should return to Kirman," I whisper for Shahryar's ears alone. "With the other Seljuk maliks under attack, Sultan Toghrul imprisoned, we have no allies. And Malik Dinar knows, for his Oghuz have become brazen."

"Shahzaman too writes of the raids, and Ishaq begs me to return," Shahryar replies heavily.

"With Baba gone"—I choke—"you here, and the Seljuk Empire becoming dust, why wouldn't the Oghuz grow bolder?"

He sighs, and his horse whickers sympathetically in response. "I have feared that leaving Bam was error, but I was . . . in a fog."

And who made that departure necessary but me?

"How can we battle the Crusaders with Sultan Saladin," Shahryar continues, "if my patrimony burns? How can Kirman's soldiers fight for their Malik when their Malik does not fight beside them? How can Bam hold when I am gone?"

He purses his lips. Is he recollecting how his own city seethed against him prior to his departure, the sigh it heaved when it shut the South Gate behind him?

"What do you think Sultan Saladin will say?"

Shahryar fixes his gaze ahead, where, somewhere in the distance, Sultan Saladin rides at the front of the great force that he assembled through his will and Allah's assistance alone. "When the time is right, I can only hope he sees my dilemma, king to king."

Suddenly, I notice that Marwan ibn Hatim, the Caliph's representative, has sidled close, his expression too carefully bored. I have not forgotten the bonds between Caliph an-Nasir and Malik Dinar. Loudly, I announce, "As you say, O Malik, I will continue my tale."

"O Malik, it is said that the King told Jauhara and Kushyar: 'I was thrust into this land, into the snow. As I brushed the powder off my arms, my skin revealed itself, dark and taut once more. I dove into the snow and when I emerged, my flesh was again my own.

"'I looked back, and the tear through which I had entered was sealed. This castle rose in its place, and its immense red doors swung open, engulfing me in warm air.

"'With nowhere else to go, I walked in. A servant greeted me. A great plague had swept through the palace, he reported, killing the royal family, and the remaining servants could not decide who would be king.

"'More servants gathered where we now sit, to see this strange guest the snow had blown in.

"'"Are there no other emirs?" I asked, and the servants were surprised. No one else remained: just them, farmers, and then snow as far as a man could walk until he died. "How do you know they are dead?" I asked. "They never came back," the servants responded. "But perhaps they've gone Elsewhere," I said, and to that there was no response.

"'When I awoke the next morning, a white sun was shining through the window and two dozen white faces were watching me.

"'"We have decided," the man who had welcomed me said, "to make you our king. It is the best way to avoid animosity among us."

"'"But I know nothing of this land," I protested. "My ignorance makes me ill-suited to rule." We argued until the sun dipped low and stained the snow red, when finally I was convinced to take the crown. "For one year," I said. "And you will form my council of advisers. If you do not find me suitable, unmake me and choose among yourselves."

"'A year passed, and it was agreed, not just by the servants but by the farmers, that my reign was acceptable. I have ruled Here for a century. But never before has someone from my home found me,' said the King. 'So tell me: How did you come Here?'

"Jauhara briefly recounted the wall of water and the boat she, Kushyar, and the parrot had taken to be borne into this world. Jauhara yawned. The King gestured for a servant, who led them up a dizzying series of glass staircases and into a great bedroom with two wide beds and a hot fire jumping in the hearth. Through a tall window, Jauhara could see the two moons. The orange crescent had swollen into a gibbous moon, while the blue moon remained spherical.

"The servant moved to close the door, and Jauhara leapt up. The parrot flapped from her shoulder. 'We are meant to share these rooms?' She hoped she did not sound worried or girlish, but the servant gave her a strange look.

"'My master thought you would appreciate having your friend near on your first night in a new world.' Bowing, he shut the green lacquer door.

"Jauhara grabbed soft wool pajamas from the bed closest to the window and said to Kushyar, 'Turn around while I change, and I will do the same for you.'

"But Kushyar, curious to see his confusing companion, peeked for the briefest moment over his shoulder. He saw Jauhara, as she was, in firelight and moonlight, and his heart began to race.

"For the next three days, Jauhara, Kushyar, and the parrot investigated Here. By their fourth night, they had explored the red-roofed villages up to the mountain, exhausting the outer bounds of the new world.

"That night, Jauhara fell into a catatonic slumber that plunged her into the deepest recesses of her dreams. In the dark caverns, a fit of ghastly shapes—a man with an alligator's head, another with a falcon's, a woman winged like a bird—circled and snapped.

"Initially, their focus was shrouded, but as she pushed closer, she recognized them, one by one: her mother, father, brothers, and sisters wrapped in glittering gold chains. She tried to call out, but no matter how she strained she was strangled.

"Panicking, Jauhara propelled herself upward and surfaced with a gasp. When she opened her eyes, Kushyar was watching.

"'What's the matter?' he asked.

"'I had a dream,' Jauhara murmured, her heartbeat racing in her ears. 'Of my family. They were . . . something was terribly wrong.'

"'It was just a dream,' Kushyar said. He knelt beside her bed, but dared not take her hand or move her tangled hair from her face. 'Nothing to fear.'

"Jauhara tried to believe him, but the disquiet would not leave her bones. 'It was something more.' Despite herself, Jauhara became teary-eyed, longing for her family, her quick-witted mother and her wise, warm father especially. 'I need to go home.' Her conviction brooked no opposition.

"The parrot hopped onto Jauhara's shoulder. 'I know a way,' he said.

"Kushyar's mind leapt, and he knew: 'Beyond the mountains. No one returns past the horizon.'"

***

Sitting beside ibn Shaddad in Sultan Saladin's tent in the Ramla encampment, I fold my legs beneath me, grateful for the warm brazier that the Sultan's steward placed nearby. Despite the two dozen emirs in the room, the tent is cold, and whenever the tent door opens a sharp wind whistles through, flicking the smoking brazier. The last man to enter is Saifuddin, who, despite his celadon tunic, looks wan, deep furrows edging his mouth. Heavily, he lowers himself onto a violet cushion beside his brother.

"We have learned from an escaped prisoner of war that the Franks intend to emerge from Jaffa and field ten thousand horses against our army," the Sultan says. "We march tomorrow."

I look first for Atsiz, who takes the news solidly, with a rueful, upturned mouth. Our eyes meet. It is enough to heat my skin like a furnace, and I look away first. Beside him, Shahryar is impassive. Rapidly, I scribe the conversation into the chronicle, leaving a swirling trail of wet ink on the page.

"I will send heralds throughout the camp," says the eagle-nosed general Behaddin Karakush.

The conversation shifts to strategy for the upcoming battle, and I take close notes. Should I be scribing in such detail? But then, this chronicle is being written so that generations from now, generals and scholars can know of the sacrifice and heroism of the Seljuks in this holy war and how they aided the great Sultan Saladin in bringing the Frankish armies to heel.

After the council, Shahryar and I walk through the camp. I frown, seeing a lamp oscillating within our tent and a dark shadow on the wall, but Shahryar's mamluk stands easy outside. We remove our slippers.

"'Asr bikhair, Malik. The Khatun's companion Mahperi awaits within."

The shadow grows. "O, Shaherazade!" she exclaims. Her cheeks are flushed. "I hoped to speak with you but," her eyes flash toward Shahryar, "we can talk tomorrow."

She flits away and the Malik removes his turban. There is an intimacy in seeing him bareheaded, after doffing the armor he wears before the world. I remove the silver diadem with its beaten disks, which has been digging into my scalp, and fold away my daffodil-colored veil. Does he think the same about seeing me so?

I should not be so unsure of what to say to my husband on the eve of battle, but suddenly the silence between us is overwhelming. I light sour orange incense and finger the uneven edges of my chronicle. I clear my throat. "Are you nervous? About battle, I mean."

He does not respond immediately. I fear I have trespassed.

Shahryar sits on the bed, hands on his knees. "If I think about the magnitude of what I am doing, yes. When I think about what a 'battle' entails. But I don't really think about it."

"What do you think about?"

He purses his lips. "I think: I must go to sleep because I must rise early. My horse needs to be ready since I have to ride tomorrow. And so on."

I think of my unceasing worry about pleasing Shahryar, about concealing Atsiz, of my persistent fear that the worst is an inevitable misstep away. "I don't think I could cabin my thoughts so."

Shahryar blows out the lamp Mahperi lit and lies back. Wispy smoke swirls above its spout like an emerging djinn. "There is no other way. Otherwise, fear will choke you."

"You will be fine," I say, resting my forehead against his, and marvel at myself. Here I am comforting this man in the face of death, who threw it at me day after day, who hurled woman after woman into its maw. But he is different now. *Can a man really change so much?*

"I don't want to think about what will be or will not." He stares past me.

"Will you continue your tale?" he says, drawing a curtain between us.

Before I let the curtain fall, I say, "Tomorrow, send messengers from the battlefield to me."

Shahryar does not answer.

"O Malik, it is said that when Jauhara told the King of their need to return, he was sorry to see them go but did not delay them. He knew nothing of what lay past the mountains, but his servants loaded the trio with thick fur cloaks, ice picks, dried meats, and warm boots.

"The King himself drove them to the foot of the mountains in his wolf-led sleigh and embraced them as they dismounted. 'May Allah protect you,' he said.

"As the King's sleigh jingled away, Jauhara looked at the mountains scraping the blue sky and remembered the green grass from which they had slid into this world. That grass was somewhere past the tops of those mountains, and past that grass was al-Askar's heat, the Nile's lushness, her family's love.

"Though they climbed high, the grassy sky and the worlds beyond remained out of reach. This high in the mountains, the sun did not set, but after twelve hours passed, by Kushyar's count, the parrot found a shelter of rocks.

"Ahead, the path was slick with ice and so steep that it was near vertical. Jauhara did not know how they would continue, but no one spoke of the impending impossibility. Jauhara lit a fire against the biting cold, and Kushyar assembled the furs into a small lean-to for the three to sleep in.

"When Jauhara awoke, she was not alone.

"With a start, she met a large topaz eye. The round black pupil reflected Jauhara's frightened face, but the immense hawk's head tilted as it retreated from the lean-to. Heart racing, Jauhara peeked out. The grass gleamed above against an incandescent sun. She saw Kushyar, the parrot lucent on his broad shoulders, talking to *someone*. Beside that someone perched an elephantine bird of prey, beak sharply curved, talons long as tusks, and a jewel-plumed tail. With a gasp, Jauhara recognized it from an illuminated bestiary: a *rokh*.

"'Sabah al-khair,' Jauhara said.

"Kushyar and the long-bearded stranger replied, 'Sabah an-noor.'

"Jauhara eyed the rokh, but it nestled peacefully beside the long-bearded stranger.

"'Jauhara, this is Bulukiya,' Kushyar said, and Bulukiya raised his hand to his heart. 'He too is not of this world.'

"Jauhara's eyes widened. 'Are you from Egypt? India? Abyssinia?'

"Bulukiya shook his head. 'My country is called Wakwak, an island at world's end, named for a tree that grows in the courtyard of our princess's palace. Its greatest wonder is its fruit: it bears heads, human heads, of beautiful men and beautiful women. At sunrise and sunset, they announce the day's arrival and departure by crying "Wakwak!" At the tree's center hangs the head of a gray-haired woman, gifted with wisdom and prophecy.

"'But I ramble—tell me of yourselves.'

"Jauhara explained their task. 'But the path ahead is impossible. Tell me, does this snow ever melt?'

"Bulukiya chuckled. 'Never, but that path is not impassable for everyone.' Bulukiya pointed to the rokh circling the verdant sky, casting shadows like immense clouds. He looked at the rokh beside him. 'Will you do it?'

"The rokh beadily examined Jauhara, Kushyar, and the parrot, taking particular note of the last. The parrot met the giant raptor's scrutiny equably, until the rokh whistled its assent.

"Jauhara and Kushyar mounted the rokh, legs gripping its feathered back. With fearlessness Jauhara found she could not match, the rokh beat its great wings, each flap a thunderclap, as it ascended to where the mountaintop brushed the grass sky."

* * *

Sitting in front of Shahryar's tent with Dunya, I coax one of the camp's many cats, fat on bones and scraps, to me. It rubs its orange head against my knuckles, twining its purring body around my legs. To the north, Ramla's White Mosque, built by the Umayyads four centuries ago, pearls like a moon in the pink dusk. Its minaret stretches into the sky, wreathed by a flock of star-dusted starlings. The muezzin starts the call for the Maghrib azaan and the starlings scatter, a stormcloud punctured.

"Any news?" Dunya asks. She looks over her shoulder for sign of the returning army—whickering horses, the heavy-footed thump of tired soldiers—but the camp is still.

Shahryar has sent but one messenger to inform me that the battle has been joined. "Nothing further."

I fear what that could mean, and I pray for Shahryar, for Atsiz, for the Seljuk warriors and Saladin's men, even as I imagine them swept away by a great white wave emblazoned with a bloodred cross. Silently, we watch the sun sink low and burn red.

A shadow startles the cat, who bounds away as Shahryar collapses on the rug beside us, smelling of musk and sweat and blood. The returning army tramps through the tents with dented armor and fresh wounds, poulticed and wrapped.

I feel a swell of relief. "Assalamu'alaikum, Shahryar. Welcome back. How did we fare against the Franks?"

Shahryar unbuckles his dirty breastplate. Beneath, his blue tunic is stained with sweat and grime, but save for some scrapes on his hands and a graze on his cheek, he appears unwounded. In the tent, one of his man-servants prepares a bath steaming with chamomile, and another collects the armor to be cleaned and polished. I gesture for a servant to bring him tea.

"Not well."

"What happened?" Dunya asks. A warm wind plucks at her jade veil.

"A rout."

I remember the carnage of Arsuf, the blood-dark earth, limbs and corpses scattered like stones on the ground, the sweet stink of rotting flesh filling my nose. I shake the images from my head.

At my expectant silence, Shahryar continues. "Saifuddin led an army of Saladin's mamluks, Seljuks, and a green company from Rûm to the Frankish army's camp. At once, the mamluks rode forward, volleying arrows. But when the company from Rûm followed, they flailed. Their rashness and inexperience sowed confusion among our men."

I flinch. "What of our emirs? Emir A—Atsiz?"

Does Shahryar catch how I caress his name? He gives no sign. "The emirs survived intact."

"Alhamdulilah. And the Franks?"

"Bore down on us as one man, even as half of our party milled in turmoil. We could do nothing but flee. The Seljuks and mamluks on their swift horses escaped, but the soldiers from Rûm were taken prisoner."

I breathe a prayer for the captives, recalling Malikric's massacre of the prisoners at Acre. "Did we take any Frankish lives?"

"Only three." Shahryar stares gloomily at the minaret, dotted with black birds in the darkening twilight.

I wince. Another humiliating loss. We could lose this war. Despite Saladin at the army's helm, despite all we have done to be here. We could lose. I bury the thought. "I am grateful that you, at least, returned to us safe, subhan'Allah."

Shahryar clears his throat, thick despair clouding his eyes. "Let us talk no more of war. Come, tell me your tale."

———

"O Malik, it is said that after days of the mountaintop hovering just out of the rokh's reach, Jauhara's head brushed soft, tall grass. She resisted the urge to look down—even the thought made her gall rise. Dismounting from the rokh, Jauhara gingerly touched the grass sky.

"'What do we do now?' she asked the parrot.

"The parrot swooped over the mountain and flew against the grass, its jonquil crest skimming the blades. He hopped onto Jauhara's shoulder. 'Close your eyes, clutch the grass, and pull yourself up and through. Think of where you want to return. So long as Kushyar and I are touching you, we will emerge wherever you are.'

"The first time Jauhara reached up, her arms shivered so much she had to shake them like a wrestler preparing for a match. The second time, her grasp slipped, her palms slick. The third time, she gripped the grass and Kushyar boosted her until she could pull herself up. She thought furiously of the throne room of the al-Askar palace, the smell of dust and jasmine and rose swirling between 'Asr and Maghrib, the soft steps of servants on marble floors, the caroling laughter of her siblings, and the taste of spiced lamb and warm bread, fresh from the palace ovens.

"When Jauhara opened her eyes, she was home.

"Kushyar and the parrot stood with her.

"The palace did not smell as Jauhara remembered—it was mustier. The air was hotter, the hall smaller. The feeling of *home* sat tight on her shoulders, like a robe she had outgrown.

"As planned, Kushyar, Jauhara, and the parrot split up, Kushyar and the parrot vanishing down a corridor. But before she could slip toward her chambers, a matched pair of guards, squat and round as peas, confronted her. They looked Jauhara up and down, taking in her fine furs. 'Identify yourself.'

"'I am Sitt Jauhara, daughter of Governor 'Omar.'

"Jauhara expected them to demand proof, but the rounder one obligingly said, 'Then let us take you to your father, ya Sitti.' As he spoke, Jauhara noticed a queer silver rheum filming the guards' black eyes.

"Jauhara's heart clutched. 'He's here?'

"'But of course,' the guard answered.

"Relief swept Jauhara—tailed by embarrassment at how she had fled worlds on the heels of a nightmare. *How Kushyar will laugh*, she thought.

"With each step, the palace grew more familiar: the gardens flushed with anemones, the arching honeycomb vaults that echoed their footfall. As her home solidified, her stomach tumbled, a stream cascading over stones.

"Jauhara held her breath as they entered the throne room. Its green-and-gold-striped dome yawned above, and the white marble floor, which her father had swept a lifetime ago, gleamed beneath her feet.

"And on the throne of the governor of Egypt, her father's throne, sat a strange and beautiful woman, with carob-brown skin and great rainbow wings that flapped lazily, stirring the perfumed air. Jauhara recognized her: the creature from her nightmare. Jauhara shrank, but her father's court swayed around her. Great and wise men showed faces pleasantly blanked.

"Jauhara grabbed the guard's shoulder. 'Where is my father?' she demanded.

"The guardsman gestured toward the creature. 'But there he is, ya Sitti.'

"The woman's gaze, too human to be human, licked Jauhara up and down.

"Neck prickling, Jauhara began murmuring Surah ad-Djinn, the Qur'anic chapter her parents had embossed onto each of their children's tongues. As she recited, the atmosphere tautened, the court began to stir. But with a snap of her fingers, the woman stilled Jauhara's lips and the surah's work dissipated.

"The creature extended her long hands toward Jauhara, and when she spoke, her voice was 'Omar's, full of sorrow. 'Ya *binti*, my beloved Jauhara. How do you not recognize your own father?'

"Jauhara tasted bile, salty and bitter. She glanced around only to meet the silver-veiled glares of a disapproving court.

"Swallowing, Jauhara thought quickly. 'O Abbi,' she proclaimed. 'It has been a long journey. Forgive me for not recognizing you.'

"Approaching the dais, Jauhara clutched the creature's hand and kissed it. A jolt of raw power, like lightning, like the rush of the Nile, raced from Jauhara's lips to her spine. She placed the creature's hand against her forehead, and a buzz rocked through her skull.

"The woman did not betray bemusement at Jauhara's performance. 'There is nothing to forgive, habibti,' and Jauhara trembled to hear mercy in her father's voice spoken from the woman's devilish mouth. She stroked Jauhara's hair, and Jauhara's head clanged with power. 'You and I have much to discuss.'"

***

I jump as Mahperi skulks into Shahryar's tent. "I was hoping you would be here," she says. She spots the letter in my hand. "Word from home?"

"From Hanna. Another Oghuz attack, so close to Bam she could see it from her home."

A smoldering strip of living orange on the horizon, a sunset in the dark of night. Smoke rises like vapor and burns my nose. Children's screams sear my ears. Every day they draw a tighter circle around Bam.

Seeing darkness bloom on my face, Mahperi loops her delicate fingers around my wrist and pulls me into the sun, shining high in a cloudless cornflower sky. Inhaling, I smell a nip of frost.

"Pader and Mader haven't written a word of it, of course," Mahperi says as she skirts around ashen campfires, leading me north toward Ramla. We pass the makeshift stables, which the Frankish captives muck in their chains. One captive, handsome and blond, catches Mahperi's eye and bows mockingly. She flushes.

"Impertinent swine!" I mutter, but Mahperi says nothing.

We continue walking until we reach the pulverized remains of Ramla's Crusader castle and rubbled walls, gray hills of crushed bone.

Mahperi's father is an important bureaucrat, a thin man whom I have never particularly liked. Mahperi's grandfather had been a *nadim*, the closest companion of Shahryar's grandfather, renowned for his polo skill and heavy head for liquor. But while Mahperi's grandfather had been grand and athletic, his son proved an asthmatic autocrat. That Mahperi wailed and banged to escape Bam does not surprise me—that her father permitted it does.

I follow Mahperi to Ramla's church, a boxy building of mottled sandy stone built by the Crusaders. Unlike a mosque, the church bears no soaring minarets or curving domes, but an iron double door is wedged open beneath a tall, pointed arch.

"Your parents don't want to frighten you," I say, peeking in.

Within, scant light filters tiredly through small, occluded windows. Peaked stone arches cascade over rows of wooden benches, the church ghostly since the city emptied of Franks. Although the church cannot be more than a few decades old—built after their last Crusade—it smells ancient, green and wet. Moss pebbles the stone floor.

It feels disrespectful to enter a house of God shod, but I know it is the Christian custom. Still, I pull my veil more firmly over my hair and keep my footsteps soft, passing a stone font holding mildewy water.

Mahperi laughs dryly, revealing a crooked tooth in the corner of her smile as she follows me into the church's chill dimness. "Oh, Pader has no qualms about threatening me in his letters for shaming him by leaving Kirman unwed and under the protection of a woman barely out of girlhood."

"But didn't he permit it?" My question echoes through the arches.

On the apse wall at the nave's end hangs a dark wooden cross. It shakes my breath to see it, this symbol of a brother faith that assails us again and again, stealing our land, bloodying our people, all in the name of the God we share.

Mahperi tugs at a stray lilac thread curling on the cuff of her trousers. She pulls and pulls until it is as long as her forearm. When it gives no sign of breaking on its own, she wraps it around her finger and snaps it off. "Only after I threatened to hang myself. Your baba was called, and he convinced him that no harm would befall me if I joined you." She rubs the thread into a little purple ball between her palms, unperturbed.

Her melancholia raises the hair on my neck. Before I can say anything, Mahperi turns back to the door. The lilac clump of thread remains fisted. "Are you coming to Sitt Jalaliyya's dinner tonight?" she asks, cheery again.

Discomfort burns my ears. "No." I clear my throat. "I was not invited."

"Oh." Mahperi's eyebrows, thick and fluted, rise. "She probably forgot."

I look at Mahperi sidewise, and she has the grace to drop her head. Have I annoyed Sitt Jalaliyya? As I walk back to the clear sun, I cannot imagine how, but it does not sit well with me.

After all, Sultan Saladin's daughter-in-law is no mean enemy to make.

Twenty-Seven

◇◇◇◇◇

I wipe my palms on my violet robe, the black-and-ivory-banded sleeves sliding down my wrists as Shahryar and I stand like supplicants before Sultan Saladin, who sits cross-legged on his gilded throne. The Sultan returned from battle earlier today, and its wear shows in the shadows on his face, the fresh cuts on his hands.

"Did you not think that leaving Kirman would be a risk?" Saladin says with more bite than I had anticipated after Shahryar's plea. The brazier beside him smokes, its embers glowing against the black-and-gold brocade of his overcoat. "You knew when you departed that your lands were overrun with Oghuz and Khwarezmids and that your own Sultan Toghrul was falling under their weight. Or were you too eager to flee your sins to consider politics?"

Shahryar snaps back as if slapped. How many men has Shahryar met, each powerful in his own right? Yet not one has challenged Shahryar, turned him away, rejected his company.

Or perhaps the killings of his wives did not matter in the face of the gold and soldiers Shahryar could offer.

Sultan Saladin exhales and, as surprisingly as it appeared, the moment of reckoning disappears. "Only Allah may judge."

I wish the Sultan had pressed on it. How would Shahryar respond if the great Sultan Saladin had confronted him, wrenched his arms and pushed his knee into the back of his sins?

"But," Saladin continues, "your departure would only fan rumors of betrayal and embolden Malikric."

"Betrayal?"

The Sultan looks at me coldly. Gone is the man who reminded me of Baba. Here is Saladin as his enemies know him: clever, fearsome, and focused on victory.

"Betrayal. Ambush after ambush thwarted. The Franks arraying their battle lines as though they know precisely when and how to expect us. This very morning, we ambushed a Frankish foraging party in the valley, but their cavalry was waiting. Our victory should have been easy, but we were defeated.

"Our spies say that Malikric believes we are weak and that our own men think we are lost and pass information to the Franks so that they may be remembered by the victors. How long before that becomes true?"

"And if we leave . . ." Shahryar says.

"It looks like *fitnah*, like weakness, like the entire Seljuk army has lost faith."

"O Sultan, that's untrue!" I say.

Sighing, Sultan Saladin thaws. "That is how it will be seen, by my army, by the Franks."

"We came to you of our own accord," Shahryar says in a low voice. If I listen closely, I can hear the almost-growl of a threat.

Sultan Saladin's sympathy flashes away, a ship sinking into the sea. "And you became part of something greater. A man enters a marriage of his own will, but once he does, he cannot abandon his wife simply because he was free before."

Shahryar flinches.

Hastily, I say, "We understand, ya Sultan. But you must also understand us. Here you stand with the greatest army in the ummah. We are
all that remains between our people and their destruction. We would pay
almost any cost to ride against the Franks with you, but it cannot be this."

The Sultan's tilted eyes soften.

"Some more time then, Sultan Saladin," Shahryar says. "A victory or
two on the field. Enough to show that there is no traitor, that your army
is still strong, and that the Seljuk army's departure has nothing to do with
a loss of faith."

"Perhaps then. I will remember the safety of your home and your
people in my prayers."

Dismissed, I press my hand to my heart and nod. Shahryar does the
same, and Sultan Saladin returns the gesture. I feel his eyes on our backs
as we depart.

Wispy clouds draw a diaphanous veil over the gibbous moon that shines
on Ramla's mosques and church. Shahryar does not speak, wrapped in a
coat of dark thoughts. Is he surprised that Sultan Saladin did not immediately release the army? I certainly am, a little. Will we truly fight here,
not as free men but slaves?

Or perhaps Shahryar dwells in the Sultan's cuts about *sins*. Is he shocked
that a man as renowned for his honor as Sultan Saladin feels repulsion at
his misdeeds?

But Shahryar's sins were not so grave that the Sultan refused his aid.

I do not want to think about that. I do not want to think about how
Baba could find no way to curb Shahryar's rampage, how Dunya excused
his execution of Fataneh, my instinctive sympathy for the Malik when I
discovered her infidelity, my eagerness to find the goodness in him and
the evil in her. How almost a year has passed, and no one has held a mirror to him and demanded a reckoning.

Who would?

Who cares enough about Altunjan, Shideh, and Inanj? Who cares
enough about Shahryar?

My hands shake as I light the silver and bronze lamps in our cold tent, the nascent flames burning the whites of my fingernails. As I bring icy hands to my clattering mouth, I cannot silence the question pounding in my head—is it for me? Is it for him? I give it voice: "Why did you do it?"

His head jerks, yanked by a puppeteer's strings. "Do what?"

My blood rushes so loudly and so thickly I cannot hear or see. I am tempted to change the subject, to pretend that I forgot my question. We have come so far. Before I can decide, my mouth moves. "Kill them."

The veneer cracks, an iron shield split by a steel sword, and there are his guts, wet and warm. But in a blink the vulnerability disappears. His answer snaps back, clipped and brutal. In his cold, hard face, I cannot find the Shahryar he has slowly begun to become again.

"Does a husband not have the right to kill his philandering wife? The laws of Allah and man allow it." Hands steady, he pours wine into a milky goblet rimmed with gold leaf.

"But they cannot. Not as you did." The lessons memorized from my tutor spill from my tongue. "By the shari'ah an adulterer may be punished, but only if the accusation is corroborated by the testimony of four witnesses. Who saw the act as clearly as a qalam dipped in an inkwell. You did not have that."

He hurls the goblet, and the wine seeps into the rug. "I saw her. I saw her with my own eyes fucking a slave." His voice rattles the tent, rattles my bones. "I saw my own wife in my own garden with my own slave. I confronted her with the li'an before the court, and she did not deny it. Then there was you."

"Me?"

He's guessed. He knows. I cannot meet his eyes.

"I know the note was yours," he whispers, closing the space between us, raising the fine hair on my nape. His breath hot on my face, he spits my quatrain's opening, sing-song: "'O Malik-e-Kirman.'"

I fall to the bed.

"Without the note, I would never have searched for her. Without that note, I would never have found her. Without your witness, I would not have executed her." He catches my horror and says gently, as though to comfort me: "She broke the law and lawbreakers must be punished. Your words brought a criminal to a just end."

My words.

"If I had known . . . if I had known that's how it would end, I would not have . . ."

"What did you think your accusation would lead to? Did you think I would let them believe that I was my wife's fool? That I was weak? Do you not think that would have invited the world on us—not only the Oghuz, but the Khwarezmids, and the Caliph, and other Seljuks too?"

How to tell him that I had not thought of Fataneh and her fate, that I had only considered the burden of keeping such a great secret and the risk to myself and my family? That if I had thought of her at all, it was to assume some blurry fate like exile, where Fataneh slowly disappeared from our memory like a dream in daylight? And I had not thought, not once, of how this would tear the Malik's heart. Suddenly, that Shaherazade feels like a child, a naïve stranger with a narrow world.

But there is more than Fataneh, more than Shahryar, more than me.

I stand. "What of your other wives, Shahryar? What were their crimes? Altunjan. Shideh. Inanj." I drop each of their names like a stone into a pond. Each lands with a satisfying weight. "What crimes did they commit?"

He does not reply.

"Were you planning on murdering me as well? The daughter of your vizier, a girl you watched grow up?"

"I paid them generous mahrs; I gave handsome wedding gifts to their families and blood money after their deaths." He is granite, certain and implacable.

I should be afraid, but I feel fury, Baba's slow anger, rise. My thighs tremble and my voice quavers. "You think that is it? That payment absolves you of remorse?"

He blinks, unmoved.

I want to weep for him and for my love. For the man I thought he was and would be again. I wish I could pick him from the spaces of my mind, from the pauses between my breath, from the beat of my heart, the way a woman picks out embroidery. I would grasp each thread and pull it out, piece by piece, with careful tugs, until there was nothing left. But it's not so easy—he is so snarled in me, woven over and over again.

"How can you claim to know what I feel?" His voice is high and at the last word it cracks.

"Who knows you better than I?"

I flinch as he slaps a trunk. His palm retreats scarlet while the wood gleams on. "You do not see half of what you think you do!"

I take satisfaction in keeping my voice level, even as his face purples. "Then give me something to see, Shahryar."

Without looking back, I stride away. My breathing is hard and quick, and each step feels like I am dragging against a tightly held leash. I pull and pull until, finally, it snaps.

✲✲✲

Rain taps against the tent I have shared with Dunya and Mahperi the last three nights. It collects at the seams and drips to the rugs. The brazier has been moved three times already, and although the tent isn't warm, it is smoky and smells of char and minty camphor. The glass lamp hisses and puffs as a fat drop of water splatters onto it. I burrow deeper into my fox-fur blanket. A hot glass of tea warms my icy hands.

I try not to think of Shahryar.

Water plops onto my head. "Mahperi, can you toss me the fur hat in that trunk?"

Mahperi throws me the cap, and I pull it on before a second cold drop can scuttle down my scalp.

Seeing my long face, Mahperi says, "It's the weather." She pats my knee. Her hand is cold even through the thick wool of my trousers. "It makes me gloomy too."

"You should tell us a story," Dunya says, lowering the painted playing cards she has been shuffling. "A story just for us, not one of Shahryar's leavings, to cheer us up in this dreary weather." As if to underscore her point, rain hails onto the tent. The drips become rivulets.

"Take us somewhere warm!" Mahperi adds.

"Only if Dunya plays the tar."

Dunya draws the tar from its case, its body like two hazelnuts attached at the tips. She tilts her head like an attentive sparrow as her fingers stride and pluck across the instrument with expert grace.

"Is Córdoba in the summer warm enough?"

Dunya strums a soft, improvised Andalusian melody. I can feel the sunshine on my face and smell the bright zest of oranges.

Some time ago, it is said, there was a scribe to the Caliph of Córdoba who had one wife and one concubine. The wife was the daughter of a scribe who was the son of a scribe married to the daughter of a scribe. The concubine was a Berber girl with round black eyes and striking copper hair that spiraled to her thighs in even thickness.

"On her chin was tattooed a palm tree, a straight line extending from her lower lip, diamonds above forming its leaves and diamonds below its roots. This was considered a great beauty. A second tattooed palm rose from between her eyebrows, two fronds extending toward her crimson hair and two roots stretching to her black eyes. This too was considered a great beauty, and there could be no doubt: Tazurt the concubine was beautiful.

"Born in the neverending sea of the Sahara beneath a horizonless sky, Tazurt the concubine had been captured in a fight between her tribe and the Córdobans and taken, weeping, to Andalusia by dhow.

"The scribe's wife was kind to the girl when he brought her home from the souk. She tenderly washed the long red curls, told Tazurt what to expect when her husband came to her in the night, and pressed upon her husband oils to ease the girl's defloration.

"And so Tazurt lived. Not happy and not free, but grateful for the small kindnesses in her life. At night, she dreamt of a sky filled with stars and galaxies, so clear she could see the edge of the universe.

"At that time, Córdoba had many princes, but one, a middle son of the Caliph Abd ar-Rahman, was infamously debauched. No tavern was unknown to him, and it is said his harem numbered one thousand and one beauties—although what was that compared to his father's harem of six thousand?

"One evening, as Tazurt left the souk, her hands full of packages, a gang of men approached her. Tazurt's heart stopped in fear. She thought to herself: *I can throw the packages at the closest men and run screaming back to the souk. It is not far. Someone can help.* She tensed, ready to flee, when the prince spoke. 'You are a vision, a *houri. Who* are you?'

"Tazurt inched away from the men. Each was dressed magnificently: fulgent silks of amethyst, carmine, and emerald, glinting with gold embroidery. They were veiled in the custom of Almoravid nobility, so that Tazurt could only see their eyes.

"The prince, sensing her discomfort, dismissed his coterie. When they were alone, the prince looked around to ensure no one was watching, and swiftly dropped his veil so Tazurt could see the almond complexion of a man who had never faced the sun, the soft jaw of a man whose father still cared for him, the plump red lips of a man accustomed to the pursuit of pleasure. 'I am Abd al-Jabbar. The Caliph's son.' He veiled himself again, leaving only his blue eyes visible, the inheritance of a Basque grandmother. 'Tell me, fair maid, who are you?'

"'I am a concubine.' She ducked around him. 'Please sidi, I must return to my master.'

"When Tazurt left her master's home the next day, she found the veiled prince waiting for her at the souk's entrance.

"'I have not been able to sleep since I saw you,' he said, oblivious to the crowd warily skirting him. 'I have stood since Fajr awaiting your return.'

"Tazurt passed him, avoiding his Basque blue gaze.

"'Tell me your name,' he pleaded. When she did not answer, he continued. 'Come to my palace. I can give you everything, every comfort. You would be very happy.'

"'I am already comfortable.' A breath of air rustled the waxy leaves of the orange trees skirting the Great Mosque and lifted Tazurt's veil, revealing her copper curls.

"The prince clutched his heart. 'Let me have you. Tell me who your master is, I will buy you.'

"Tazurt sped away, weaving behind a fruit stand, leaping past a cloth merchant, until the river was in sight. The prince grabbed her arm and held fast although she tried to shake free.

"'How can you, a concubine, ignore me?' he demanded. 'I am a prince. The son of the Caliph. You cannot imagine the gold I have. Oceans of it! The women I possess! Each more beautiful than the last! The treasures I own: a lamp with a djinn locked within, a rug that can fly across the sea! And you think I cannot possess you?'

"*A rug that can fly across the sea?* Tazurt thought.

"'I do not believe you,' Tazurt said quickly. 'If you are truly the Caliph's son, then very well: I will give you my master's name and you can buy me. But you must prove it.'

"Abd al-Jabbar laughed. 'Is that your only requirement? Any of my companions can attest to who I am.'

"'How will I know that they are not lying for your sake?'

"'Come with me and I will show you the palace of the Madinat az-Zahra where you will live.'

"'I cannot travel out of the city,' Tazurt said, finally wresting her arm away. 'Besides, how will I know you have not simply bribed the guards to allow you in? If you bring me before the Caliph, I will believe you.'

"Abd al-Jabbar flushed. 'Bring another man's concubine so that my father might bear witness to my identity? And become the laughingstock of the court?'

"'Very well. You claim you are a man of great wealth, with countless treasures?'

"'I am.'

"Tazurt pointed to the bridge that swooped over al-Wadi al-Kabir and connected the Great Mosque, with its persimmon-striped arches, to the Alcazar's palm gardens and deep green pools. 'Meet me in the center of the Roman Bridge at midnight with your flying rug. If you are indeed the Caliph's son and possess such a gift, I will give you my name and that of my master. Is this acceptable?'

"Abd al-Jabbar, more astonished than anything, nodded.

"Tazurt held a finger up. 'One more thing. You must come alone.'

"Abd al-Jabbar murmured his agreement. Tazurt, suddenly breathless, hastened into the souk, looking over her shoulder until the crowd was too thick to see the prince, who was still rooted where she had left him.

"After finishing her shopping, Tazurt returned to the scribe's home, giving the cucumber and celery for the night's *barida* to the cook and the thread to the wife's maid.

"Clenching her jaw to restrain her excited grin, Tazurt pulled from her trunk her thickest wrapper to keep her warm in the sky and over the sea. In its pockets, she placed a knife pilfered from the cook and a pearl comb and ruby ring gifted from the scribe. This was the sum of her possessions from her three years in Córdoba.

"She spent the rest of the day half-heartedly stitching her mistress's torn shawl and walking listlessly around the house. When the scribe returned home, she was distant and pled her menstruation. After 'Isha, the home darkened, the scribe joined his wife in their room, and Tazurt slipped into the street.

"It was late, but Tazurt was not alone on Córdoba's illumined streets. A few men passed her but paid no mind. When she finally saw the moon glinting on the river, she released her held breath. A lone figure stood in the bridge's center. Tazurt was too far to see whether the rug was with him. Feeling the knife in her pocket, she met the prince on the Roman Bridge.

"Seeing her, the veiled prince said, 'I brought the carpet.' Looking down, Tazurt saw she stood on a rug. Even in the moonlight, its unique beauty was obvious: set against an ocean-dark blue, a tawny honeycomb pattern was stamped through the center and bordered with all manner of astonishing flying creatures: *buraq*, griffins, *anqa*, rokhs.

"Nonetheless, Tazurt said coolly, 'You have brought a carpet, but have you brought a flying carpet?'

"The prince sat at her feet. 'Up!' The carpet rose beneath Tazurt, who nearly fell off, and hovered above the bridge.

"'Ya Allah!'

"The prince laughed at the expression on her beautiful face. The tattoo in her forehead's center darkened as she furrowed her brow. Carefully, Tazurt sat cross-legged, far from the edge. 'Can it truly cross seas?' Her palms flashed hot and cold.

"'Indeed,' the prince said, basking in the concubine's awe.

"'Fly it over Córdoba then.'

"The carpet rose higher and higher and wheeled over the Great Mosque and its green gardens. From so high, the Mosque looked like a child's toy. *Surely, this is what Allah sees!* Tazurt thought.

"'Can I make it fly?' she asked.

"The prince, sure of his victory, said, 'Just command it.'

"'Fly over the Alcazar,' Tazurt said, and the carpet zipped across the shining al-Wadi al-Kabir. Her eyes wept with cold and wind.

"'Do you believe me now?' the prince asked.

"'Yes, I believe you. You are indeed the Caliph's son.' The carpet hovered above the Alcazar's pools, and she let the prince lower his veil and kiss her. As he fell into easy bliss, Tazurt opened her eyes and, with a great heave, pushed the prince. He scrabbled at her hands, and she clawed him away before tipping him into the dark pool.

"'What are you doing?' the splashing prince demanded, but under Tazurt's command, the carpet ascended. 'Take me home,' she whispered, bundling her wrapper close. The wind whistled past her ears as the carpet raced through the stardust sky into the endless horizon."

Dunya picks the last two notes, and they float lazily.

"Would her family really take her back after she had been used as a concubine for so many years?" Mahperi asks.

"Perhaps they would be so relieved to see their daughter they would ask no questions. Or if they asked questions, their relief would be greater than their shock."

"Or perhaps her family would cast her out," Mahperi says.

"And then Tazurt would take the rug and make a new life elsewhere. But I think her family would be overjoyed."

Mahperi inclines her head. "You are the storyteller—and the women in your tales are always lucky."

I feel my mouth shrinking.

Catching my eye, Mahperi quickly adds, "Oh, don't be hurt, Shaherazade. It was a lovely story. I was simply thinking that your happy ending would not be so easy in truth."

"It's not truth, Mahperi," Dunya says. "It's a story."

"You're right, Mahperi," I say, "Tazurt was lucky. She was not raped on her voyage to Córdoba, the scribe's wife was kind, the scribe was not rough, the prince did not abduct her and dispose of her, and she found a magic carpet that could take her home. Others can have their grisly tales. I give my Tazurt hope."

Twenty-Eight

◇◇◇◇◇

At last invited to one of Sitt Jalaliyya's feasts, a reception for a Frankish ambassador, I feel shabby, spying her diamond-and-pearl diadem wink boldly. She sits beside al-Afdal at a high table facing three rows of tables weighed with pigeon stewed with quince, lamb sour with pomegranate juice and sumac, kid in a sauce of asafetida and citron, rice with white beans and cassia, puddings of bread and rice and rose water and cinnamon, and spikenard-spiced peach sharbat. The aromas make my stomach rumble.

A small table for the Ayyubid and Seljuk noblewomen, all silken and lustrous, is set apart by carved wooden screens. Dunya, sitting farther down with Mahperi, waves me over. Nervously, I look for Shahryar, but he is not there. I recall Sitt Jalaliyya's distaste for my husband.

Dunya giggles as Mahperi's forehead and nose flush. Catching my eye, Dunya says over the *ney* strains of a popular melody, "Come, Shaherazade, help me guess. Mahperi has a suitor and she won't tell me who."

"A suitor?" I am surprised at the sternness in my voice—why do I sound like a matron of forty?

It is said that a djinn fell in love with a temperamental daughter of Damascus, who said unto him, "I will love you only if you become a horse," and so he became the finest thoroughbred stallion in Sham. "No," she said, "a palace," and he transformed into a marvelous marble palace, dripping with sculpted stucco. "No," she said, "a baghla," and he morphed into a deep-bellied baghla with billowing lateen sails . . .

"He's not a Seljuk, that much I have discovered."

"Oh stop, Dunya!" Mahperi wails.

"Do you think it's Saifuddin?" Dunya elbows me, glancing at the Sultan's brother who leans over to Saladin, his rose-colored turban bent in serious conversation.

"You're being disrespectful, Dunya." But I cannot deny how good it is to see my sister light and mischievous once more. "How did you meet him, Mahperi?"

But Mahperi only buries her pomegranate-red face in her hands.

"Well, you'll need to tell us soon enough." Dunya bites into her rice, her ruby and gold rings sparkling as she waves. "You'll want to get married, and when you do, you'll need Shahryar's blessing, and to get Shahryar's blessing, you'll need Shaherazade's intercession."

Biting my lip, I consider how much my intercession would now be worth. My husband and I have not spoken in a week. Each passing day raises the chasm harboring the fears of my first married nights closer to the surface.

Taking mercy on the writhing Mahperi, Dunya changes the topic. "What do you make of Malikric's conference with Saifuddin?"

The camp hums with news of Saifuddin's meeting with Malikric at the front lines, in which they sat together nearly the whole day, each eating dishes of the other's homeland, and then parted on good terms. I cannot understand how these men meet as friends one day and converge the next to kill each other. It reminds me of ibn Shaddad's odd tale of dancing warriors and the boys' battle.

"I heard Malikric hopes to meet with Sultan Saladin," Mahperi offers. "Do you suppose it will happen?"

As she speaks, I feel my neck prickle and turn to see Sitt Jalaliyya watching me inscrutably. Turning away, I shrug off the itch of her gaze.

"Sultan Saladin sent an emissary to the Lionheart to decline," an older Ayyubid noblewoman supplies, "saying that kings should not battle each other after breaking bread and promising to meet once the war is settled."

Dunya and Mahperi fall silent. I look over my shoulder as a servant, a carnation veil draped over her black curls, approaches us. "Sitt Jalaliyya requests that I bring you to her tent," she says to me, her harelip wobbling with each word.

When Dunya and Mahperi follow, the servant says, "Sitt Jalaliyya wants only her."

I cannot imagine why. "They come with me."

The girl rolls her eyes and leads us to Sitt Jalaliyya's tent. Whispers buzz. I glance to the high table and meet Sitt Jalaliyya's frosty eye.

In the tent, I take a low saddled seat while Dunya and Mahperi sit on floor cushions embroidered with blue and red flowers. Dunya runs her fingers along the silk weave of the rug beneath her. The servant girl clears her throat and Dunya snatches her fingers away.

"Saladin's daughter-in-law does not stint," Dunya whispers. Indeed, every piece in the tent, from the teak trunks to the gold necklaces scattered on her bed, is of the finest workmanship.

The tent opens, and I smell the floral attar of *ghaliyya*. Sitt Jalaliyya enters, her diamond-and-pearl diadem shining like a starstruck halo. Al-Afdal, who seems as surprised to see the three of us awaiting his wife as I am to see him, follows her. Sitt Jalaliyya takes a leather stool across from me and regards me down the length of her nose.

"Why have you summoned me?"

My question sounds petulant. I should have waited for her to speak.

Sitt Jalaliyya does not answer immediately. She scans the room—her eyes moving from me to Dunya to Mahperi to her husband. Ruefully, she twists her mouth. "There have been rumors about you, Shaherazade Khatun."

Atsiz.

My head thunders. "You should say what you mean."

Pearl strands click as she tilts her head askance, a cat waiting for a mouse to emerge from its nest. "I hope my husband can enlighten us."

Her husband?

"I cannot begin to imagine." Al-Afdal's mouth twists into a laconic half-smile. "Nor do I have the leisure for your harem intrigues."

"I have held my tongue only for the sake of our cause—but no more, not when *you* have the impudence to attend my dinner without your husband." Sitt Jalaliyya's eyes dart to al-Afdal and then to me.

"Do you think"—I swallow down relieved, frenetic laughter—"that your husband and I . . . ?" I would thank Allah that her accusation missed its mark if that did not seem sacrilegious.

Her long face, with its high cheekbones and higher forehead, reddens with choler, reminding me that a false rumor is still dangerous.

Before she can speak, al-Afdal says, "Have you taken leave of your senses, Jalaliyya? You believe that I am carrying on with the wife of one of my father's allies? I have spoken to the girl, what—once? Twice?"

Sitt Jalaliyya applauds. "Very good. Almost believable. As if I don't smell strange attar on you when you return at night."

Now, it is al-Afdal's turn to flush, and my stomach sinks. If I am captured in some tangle of *his* infidelity . . .

"This seems like a matter of your own marriage," I say, "in which I have no part. We will leave." Rising, I gesture for Dunya and Mahperi to follow, but the harelipped servant blocks the way.

"Sit," Sitt Jalaliyya snaps. Mahperi falls to the floor, although Dunya and I remain straight-backed and standing.

"You deny it, but one of your own trusted companions has testified to the truth."

My own confusion is reflected in Mahperi and Dunya's furrowed brows. What enemies do I have? It does not matter—there is false testimony that I am an adulteress, testimony so believable that even the Sultan's own daughter-in-law is persuaded. I try to master the panic that threatens to glaze sight and sound.

"I swear to you, whatever you have heard is false and whoever has told you this is a liar."

Fataneh's blood rises to my ankles.

Sitt Jalaliyya's long fingers remain clenched. "Then why would Mahperi Khatun, your companion so trusted that she sits here, tell me this?"

The ocean crashes in my ears and my mouth fills with its salt. I whip around. Mahperi folds her legs to her chest, fixing her gaze on her bare feet. "Mahperi?"

I wait for her to call Sitt Jalaliyya a liar, but yards and yards of cotton seem to have replaced her tongue.

"I cannot understand you." I bite each word. *Who is she, this liar I have known my whole life? Who has traveled with me across worlds, across oceans of sand, through nights and days?*

Mahperi traces the carpet's red-and-blue arabesques. Her mouth quavers, but she says nothing. I want to shake her until the teeth clatter from her mouth and her reason for these falsehoods tumbles out with them. Finally, Mahperi shakes her head and whispers, "I lied." She covers her face.

Sitt Jalaliyya plies Mahperi's hands away so we can all see her blotchy cheeks, shining nose, running eyes. I despise her for her fragility. I think of captured Fataneh, composed to the end.

"Do you swear it?" Sitt Jalaliyya demands.

"*Wallahi,*" she murmurs.

"And this is no ploy?" Sitt Jalaliyya turns to us.

Shaking with anger, I say, "I swear it."

"I vouchsafe my sister's word." Dunya leans forward, daring Sitt Jalali-yya to find a lie. "I swear it by the Qur'an."

"Girls get bored in battle," al-Afdal says, "and they spin deceit for their own amusement." He gives Mahperi a withering look, and she crumples further.

Sitt Jalaliyya glances sharply at Mahperi. "The punishment for a false accusation of *zina* is lashing. I hope you rebuke your *companion* strongly, Shaherazade Khatun. For your own sake."

Mahperi stands, her arms crossed over her stomach, head bent. Although she weeps, I cannot tell if it is for herself or for the gamble she played with my and al-Afdal's lives. Why would she do such a thing? What would have happened if Sitt Jalaliyya had taken her claims as true and lit a fire with this rumor that ran from Shahryar to Sultan Saladin to the troops themselves? Shahryar and Sultan Saladin would have been divided; al-Afdal exiled; I murdered; and the discord would have spiraled from the commanders to the army—fitnah enough to crack our resis-tance against the Franks.

This last thought clicks it into place.

"Did a Frank put you up to this?"

She does not deny it. She presses her lips, and the rage I have reined in slips. My hand burns and a red print blooms on her cheek. I remember that we are in Sitt Jalaliyya and al-Afdal's tent, and yank Mahperi out. Her arm feels like rubber. Dunya follows quietly. Al-Afdal and Sitt Jalaliyya are left in shock. Without a doubt, Saladin will know soon.

In Dunya and Mahperi's tent, Dunya lights lamps that shine on the wet kohl that has tracked down Mahperi's cheeks. But in my heart, where there would be sympathy, there is only marble and steel. Mahperi sits where I point on the rug. She hugs her crisscrossed legs to her chest, burying her lying face between them.

I search for the prisoner's name, the one who'd made Mahperi glow, the one, I realize, who had bowed to her as we'd walked to the church. "Did Humphrey of Toron tell you to lie to Sitt Jalaliyya, Mahperi?"

Her jaw juts in stubborn silence.

"Tell me, Mahperi. Tell me the whole truth. You will have an easier time of it with me than with Shahryar or Sultan Saladin."

She clutches her legs tighter, her green trousers peeking beneath the spilling pink of her robe. She looks like a little girl, and I remember running through the citadel with her, our arms full of hyacinths from the gardens, our mouths sweet with halva.

"How could you do this?" Dunya demands, crouching beside Mahperi, her indigo tunic pooling around her. "How could you betray Shaherazade? How could you try to derail Sultan Saladin's efforts? All for what? A Frank? A *married, lying infidel?*"

Mahperi hides her eyes.

"And he told you to spread the lie about Shaherazade?"

"Yes."

"Did you not consider the danger to me?" I ask.

She buries her face in the mountains of her knees. "I don't know."

"And you had no care for our cause?"

Mahperi raises her head. "Why would I care? What difference is it to me if the Franks rule Jerusalem or if Saladin does? I have never been a Dunya to you, or a Hanna or a Laila. But Humphrey promised me that I would be one of his wives once the Crusaders won."

Is this my fault then? Should I have cherished her more deeply, or put her in the path of someone who would have, instead of leaving her vulnerable to a snake like the Frank? The steel in my heart begins to bend.

"Franks don't have multiple wives, stupid," Dunya snaps. "The best you could hope to be is his Saracen concubine—which I suppose you are."

"Dunya . . ." I warn. "Did he put you up to anything else?"

"No, Shaherazade," Mahperi whispers.

I do not know if I believe her.

"I warned you, did I not, to be wary of him?"

She slumps. "Yes, Shaherazade."

"Yet you let him use you, let him corrupt your very soul?"

"Yes, Shaherazade."

For all that she was willing to do for him, she does not defend Humphrey, does not deny that he lied and used her, does not claim that he loves her. How easily she is persuaded that he never cared for her.

I take her hand, wet with tears. "You must go before Sultan Saladin, Mahperi. Tell him everything."

Dunya's arms are folded, but even she frowns as Mahperi begins heaving deep, shuddering sobs.

Despite my fury, I feel tears rise. "Dunya, go with a mamluk and bring the Malik to Saladin's tent."

After Dunya departs, I say to Mahperi, "Be honest with the Sultan. He will be merciful."

"And you?" A sob scratches Mahperi's throat. "And the Malik?" She falls to her knees, pounds the earth, weeping so loudly that surely the sound careens across the camp. "And Pader—?" The rest dies in a gasping gurgle.

My hand hesitates briefly at her cheek before I slap her a second time. "Be calm, Mahperi." I hold her face. "You plotted against Saladin and his army. Meet him with some dignity."

Like Fataneh. Chin raised, eyes clear and unfaltering.

She fights to control herself, but bubbles into tears again. I wipe her face with my veil and guide her outside. For a moment, I am again in Bam, swaddling Altunjan in soft words and sending her to death.

I swallow and hold Mahperi's shaking shoulders. I meet her gazelle eyes, large and frightened. "Mahperi: so long as you are honest and forthright with the Sultan, no harm will come to you. You are my liege woman and under my protection."

Her nails scrabble at my arms. "Oh no! Shaherazade! Humphrey cannot know that I have betrayed him. Please. I have told you. Do not make me confess before Sultan Saladin."

Her weeping resumes, but I feel my anger rise and my patience wane. I wrap Dunya's weasel-lined cloak around me and yank Mahperi out of the tent and to her fate.

As we approach Saladin's glowing tent, Mahperi twists away like a fish on a line.

"I cannot protect you if you do not cooperate," I hiss.

She slackens, her courage dying after one half-hearted escape attempt.

How do events always manage to spin so wildly out of my control and always in the same way? But not this time, not for this girl I grew up with. I squeeze her clammy hand. She is a traitor and a fool, but she has also been my friend since childhood, who crossed the world to be my damsel. I cannot abandon her, not now. I am Shaherazade Khatun, and it will be so. I raise my chin and will myself to believe my bravado. My heart beats in time with Mahperi's as we enter.

Humphrey of Toron stands in front of a tribunal of Saladin, al-Afdal, Sitt Jalaliyya, and Shahryar. His shoulders are relaxed, his face a mask of arch amusement. Mahperi and I join him. I wrest my hand from Mahperi and take the empty cushion beside Shahryar. He does not acknowledge my presence. From my seat, Mahperi and Humphrey look small. She sidles to him, but he stands stiffly. She pulls away.

"My son and daughter-in-law have relayed the most . . . perplexing tale." Sultan Saladin's almond eyes are sharp and weighing, prepared to peel skin and muscle and bone to arrive at the truth. "Shameful rumors regarding Shaherazade Khatun and my son, Mahperi Khatun spreading them at Humphrey of Toron's behest. Lies disseminated to cause fitnah in service of the Franks."

"Your Grace cannot believe that I would dishonor your hospitality and gentleness so," Humphrey says in silky Arabic, turning his hands upward in honest supplication. "Even if you would believe such insolence of me, at least credit me the wit to not entrust this task to a woman." He pauses. "Mahperi Khatun is prone to moods and to see truths for untruth and untruths for truth."

I am overcome with the desire to rip his wet, lying tongue from his wet, lying mouth.

"You are very familiar with her ways," Sitt Jalaliyya says. Her eyes are serene above the veil she has drawn against the infidel, her point sharp.

Shahryar's attention darts between Sitt Jalaliyya and Mahperi. Even after all these months as his wife, I cannot guess his thoughts.

"I saw her but in passing in the Seljuk Khatun's company, but I am a keen observer."

I do not know if Humphrey's lies have satisfied Sultan Saladin, whose visage is carefully equanimous.

"Mahperi Khatun, did you falsely tell Sitt Jalaliyya that Shaherazade Khatun and my son were unlawfully involved?"

Mahperi looks at the floor and then our knees. "I did, O Sultan." Without prompting, she speaks an unstinting truth, detailing her loneliness, chance meetings with Humphrey that grew into something more, the promises he slipped into her ears, treacherous notes he slipped into her hand. "I lied to Sitt Jalaliyya and I carried messages between Humphrey and Frankish scouts."

The Frank's lips whiten until they match the color of his face.

"What messages?" Sultan Saladin asks gently.

Drawing a breath, Mahperi wraps her arms around her waist. "Humphrey asked that I read Shaherazade Khatun's chronicle after council and convey battle plans and discussions to Humphrey, who would write messages for me to provide to Frankish scouts."

Humphrey looks as though he would cleave Mahperi from skull to navel. Cold sweeps through me as I think of the times I found Mahperi waiting for me in Shahryar's tent or when I left the chronicle visible, of the times I never thought to ask.

Mahperi's treachery pulses between us all.

Sultan Saladin's sympathy winks out like a doused lamp. "This is treason. For this, you should face death."

Mahperi blanches and looks at me beseechingly. I know what I promised her, but I resist keeping my word for her, who cannot fall to her knees and beg forgiveness herself. But there sits Shahryar, whole and well, and sometimes mercy is not fair. A hundred wasps buzz in my stomach.

"Mahperi has committed a grave crime and she has confessed," I pronounce. "If you were to ask, O Sultan, she would kneel before you and beg your mercy."

Mahperi folds her legs beneath her, as in prayer, and clasps her hands. "O please, Sultan Saladin. Take mercy upon me. I have sinned and I have erred and I am not deserving of your mercy, but still, I beg it."

"She has been a fool and so should be punished, but she is no soldier," I say. "She is a sheltered girl, brought into a wild world, who fell into a Frankish snare. A soldier can be caught in an enemy's trap and so Mahperi was caught. But a soldier would not be executed for that."

"But you still think she should be punished," Sitt Jalaliyya notes. "One does not punish a trapped soldier."

I think quickly. "A soldier trapped because of his foolishness deserves a reprimand."

"What *reprimand* do you think would fit Mahperi Khatun's . . . misstep?" Sultan Saladin asks, turning to me.

If I am to credibly guide Mahperi's sentence, then I cannot be lenient. Even from where I sit, I can see Mahperi shake. I glance at Sitt Jalaliyya. "The punishment for a false accusation of zina is lashing. Send Mahperi Khatun back to Kirman in shame. Bar her from Ayyubid lands. Write to her father of what she has done."

As Mahperi begins to sob again, I think that perhaps I have devised the cruelest punishment of all.

"What do you think of this, Malik Shahryar?" Sultan Saladin asks coolly. "Your negligence too is to blame here."

My fingernails dig into my palms.

Shahryar hangs his head, but I do not miss his hard glance toward me. "I beg forgiveness that I brought her to you, O Sultan. The girl is a traitor, but a fool and a young one at that. Shaherazade Khatun's sentence seems just."

Sultan Saladin stares at Mahperi and she shrivels beneath his gaze, a snail scattered with salt. "I will consider it."

Before I can offer, Sitt Jalaliyya, cutting her eyes at me, persuades Sultan Saladin to place Mahperi in her charge. Humphrey is decreed to be gagged and bound hand and foot at all times.

As for Humphrey's life, there is no question of its security.

Twenty-Nine

◇◇◇◇◇

The muscles in Shahryar's bare shoulders tauten as he whips his sham-shir over his mamluk's head, bringing the blade to a halt before it splits the man's skull. The mamluk's pulse hops like a hare in his throat as he exhales. Shahryar turns at my gasp, handing his sword to the mamluk. He regards me expectantly, and I manage the courage to ask, "Have Sultan Saladin or al-Afdal said anything of Mahperi?"

Shahryar shakes his head.

Two weeks have passed since Mahperi's trial, and camp has moved from Ramla to the ancient hills of Tel Jezer, where almost two decades ago the Franks routed Sultan Saladin. Sitt Jalaliyya has permitted Dunya and me only one glimpse of Mahperi, hands bound in a rough tent, eyes swollen. In the meantime, and perhaps directly due to Mahperi's impris-onment, we have begun winning skirmishes against the Franks, our camp brimming with red-faced Frankish prisoners. I try not to think about the Muslim lives that Mahperi's betrayal has cost.

Whether the Sultan's delay shows an inclination toward mercy or a time for contemplation before execution, I cannot guess.

"Have you spoken to Saladin on her behalf?"

Shahryar shakes his head again.

"Will you go? Please. Her father placed her under our protection."

"I am not alone in the blame."

Shame heats my neck, for I know I failed Mahperi as Khatun, failed her father who entrusted her to me despite himself. I think now, too late, of the measures I could have taken to safeguard her. "I know, Shahryar," I whisper.

He grunts.

"We must make this right, and perhaps I should not say this . . ."

"Please, do not begin holding your tongue now." There is vinegar in his voice.

I take a breath. "You murdered three girls without right and without cause.

"You sinned and flouted the law: but you will not be punished in this world and even rivers of gold would be inadequate blood money to recompense their families. But you *can* save Mahperi and balance the scale against one of the lives you took."

Shahryar stays quiet.

"Tell Sultan Saladin that Mahperi is your liege woman and only you can decide her fate. Tell him it is time for the Seljuk army to be released. He may be commander of the army, but you hold power over your own people."

Shahryar raises his eyebrows. "You want me to challenge the Sultan?"

I cannot help my hard stare. How easily he exercised despotic power over Bam in the days of his rage, and how he quails now at asserting his rights before the Sultan. Before I know what I am saying, I tell him: "Mard bash."

As I storm away, anxiety replaces anger, fizzing from my stomach to my ears. The buzz of heady rumor, that the Khatun publicly upbraided the Malik, follows me through the camp. Smoothing my brow, I try to appear as if all is peace, but my blood simmers. I feel tugged toward *something* that can cool it.

Finding myself standing before his tent, I realize who I am looking for: Atsiz. But he's not here. The sun warming my braids, I drift around the camp, even going so far as to stroll past Nurani's tent.

Deserted.

I imagine them at some assignation spot, and then viciously thrust the thought away.

My mamluks trailing me, I leave the camp and stride over Tel Jezer's endlessly voluptuous emerald hills, passing a long-bearded shepherd tending his flock of cotton sheep.

And there, like a shepherd from a tale himself, sits Atsiz, leaning against a thickly twisted olive trunk, book in hand. I squint. *Leili o Majnun*, Nizami's new verse about the Bedouin poet driven djinn-mad by his love for the unattainable Leila. Seeing me, Atsiz pockets the small book in his forest-green overcoat.

He rises. "Durood, Shaherazade Khatun."

My heart hammers. "Salaam, Emir Atsiz."

He appraises me, our last conversation filling his leaf-green eyes and the space between us. But then he asks, "What is it?" and his voice, deep and tender, sweeps the discomfort away and once more, we are only Shaherazade and Atsiz and all is easy between us.

I tell him of what passed with Shahryar. "Ay Atsiz, why does Shahryar delay seeking the release of Mahperi and the army?"

Sighing, Atsiz runs his fingers through his dark hair. "I do not know, but Sultan Saladin . . . rebuked Shahryar again for allowing the Mahperi situation . . ." He searches for the right word. "To fester."

"He must be persuaded."

"You don't need to convince me, Shaherazade," Atsiz says heavily. "The emirs are united, and even Shahryar agrees in council. His bravery is second to none on the battlefield, but he delays presenting his claim to the Sultan and does not tell us when he will."

I think of the hot breath of the Oghuz on Bam, fine sand spilling through a sandglass, Mahperi, small and alone, as the great men of the world decide whether she will live. "Will you try again?"

Atsiz bows, his fingertips touching his heart. "I am your servant. In this, and in all things."

Despite the autumn chill and the softly crushing weight of the world, I feel my skin heat, as though brushed by a djinn's fiery fingers.

* * *

He has done it. Shahryar has done it, with all the finesse of an ax. I rush toward Sultan Saladin's tent, Atsiz's hastily whispered story ringing in my ears.

Trampling into the Sultan's tent, Shahryar declared before al-Afdal and Saifuddin that the Sultan had usurped his power by preventing him from deciding Mahperi's fate, violated his sovereignty by keeping the Seljuk army in Palestine. Sultan Saladin allowed him to speak, and once Shahryar had spent himself, Sultan Saladin directed his mamluk with an imperious flick to escort Shahryar out and decreed that Shahryar was enjoined from his presence.

I did this. Pushed Shahryar, once more, to the brink of destruction. Asked his closest emir to pressure him. Spat *Mard bash*, knowing what those words conjured.

And now, I must fix it.

A mamluk stands guard outside Saladin's softly glowing tent, the ocher Ayyubid banner fluttering above.

"Is Sultan Saladin within? I have come to speak to him about my husband."

The mamluk goes inside, and I hear the ghosts of my words echo within. The mamluk reappears and bows. Torchlight catches on the red acne scars pocking his cheeks. "Marhaba."

Without emirs and princes and maliks and traitors crowding it, the tent extends in vast emptiness. A glass of tea steams in Saladin's large hand, his broad fingers decorated with silver scars from a lifetime of war. Ibn Shaddad sits on a cushion, his thick chronicle spread in his lap. His qalam swims over the page, leaving a swirling trail of black ink. I hesitate, but instead of turning me away, Sultan Saladin and ibn Shaddad rise.

"Welcome, Shaherazade Khatun," Sultan Saladin says with a warmth that pushes me off-balance.

A servant offers me a glass of tea. I clutch its heat between my breasts.

Ibn Shaddad's hand remains poised over the chronicle, and I am tempted to ask him to lower it. But if ibn Shaddad writes of this, no matter how I die—a husband's sword, a Frankish mace, an Oghuz arrow, or illness and old age with no renown—I will live in the annals of history, a woman, like Turkan Khatun, who dared enter the world of men.

And my tales? Crafted in the belly of the harem that saved my life and the lives of other women? But women's achievements are not accorded the same glory as men's. But then: a woman's words can drive a man to break with his commander; a man's actions can spur the spinning of tales in the harem, tales that spin out and bring me into the womb of war, before the greatest commander Muslims have known since Prophet Muhammad himself.

I meet the Sultan's eye, and my head lightens into a storyteller's trance. "O Sultan, I have come to ask two favors. I know this is much to ask, so in return I offer a tale. I know that is a poor exchange, but I have little else. O Sultan, if you are amenable: Will you hear the tale first or my requests?"

Silence stretches until my neck grows hot.

"Let us hear your requests, so we can judge whether your tale is fair compensation."

I am pleasantly surprised that he did not cordially eject me.

"The first of my requests is that you spare my friend's life. Let me send her far from here, back to her parents, where she can do no further damage."

"She would be safer under my care."

I envision Mahperi in a tower surrounded by a flat, golden plain.

Months and years pass, and still Saladin fights the infidels and still she cannot leave. The door creaks in the wind and she thinks of jumping. Perhaps she will land on her hands and knees like a cat and run and run until she reaches Kirman. Or perhaps she will break her neck. She retreats from the ledge. How can she face Allah's judgment after her treason? Her back prickles and a silken cord snares her throat until her eyes blacken and the Ayyubid house is discharged of responsibility for a little-known noblewoman of a little-known province of a sultanate burning itself into ashes.

"What is your second request?"

"Release the Seljuk army, O Sultan. Have mercy upon us and release us to fight for Kirman."

Sultan Saladin wears his judge's mask, calm and patient. "These are weighty requests. I hope your tale can meet the burden."

I know Sultan Saladin is a good man, a just man. But he is a man single-minded in his thirst for victory; his destruction of Ascalon, Ramla, and an-Natrun proves that. Single-mindedness is required for greatness, and Sultan Saladin is, above all else, a man anointed for destiny.

I close my eyes and feel gold and silver, moonlight and starlight, pulse through my veins, course through my legs, flicker to my fingers, dazzle my eyes, rob my breath. If this is a thousandth of what the Prophet felt when the Angel Gibrail embraced him in Mount Hira, then I can understand why he fell to his knees and wept.

In the name of my Lord, I recite:

———————

"O Sultan, they say—and Allah knows better—that there is a story of past times and past peoples that is best suited to men of intelligence and understanding. In the city of Mogadishu resided a druggist called Hassan. He had one good eye, one good ear, one wife, and seven children, alternating boy and girl.

"Hassan was Mogadishu's most prominent pharmacist and princes numbered among his customers, so he was unsurprised when, late in the evening, a man and a woman in glittering vestments entered his premises. But he *was* surprised by their beauty: sable, lustrous, and perhaps, infernal.

"The woman reached for Hassan and he felt himself fall into a languorous spell, as though he had spent too long in the sun or drunk too deeply of palm wine.

"'You do not recall us,' she smirked.

"'I do not, milady.'

"Hassan woke the next morning, in his own bed, with no recollection of how or when he reached home.

"'You have been here all night, my love,' his wife said. But on each of his fingers he found rings: ruby, emerald, sapphire, diamond. He gawped and his wife exclaimed, 'Is my husband a gambler? A thief?'

"Hassan could only stare at the small fortunes gleaming on his fingers. Although his wife was suspicious, she tucked the jewels away for the mahr of their sons' weddings and trousseaux of their daughters'.

"Hassan continued his day normally, weaving through the bustling streets to his limestone pharmacy. He lost himself in the rhythm of weighing powders and stirring liquids and greeting customers until the Maghrib azaan echoed. As he prepared to close his shop to join the prayer, a man and woman arrived.

"Hassan recognized them immediately, as dreams—nightmares—come to life.

"'You recall us,' the woman said, and the languor enfolded him again.

"Hassan awoke the next morning, in his own bed, with no recollection of how or when he reached home. 'You slept here all night,' his wife said, concerned. But on his wrists shone two ruby-studded gold cuffs. His wife bit them and they were indeed soft gold.

"Hassan returned to his pharmacy, and when the sky flushed dark, he mixed a tonic for wakefulness and memory and drank.

"'Why can I not recall you?' he asked when the man and woman entered.

"Smirking, the woman extended her hand, and Hassan followed the pair through winding streets until he grew dizzy, until the city lost its familiarity, until he squeezed through a sliver of an alleyway and was greeted with great green palace gates riveted with gold bolts. 'I remember this,' he murmured.

"'Of course you do,' the man said with a strange expression.

"The moonlit castle grounds were empty save for a large fountain, shaped like an eight-pointed star, that sprouted in the center. Without a word, the man and woman vanished into the pool. As the castle walls began to dissolve, Hassan ignored his misgiving and jumped in too.

"But the fountain's warm water only licked Hassan's ankles, and Hassan stared in horror as around him *something* became *nothing*. His stomach lodged in his throat as the marble gave way, and he fell into the fathomless dark for so long that time grew filament-thin then river-wide. When Hassan began to think that perhaps this was death after all, he thumped onto soft earth.

"The man and woman appeared. 'Yalla, our master waits.'

"Each step through the stygian tunnel touched a memory, and fear curdled in Hassan. As they pressed deeper, the tunnel warmed and then became hot, and the pharmacist shielded his eye against the heat. Still, they walked, until Hassan could go no farther and they stopped at a black wall four times his height.

"The wall rippled and a giant golden eye opened.

"'We have brought the pharmacist, ya Falak,' the man said.

"The man and woman had deposited Hassan before a man-eating serpent coiled around the earth's heart beneath the Realm of Fire. The Falak unhinged its jaw, and in its maw Hassan saw stars and galaxies and universes, endlessly spiraling, ready to emulsify him into dust.

"Instead, the serpent spoke, and its voice was slick and deep: 'Have him prepare my medicine.'

"Hassan noticed the pharmacist's station in the corner, ready with strange herbs and unfamiliar powders.

"'What am I making?' Hassan asked, trying to smooth the splintered edges of his words.

"The woman looked at him askance. 'What you always make, druggist.'

"Hassan stared at the station, his neck and ears prickling. He regretted taking his potion and avoided looking at the serpent, but felt its great eye upon him. He thought of his wife and his seven children, of death, and of being smashed into eternity without even a grave in which to await the Day of Judgment. He stared harder at the jars—jade liquid, lapis powder, purple herbs—willing recognition to stir. He fingered each container and when he picked up an indigo powder, something rang in him: the first ingredient. Step by step—indigo powder, dried green herbs, yellow blooms, silver liquid, black powder—Hassan measured and stirred, led by dream memory, until he held an opalescent elixir.

"Hassan handed it to the man. 'But what is it for?' he asked.

"When the Falak spoke, Hassan saw only a snake's white-ribbed cotton mouth. 'I am the Falak, the swallower of universes, destroyer of worlds. Only the One, the Maker of all the Heavens and all the Earths, is more powerful. Only He stops me from consuming this world and its universe. But with your elixir, my power will match his.'

"Thus midwifed Hassan the greatest blasphemy of the age.

"Hassan's fear-dried lips rasped as he began reciting the Verse of the Throne:

'There is no god but Allah, the Living, the Eternal
'Neither slumber nor sleep overtake him
'Whatever is in the Heavens belongs to him and whatever is
in the Earth . . .'

"Ya Allah, Hassan prayed, *Please draw Your eye upon this evil and halt it and forgive me for helping it.*

"The Falak vibrated irritably. 'The druggist invokes Him. Return him to his home. When you bring him tomorrow, he must not behave like this.'

"Hassan woke the next morning in his own bed, a thick gold band twinkling with black cacherons tight at his neck, suffocated by the realization that he would be abducted night after night until the Falak's strength equaled Allah's and the serpent decimated Creation in his starred bowels.

"Weeping, Hassan implored Allah for mercy and, in his good ear, he heard: *You cannot let this happen.* Whether it was an angel or his own soul, Hassan did not know. He knew only that he had no choice but to obey."

Sultan Saladin stares, mouth parted, and even ibn Shaddad has lowered his pen. I feel as if I have run up and down the tel of Bam seven times.

"And then?"

"I have made two requests, O Sultan. If you grant them, I will complete the tale."

Impatiently, he drums his knees. "I cannot release a military force on the back of an unfinished tale."

Demurely, I look at the crimson carpet, tracing a dark vine to where it bursts into woven gold-and-blue blossoms. The drumming amplifies.

"Not when Malikric is poised to march on Jerusalem."

I try to stifle the voice—Shaitaan's whispers—reproving me that I am a fool to dream that I can succeed, so arrogant as to believe that my stories have cachet in the realm of soldiers and dinars.

"However, I will transfer your friend to your custody. But my steward will oversee her return to Bam."

In my shock, I am cloud-light; I float to the tent's ashen ceiling and then higher still, into the cold night sky. "Yes, O Sultan," I say, and quell the *waswasa* admonishing me that I cannot accomplish for the Seljuk army what I have for Mahperi.

The following evening, the man and woman did not fetch Hassan and he prayed that he was rid of them. But they came the next night and though he drank his potion, Hassan woke the next morning in his own bed with no recollection of how or when he had reached home, a gold coronet on his brow.

"That day, Hassan remained home, starting at shadows. In the evening, no one came, and Hassan dared believe that his small subterfuge had deterred the Falak. To be safe, Hassan hid for a second day, but he heard a knock after Maghrib. Before he could cry a warning, his eldest daughter, Iman, opened the door and called for him.

"On his threshold stood the woman and man. At his stern look, Hassan's daughter fled.

"'Why do you hide?' the woman asked, her smile pearly and pointed. Hassan shuddered with quicksilver fear at bringing the beast's servants to his home.

"'I have been ill. Are you customers?'

"'You do not remember us?' But Hassan could tell the man sensed his lie.

"'I have seen you before. In my pharmacy,' Hassan answered carefully, and the couple seemed satisfied.

"'Come,' and Hassan could not refuse.

"Hassan woke the next morning in his own bed, with no recollection of how or when he reached home, his arms laden with lapis-studded bangles. As he willed himself to remember but produced neither glimmer nor shadow, his eldest daughter entered.

"Lanky-limbed, Iman had Hassan's face and a mind for algebra and geometry that took her tutor's breath away. Had she been born a boy, perhaps she would have been sent to the Nizamiyya in Persia or Al-Qarawine in Fez. But as a girl, Iman kept her father's accounts, and soon, when she married, she would do the same for her husband.

"'Where did you go, Aabe? I watched you leave,' Iman said. 'And although I waited all night, you did not return until Fajr. When I opened the door, you did not see me, but walked in like a man entranced.'

"He patted her clay-smooth cheek. 'Do not worry, my daughter. It is nothing,' for Hassan hated nothing more than seeing worry for him cloud his own child's eyes.

"But Iman did not believe her father. Before sunset, she donned her wrapper, tucking a sharp kitchen knife inside. She walked to her father's pharmacy, calculating degrees and hyperbolic functions for the lines of bakeries and butcheries, the angles of homes and madrasas, and the curves of coral archways and mosque domes.

"Approaching her father's pharmacy, she smelled its distinct mix of earthy herbs and sterile chemicals. Her Aabe's shadow bobbed on the pharmacy's packed-earth floor, and her heart swelled with affection.

"As Iman lurked, a man and woman, their beauty so otherworldly it bordered on ghastly, entered the pharmacy. Recognition shivered through her. Iman slunk deeper into the shadows and they reappeared, her father behind them. Moving at an improbable speed, they flickered in and out of Iman's vision like a mirage. Iman hastened to keep pace, but when she was almost upon them, they blinked out like a snuffed lamp.

"By now, Iman was in the unfamiliar deep of Mogadishu. She paced between the white coral homes, but saw no one; she patted the earth, but felt nothing.

"Then, she saw it. A single line, hair-fine, finger-long, of silver scar tissue in the air. Iman touched it and flinched as it burned hot and white. Examining it, Iman saw it was a string made of hundreds of twisted infinitesimal threads. She plucked one, and the line became a peephole that winked away.

"Steeling herself against their heat, Iman pulled the threads until a window opened, just wide enough for her to slip through.

"Iman entered a world of frosty lightning and thunder. She flinched as the sky flashed bone-white. Rain, cold and hard and unceasing, the likes of which she had seen only during the monsoon, lashed her wrapper. Before her was an eight-pointed fountain, filmed with rainwater, and around her, tall ramparts. Iman turned around.

"She was alone, the silver scar gone.

"Always rational, Iman paced the slicked black stone perimeter. She found the immense soaring wall to be unbroken by gate, door, or window. Shrinking, Iman sought what little shelter the wall offered and began to think. First, an exit had to exist, for if not, she would have found her father. Second, the walls had to serve one of two purposes: either to keep people in or to keep them out. Now, Iman reasoned, if the purpose was to keep people in, she would not be alone. Therefore, the wall must be barring people. But why? Because something within required protection, but other than Iman, there was only the fountain.

"Iman approached the fountain, stroked the slimy marble, tasted the silty rainwater. She rapped her knuckles on the marble and waded into the fountain's center. The water, surprisingly tepid, reached her ankles. But she could find nothing. She knew the key to her Aabe lay here. If it did not, then there was no answer and her Aabe was gone, and that Iman could not accept.

"Frustrated, Iman stomped her foot, and when she did, the water splashing at her shins swirled, lilac, cyan, jade. Gasping, she jumped and jumped until the water turned white, until her feet did not meet marble, until warm water filled her mouth, until white went black.

"Iman reemerged in a dirt tunnel, the only light a faint glow at its distant end. Heart drumming, she padded toward that beacon until the heat, hotter than the most scorching Mogadishu sun, dried her soaked wrapper. Still, she pressed on until she thought that somehow her calculations had erred.

"Then, the tunnel expanded into an illuminated cavern dripping with crystalline stalactites. With a jolt of relief, Iman saw her Aabe, but her heart sank at his vacant face. She spotted the man and woman standing at a gleaming wall of black-green jewels.

"The wall winked a great elliptical eye and flickered its black tongue. Iman barely bit down her scream.

"Sibilant, it announced, 'Another of the *Bani Adam* is here. Find her.'

"Hassan's head snapped up as Iman squirreled herself between two crystal pillars, but, in moments, the man and woman hauled her out with matching terrible smiles. As Iman tumbled before the serpent, her father dashed forth, sheltering his daughter's body with his own.

"'Ah,' the Falak said.

"The earth shook, and crystal stalactites rained on Iman and Hassan. The serpent opened its maw to reveal starry purple depths. 'Traitors.' The Falak lunged, its hot, scaly skin brushing Iman's cheek. She shrieked as it burned.

"'No!' Hassan yelled. 'We have done nothing—she has done nothing! If you must punish someone, punish me, but O Falak, spare her!'

"Iman thought quickly. 'O Falak, I have heard of your greatness and have been searching for you.'

"The snake fixed its eye on her. 'You have?'

"'O Falak, I beg you, let me be your handmaiden and serve you eternally.'

"'A lie.'

"'A lie? No, O Falak. Let me tell you true. I am a girl, but brilliant, I swear to you. Are you familiar with the mathematician al-Khwarizmi? I mastered his equations when I was eleven. Had I been a born a boy, I could have left my home, studied the mysteries of the numbers that compose our world, and left my name for history. But I am a girl, and my destiny is to tend to home and family. But with you, O Falak, I can serve greatness at last.'

"The Falak's tongue flicked out and tasted the truth of her words. 'You may be clever as you claim: you did find your way here.'

"The serpent opened its white mouth, and Iman braced herself. Instead, she heard a squeal and opened her eyes in time to see the beautiful woman vaporized in the snake's mouth.

"'Do not retreat now,' the Falak said.

"'What will you have me do?' Iman asked, imagining the worst: flinging her Aabe into the serpent's mouth, bringing her mother and siblings as sacrifice.

"'Take the druggist home with Wajdi. Wajdi, ensure, as always, that he remembers nothing. This time, give him our heaviest gold necklace. He has provided us much tonight.'

"'Wajdi ran his hands over Hassan's good eye, dazing him, and swept him out by the elbow. Iman scurried behind as Wajdi flowed through the tunnel and, with a murmured enchantment, created a silver door to the fountain. Wajdi pushed her father and Iman into its warm eddies and spoke again, opening mercurial threads to their home.

"'Careful,' Wajdi said, smiling cruelly, as he pushed them into Mogadishu. 'These windows can slice a man through.'

"Wajdi nudged Hassan toward the door and whipped back into the street, his black cloak flying like a thunderhead. Iman hastened to follow, fastidiously noting all that Wajdi did to arrive back at the fountain—where he stopped, his words, his gestures—and chanting them in her mind as she had memorized Qur'anic verses and algebraic formulae.

"'Ay, Wajdi,' Iman said as the fountain shimmered at Wajdi's familiar presence. 'Why did you find my Aabe?'

"'For the first time, Wajdi looked at Iman. 'Why so curious?' he asked.

"'We serve the same master. I should like to know what we do.'

"'We—that is, Roshnara, the girl that was once you, and I—tried for many years to create the elixir that would strengthen the Falak, but we are not chemists. Sometimes, our concoctions did nothing. Sometimes, they burned the Falak, dimming his stars. Tired of our incompetence, he sent us to find one able to do what he needed.'

"'But what happens to us when the Falak swallows the world? Will he not consume us too?' Iman asked.

"'Puckering his aristocratic brow, Wajdi decided, 'Of course not. We are his chosen.'

"'But where will we go when Creation rests in his belly?' Iman insisted.

"'Wajdi, as handsome and evil as he was stupid and blind, refused to figure the answer.

"'Instead, he whispered excitedly, 'Tomorrow, the Falak will take his final dose and become as strong as the Creator.'

"'And then?' Iman asked.

"'There will be no after.'"

"And then, Shaherazade Khatun?" Sultan Saladin's fingers curl at the edge of his scarlet cushion.

"My tale nears its end: O Sultan, say you will release the Seljuk army and I will finish it."

My heart falls as the Sultan shakes his head. After all this, what else did I expect? That a story would wield power over politics, over war? I've saved Mahperi's life. I do not know how I expected more.

His dark, almond eyes are emotionless. "I told you that I would not release an army on the back of an unfinished tale, Shaherazade Khatun."

The burden of my failure digs into my shoulders, nestles in my neck. Bam will be reduced to ashes without even a fight from its army, and my best, for I have given my best, couldn't sway its fate.

"Do you not trust me? Frankish kings and Arab emirs trust me, but you do not?"

I look at him and hope he does not see my tears. Men can weep for battles and comrades and their tears are not taken for weakness, but women do not have such luxury.

"Finish your tale and I will decide."

I want to say: *All I have is this tale. If I give it to you without securing my army's freedom, then what am I left to bargain with?* Instead, I clear my throat and begin again.

"That night, as she lay in her cot, Iman's mind whirred. When Wajdi's breathing softened into sleep, Iman crept into the tunnel, slinking until she came upon the dozing Falak twirled in the crevasse. As Iman approached, its eye opened, shining like yolk and fixing Iman like a hunter sighting a deer.

"'Have you come to slay me?' The Falak chuckled, an earth-shaking sound that grazed Iman's bones.

"When Iman found her voice, she said, 'O Falak, I come because Wajdi has told me that the potion my Aabe brews will make you the Creator's equal in strength.'

"'Do you fear that, *Bint Adam?*' the Falak asked.

"'O Falak, it is simple mathematics. Even a child could do the sum. If you are as strong as the Creator, then you negate Him. But the Creator has all of Creation, an army of angels and djinn. And you? All you have are myself and Wajdi. You see, you are outmatched.

"'And so, you have two options. Amass your own army, of demons, *nasnas, marid*, and ifrit, those sworn enemies of Allah, but that could require centuries, time enough for Him to destroy you. Or . . .' Iman let her voice trail off tantalizingly, inviting the Falak to complete the equation.

"'I must become stronger than the Creator.'

"Iman was astounded that the earth did not crack at the heresy as she said, 'Yes.'

"'It cannot be done,' the Falak replied, rearing its head as though something deep within that still commanded adherence to the Almighty was repulsed. But greed and pride muffled that short-lived protest. 'Tell me how.'

"Iman's heart raced. 'You know my Aabe's skill. He will be able to do this. I will persuade him to do as you command.'

"'Then do it,' the Falak said, 'but if you fail or lie, I will consume all you hold dear and it will be nothing to me.'

"Iman nodded coolly, grateful that the Falak did not flick its tongue and taste her putrid fear. At the tunnel's end, Iman found that Wajdi's enchantments rested easy in her mouth and she tumbled from the Falak's lair to the moonlit marble world of the fountain and then onto the threshold of her home. She tried the door and found it locked, so she rapped softly until Hassan opened the door.

"'Child . . .' Hassan caressed her cheek in wonder. 'I thought you had become his.' He peered behind her. 'Are you alone?'

"Although Iman wanted nothing more than to collapse into her father's arms, she said, 'Aabe, time runs short. The Falak prepares to consume the world.'

"Hassan tightened Iman's wrapper around her shoulders as if she were a small child being bundled against a chill night. 'Then we must flee. I will rouse your mother. Get your brothers and sisters. We will disappear.'

"Iman liked the thought. She imagined hiding with her family in a warm, nondescript village in the middle of a sunny savanna. Her mother would bake bread and her father would create tinctures. But although her father was a good pharmacist, surely others in the world were as skilled—better even. The Falak would find another, begin the process again, and at its conclusion blow the world out like a candle.

"'Aabe, there's nowhere to hide if it succeeds.'

"Hassan remembered the whisper in his good ear. 'I will not let that happen.'

"'Aabe, listen: the Falak can be hurt. Wajdi—the man, mentioned this. That potions burned the Falak. If so, then perhaps it can be killed.'

"Hassan touched his daughter's shoulder, already considering the poisons and acids in his pharmacy. 'Run back, Iman, before they doubt you. I must work tonight.'

"The next evening, Iman and Wajdi presented a trembling Hassan to the Falak. He offered a green glass bottle filled with a black potion, its dark so heavy that it absorbed the cavern's little light.

"'This will make me stronger than the Creator?' The serpent's voice vibrated with greed.

"'Yes, O Falak.'

"With difficulty, Hassan kept his hands from quaking and handed the medicine to Iman, who poured it into the Falak's boned mouth. The liquid slipped down the serpent's gullet and the Falak waited for the Almighty's power to flow through him like honeyed mead. Instead, it felt pain spear its insides. The Falak shrieked, its cry shaking the earth.

"Uncoiling from its nest, the Falak jerked toward Hassan, but before the serpent could reach him, spasms rocked it from nostril to tail. Rearing its great head in fury, the Falak lunged at Iman and snapped her into its jaws.

"As the Falak murdered his daughter, Hassan's vision blackened and he was holding a wailing, newborn Iman; then he was watching with pride as Iman took her first tremulous baby steps in his pharmacy and, in a blink, grow tall into womanhood, her mind always whirring. Then, he saw Iman follow him into the earth's foul bowels to safeguard him as he cried *No!*

"Inside the Falak, Iman floated outside of all. She felt no panic, just wonder at the velveteen blackness and the infinite dazzle of stars too distant to touch. After minutes—or hours—of hovering, Iman kicked up. To her surprise, she found that the endless universe ended, warm and soft, beneath her hand.

"'This is not what you think it is.'

"Iman whipped around and gasped when she saw Roshnara, who had once been Iman, hovering in the spectral light.

"'What is it then?' Iman asked.

"But Roshnara did not answer.

"Perhaps this was death. Iman had passed from worlds into worlds and at last into a world without escape. Not the heaven she was promised nor the hell she had been warned of.

"'Where are we?' Iman tried again.

"Roshnara shrugged. 'Does it matter? There is no way out.'

"But Iman touched the knife in her pocket and knew that it did.

"In the cavern, Wajdi tackled Hassan, pressing his knee into the pharmacist's back.

"'Will I have to swallow each of your family members before you obey?' the Falak demanded.

"Hassan thought of his wife, his wise pillar, his four sons and three—no, two—daughters, each clever and kind, his parents, siblings, cousins, aunts and uncles, the vast clan that had given Hassan all he had. He weighed his love for these people against his love for Allah and knew that he could not aid the Falak.

"But Hassan did not have the chance to answer. The Falak shrieked as fat black drops fizzed at its neck. Frenzied, the Falak smashed its spine against the tunnel. Crystals and earth rained from the cavern, knocking Wajdi off Hassan.

"From the Falak's neck, a head, matted with inky blood, emerged. Iman, hauling herself out of the wound. Before the Falak could break her body against the wall, Iman rolled to the ground, Roshnara tumbling out after her. With a frantic snap of its tail, the Falak struck Roshnara cold.

"Clambering over dirt hillocks, Hassan pulled his daughter up and pushed her through the disintegrating tunnel as the Falak reared. They ran. Having seen the vastness of all that the Falak contained and knowing that no amount of her father's poison could destroy it, Iman thought quickly as, behind them, the starry whirl of the Falak's mouth opened.

"Its hot breath on her legs, Iman opened a gate into the moonlit world. Hassan pushed his daughter in first and leapt in second. Although Hassan called for her to run, Iman waited at the gate's mouth, the iridescent fountain water warm at her ankles. Yellow eyes wild, the Falak rammed itself through the filament gate, ready to crack Iman in two.

"'Bismillah,' Iman whispered, grasping the hot threads. She pinched.

"The gate snapped.

"As Wajdi had warned, the hot, silver fiber cut through the Falak's thick neck, its howl resounding against the ramparts and piercing Iman to the bone, still echoing even as the Falak's head thudded to Iman's feet, glassy eyes staring dumbly at the ultramarine sky.

"And Hassan heard a whisper in his good ear, softer than the brush of a dove's wing: 'You have done well.'"

I cannot tell if Sultan Saladin has enjoyed the tale, if he will consider it a worthy ransom for an army. He does not praise it. He does not applaud. He only watches me, circumspect.

"What if I return the Seljuk army and Kirman has already fallen? What if the Seljuk army returns to Kirman and the Muslims collapse before the Franks?"

He points my own fears at me as though they are lances.

"If the Seljuk army does not return, Kirman, one of the last strongholds of Seljuk power in Persia, will certainly fall. If it falls before we arrive, then it is as Allah wills, but we cannot be idle; we must tie our camel. And, O Sultan, how can a few hundred men decide the success of our struggle against the Franks in armies that field thousands upon thousands?"

Sultan Saladin sits impassive, and my heartbeat ascends from my breast to my ears until it is all I can hear. My attention focuses on an absurd detail—the Sultan's calves, exposed by his raised trousers, are as smooth and pale as a maiden's.

"The Seljuks may return to Kirman, but a force of one thousand will remain as a sign of the Malik's support."

I calculate quickly. Of the five thousand soldiers with which we left Kirman, only four thousand arrived in Palestine, almost a quarter succumbing to the fever that took Faramurz. Since then, we have lost nearly five hundred men. Each soldier is precious, worth his weight in gold.

"Two hundred and fifty," I counter, a fishwife haggling in a bazaar.

"Five hundred horsemen," the Sultan replies, settling it.

Sultan Saladin rises and bows, hand over his heart. I bow in return, my skin thrumming, my body pounding. Leaving, I glance at what ibn Shaddad has been writing in his chronicle: a description of a meeting between the Sultan and a Frankish ambassador that day.

Thirty

◇◇◇◇◇◇

$\int$ entries watch me leave the camp's bounds. Beneath the pale moon, I pass the ancient bleached boundary stones that dot Tel Jezer's hills. Looking over my shoulder so I do not lose sight of the camp or my following mamluk, I draw my cloak against the night's chill.

I hear Shahryar before I see him.

Hiss. Thud. Hiss. Thud.

At the edge of a copse of tall pines, their bottlebrush tops profiled darkly against the sky, Shahryar pulls the string of his short, recurved bow to his ear and lets the arrow fly. It thuds into a pine's knot, joining several of its mates. In quick, angry succession, Shahryar lets five more fly, each arrow splitting the one that landed before. When he has emptied his quiver, he goes to the tree and yanks the arrows out. With a yell that cuts through the quiet wood, he cracks them over his knee and hurls them to the ground.

I step back, and my boot snaps a twig. With alacrity, Shahryar withdraws his shamshir, the blade glinting white in the moonlight. He sees me, my hands raised, eyes wide. "Oh, it's you." The sword whistles as it slips into the scabbard.

Although his body has relaxed, even in the scant illumination of moon and stars, I can read the rage in his soot-colored eyes and taut lips.

Tongue dry, I glance at Bahram. But what can the Circassian mamluk do?

"Why are you here, Shaherazade?"

I take a breath. "I have done something, but I have done it for you and I have done it for Kirman."

His hand curls over the shamshir's hilt. "Say it."

I swallow. "The Sultan agrees to return Mahperi to our custody." I pause, but he says nothing. "He has also agreed to release the Seljuk army, save for five hundred horsemen. We can return."

I know I have trespassed. I made Shahryar angry, caused him to flounder before the Sultan. And now, not only did I seek to repair that harm, I had the audacity to succeed. To do what Shahryar could not, extract our men from our alliance with the greatest commander and Sultan of our age, so that we may fight the Oghuz for our homeland.

A shoot of pride, tender and green, springs up.

What would Baba think? Briefly, the warmth of his pride enfolds me.

Shahryar's face could be carved from a glacier, for its coldness, for its rigidity, for how much mind it pays me. "Continue your tale."

"Will we return?"

"Continue your tale."

"But—"

"Continue your tale."

"Malik, that evening, when the Maghrib azaan should have rung from al-Askar's mosques but did not, Jauhara joined the devil for dinner.

"Mosaics of palms and peacocks glittered in the great hall where servants set the long table with Jauhara's favorites: rabbit stewed in quince and mint, milk pudding savory with chicken and yellowed with saffron, crisp white bread, and sesame-sweet *zalabiyya*, fried and latticed. At the table's head, in her father's seat, loomed the woman. Each beat of her irised wings expelled a breath that resounded through the hall.

"'Sit, Jauhara,' the woman directed.

"Heart hammering, Jauhara sat. Her damp palms sliding on the silken cushion, Jauhara demanded, with all the courage she could muster, 'Who are you? Where is my family?'

"The creature smiled, revealing pointed teeth that smoothed until their edges were blunt and human. 'Eat, Jauhara,' and snaked into the woman's voice was 'Omar's.

"Jauhara's hands shook. 'Who are you?' she repeated.

"'I am al-Maut,' the creature answered and Jauhara shuddered for the name meant *death*.

"'What are you?' Jauhara asked.

"'I am a descendant of angels fallen from Paradise, I and my siblings, marid all. For four thousand years, bearing different faces and names, we were the gods of this world's most powerful empires. From their worship, we drew power. Their sacrifices and priestly rituals made us divine.'

"Jauhara leapt up. 'You are a false god! You cannot exist. You do not exist!'

"Then, Jauhara noticed them slinking from shadow, men and women, tall and graceful as al-Maut. Some were winged like her, although none were as brilliantly plumed. They congregated around her: a jade-colored man with storm-gray ostrich wings, a blue-haired man with darkly lined eyes and the wings of a peregrine, a golden-skinned woman bearing tall cow horns and no wings at all. Men and women, marid and false gods all, spilled forth until every corner of the hall glowed with their phosphorescent bodies. They watched Jauhara with steady, unblinking marid eyes.

"'The Creator trapped us,' said al-Maut, lip curled, 'suspended us in sleep as punishment for our *lies* and *pride*.' At each of the sins, her siblings howled like jackals in the desert night. 'But someone spoke the sorcerous words and now here we are, awake. Was it you?' She smiled, and her teeth formed points, scythe-sharp. 'It was. I can feel it—the tear in your soul from working the ancient magic.'

"Unconsciously, Jauhara pinched the flesh above her heart as though to seam the rip. 'Where is my father? My mother? My brothers and sisters?'

"'For now, they are spelled into sleep. As for their future, the choice is yours.'

"'Mine?' Jauhara asked.

"Al-Maut chuckled softly. 'We have no quarrel with you. Far from it. We owe you a great debt. Without you inviting our magic back into this world, we would not have woken.'

"Jauhara's stomach curdled.

"'And we have a use for you.' The other marid, flanking al-Maut, looked at Jauhara hungrily.

"'You already control the palace and the city.' As Jauhara spoke, the truth of it filled her gut with arsenic. 'What do you need me for?'

"Al-Maut waved at the spelled servants. 'We cannot grow on this, cannot feed on this. We are not meant to reign as kings but to be worshipped as gods. But—"There is no compulsion in faith." We need free-souled men and women to choose us.

"'Someone must rule, a prophet who will bring us to their people.' Al-Maut met Jauhara's eyes, and thunder clapped in Jauhara's skull. 'Kneel before us, Jauhara. Raze His mosques, raise our temples, turn your people to our worship, and see the heights to which we will elevate you.'

"Despite the penetrating eyes and vicious claws of the marid, Jauhara said, clear and calm, 'Never. There is no god but Allah, I proclaim it.'

"Al-Maut was undeterred. 'You've searched worlds and what have you found? You've come home and who will you be? You've tasted carving your own destiny. Will you once again be a governor's obedient daughter, a man's wife, a child's mother?' Al-Maut slammed her palm against the table. When she raised her hand, the table was riven. 'I can give you so much more.'

"Despite herself, Jauhara felt a tendril of temptation curl through her belly. 'If I do not agree?'

"Al-Maut shrugged. 'Then you are of no use to us. We will destroy you and your family as well.' The marid snapped their jaws, rolled their sinuous necks.

"'And if I agree?'

"'Then we will return this land to its ancient splendor, hand in hand, and your family will be safe.'

"*Ya Allah, please forgive me*, Jauhara prayed as her lips parted: 'Yes.'"

"I cannot return," Shahryar says quietly, and I almost miss his words for an owl's long hoot.

I smooth the shock from my face. "Will you lose your home without fighting for it?"

"Who am I to fight for it? Better put my sword in your hand. My own wife." He chuckles joylessly. "My own wife, who is little more than a child, can maneuver Sultan Saladin into releasing *my own* army. If Fataneh cuckolded my bed, you have cuckolded my kingship."

"No!"

"Then what did you do? Promise him favors? You're comely enough."

Nausea claws at my throat and I crumple my viridian farajiyya, the silk squeezing through my fingers like clay. "No! The Sultan considers you a fellow ruler, a serious ally and adversary. But I am a girl, so far below his notice that to give me something is like giving a gift to a child, not surrender to a fellow king."

Shahryar's anger evaporates, leaving a viscous moroseness. "Why fight only to lose? Why risk lives when victory is not possible? For my pride?"

I take his hand. To my surprise, he does not resist. "For your pride? Shahryar, your subjects await your return so that you may rescue them from Oghuz violence. Will you hide while they—fathers and mothers and children—are slaughtered? Kirman is greater than you."

He looks upward, watching bats flap in shadowy silhouette.

"Are you afraid?" My words leave clouds of warm breath. I think of the other women, khatuns and queens and sultanas and wives, who have endless patience to rightly guide their men, to save them from themselves, and who do it unseen. "You are a malik who has felt fear. You have risked your life in battle. Why do you balk now?"

"I am cursed, Shaherazade." He speaks as though tapping something that has been long fermenting. "I have been cursed since I killed Fataneh. Since I killed the other girls. The Oghuz are a trap. Her trap. She lures me back to kill me." In his face, I read deeply sown seeds of fear.

I am tempted to touch his cheek, to try to wipe that fear away. Then, I think, he deserves it. He deserves each bone-splitting fear, he deserves his sins to be driven into his flesh like nails, to feel a hundredth of the pain he inflicted on his wives, the terror he plunged into his subjects' hearts. But it cannot break him. Not now. Not yet.

"It is He, not Fataneh, who controls men's fates. This is not a curse. Repulse Malik Dinar and the Oghuz, secure Kirman, and lead it to prosperity."

"You should have been born Malik." Shahryar says it as if someone has cracked his rib cage, sliced his back, and pulled his spine cleanly out from between shining red flaps of flesh. Or perhaps Fataneh was his spine all along, the invisible hand pushing him to fulfill his duties.

"But it was you." After a pause, I add, "And Allah does not err." I squeeze his arm. "You know what is right. And I know you have the courage to act upon it."

Even as I say it, I am not certain I believe it.

✳ ✳ ✳

Aided by two strapping servants, Gulnar has brought a bath just large enough for two into my tent. Fog rises from the hot water, slick with sweet jasmine oil.

Sighing, I slide into the hot bath. With the braziers burning, this is the first time in weeks I have felt warmed through. I skim my fingers over the water as Dunya steps in across from me.

"Do you remember hamaams so large that you could swim in them?" Dunya asks.

I flinch as Gulnar pours another bucket of hot water. "I remember *everything*," I say, submerging my head into a world of distorted echoes.

When I float up again, Dunya leans forward. She glances at Gulnar, who is murmuring benedictions and clicking her tasbih's translucent jade beads.

"I think I may have dreamed Shahryar," I whisper, giving voice to the fear that has been twining through my veins for days. "Where did the Malik of our childhood go? Did he ever exist?"

"Do you no longer love him?"

As I rise, warm water trickles down my chest and legs and onto the rug below. Wrapping myself in a towel, I reply, "I do not know what I loved, Dunya. I thought he was so much more." The words sit soft and heavy.

"A weak man is an opportunity for a strong woman."

I consider the point and find it repulsive. I do not want a manipulable husband or a temperamental, murderous one. I want Shahryar to be a strong and just ruler, who takes my counsel when it is right, with whom I can rule over a prosperous and peaceful land.

I want him to be how I imagined. That he is not hollows a cavern in my chest.

A flurry of heavy steps squelches mud outside and Fakhruddin calls out, "Shaherazade Khatun! May I enter?" Gulnar whirlwinds Dunya and me into layers of tunics and overcoats, trousers and veils, crowning tiaras and cinching sashes.

"Enter, Fakhruddin."

At the sight of our wet faces and the still-steaming tub, Fakhruddin hovers at the entrance. His thinning gray hair is damp with perspiration, but his eyes shine. "The Malik has conferred with Sultan Saladin and the astrologers and announced the Seljuk departure. We will start back after Jummah."

In three days.

Outside, Seljuk soldiers have already begun collecting and packing belongings flung between soldiers over months of marching and war. A soldier catches my eye and smiles, revealing a gap in his bottom teeth. Behind him, I see Atsiz and my heart leaps. I almost turn away, but he strides forward. Fakhruddin watches stiffly.

"It's true then?" I ask.

Atsiz laughs softly, and the sound caresses my neck. "Why do you seem so surprised? This was your doing, Shaherazade Khatun." Atsiz's green eyes darken. "You are remarkable."

The way he says it feels too intimate to be expressed before Dunya and Fakhruddin. I cannot look at either of them, not when Atsiz's praise warms my stomach and curls my toes.

"Do you think we can win?" Asking the question, I realize that of all those I can ask, his opinion is the one that matters the most.

"We must." His hand hovers above my shoulder and then, perhaps remembering Dunya and Fakhruddin, it retreats to the pommel of his sword.

Suddenly, his nearness, combined with Dunya's and Fakhruddin's presence, overwhelms me. There is something dangerous here, I sense it now. "Mutashakaram Emir Atsiz, for your views. And thank you, Fakhruddin, for delivering this news. I must find my *husband*, the Malik."

In the mêlée in the camp, dodging soldiers careless with their slung bows and long-legged horses, I cannot find Shahryar.

I turn toward the Ayyubid encampment, sidestepping rushing men and strewn property to find Sitt Jalaliyya and seek Mahperi's release into my custody at last. I will take that girl home, and all that happened, the Frank, her treachery, can remain here. I will secure for Mahperi a good marriage, to a kind man, with a home in a small town or deep in the country, where she can live in peace, away from harm, away from her father, away from dangerous intrigues. Perhaps I could someday forgive her or even trust her again.

But I do not need to trust Mahperi to keep her safe.

Before I can find Sitt Jalaliyya, she finds me, ashen faced. "O Shaher-azade Khatun . . ." Tears shimmer in her large eyes and her curved nose shines red. I do not want to think about what could make iron-backed Jalaliyya weep. "Mahperi Khatun is . . ."

Fled, Mahperi has fled, with the Frank, untrustworthy to the end. Mahperi somehow learned of Atsiz, and spilled to Shahryar a true story, to secure her own freedom.

"Dead. She is dead."

"What?"

Pretty, moon-faced Mahperi with her fluttering spiral curls, always reaching for love, always finding it out of her grasp. The friend who followed me to the ends of the earth, who was always a second thought. Whom I considered a traitor even in death. And Jalaliyya, who demanded that Mahperi be submitted to her supervision.

"She was in your custody, Sitt Jalaliyya," I say quietly, holding myself tightly so I don't scream. "You had charge of her, you were duty-bound to care for her. Now you tell me she is dead."

The pieces of Sitt Jalaliyya's face distort—the skin around her eyes trembles, her mouth shakes, her cheeks vibrate. Touching my hand, she says softly, "She hanged herself. I had told her, just an hour before, that the Seljuks would be returning to Kirman. A maid found her in the tent." She swallows. "I would not have wished this end for her."

But sympathy for the dead is easy.

"Did the guards hear anything?"

Jalaliyya shakes her head. Could Mahperi have really hung a noose without shaking the tent, without making noise that would arouse suspicion?

Jalaliyya follows me into Mahperi's tent. Someone, maybe the guards, finally taking action, has cut Mahperi down and laid her on the cot. A blanket covers her up to her neck. Her eyes are closed, her mouth puffed. For all these months at war, I have never felt nearer to death—I think the last corpse I saw so close was my mother's.

Mahperi does not look like she is sleeping, as some say death appears. She looks empty, her marrow and matter sucked out. I fold back the still-warm blanket over her still-soft chest, revealing a date-colored bruise cutting a sinuous line around her neck. An easy disposal of an inconvenient woman. The noose, as easily a tool for suicide as a weapon for murder, woven from a cotton sheet, coils neatly beside her.

Warily, I eye Jalaliyya, who appears genuinely distraught.

"She will have to be buried and a *janaza* prayed before we leave," I finally say, knowing that is the right thing to say and taking refuge in propriety. I bury my suspicion and wonder if I am guilty of the same sin as so many others—putting men's machinations ahead of women's lives.

"Yes, of course. My father's steward will arrange it." On that excuse, Jalaliyya escapes, leaving me with a dead girl.

"To Allah we belong and unto Him we return," I murmur, wiping my tears. I draw the sheet over Mahperi's head. I feel as though I am shrouding a stranger.

PART FOUR

Thirty-One

◇◇◇◇◇

We traveled back, over sand and sea, leaving Saladin, his army, and the Franks, our faces forward to Bam and the Oghuz, our journey near four months' gone. As Jauhara traveled from west to east and back again, we reverse her path. The dust in my mouth and the sun on my head are companions as familiar as Dunya.

The sareban and his navigators drew a path that arced us wide over Baghdad to avoid Caliph an-Nasir. We are days away from Kirman, and tonight I sit in the same caravanserai, nestled between bare, winter-struck mountains, where we stopped a year ago. Then, it seemed a new piece of a new world; now, it is a palm's-length from home.

We—the Seljuk nobles—dine in a domed pavilion, where the caravanserai's proprietor, a heavyset man with a ring of black hair clinging to his skull, directs the servers to lay out honeyed plum sharbat, thick, round bread steaming in baskets, pounded beef ground with almond and sumac, and lamb sweet with dates and apricots.

Conversation from the other travelers hums through the pavilion. For the first time in weeks, we crowd together, smelling not of sweat and dirt but of fresh bathwater and scented oils from the caravanserai's hamaam. I pull my squirrel-lined cloak tight against the cold mountain wind that makes the fire pop. Down the table, I see Dunya. Beside her, where Mahperi should be, is Nurani. My chest squeezes.

Placing a fist over his heart, the proprietor bows before Shahryar. "Malik Shahryar, I hope this meal is to your liking. We are pleased that you have returned at last."

"And I am happy to be home," Shahryar says with easy grace. Without Saladin's shadow and close to his own patrimony, Shahryar expands, a flame given air. "Tell me, what news from Bam?"

The man's lips thin into his round face. "It pains me to bear this news, O Malik, but I have had it from merchants that the Oghuz have besieged Bam for almost a month. Their chieftain, Malik Dinar, has drawn a tight snare around the city—nothing in, no one out."

I try to exchange a worried look with Atsiz, but he stares fixedly at Shahryar.

"Has there been any fighting?"

"I have heard that arrows have been exchanged." The proprietor leans forward, a knowing glint in his eye. "I'm not a military man, but I guess that the Oghuz are waiting for Bam's resolve to weaken. They think that because you are gone, Bam will lose its nerve."

I remember Bam's nerve when Shahryar was within its walls, how it edged to an uprising, to drowning the citadel in blood and fire.

"How many men do the Oghuz have?" Atsiz asks, folding a morsel of lamb in nan.

The man eyes our army ringed by the caravanserai's crenellated mud-brick walls, scarred, dirty, and tired. "I can only say what I have heard, but it is many thousands more than this."

Shahryar thanks the proprietor. Recognizing the dismissal, he bows and backs away.

Shahryar sees my worry and, once the proprietor is out of earshot, says, "Even if Malik Dinar has more men, our soldiers became warriors learning how to battle for Kirman. A soldier at home in his land can out-match his enemy."

"And Malik Dinar's soldiers are raiders of farms and villages," Atsiz adds. "Our men are blades freshly sharpened by battle with the Franks and training with the Ayyubids."

Shahryar says to Atsiz, "The Arg-e-Bam has provisions—grain and nuts and dates—to last years. And water flows into the city from the mountains through underground canals and the Chelekhoneh River. The citadel's walls are thick, designed to withstand a siege."

"You must decide," Atsiz says. "Do we treat with the Oghuz or do we fight?"

The two have been tossing the question back and forth since we left Palestine. What do we offer in negotiations, what can we lose, what would the Oghuz accept? Or do we fight—our tired, battle-weary, march-fatigued Seljuks against their lounging besiegers? The answers always change, for no answer is good.

"I have not received good information on the number of Oghuz. The scouts have not yet returned. Malik Dinar has at least seven thousand. Perhaps eight. We are returning with just over two thousand Seljuk soldiers. One thousand remain in the garrison at Bam, and Shahzaman brought one thousand from Samarkand."

"War hurts us more than them," I counsel. "If we can reach a resolution without bloodshed, without risking lives, I think that is better."

I try to catch Atsiz's eye. As always, he is looking elsewhere. If I had not been alert to it, I would have missed the smooth avoidance, eyes too consistently averted to be by chance. I do not know why, but after Mah-peri's death, he began to hold himself apart. His distance aches.

Still no engagement has been announced between him and Nurani. That leaves me with a wan satisfaction I take no pride in.

"If we move to treat, we lose the advantage of surprise," Shahryar counters.

"You can always treat after an attack," Atsiz says.

"And if we lose the attack? Why would the Oghuz treat then?"

"I am sure Malik Dinar values the lives of his own men as we do ours," I answer. As Shahryar considers, I say, "And should we lose and treat, Malik Dinar may agree to let you remain the Malik of Kirman if you take him as your suzerain. They're a raiding folk—they could be persuaded to accept tribute."

Atsiz and Shahryar look at me as though I've blasphemed. But men are emotional about land and fealty.

"What difference if your overlord is a Seljuk Sultan or an Oghuz warlord so long as peace is kept?" I press.

"That way of thinking leads to defeat." Shahryar tiredly rises, leaving me with Atsiz. He does not ask me to join him. Since I orchestrated our departure from Palestine, during the long months of our journey home, Shahryar has receded from me, neither cold nor warm.

Atsiz and I don't speak as Shahryar passes now-empty market stalls in the caravanserai's courtyard and disappears beneath the arcade to his room. But something snaps between us, like the air alive before a thunderstorm. I want to break the silence, but my voice catches and my thoughts are a jumble, none of them right.

The quiet stretches.

Atsiz stands. "Shab bikhair, Shaherazade Khatun." Bowing, he vanishes through the pavilion's carved wooden columns. Had he been waiting for me to speak? Should I follow him? My heart thumps, my face feels hot, and I cannot name the force that impels me.

His broad back, lit by the gibbous moon and whorled stars, reminds me of that long-ago moonlit desert ride and fills my heart with a confused *something*. "Atsiz!" I whisper. "Ay Atsiz!"

He turns and even in the guttering torchlight I catch the softness in his face.

It is enough.

I rush to him, touching his sharp-cut cheek before the softness disappears. "O Atsiz. Why have you avoided me all these months?"

He catches my hand and lowers it to my side, holds on to it a moment longer than he must. "You know why." He averts his gaze.

"I am not a mind reader."

Atsiz raises his golden-green eyes, and my heart drops. "You know why," he rasps, and suddenly, we, together, at once, timed with astronomical perfection, pull each other in. My hands are in his hair and his lips are on my neck, my face. My mouth seeks his, his strong arm encircles my waist, his hands tangle themselves in my plaits and veil, and it is as if all of my pieces are in one place. The stars fall from the sky and settle softly at our feet and I am awash in the glow.

A heavy tread falls on the ground and I spring away, shoving Atsiz. He frowns, hurt, before seeing what I see: my mamluk, Fakhruddin, with a hand on his blade.

He looks at me and then Atsiz and then me and then Atsiz, and I can almost hear the abacus beads click in his mind.

"I could not have imagined this of you," Fakhruddin says in a deep, disappointed voice. "Shaherazade Khan, wife of the Malik, daughter of Vizier Muhammad."

"Fakhruddin—" Atsiz begins jocularly, stepping forward, but the mamluk stiffens. Atsiz's easy hand moves to his scimitar.

"Didn't I warn you, Emir Atsiz? When you came to Shaherazade Khatun's tent on the day of Mahperi Khatun's death, did I not warn you to cease your familiarity?"

The disappointment Baba would have felt ties my tongue, and the brunt of what I have done—been unfaithful to my husband—my murderous, dark, confused husband—strikes me. This is no longer a game of whispers in the dark, potent silences, and significant eyes, of nighttime rides and slipped poems.

After a year of threading a needle indescribably fine, of securing my life and the lives of all the women whom Shahryar would have married after me, I slip. I want to fall to my knees. Will Fakhruddin show mercy then? Should I bribe him or will that only cement his view that I am a fallen woman? Atsiz's blade glints and I find steel in my own voice.

"Your choice is easy, Fakhruddin. You vow by Allah that you will not breathe a word of what you have seen. Or Atsiz will kill you here."

Whipping his scimitar from its scabbard, Fakhruddin, despite his age, drops into a loose fighter's stance, his sword hanging lazily from his hand; Atsiz still does not draw his blade. "I will not be an easy murder." He nods at the pavilion. Can they see this, even through the hazy dark? "But I will not distract the Malik before he must meet the Oghuz. Your secret," he regards me and Atsiz distastefully, "is safe. Shaherazade Khatun—you have already disappointed your father's legacy with your infidelity; do not compound your sin."

Without looking back, I flee to Shahryar's chamber and slip in bed beside his sleeping form. I swallow nausea. Is this how Fataneh felt, as though all the walls and doors were closing around her? And I reacted just as she did, with threats of murder, twisting Allah's name with my own sins.

Will Fakhruddin react as I did?

I breathe deeply. I have time. Fakhruddin will not say anything until the Oghuz are defeated. I will figure this out, but *I will not die*. Repeating those words over and over again like a lullaby, I rock myself to sleep.

Thirty-Two

The caravanserai shrinks against the mountains as the caravan heads east. If I ride Andalib toward the front of the caravan, Atsiz retreats. If Atsiz rides left, I go right, a seamless, unspoken, unnoticed choreography.

Now, I'm near the caravan's head, close behind my husband. I can't look at him. I keep Fakhruddin in my line of sight.

I find Fakhruddin in his tent, his soft snores like a cat's purrs. I slink beside him, fall to my knees, and before he can awaken I open his mouth, pull out his wet tongue, and slice its juicy meat until it falls in my hand, crimson and pulsing. He screams, loud and bloodcurdling, the scream of ghouls whipping through houses, of habub whirling through the desert.

The thought is so repulsive, I flick my fingers, hurling it away, but I can't shake the metallic taste in the back of my throat, the feel of Fakhruddin's bloody tongue lodged there. I take a long draft of lukewarm water from my canteen and wash the bile from my mouth.

"Isn't it bizarre," Dunya says, riding up beside me. I jump in my seat. "To be returning to Bam? Leaving everything that has happened behind?" She has dark shadows under her eyes that even the emerald diadem that was our mother's cannot brighten.

"Did . . ." I begin tentatively, trying to suppress every disturbing thought and turn to my sister's light. "Did the caravanserai remind you of Faramurz?"

She smiles softly. "Of course. He was everywhere. It filled me with—oh, I don't know. Nostalgia and memory and all the feelings that I felt with him and—here is a place, where Faramurz was and where I fell in love. It exists, a real place, not just drifting desert, and he is seeped in every part of it." Dunya glances at me. "I understand now why Baba had to move into the citadel after Mama died. He could have spent his life chasing her shadow in our home."

I think of Baba—not only in our rooms, but in the courtyards and the halls of the Arg-e-Bam. Here he counseled me to patience; there he watched me get married. Every echo only reminds me of Baba's shame at seeing the daughter he thought a heroine turned into an adulteress. I gingerly daub my tears with a banded sleeve. At Dunya's look, I say, "Just thinking of how full the citadel will be of Baba's shadow."

Then I see smoke coiling a hundred paces ahead, above the burned bones of a village. Gulnar, who has ridden up, gasps, the blood draining from her round cheeks.

"Ay Khoda," I murmur.

"Halt!" Shahryar bellows, raising a fist toward the sky. At his command, his mamluks race their horses through the caravan, flashing armor and leather cuirasses, echoing his order until the soldiers and wagons stop in confusion. Shahryar directs scouts to investigate, and two lithe men dash into the charred ruins.

The village was small, nestled in sand and rock. Smoke has blackened its rosy adobe walls; fire has caved in its cupolas. The surrounding grove, likely pistachio, has been torched, cinder burying the neatly arrayed stumps. In some ways, it's a small devastation. Fighting the Franks, I saw great cities collapse into white dust. But then, this is Kirman. This is my homeland.

And it is aflame.

"This is what my village looked like," Gulnar murmurs. "When I was stolen. Burned black, homes and bodies."

I quell my surprise. I have asked about Gulnar's childhood but once, when I was younger, and she fidgeted uncomfortably as if I had encroached upon something private. I know only what Baba told me when she arrived, a knock-kneed girl of fifteen—that she came from a farming village in Transoxiana. Only when my mother died did Gulnar say that she too had watched her own mother die. Then, as now, Gulnar says nothing more. Her hands, already unsteady on her horse, quiver. I hold her hand tightly and look straight ahead. If I glance at her, I know I will weep. After a moment, she breaks my hold.

Drawing my blue veil over my mouth against the smoke, I click my tongue at Andalib, who moves closer to Shahryar. "Do you think it is the Oghuz?"

"Most likely," Shahryar answers. "Or bandits. Or some other band of wild men."

"Bandits don't do this," Atsiz says softly.

Grimly, we await the scouts' return.

The scouts, young men browned in the sun, approach Shahryar. The mouth of the taller one quirks with emotion as he speaks. "The village is empty, O Malik. But we saw at least thirty corpses of men, violently killed, leaving the village red with blood. The women and children are gone, most likely taken as captives."

The second scout adds hoarsely, "The stores have been raided. The food and water are all gone. But the bodies show no decay. The marauders are likely only a few days ahead."

I think of Gulnar, who watched her mother killed in a raid, who, like the women of this village, was stolen. Their fates are not hard to guess. Perhaps the dead men are the lucky ones after all.

"Malik Dinar must have sent an Oghuz raiding party to support the siege of Bam," Shahryar says.

"If the Oghuz are ranging this far to support the siege, it must be bad." I dread to think how many more towns and villages like this we will find.

"Atsiz, gather some soldiers to bury the dead," Shahryar says. Tears pearl in his eyes. "That is the least we can do."

Dunya, Gulnar, and I huddle against a rising cold wind while Atsiz and his soldiers drag the corpses from the rubble down the village streets and line them up, until the row of bodies reaches long, an unending string beaded with our countrymen. Even at a distance, I can see that the bodies are red, raw, charred. Gulnar retches, and a responsive brackishness fills my mouth. I clasp her hand, and this time she lets me.

Their shovels scraping against sandy earth, the soldiers dig the graves and bury the burned men, one by one, near the burnt pistachio grove. In another life, it would have been just beginning to green with springtime buds, Nowruz around the corner. The wind whips the dirt from the grave mounds. We do not have enough time to complete the death rituals, bathing the men in clean water and shrouding them in white cotton. Nonetheless, the entire Seljuk army assembles behind Shahryar, who raises his hands behind his ears and leads the funerary prayer, one act the Malik of Kirman can still perform for his slain subjects.

The soldiers' cries of *Takbir!* dissipate weakly into the desert.

* * *

Sleeplessly, Shahryar and I twist and toss. When I close my eyes, corpses, burned black and red, climb on top of me, suffocating me with their hot, stinking flesh. Shahryar's hand grazes mine and, although I fear he'll divine my guilt in my racing pulse and moist palm, I clasp it tightly.

"O Shaherazade, will you continue your tale?" he whispers, asking me for only the second time since we left Saladin.

And I am grateful to leave my world for another.

"O Malik, it is said that the day after she returned to Egypt, Jauhara stood behind al-Maut on the dais. Al-Maut, masked with 'Omar's face, announced, 'O my brethren. It has been my honor to guard Egypt as your governor for these last twenty years. But I have decided, difficult though it is, to step down. My daughter, Sitt Jauhara,' al-Maut curled her talons over Jauhara's shoulders, 'will succeed me.'

"Al-Maut had begun slowly lifting the enchantment of easy compliance from the court, and the announcement sparked through the men like catching tinder. 'Ya saidi!' a chancellor named Abdurrahim, who had been 'Omar's longtime confidant, called. 'This . . . girl child to rule in your place? Are you ill? Are there no men left?'

"'She is wiser than you credit her. Under her reign, Egypt will become what it once was,' al-Maut said, and 'Omar's voice resonated with conviction. 'For your love of me, I ask that you give her a chance.'

"Chastened, Abdurrahim fell back. 'For love of you, ya saidi, of course.' But when al-Maut looked away, he glowered at Jauhara.

"The gilt robes of state gouging her shoulders and dragging at her ankles, Jauhara stepped forward. She feared she looked like a child dressed in her mother's clothes. The bargain she had struck churned through her stomach like a storm-swept ship.

"Jauhara spoke the words al-Maut had put in her mouth: 'I will rule here where my father did and my grandfather before him. I will return Egypt to its ancient splendor, to the power it held when it was the most feared land on this earth.'

"Jauhara tasted ash.

"And so, in the first week of Jauhara's governorship, Jauhara, strung like a puppet, defunded the *awqaaf* that benefited the madrasas and mosques, banned the azaan, and closed down half of the city's mosques, decisions met with uproar in the court and in the streets. But Jauhara, swept in the rushing river of al-Maut's demands, had no choice but to hold steady.

"The thought of how hard her father and mother had fought against the very evil Jauhara offered al-Maut on a gilded platter hounded her night and day, souring her meals, slicing through her dreams like a knife. As the palace of al-Askar slumbered, she wandered its black halls and pearl-gleaming gardens veined with Nile-fed canals.

"Out of the corner of her eye, Jauhara saw a flash of white, like the wings of a mourning dove. She blinked. She saw it again. Removing her silk slippers, her feet sinking into the garden's soft loam, Jauhara crept closer.

"Under the moonlight, dozens of men and women in bleached linen robes processed, holding burning incense aloft. They were surrounded by marid—al-Maut, the falcon and the jackal, and the crocodile, who quavered with anticipation.

"Ringed by the acolytes, a shivering, shadow-eyed boy struggled against the gag in his mouth. Jauhara stared blankly before recognition slapped her.

"Her brother, Bishr.

"An acolyte took Bishr's arm, gently, gently, and Jauhara thought: *They will free him, they will return him to me, have I not done as al-Maut required? Have I not been loyal, have I not been obedient? Has not their power grown and Islam waned?*

"Husky chanting in a strange tongue curled with the incense smoke to the black sky, as al-Maut gripped two stone blocks in the palace wall and pulled. The wall parted like cotton curtains. Al-Maut ducked in, followed by marid, acolytes, and Jauhara's brother. As the stones closed, Jauhara ran, but under her searching hands the mortar was unbroken. She pulled until her nails cracked, slapped the wall until her palms flamed scarlet, but still the blocks did not budge.

"Red-eyed, Jauhara shivered through the night, concealed behind a bush. As the sun rose, the palace walls parted and the marid and acolytes streamed forth. Jauhara could see stains—black? crimson?—splashed on their white robes.

"Bishr was not with them."

Thirty-Three

✧✧✧✧✧

We are three days past the burnt village, four days to Bam. The caravan is somber. We'd thought we would return as valiant rescuers. Now, I fear we are entirely too late.

I look back at Atsiz and Shahryar and think, *I am but twenty, and so much of my life is doused in shadow.* The vise tightens and I kick Andalib's black sides. My veil whips off and my crimson overcoat billows in the cool evening air as Andalib flies forward. I inhale the sweetness of burning smoke, the acridity of bodies pushed together, and leave them behind. Andalib rushes away from the sinking sun, and I slow her only when the army has faded into a glimmer of torchlight. My heart jumps as I hear hoofbeats. I turn Andalib around. It is only Dunya, who smiles.

"Must you always rush off into the night, Shaherazade?" she says, amused. Dusk's soft roses and violets glow on her flushed cheeks, matching the jewels of her diadem. Her dark, tilted eyes sparkle, and my sister's fresh beauty strikes me. Her smile fades. Everything feels too heavy for such levity.

If I confessed my fears, she would reply with a logician's coolness—that I am but one factor in a series of independent choices that yielded the carnage in the village and the Oghuz siege of Bam. And in the end, everything is as Allah wills. I know this as well as she—I drilled her in these lessons. But I do not *feel* it.

And who can deny that some choices weigh more than others?

"How far do you think I must run before I am no longer suffocated by the enormity of everything?"

She regards me sympathetically. "That depends. How far before you are no longer Khatun?"

"I will be a Khatun until I die."

I remember to be grateful that I have lasted even this long.

We head back toward the caravan in the shadow of the mountains that cradle the valley road back to Bam. As the sky deepens to dark blue, only a wisp of yellow lights the horizon. I shiver as a chill wind rises.

"Any word from Emir Özbeg about how Sultan Saladin fares against the Franks?" Dunya asks, Shaheen dancing beneath her.

I wrap my hands in my cloak. "Just that the Sultan winters in Jerusalem, while Malikric has retreated to Acre after rebuilding Ascalon." Now that we are so close to Bam, Palestine, from the violet sea to the great battles between Muslim heroes and red-faced Franks, seems like a fable.

I hear hoofbeats—the caravan approaching—but Dunya's frozen eyes run a warning down my back. Slowly, I turn Andalib.

Darkness.

Then I catch the silvery gleam of a conical helmet, the glittering whites of eyes, the dark iron shine of an arrow pointed at my heart. Why would a Seljuk soldier point an arrow at me? I understand, and my heart seizes.

"Oghuz!" I cry, and the dimpled bow creaks as the soldier draws it tighter, his elbow level with his cheek. Four more soldiers appear behind him. I look for my mamluks, but they are nowhere.

"Quiet," our attacker says in Oghuz, and his Turkic is the distilled Turkic of the steppes. "Seljuk?"

Dry winter grass cracks under Andalib as she shifts nervously. I hear the soft breathing of their horses, smell the salt-and-iron sweat of the men's bodies. My hand catches Dunya's. I cannot tell if its slickness belongs to her, me, or both.

The Oghuz soldier keeps his bowstring taut and aimed at us. "Dismount. Both of you."

Although I try to command my legs to jump down from Andalib, they stick to her. Another Oghuz rides forward and strikes me across the face, sending me tumbling to the hard ground.

My face pounds, with pain, with anger. If I wake tomorrow morning, it will be with bruises like black figs on my face and down my body. Andalib dances fitfully. Grabbing the saddle, I heave myself against her. I wish I had anything, a dagger, a knife, with which to defend myself and Dunya.

"You should be careful with us!" I call. "We are not poor creatures of whom you can make poor sport."

I may as well not have spoken. One of the Oghuz pulls Dunya from her horse, and although Dunya beats at his chest, kicks, wriggles, and screams, he hauls her over like a sack of grain. He rips a strip from the hem of her apricot overcoat, trussing her arms and legs, gagging her mouth. As another Oghuz reaches for me, the night explodes with battle cries. Seljuk soldiers burst upon us, a monsoon cloud ripping open. I hear the zip of arrows and the thud of bodies. Three Oghuz fall: an arrow in the eye, an arrow in the throat, an arrow in the chest, *thump, thump, thump.* A fourth is hit twice in the thigh and collapses.

But the Oghuz with Dunya dodges the assault and thunders away.

"Dunya!"

Shahryar barks an order, and his mamluks pursue the fleeing man. I kick Andalib to join them, but I feel her tugged back. Fakhruddin has arrived, my other mamluks at his back.

As they knot a tight circle around me, he shakes his head with almost fatherly concern. "What can you do here that a trained mamluk cannot?" A dozen other horsemen gallop after my sister's abductor.

I double over Andalib's neck, my skin cold. Dunya is all that is left to me, left of me, of Baba and Mama. Of home.

Then I remember I am not some powerless girl.

"Fakhruddin. Send my entire mamluk guard after her. Bring her back to me." He hesitates, and my mouth presses into a thin line.

"As you say, Shaherazade Khatun. Follow Dunyazade," he orders, and six men dart into the darkness, for now night has truly fallen and the world is black.

Ay Khoda, bring her back, bring her back. I will pray a thousand and one nafl for my thankfulness and sacrifice a thousand and one goats for the poor, just return her. I try not to think of what could befall her, a girl alone with a soldier in the dark.

Shahryar glances angrily at Fakhruddin. "How could you leave them alone? When we know that the Oghuz are close, that they are burning villages steps ahead of us?"

Fakhruddin bows his head, accepting rebuke.

Gently, Shahryar touches the darkening welt on my cheek. "We will find her, Shaherazade. You have nothing to fear. She is as dear to me as my own sister."

Wiping away tears, I follow Shahryar, who strides into the circle of soldiers holding burning torches that glimmer like a constellation of small suns. Shahryar looms over the bound and kneeling captive. Where the arrows rent through clothing and skin, his blood blooms and drips into the earth. His helmet has been knocked aside, revealing tanned skin, an aquiline nose.

"Who are you with?" Shahryar demands.

When the Oghuz does not reply, Shahryar pulls out his shamshir with a high metallic hiss and whips the flat of the damascene blade against the man's face, raising a red weal on his cheek that matches my own.

The man pants but does not break his silence.

"I ask you again," Shahryar says in a low voice that raises the hair on my neck, that calls to mind the man who killed Fataneh and Altunjan and Shideh and Inanj. Perhaps the Oghuz does not sense the threat, for he remains mute. Shahryar strikes him across his other cheek, and the blow stripes his face with blood, shining thick and red.

The Oghuz raises his chin, lets the blood roll from his cheek to his neck. He meets Shahryar's eyes boldly, and then Shahryar's fist knocks him out cold. For all that this man attacked us, my stomach turns. A medic produces reviving camphor, waving the minty white wax beneath the captive's nose. The man's eyes flicker open hazily and he finally reads the hard murder in Shahryar's eyes.

"We are scouts for Malik Dinar," he slurs. "We have been watching you since you passed 'Abbasid lands."

So Caliph an-Nasir's own network of spies had a hand in this.

"Give him water," Shahryar orders. A soldier passes a leather waterskin to Shahryar. Kneeling beside the captive, Shahryar tips the water into his mouth with tender, mothering hands. The scout coughs up more water than he swallows.

"Now, tell me," Shahryar hisses once the coughing subsides, "where will your companion take the girl?"

"Back." The Oghuz's tongue darts out to lick the dripping water. "He will take her to Malik Dinar, and her station will determine if she will be a concubine or a hostage."

"Where will he stop? What route will he take?"

The Oghuz laughs, a jangling, discordant sound. "We are scouts; we sleep on pallets when need requires, wherever it requires. He will slip into the darkness with the girl. There is no set route. You will not find them."

I resist the urge to bury my face into my shaking hands. First, I lost Baba. Then, Mahperi. Now, Dunya. I have lost two girls entrusted to my care. I have lost my own sister.

Shahryar holds the man's hair tight near the scalp, tilts his head back, and tips the waterskin into his mouth until the man sputters and gags, pulling away so violently that Shahryar is left gripping a clump of hair. Once the captive catches his breath, Shahryar asks, "How many men does Malik Dinar have?"

The Oghuz remains defiant. "As far as the eye can see, there are his men. Kirman is his in all but name." He cackles again. "What kind of fool abandons his province? First, your wife cuckolds you and now we do."

In the tight ring of his men, Shahryar whitens. Will he slit the prisoner's throat? But he chuckles, and his men laugh with him. "Only a fool mocks the man who holds his life in his hands," Shahryar says quietly. "Especially when that life is useless. Tell me, do you have anything else that will be of use to me?"

For the first time, the Oghuz seems shaken. Has he been fed that Shahryar is a lamb, that his iron teeth emerge only to bite the heads off his wives?

"I am a scout and I can only tell you what the scouts say. We are eight thousand Oghuz strong, and the city has weakened through the winter. Malik Dinar will take Bam now that he knows you are near. He may have already. And it is said he wants a Seljuk bride for his own."

Dunya: the virgin sister-in-law of the Malik, the daughter of the vizier, beloved in Kirman.

I stand at Shahryar's shoulder. "Never!"

"Tell me, Scout, do you have anything else?"

The man's eyes dart back and forth, but he says nothing. Shahryar hefts his shamshir, touches it softly against the back of the man's neck. When the Oghuz remains close-mouthed, Shahryar swings the shamshir upward; it sings and then rumbles as it cracks through the scout's vertebrae and slices through his soft flesh. The head falls to one side, the body to the other, and the dirt beneath drinks his blood like water.

✳ ✳ ✳

I hunch over a hot glass of tea thrust into my hand by Shahryar's steward, Yaghmur, in Shahryar's tent as a scout reports to Shahryar and his emirs. The scout's cheeks are scarlet with windburn, his trousers still muddy from the road, as though he has flung himself from his horse to this tent. He likely has.

"Bam stands, O Malik, but barely. The Oghuz have begun an earnest assault, hurling boulders at the city walls with giant mangonels."

My hand tightens. I see them trapped, Ishaq, Hanna, Leila, Arzu, Shahzaman, the townspeople, flinching as each boulder collides with the walls, praying that the citadel will withstand the assault, waiting for the Oghuz to ram through the South Gate and spill inside.

The scout continues, "Kirmani and Samarkandi soldiers fight back. They have slicked the walls with hot oil and fire their crossbows, but still the Oghuz come in waves."

"And Dunya?" I croak. "My sister?"

The scout turns to me, black eyes apologetic. "I am sorry, O Khatun, but there is no sign of her."

The emirs—Atsiz, Savtegin, and Ildegiz—share Shahryar's hard expression.

"Have the Oghuz taken the Maiden's Fortress?" Shahryar asks, referring to the Qaleh Dokhtar, an ancient fort that rises from a rocky outcropping on the plain, less than a parasang north from the Arg-e-Bam.

"Yes," the scout says, "although less than a hundred men defend it. Malik Dinar has focused the brunt of his army on the siege."

"Malik Dinar means to take Bam before you return," Atsiz says after the scout departs. "We must march tonight."

Shahryar stares at a map of Kirman, the province's borders marked in lapis, the mountains russet mounds, roads leaf-green slithers, names inked in black and red naksh, and Bam, its crenellated walls and adobe domes painted lovingly in gold and crimson.

"While Malik Dinar's eyes are on Bam, we will take the Maiden's Fortress." Shahryar points to an orange castle north of the citadel. "Replenish our resources, draw his eye from Bam, and stage an assault on his rear while Bam renews its defense. Then, we crush him between us."

"Yes . . . that may work," Emir Savtegin says, rubbing his smooth, hairless chin. "So long as we take the Fortress tonight, as quietly as possible, and attack Malik Dinar before he can reorient his forces."

"Tonight's clouds will give additional cover," Ildegiz says.

When Atsiz does not object, Shahryar says, "Savtegin, ready two hundred of our quickest, strongest soldiers. We will strike before Malik Dinar realizes we are upon him."

As Savtegin leaves, Shahryar, Emir Ildegiz, and Atsiz cluster over the map, murmuring about strategy and defenses, their fingers gliding over green roads, the orange Maiden's Fortress, the gold citadel of Bam. Once the Seljuk course has been finely tuned, Ildegiz and Atsiz depart, determined. Atsiz and Shahryar will lead the battle for the Maiden's Fortress, while Savtegin and silver-headed Ildegiz will remain with the army, ready to join them when they succeed.

I follow Shahryar out of the tent as he works through the camp, clapping soldiers on the back and announcing that the Seljuks return to Bam tonight. The caravan thrums with excitement. An older soldier, his beard and hair streaked gray, kisses Shahryar's hands. Shahryar shines.

On the eve of *his* battle, to claim *his* right, I glimpse the Malik I knew as a girl.

As word spreads, the two hundred chosen bind their breastplates, don their gleaming conical helmets. Under Emir Savtegin's guidance, they array themselves with shields and shamshirs into neat lines, these travel-weary, battle-tired Seljuk soldiers who must face death for the umpteenth time at their lord's command.

Between the soldiers congregating around Shahryar, a young man, in whose tender face, for a breath, ripples Faramurz, bows to me. He claps a fist to his heart. "Make *du'aa* for me, O Khatun. Pray for us all."

Another face ripples above his, a premonition, lifeless as the broken bodies after the Battle of Arsuf. I can think of nothing I want less. "You have my word." My throat closes with emotion.

His eyes, brown as rich earth, glisten. "Then I know we will not fail."

***

In his tent, Shahryar, assisted by his manservant, straps on his armor, gilded with protective Qur'anic verses. On the map still spread out on the crimson rug behind him, Bam glitters, gold and scarlet.

"If I fall, I have ordered the emirs to rally the army to you."

Bells roar in my ears and ring in my bones. "What do you mean?"

"If I die or am captured, you must lead the Seljuks." He delivers this edict as an afterthought, but one of many items to address before riding into war.

"Shahryar." My shoulders are heavy as though strapped with a steel-plated cuirass, the left weighed down by Shahryar's trust, the right by the future of the Seljuks of Kirman. I see myself astride Andalib at the army's head, banners undulating, my face veiled by iron.

I am wise enough to know this is not the kind of power I seek.

"You honor me, Shahryar. Immensely. That you would think me capable is the highest praise." My nose burns with unshed tears. "But *you* are the Malik of Kirman. Remember this. If you lose, we die." The words fall hard.

The blood vanishes from Shahryar's face. "We will not lose." Mouth twitching, he strokes my chin then pulls away.

Briefly, like a habit, I wish he had done more.

"Will you continue your tale?" he asks roughly.

I think of the times I have sent him to war with a story in his heart.

Each time, he has returned.

"In the following weeks, darkness welled in Jauhara. It was quicksand, it was a wave, and it enveloped Jauhara until she could not breathe. Night after night, she crouched in the garden, waiting for al-Maut and her acolytes to return, for Bishr to reappear.

"But they did not.

"At yet another dinner, where the marid feasted and Jauhara could not swallow, she mustered the courage to ask, 'O al-Maut. It has been a month. Have I not done your bidding in all things?'

"Al-Maut stopped chewing. 'You have been obedient.'

"'I have,' Jauhara agreed. 'Against my own heart and my own faith. Have

I not silenced the muezzins and wrenched the veils from the women? You promised me power, and yet you control me entirely. You threaten my family, but I have not seen them. Do you even have them, al-Maut? Do they'—Jauhara's throat dried—'do they even live?'

"Torchlight guttered and sank the hall into shadow. 'Do you doubt me, Jauhara?' al-Maut whispered coldly. The other marid chittered, rat's claws scraping against the ground. 'I, who am truth and justice? You doubt *my* word?'

"Jauhara thought of the Sufi al-Hallaj, strung up for his blasphemous declaration, *I am the truth*, that which only Allah could be. 'If you speak true, then prove it to me. Prove it and I will be your devoted slave.' Jauhara's tongue tripped on the vow.

"'Soon, Jauhara, soon. But tonight, I will show you something else. Something I know you have been longing to see.'

"After the marid finished feasting, Jauhara found herself with their white-robed acolytes in the garden of the palace of al-Askar, an apricot moon looming above. The acolytes avoided Jauhara, but she spotted among them great men of the land—her father's erstwhile chancellors and advisers, muftis and imams. Jauhara trembled at how quickly they had lapsed into ignorance.

"The gravelly chanting that Jauhara recognized rose again, and the rancid sweetness of the incense spun her head. She stumbled, and a strong hand caught her arm. Surprised, she looked up.

"It was Kushyar.

"Save for a flicker, Kushyar betrayed no recognition.

"'Careful, saiditi,' he murmured, setting her aright as Jauhara flushed with shock. The parrot did not appear to be with him. Jauhara's gaze bored into the back of Kushyar's head, as though she could part hair and bone and perceive his intent.

"Al-Maut split the palace stones and led them down sand-dusted steps. Their shared breaths warmed the narrow stairwell.

"Light, harsh as the midday sun in the desert, burst upon them. Jauhara shielded her eyes. They had entered a gold-plated room, fragrant with incense. On the walls gleamed lapis and gold glyphs and etchings of men with animal parts, animals with human parts, all nauseatingly swapped and disjointed.

"One panel depicted a human heart, balanced on an immense scale against a reddened knife. As if drawn from the panel, gold-and-ebon scales, as tall as three men, rose in the chamber's center. The scales tilted to the left, unbalanced by a clean gold knife.

"Jauhara thought of the acolytes' stained robes. Her missing brother. Her vision blurred.

"Al-Maut strode to the room's center, her steps chiming against the gold floor. 'My priests and priestesses,' she said fondly. 'Look how we grow. Where there were none, today there are a hundred. We grow in number, and we grow in *power*. Already, the people forget Him and remember us.'

"The marid hissed in pleasure.

"'But power requires more than will. It requires sacrifice. It requires blood. Noble blood. *Her* blood.' Al-Maut extended a long finger toward Jauhara. 'Bind her.'

"Priests—her father's own friends among them—lashed her hands and feet. Jauhara knew no more."

With anxious hands, I comb Andalib's mane, curry her coat as she blinks patiently. Her sister, Shaheen, softly butts my shoulder as though to ask, *Where is my rider? Where is Dunya?*

Together, we listen to men prepare for battle: the creak of armor, heavy booted feet marching in neat lines, the snorts of battle-trained horses. What happens if Shahryar is felled? I try to remember that he is a malik, trained in strategy by atabegs and emirs and Baba since he was a boy, that he has refined his warcraft by studying Sultan Saladin, the greatest military mind of our age. And who is Malik Dinar? An untutored barbarian brought up far from civilization who thinks victory requires only brutality.

Then again, Malik Dinar is also our cousin, a mirror into what we would have been if, nine generations ago, Seljuk bin Duqaq of the Qiniq clan of Oghuz Turkmen had not liberated a small Muslim town from another Oghuz chieftain and converted to Islam, thereby taking the first step in eternalizing the Seljuk name. We had been nothing, one of twenty-five Oghuz clans that raided the steppes, but in two generations, we became overlords of the caliphs, the Sultans of the East and West, the khutbahs in 'Abbasid Baghdad read in our Seljuk names.

Perhaps Malik Dinar is not our mirror, then—he is our past.

As I turn to brush Shaheen, a tall shadow slips in beside me, soundlessly as a Hashashin. Stumbling against the horse, I open my mouth to scream for my mamluks who must surely be close, who would not be foolish enough to let another Seljuk noblewoman be kidnapped.

"Ay Shaherazade. It's me."

Atsiz, who is as dangerous to me as all the Oghuz. I collide with his warm body, the smooth leather of his jerkin, enveloped in his scent of musk and soap. Despite everything, I have never felt safer.

"You cannot be here." I pull away, my pulse leaping at each step of human and horse.

"I wanted to give you something."

In my hand, Atsiz places a cold, smooth object. I run my fingers up and down—a small dagger, no longer from wooden hilt to metal tip than my forearm. I trace the bone handle, inlaid with silver.

"This was the first weapon my father gave me. You will be with the army, with your mamluks, you will be safe. But in the end, you should be armed."

I want to bring his face to mine and kiss him as we kissed in the caravanserai. I want to remove the layers that separate us and feel his skin heat mine until we are two seamlessly fused bodies. I want us to be two people, simple folk, for whom such things are possible. Instead, he may die tonight and everything between us will have been stillborn.

My voice tight, I say, "Mutashakaram. I will keep this safe for your return."

He sighs. "It is a gift."

Surprising myself, I grip his face, his beard prickling my palm. His breathing grows ragged. My heartbeat almost drowns my voice. "Bring yourself back to me whole. That is the only gift I seek."

"Ay Khoda, I swear it."

With that, he is gone.

A short time later, I hear the pounding of hooves on earth and know that the Seljuk vanguard is gone too.

Thirty-Four

⬦⬦⬦⬦⬦

Nervously rubbing the dagger's bone handle, I wander the dark encampment. Soldiers stir uneasily, their tents packed, lying on thin pallets that can be quickly folded if we must move. They greet me faintly. It is almost Fajr. Shahryar, Atsiz, and the army must be near the Qaleh Dokhtar by now, skulking in the scrub, skirting sentries, sneaking through the dark, swords in hand. It will be hours before we know anything, but still, I keep looking east, as if I could scry through the miles of desert and mountain, through the night-dark, and into the heart of their battle.

And if they lose?

If Malik Dinar takes Shahryar's and Atsiz's heads and mounts them on pikes to rot on the Arg-e-Bam's ramparts, could I lead Kirman's army? Where would we go but back, to throw ourselves on Sultan Saladin's mercy or dissipate like dust into Azerbaijan's reaches or Georgia's mountains, like many a defeated Persian noble? But I know I cannot depart this land without Dunya.

Silver bubbles foaming in her wake, the seamaid Neda halted before a towering mountain checkered with waving seagrass. Water distorted the shrill cries closing in.

Neda leapt.

She climbed leagues as quickly as her legs could pump and when she reached the place sunshine warmed the ocean, she looked down, past sloping hills, undersea forests, and shimmering schools of darting fish. She had escaped. But relief lasted only a moment before a net snarled itself in her sable hair and webbed fingers. Flailing, she only knotted herself tighter as unseen hands reeled her to the surface . . .

I return to my tent and lay out my copper prayer rug, woven with turquoise blocks and cobalt diamonds. Rubbing clean earth on my face and forearms, I perform *tayyamum*, and so purified, as I promised the soldier, I fold my hands across my breast and pray for Seljuk victory, for Shahryar's safety, for Atsiz's safety, for the safety of all the soldiers whose names I do not know who would die for us.

✷ ✷ ✷

Under a woolen sky, three thousand Seljuk soldiers fly. I bend low over Andalib's neck, racing to the Qaleh Dokhtar, which, mamluks report, Shahryar wrested from Malik Dinar's soldiers in a quick and quiet ambush. A first victory, and an omen of Allah's favor. Shahryar survived, Atsiz survived, and I release a breath I did not realize I was holding.

Andalib's sweat seeps through my trousers, and I can feel her quavering at the furious pace that Emir Ildegiz has set for hours. Unshaken, Nurani and Gulnar keep pace beside me, their braids and veils streaming behind them like war banners. Overhead, the clouds crack open and auspicious Mars winks like a ruby eye.

My breath quickens. There, through the half dark, pricks the Qaleh Dokhtar on the horizon. The fortress sits on a rocky outcropping, its six stone towers illumined in firelight. Parasangs south down the plain, the torches and fires of Malik Dinar's army shimmer, ensnaring Bam in a flaming noose. Somewhere there too is Dunya. Can she feel me pass, our twin souls grazing each other? We are so close that I could spin Andalib south, careen through the great Oghuz army, pound at Bam's gates, and finally be home.

Thighs aching, I train my eyes ahead. At any moment, the Oghuz army can turn toward us, nock its bows, and fell us in a hailstorm of arrows. As the wind whistles past my ears, I flinch. But the night is our friend—we ride without torches, and at a distance, we are little more than shadow. Perhaps that too is a signal of Allah's favor. I urge the flagging Andalib faster.

As we near the Qaleh Dokhtar's east gates, the soldiers within cry out in recognition and I relax with relief. The wooden gate is cranked open, and the Seljuk rear guard gallops into the bailey until there is not room to breathe. I am smashed between my mamluks; a mail shirt digs into my cheek. The courtyard stinks of men, sweat, and horses, but I can't help but join in the soldiers' cheers.

"Takbir!"

"Allahu akbar!"

The cries rattle through my chest and against the fortress's old walls.

Drawn by the thunder of hooves and the cries of men, Shahryar appears on the stairs. His grin splits his face. Musicians beat their drums, blow their pipes, and rattle their tambourines before their magnificently smiling Malik, who clasps their shoulders, kisses their sweaty foreheads, a beaming warrior king. His boots are muddy, his hauberk bloody, and his long, black hair is matted with sweat.

But he is whole. I look, too, for Atsiz in the throng, but I do not find him.

Shahryar leaps to the ramparts and bellows so that the soldiers in all corners of the fortress can hear. "My Seljuk brothers, today, we have taken our first step to reclaiming our home. Tonight, we rest. Tomorrow morning, we smash the Oghuz flies against Bam's walls, ride on them with our horses and bows until we crush them to dust. *That* is the fate of those who would seek to wrest Kirman from the Seljuk."

My ears ring as the men whoop, and the trumpeting of horns and percussion of drums echo in the courtyard, drowning my own giddy cheers. Shahryar grins beatifically. When his eyes find mine, he raises a satisfied eyebrow. I smile in return.

As the soldiers' celebration quiets, Yaghmur and the clerks begin working through the soldiers to task them with clearing the dead, cleaning the castle, and setting up bed for the night. With difficulty, I weave through the tight morass of soldiers.

Spying Shahryar disappear up the stairs, I push through the milling soldiers to follow.

Despite the dry stones, the dark stairwell smells moist. Slipping even in my riding boots on the worn steps, I scrabble against the rough wall until a doorway opens to the rampart. Concealed in the archway, I watch as Shahryar and Atsiz—who is dirty but unwounded—and Emirs Ildegiz and Savtegin stand expectantly beneath a tower.

I sidle in between Atsiz and Shahryar. They seem surprised to see me, but they make room.

First, there is only darkness.

"What are we waiting for?" I ask, but no one answers.

Then, the tower blazes like a candle, the beacon within lit. The men turn toward Bam, but no responding light flares. We watch and watch, but nothing happens. A breath of disappointment passes through the emirs. But even as they turn away, Shahryar does not stop watching.

And then, the citadel's Fire Tower lights up like a flaming sun, illuminating Bam's crenellated walls and winding steps, the citadel, madrasas, mosques, and homes.

The merry signal flame feels like a touch, as if we reached out to Bam, and in response, she wrapped her fingers around ours. What must they be thinking, to know that we have returned at last? Would I recognize the soldiers who lit the beacon? Does Dunya see this and know what it means? Do Leila and Hanna and Ishaq?

If we win against Malik Dinar, will that heal the place the Malik once held in Bam's heart? Staring at Malik Dinar's vast army that sinks almost half the plain into black, I think, *one at a time.*

* * *

Shahryar's room in the fortress is small and dank, but Yaghmur has appointed it with his rugs and cushions, imbuing it with a comfortable familiarity. Despite the tight quarters and short time, Yaghmur and the cooks have managed a meal for the emirs of pullets roasted with olive oil, game meat cooked with raisin juice, and pilau. Atsiz and I flank Shahryar on his right and left at the head of a low wooden table riven by a deep crack running through its center. We do not look at each other.

As servants lay out the steaming dishes, I prompt, "O Malik, tell us of how you struck a blow to the eye of the Oghuz and wrested the fortress from them."

Downing a chalice of wine, Shahryar rakes his fingers through his dark hair. "We rode from the camp through the dark. Malik Dinar had set a scout on our tail, but Savtegin shot him clean through the neck. We raced on to the Qaleh Dokhtar, which the flea-bitten Oghuz had taken in name only—thirty if not fewer soldiers held it. Ay Khoda, I swear, when we rode up, minutes before dawn, they had not even locked the gate. And what are thirty Oghuz before two hundred Seljuks?"

The emirs thump the low table. The glazed turquoise dishes bounce and ring.

"Before they could scream, we slit each Oghuz throat. It was done that quietly and that easily, as though Allah Himself had cloaked our efforts in velvet. I'd guess that Malik Dinar is only now hearing that the Seljuks have returned to Kirman, killed his men, taken back their fortress, and stand ready to thrash the Oghuz against Bam's walls." Shahryar leans back with a satisfied smile, a leopard with an antelope in his jaws.

"Before first light," Atsiz says.

"Before first light," Shahryar agrees, finishing his chalice. "While the Oghuz gnats still sleep."

The conversation hums, but with battle imminent and Shahryar dozing, the emirs trickle to their makeshift chambers. Gently, I shake Shahryar awake, guide him out of his clothes and into a soft cotton tunic for sleeping.

"I did well, didn't I, Shaherazade?" he asks, nuzzling his cheek against a pillow.

My heart wells with tenderness for him, this tired man whose shoulders bear the weight of our civilization. Hesitantly, I kiss his forehead and feel a flicker of relief when he does not pull away. "You did marvelously. And tomorrow, you will do marvelously again, insh'Allah."

"Insh'Allah," Shahryar echoes. "Insh'Allah, tomorrow night, we will sleep in the Arg-e-Bam." His voice cracks with longing, and I bury my face against his chest. To think we could be back in those familiar halls that soon.

Extinguishing the bronze lamp, I lie beside Shahryar and feel him flip toward me.

"Continue your story," he murmurs. "Just until I fall asleep."

"O Malik, it is said that when Jauhara awoke in her own bed, Kushyar, still garbed as an acolyte, resolved before her. Jauhara watched him distrustfully. Nonetheless, she licked her dry lips and asked, 'What happened?'

"'A sacrifice of your blood,' and the voice was not Kushyar's, but melodious, birdsong bound with trumpets. The saffron-crested parrot hopped onto Jauhara's woven bedspread. 'That is why al-Maut holds your family. They are Egypt's ruling family and you are the awakener of the marid— there is power in their blood and yours. Power that the marid can use to restore their own.'

"'Why did she not kill me?' Jauhara gasped, rubbing her bandaged arms.

"'Because it is not yet necessary. But some blood is weaker than others,' the parrot said.

"'Bishr.' Jauhara dropped into a well, black and deep, with the water fast rising, to her chin, above her head.

"'Yes,' the parrot said sadly. 'And before him, your sister Ruqaiyya.'

"'*No.*' Jauhara heard strums of the stringed *simsimiyya*, which would sing under Ruqaiyya's deft fingers. She smelled Bishr's *khabis gharib*, the honey and walnut oil pudding he prepared so expertly that no other cook in the palace would make it.

"'That is why she has gathered your father's friends as her priests,' Kushyar said. 'The sacrifice cuts deeper for the love they bore your father.'

"'May Allah curse them!' Jauhara exclaimed. 'And you, Kushyar? You joined her, too. Are you any better than my father's betrayers?'

"Kushyar's eyebrows rose, and the parrot unfurled a wing on Jauhara's hand. 'He has joined them to learn of the marid.'

"'And what have you learned?' Jauhara said coldly.

"'Your parents still live,' Kushyar said. At his words, a knot burst in Jauhara's chest and great hiccups—relief, fear, and desperation—shuddered through her.

"'Where are they?' Jauhara asked once she regained her breath.

"'Only al-Maut's most trusted priests know,' Kushyar said. 'But they are somewhere near, in al-Askar.'

"'So al-Maut lied to me. She will kill my family, one by one, and use their blood to drive Egypt into jahiliyya.'

"'Ya Jauhara,' the parrot said. 'The descent has already begun.'

"Jauhara saw Ruqaiyya's and Bishr's faces and knew that her compliance was finished.

"In the evening, after Kushyar and the parrot had left, al-Maut visited Jauhara in the guise of a woman. 'Were you frightened by what you saw, Jauhara?'

"Jauhara said, 'O al-Maut, I had a vision. You and the other marid stood high atop the pyramids in the desert of Giza and all of Egypt knelt before you as the sun rose high. And I? I stood on the pyramid beneath you, and I knew it was my rightful place.

"'You need only to command. I am with you, with my whole heart.'

"Al-Maut dug her nails, long and sharp, into Jauhara's chest, so deeply that Jauhara thought that al-Maut would rip it out, but Jauhara met her eye and did not flinch.

"'If I have your heart,' al-Maut cooed, 'you must prove it.'"

Shahryar's breath comes at easy intervals, and I allow my voice to trail off as something pelts the window.

Quietly, I slip from bed and peer through the window. Atsiz stands in the bailey, cupping gravel, his arm poised to throw. Sighting me, he points inside the fortress. My brow furrows, but then I understand. Padding to the door, I slide past the mamluk guards with a cool nod.

My heart hums against my breastbone, one unceasing beat until I am alone and out of the guards' sight. I should not be doing this, but I feel both in my own body and apart. In the hall's half darkness, I jump at a shadow emerging from the stairs.

Atsiz places a finger against his lips and beckons. I wait for him to speak, but he only gazes at me with such tender focus that I can no longer bear the silence or space between us. I withdraw his dagger, warm from the hours at my side.

"Mutashakaram for this loan." I try to return it, but he fends me off.

"It's a gift. The least I can do for you." His green-gold eyes shine.

"I cannot keep it. You know that." But I want to keep it, this token of his affection. If I cannot have him, then why can I not have this? But the answer to both questions is the same.

"I want you to," he says, and for a moment, I hear, "I want you," and my blood runs cold and then very, very hot. Suddenly, the dagger feels like fire against my fingers, ripe to burn.

"Take it back!" I shove the dagger at Atsiz. He wraps his fingers around my hands and I am like a fly captured in the sticky, silver thread of a spider's web. My pulse hammers hard enough to burst through my throat.

Suddenly, Atsiz's hands drop away and I grasp only air. Feeling hot breath down my neck, I spin around.

Shahryar.

His flint-sharp eyes catch on me, on Atsiz. "What is this?" he asks. Wine wafts on his words.

Atsiz proffers the dagger to Shahryar as though it can bear witness to the truth. "I gave this to your wife for protection while we took the Qaleh Dokhtar."

I expect Shahryar to say, *You overstep, Emir Atsiz. She is my wife and I protect her as I please*, but he only looks at me.

"I was returning it to him. That is it. By Allah, I swear to you."

Even as I say it, my chest twinges, but Shahryar relaxes. He believes us, and perhaps, despite himself, we are two of the only people he can trust.

Should I confess my sins? They are not so vast. Court romances that live in chaste imagination are not uncommon. And then what? Do I tell him of the physical embrace? The division in my heart?

Then I remember who Shahryar is, and I have come too far to lose my head.

"Atsiz, do you swear it?" A childlike naïveté rings through.

Pale but steady, Atsiz answers, "I swear it too."

Shahryar's face fixes into a cold, bronze mask. "Then you both have forsworn yourselves. You think I do not know what has passed between you beneath night's dark when you thought you were alone?"

Here is each nightmare, each foreboding, come to life. I dig my fingernails into my thigh, scratching past robe and trousers, but I do not wake. *How could I have been so foolish?*

Quick as a snake, Shahryar fixes me to his side and calls for his mamluks. I hear their thudding steps, their fish-scale armor ringing like raindrops as they appear. Shahryar points at Atsiz, who stands stiff-necked, a soldier taking his censure.

"Take him to the dungeons."

Atsiz faces Shahryar as the mamluks pin his arms. "I will not resist, for you are my commander and my fealty is always yours. I beg your pardon for my trespass. But you are making a mistake, and I fear it will be grievous for our war."

Our eyes meet only briefly as the mamluks lead Atsiz away, and in them I read apology, regret, fear, and underneath it all something warmer and deeper that we have not yet spoken.

Wresting my arm, Shahryar jerks me into his small chamber.

"I don't know what you think I've done." I try to keep the quaver from my voice, to sound honest and sincere. "But I am no Fataneh Khatun."

"Do not say her name," he growls, thrusting me inside. He pulls the heavy wooden door shut, peering at me through a sliver between jamb and door. "Little Shaherazade, I thought you cannier than this. Oh, the rumors that swirled, brought by your own mamluks, by others with no reason to lie. Mahperi picked the wrong man, but she wasn't entirely mistaken, was she?"

My ears throb, my cheeks warm, and fear, thick as wool, scours my stomach. Before I can muster my defense, Shahryar locks the door. The wood is so thick that I cannot hear his footsteps disappear down the hall. I could scream, but even if the sound broke through, who would come? Even my own mamluks have betrayed me. It is no less than I deserve for acting recklessly when I knew I did not have that luxury, for sinning when I knew better.

After everything—leaving Bam and Baba, a year in caravans and tents, Mahperi's death and Dunya's abduction—I too will end as Fataneh did. I think of the philosopher, al-Jahiz, smothered beneath the weight of his own books.

I cannot slow my breath. Was I seized by the same lunacy that possessed Fataneh when she took her lover again and again? Or was it Fataneh herself, her spirit clawing out of the grave and quickening my feet to wreak her vengeance for a poem slipped beneath a door, a head tumbled in a straw basket?

I rush to the thick glass window. Heave it open. Let the cold, dry air caress my face. I grip the rough stone sill, inhale deeply until I steady.

Once, there was a childless Andalusian sultan in desperate want of a son. He had one wife, a Moorish princess, and while another king might have wed again, his marriage contract forbade him from doing so. Instead, he turned to the hundred concubines of his harem, but their wombs too failed to quicken. Soon, it was whispered that the Sultan—not the women—was deficient. The Sultana gave thanks, for she knew that if another woman bore the long-awaited heir, she would become nothing.

But one airless afternoon, the Sultan's steward smirked as he reported, "One of the Sultan's concubines is expecting. A child is due in the summer." The Sultana, her breath hostage in her lungs, waited while the Sultan doted on his concubine and the court's orbit shifted to circumambulate her.

The day her husband's son was born, the Sultana asked her trusted servants to quietly spread word among the city's druggists that she needed their services. Pharmacist upon pharmacist offered her tinctures to inspire the Sultan's desire, elixirs to heighten his potency, and powders to increase her fertility. But still, she did not become pregnant, and the Sultan's annoyance with her—an infertile obstruction that prevented him from marrying the bewitching mother of his son—became increasingly palpable.

When the concubine's son reached six months, the Sultana's servant brought a merchant to her receiving chamber. Seated on a rosewood divan, the Sultana regarded the merchant. He was tall and narrowly drawn, whip-like, sharp-faced. The Sultana felt a thrill of danger.

"O Sultana, I come to make you the gift of a son."

"How will you do that?" the Sultana replied, certain that he, like the others, would prove unfruitful.

"I will provide you the same method that the umm walad *used." Smiling, the merchant reached for the Sultana but did not touch her.*

"You helped the concubine?"

"I did."

The Sultana eyed him warily but did not retract her hand. "How?"

"The Sultan is sterile," the merchant said. "But I have ten children with my own wife and countless with other women whose husbands cannot produce. Lie with me and I will make you a mother as well."

The Sultana considered the proposal, considered the man, and then considered growing old and powerless, locked in the harem, no better than an old aunt from the countryside. She opened her arms. As the merchant's hands slid through her hair, over her hips, and slipped her silk robe over her pale shoulder, the Sultana remembered a feeling she had long forgotten—that of being desired.

As the Sultana and the merchant lay on the deed's precipice, the Sultana's door was forced open with a crack. A regiment of the Sultan's guards crammed into the room, scimitars drawn. The Sultan followed.

Shrieking, the Sultana pushed the merchant away, gathering her robes, but she knew, with a feeling like being dropped into quicksand, that her fate was sealed. She did not protest as the guards conveyed her to the dungeons. Because of this, she did not see the steward slip a purse of dinars into the merchant's hand or the Sultan's own wide smile.

Three stories below and beyond stretches the wide plain, cupped by rocky mountains. It folds forward until it meets the twinkling lanterns of Malik Dinar's army and Bam's moon-bathed adobe walls.

There is all of that, but no escape.

Thirty-Five

◇◇◇◇◇◇

I awake to the Fajr azaan in an unfamiliar bed. I try to move my legs, raise my neck, but I am frozen.

I am not alone.

Through the hazy dark, a shadowy form, four-winged and many-eyed—Fataneh's spring-green, Mahperi's gentle brown (or is it Dunya's?)—glides toward me.

I recognize him.

He is 'Azraeel, the angel of death. Although I scream, my throat is mute. I try again, but I am suffocating.

He is coming for me, they are coming for me, something is coming for me.

He is upon me, clawing at me, dragging me up, up, up, through the door and to the ramparts so that I may be punished for my crimes in this world and the next. Of course it would happen. How could I have thought it would not? 'Azraeel's face, carved of black and silver bone, is calm, removed, half in this world, half in the next. I pull away from his spider-fingered grasp.

I scream—

—and like a drowning body emerging from the sea, I resurface in bed. My limbs are my own, and when I whisper, Ay Khoda, the sound is mine as well.

'Azraeel dissipates, skulking through the crack beneath the door.

I remember last night again, the betrayal rank around Atsiz and me. Shahryar cutting through vine and bramble and seeing the treachery lacquer our hearts.

Is this how Fataneh felt? Mad with the stink of herself and the stink of her sins? Was it the loneliness, this feeling that the world is continuing without her like a ship floating with the tides that drove Mahperi to her end?

Rising, I open the crooked shutters to a rush of cool air. I hear familiar noises: the jangle of armor, the thud of hoofbeats. Peering through the predawn dark, I sight them: a thick ring of thousands of armored Oghuz marching upon the Qaleh Dokhtar, an orderly swarm. Stretching into the vast plain, out of arrow's reach, they trumpet war horns, beat drums, and stomp their feet. My heart thumps in time, a synchronous treason.

Ay Khoda, ay Khoda, ay Khoda.

The Oghuz have sneaked upon us as we slept.

Shadows of Seljuk soldiers race along the fortress's battlements. Shahryar appears—I recognize his broad shoulders, his assured step—leaping over the stairs two at a time. At the top of the ramparts, his neck swivels as he silently surveys the noose the Oghuz army has caught us in.

I feel the noose tighten around my own throat.

✳ ✳ ✳

Isolated in my imprisonment, I conjure Dunya, then Baba, then Mama, their soft answers emanating from somewhere beyond mist.

What do you think, Baba?

His gentle fingers lace through my braids. I fear for you, jaanem.

You always worry, Muhammad, Mama says. You will emerge from this, dokhtarem. Stronger.

I cannot believe you would do this, Dunya hisses.

Gulnar, bearing flatbread and salted goat, enters and dispels their shadows. Tight-lipped, she places the food on the table.

I lower the collection of Dede Korkut's Oghuz tales. My questions pour like a torrent. "Durood. Any news, Gulnar jaan, of the siege? Of how long Shahryar means to keep me here?" Glancing at the mamluk guards, I refrain from asking after Atsiz. I picture him kicking against a twisted, silken cord at his neck, his eyes bulging, face purpling. My lip trembles. *Audhubillah.* Then I feel the cord strangling me, envision the ugly, mottled purple that cut across Mahperi's neck. I rub at my throat.

"I cannot answer your questions, Shaherazade Khatun," Gulnar replies woodenly.

Has she heard what passed last night? Did she think that when Baba charged me to her care a year ago, I would be so feckless, so sinful? But her eyes are soft and after a quick look over her shoulder, she squeezes my hand. "I will return with your dinner after Maghrib."

Before Gulnar seals me behind the door, I beg the mamluks, "Tell the Malik I wish to speak to him. Please. Tell him I must."

I don't know what I could say to him, whether my words would quench a flame or accelerate it. Once, I enticed guards at the Malik's door with a tale, but before I can say another word, the mamluks slam the door, that handbreadth of wood dividing me from liberty.

I wish I could count on my mamluks to smash this door to splinters and redeem me of these confines. I wish that I had done so many things differently.

I choke down each bite of oily meat and stale bread. After, I retrieve my chronicle and sit by the window. I cross out lines and add phrases, soothing, at least briefly, my nerves. Can it be that I wrote this chronicle for Shahryar in a world where I was rising in his favor, where he allowed me privileges denied others, and that I took this thing of fine-spun glass and handled it like coal?

After some time, movement catches my eye. Seljuk horsemen in leather jerkins, with light cuirasses, bows slung in their saddles, and swords at their hips, ride into the bailey. I spy Emir Ildegiz at their head, his hair flowing from his steel helmet. Captains ride between the soldiers, straightening the lines. Dozens more archers climb to the battlement, stationing themselves between the crenels.

The sudden, bone-shaking beat of Seljuk drums raises the hair on my arms. Marching out the open gate and onto the plain, two thousand Seljuk soldiers take their positions on the other side of the wall. Shahryar stalks on his white stallion at the army's head, while artillerymen arrange trebuchets on the ramparts.

On the other side, Oghuz soldiers, sighting our preparations, stir. The Seljuk horsemen raise a great hue and cry, and musicians beat their tombeks and blow their horns in menacing discord. Once soldiers advance close enough, they snipe the Oghuz front lines with a volley of arrows.

Then, like released arrows themselves, the Seljuk horsemen fly.

Shahryar is lost in the sea of soldiers and suddenly a treasonous thought strikes me—

If Shahryar perishes, I am no longer a prisoner to his power.

If Shahryar perishes, then my husband is dead, the Seljuk armies dissolve, Bam is lost, the Oghuz prevail, and Malik Dinar becomes the ruler. And perhaps my life would still be forfeit. I shake the vile, disloyal thought from my head.

Ay Khoda, preserve my husband's safety from the Oghuz and from my own thoughts.

In the slurry of dust, the battlefield is a giant, worming body, like a nest of rats, men and horses and swords and arrows flailing in one mass. I hear their high-pitched screams, until the sounds become so terrible that I seal the window and turn away. Even so, the cries carry through the glass, tinny and embedded deep in my ear.

I try turning to the chronicle, but I keep losing the thread of my sentences. I pace the small chamber, counting the rough stones in the wall, the flagstones on the floor, but I lose the thread there too. I spread my rug and pray, but the battle keeps me twitching. I knock on the door, but Shahryar's mamluks do not answer. I rifle through *Kalila wa Dimna*. The screams and war drums grow louder, and despite myself I rush to the window.

The Seljuk army is in retreat.

Whooping victoriously, the Oghuz troops bear down and the Seljuk soldiers cascade back into the Qaleh Dokhtar. Soldiers stand in their stirrups to hasten their steeds; the field behind is littered with bloody dead. Broken bodies flash between galloping horse legs.

Arrows, loosed by the Seljuk archers stationed on the battlements, briefly darken the sky and then descend like locusts onto the Oghuz, felling them by the dozens as the Seljuk army fills the bailey.

Still the Oghuz come.

The gate shuts. The Seljuk bowmen keep shooting, selecting arrows from their quivers, nocking, pulling the bowstrings taut, and releasing arrows in clean parabolae in practiced unison until the last Oghuz pursuer falls or flees.

But beyond the archers' reach, the remainder of the Oghuz army stands, numerous, strong, and now triumphant.

✳ ✳ ✳

Some days after the rout, after Isha, my door creaks open and I hear the carousing of soldiers, plates clattering, goblets slamming. The faint moonlight that has picked through the window shines on the figure padding inside. My neck prickles. I do not recognize it. Not Shahryar, broad and strong, nor Gulnar, familiar and wiry. I wish for Atsiz's dagger, envisioning a Hashashin hired to make quick work of Shahryar's unfaithful wife or a nameless mamluk seeking to earn the Malik's favor.

"Announce yourself," I say, steely.

The intruder laughs, husky and familiar. "Frightened so easily, Shaher-azade?"

Her sapphire diadem glittering, Nurani surveys the shadowed chamber. "What keeps you away from us, Shaherazade?" she asks, eyebrow lifted. "The Malik claims you are ill, but the Qaleh Dokhtar *brims* with rumor."

I hear her smirk, but it cannot diminish a sunlit burst of hope—Shahryar conceals my fall. But—maybe he does so not for my sake, but because he fears rumor spreading like wildfire, windblown from east to west—to Malik Dinar, Caliph an-Nasir, Sultan Saladin—that Malik Shahryar has been cuckolded again.

"Why are you here?"

Nurani's farajiyya whispers against the floor, the embroidered ruby silk soft on stone as she circles me. "I came to see you, caught in the web you thought you'd so cleverly woven. If only Fataneh could see you." Her teeth flash white, a predator stalking.

"Not many would be so loyal to a dead adulteress."

"Would that *you* had been more loyal, Shaherazade."

"How are you here, Nurani?" I tear each word with my teeth.

"Shahryar heard you were longing for company," she drawls. "And he thought, who better than me?"

What had Shahryar said? Someone who was no liar had told him something, something that was enough to persuade him to imprison me. Someone had moved their hands and mouth to harm me, crooning the devil's *waswasa* in the Malik's ear.

It clicks together.

"It was you. Feeding lies to the Malik." Rage swallows my veins like naphtha, fury at Nurani for betraying me, fury that I placed myself in a position where I could be betrayed.

Nurani's slippers tap as she walks closer, so near that I can smell her sandalwood attar. "Lies?" She laughs humorlessly. "I saw you, you foolish girl. I saw you and Atsiz in the caravanserai. I saw you caught by your own mamluk captain. Did you think you would escape notice?"

Anger grabs my neck and shakes my voice. "You betrayed me."

"A hypocrite betrays only herself."

"I can't believe you risked Atsiz to do so."

I imagine Shahryar torturing Atsiz as he tortured the Oghuz scout: bound on his knees and whipped by Shahryar's watered blade until he bleeds.

Nurani sniffs. "The alliances of men run deep. Even now, Atsiz leads nighttime sorties against the Oghuz, surrounded by a coterie of Seljuk soldiers."

Despite myself, I gasp, as if a sharp dagger has been slid between my ribs.

"You did not understand that men will forgive each other and punish women. You sold Fataneh for the Malik's favor and her position. But you could never make it yours."

Winded, I lean against the wall, cold seeping through my fur-lined cloak. I see a tumult of images: Atsiz riding with Shahryar's soldiers, Fataneh smiling at her wedding, Atsiz and Shahryar laughing together, Fataneh weeping in her cell.

Should I claim that Nurani's arrow has missed its mark? Whatever else, Nurani was Fataneh's friend, the only one who, even after her death, speaks for her.

"I regret it," I say quietly.

A sharp intake of breath.

Honesty loosens my tongue. "In some ways, not in others. I regret that I acted without understanding, as a child, muddling through adult affairs. I regret that my unthinking caused her death. But I do not regret that I acted to protect my family or Shahryar.

"I take my part for what happened to Fataneh, but so must she take hers, the Malik his, and those in the Arg-e-Bam who stood still as the Malik went mad."

Nurani does not even pause before retorting. "Is that the pretty story you will tell yourself when you meet the same end?"

Disappointment pulses through me. I had hoped Nurani would feel the truth in my words, that even if she could not forgive me, she would understand me.

I must accept that she does not.

* * *

"My mamluks report that you have called for me."

Shahryar does not look at me, instead training his gaze on the window. Blood thunders through my limbs and my fingertips. I had almost given up expecting him. Keeping my eyes at his slippered, astride feet, I surreptitiously glance up and catch flickers of my husband: a bloodred kaftan, his dark beard, unusually unkempt, his heavy, tired eyes.

"I was not inclined, but then I considered: if Fataneh was permitted a final personal audience, then you are owed the same."

My ears ring at *final*. "Mutashakaram. I am grateful."

I wait for him to speak, but his foot drums against the flagstones. "This audience was at your request."

Although I should not, I ask, "Do you truly believe my sins are the same as Fataneh's?"

He raises his eyebrows and I fear that I have overstepped. Then I almost scoff for I *have* overstepped. I am Shahryar's wife because I overstepped. We fought against the Crusaders alongside Saladin and then returned from Palestine because I overstepped. Bam did not burn because I overstepped. I am imprisoned because I overstepped.

"There *is* a difference, Shaherazade. I loved Fataneh."

And you are nothing to me.

The sea crashes against my ears and the room spins. After all my confusion, here is the answer, plainly put. I follow his eyes to the window and think that we are on the cusp of judgment day. And the story I have told myself about Shahryar for months, for years, the secret that I have kept, bursts like a bitten peppercorn on my tongue.

"O Malik, permit me to tell you a tale. A true tale although its heart is fable.

"Once, in a great-walled desert city in the middle of a vast and dissipating empire, a girl fell in love with a king. She was no beauty, and although her father was powerful in their small world, no one feared her or even thought about her. The king was married and in love, and when he looked at the girl, if he ever did, he saw a child. Yet, she knew the king and, in her own quiet way, thought she saw the goodness deep in his soul.

"Although the king, one bloody morning, moved in part by the girl's own foolish hand, killed his beloved wife, the girl continued to love him. Even after he wed and beheaded a procession of innocent girls to purge his grief, the girl believed that despair fogged his goodness and loved him.

"When she finally married him, thinking she could save him from the rot in his soul, her heart broke upon him, night after night, over and over, like waves crashing upon sand and rock. But his hardness proved impenetrable and even the flickers of gold that appeared were blackened. She feared that he had never been as kind and gentle and strong as she had thought, but that her love had imagined those qualities for him. She realized, over time, the folly of loving a story, and the folly of hoping that she would be loved in return."

My tongue sticks against my dry mouth. A serpent, bound tightly around my lungs and stomach, has loosened.

Shahryar's eye twitches, his fingers curl, his mouth puckers. I brace myself for his reply. But he closes his eyes, unfurls his fingers, and walks out. He closes the door behind him, neither softly nor loudly.

As he leaves, twin azaan resound against the mountains, the Seljuk azaan so close that it echoes in my ear and the other, Oghuz azaan a sepulchral whisper. The call to prayer binds the distance between the two armies. Here and there, the Oghuz and Seljuk will simultaneously pray to the same god, in the same manner, so that when Allah watches from the heavens, He would see us moving as one.

I lay out my prayer rug and join. At 'Isha's conclusion, after greeting the angels on my left and right, I bury my face in cupped hands and pray for Seljuk victory, Dunya's safety, pray that the world would return to what it had been, that He forgive my multitude of sins.

Thirty-Six

The Qaleh Dokhtar's ramparts are alive with Seljuk soldiers falling into position as the emirs call orders. I clutch the windowsill as the first Seljuk volley of naphtha-dipped arrows alight like meteors in the night. *Bam. Bam. Bam.*

The great Oghuz-hefted battering ram rocks against the Qaleh Dokhtar's thin gate, more artifact than defense. I wait to hear it fissure. It holds. Our Seljuk archers fill the sky with flaring arrows, raining fire on the Oghuz in a steady, mesmerizing rhythm.

The Oghuz army does not bend.

A shouted command, and the Seljuk archers focus their fire. After a flaming pounding, an Oghuz siege tower catches, fire licking wood and man alike and casting the Qaleh Dokhtar in combustive orange. But four other Oghuz siege towers stand tall and untouched.

Ay Khoda, safeguard us all.

Almost a year ago, thinking to delay his hand, I had advised Caliph an-Nasir to wait to pluck the rose until the gardener was home. I had hoped the seed I patted into the earth would never take root. But here is the harvest—the lines of Oghuz horsemen stretching into the vanishing dark, a battering ram poised at the main gate, great wooden siege towers rolled to the Qaleh Dokhtar—no doubt funded by the Caliph's coffers.

Another siege engine docks on the curtain wall. Even as it crackles with fire, dozens of Oghuz soldiers spill from it onto the walls. They slice through the Seljuk defenders with ferocious ease, leaving empty pockmarks along the defenses. Seljuk reinforcements race to the wall, swarming on the Oghuz like ants over honeyed halva. In minutes, the Seljuks decimate the Oghuz as the siege engine crumbles, piece by blazing piece. Sweet, woody smoke fogs the ramparts, slipping its tendrils into the bailey and over the battlefield until the armies fight in and against dark and smoke.

This is how they will tell the tale of our victory. We repulse the Oghuz at every turn and our soldiers fight with greater fury, because they defend what is theirs—their land, their home, their families, their empire. We do it again and again as the sun rises, glinting on armor and outshining the burning fires. Soon, Bam's South Gate will open and its soldiers will spill forth. How can the Oghuz hope to withstand our rage?

Titanic thunder roars.

The walls shake, and before my eyes a great piece of the curtain wall descends, sapped.

Below, Seljuk archers lie broken, crushed by stone blocks. The Qaleh Dokhtar is cut open, an apple bitten by Allah's own teeth.

For a moment, all is breath.

Then, the Oghuz give a wild cry that raises the hair on my nape. The fire lights their hauberks red and they flood into the wall's split seam like a river of blood.

I curl to the floor, my hands shaking. I cannot will them to stop. My heart beats spitfire in my ears. High-pitched, jubilant ululations beat through the walls, and the thumps of a hundred battle drums reverberate like tiny earthquakes.

Other Seljuks appear at the wound, but they are not a bandage thick enough to stanch the blood, and the invigorated Oghuz fling the Seljuk soldiers aside like dolls. They work with methodical brutality, opening the gate, slitting throats, and punching through Seljuk cuirasses into soft flesh.

In the smoke and fire and fray, I do not see the other emirs. I do not see my mamluks. I do not see Shahryar. I do not see Atsiz. But I see Seljuk men splayed on the earth, wounded, bleeding, dead.

I hear screams and stamping boots racing through the hallway.

The Oghuz are inside.

The window is small, but I could pull my body through and hurl myself to the ground. But it is only three stories. Not enough to guarantee a broken neck. I could take the dinner knife and pass it over my wrists, deep enough so I bleed until the world goes softly dark. I could do this in the face of this world-altering defeat.

But the world has ended before. Many times. Each time, it begins anew.

I think of Mama, the descendant of Sassanian princesses who survived conquest by the Arabs, who survived the Umayyads, to survive the 'Abbasids, to survive Seljuk dominion. Will I be the first of my bloodline to falter and fall?

Violent knocks crack against my door, mailed fists shaking the frame. Swiping the dull dinner knife and backing into the far corner of the room, I wish I had barricaded the door with bed and table.

Yells are followed by heavy, bodily thumps. *Ay Khoda, let it be the Seljuk guards who have prevailed.* The pounding escalates, deafening thumps striking the wood. A battle-ax splinters through. My skin turns to ice.

Frantically, I look around the small room, searching for somewhere to hide: the bed and table are too low to slip under, the garderobe too exposed; there are, however, my trunks. Opening a heavy wooden trunk, I curl myself inside, beside the books and musky farajiyya and trousers, and gingerly close the lid. The small space warms quickly. As leaden footsteps beat the stone floor and I hear the harsh murmurs of Oghuz, I am con-

scious of how rapidly my breath eats the air. Praying furiously, I try not
to breathe.

There was once a boy who could blink an eye and dissolve into fog . . .

The footsteps come closer and then drift away. I hear scuffling through
my belongings, grimy hands, split fingernails digging through clothes of
ciclatoun and Dabiqi, jewels that had once been my mother's.

The footfalls stop. I have been holding my breath for so long that
purple and silver stars sparkle. When the trunk opens, my first fleeting
feeling is relief as I gasp cold air.

Rough hands haul my shoulders and the trunk tumbles, spilling books
and clothing. Bisecting conical helmets obscure my captors' faces, but
their hands and armor are black with ash and blood, their eyes glazed as
though with drink. Behind them, the door is ajar and blocked with mamluk bodies. I feel faint.

The soldier who pulled me out pushes me against the wall and brings
his face so close that his graying beard scrapes my cheek. My mouth and
nose fill with the stink of him.

"A little concubine." He strokes my hip.

Cold, black panic bursts in my eyes, drenches my ears. I try to shove
him off, but he is too tall, too heavy.

"Take me to Malik Dinar. I am not a concubine," I gasp.

A sharp brightness, silver as mercury, keen as thorns, cuts through the
panic. My nails bite against his armor and leather, but I cannot pierce to
his skin.

"Every Kirmani woman is a concubine to an Oghuz." He shoves me
harder against the wall and I think, *Ay Khoda, this cannot be it.*

The world blackens, and the man's hold loosens.

He slumps, his hand and feet working like waterwheels. The wooden
handle of my dinner knife emerges from his right eye, red rivulets weeping down his cheek. His limbs seize like a dying beetle's. My hand echoes

with the nauseating feel of the knife slicing through the silken membrane of his eyeball and into the soft, grooved tissue of his brain. His blood is warm on my gown.

The other man whips out his sword and advances. I slide deeper into the corner, but there is nowhere to retreat and my sole weapon rests in the eye of a still-twitching corpse. I wish—for so many reasons—that I had not returned Atsiz's dagger.

"I am Shaherazade Khatun," I say in Oghuz, clenching my fingers and trying to submerge the horror of what I have done. "I am the wife of Malik Shahryar. Your life is not worth my death."

The soldier hesitates. He is younger than the first—perhaps a little younger than Shahryar—bearded in patches with a tremulous, rabbit-like quality.

I lick my dry lips, draw myself tall, remind myself that I am a Seljuk Khatun—one, *the last*, in a line of women who could not be dominated. "Take me to Malik Dinar. Do you know the reward he will heap upon you, you, a soldier from . . . ?"

"S—Serakhs. I am Bakrak of Serakhs."

"Think of the honor you will bring the men and women of your home, the rubies and emeralds Malik Dinar will bestow upon you for bringing him one of the last Seljuk Khatuns as his hostage. This is how great generals, atabegs, are made of men who come from dust—a heroic capture, the wife of the toppled Malik Shahryar, thrown at Malik Dinar's feet. You will tell this tale to your grandchildren, how you elevated your family among the Oghuz when the Oghuz were remaking the world. Take me to Malik Dinar, O Bakrak of Serakhs, and make your fate."

The man glances at his still compatriot and then at me. For a moment, his eyes are shaded. Then, he raises them and they spark with jewels, flying away from the screaming men and horses and into the future I have spoken.

"Once the fighting is done, I will take you to M—Malik Dinar."

I could bow with relief.

Easily, Bakrak flips the riven table, turns it long, and barricades the door. Renewed fear throbs through me, but he only buttresses the table with my trunks. Grasping the dead Oghuz's boots, he drags him to the garderobe, a thin trail of blood marking his path. Once finished, he stands sentry and does not look at me.

Bakrak of Serakhs does not look so different from our Seljuk soldiers. The same scaled cuirass, a common stocky build, dark hair that emerges from his helmet in sweat-matted tangles, coarse hands brushed with fine hair. As much as he could be a Kirmani townsperson, he took up arms against us, perhaps ravaging villages and abducting women and children, and for what—a plot of land? A castle with walls? The thrill of conquest, the thrill of tearing a weak throat with sharp teeth?

Or perhaps he was conscripted, torn from his wife and children, his mother and father, by Malik Dinar who wanted to fatten his army with men to glorify his name. What choice did Bakrak of Serakhs—who, unlike Malik Dinar, will not live in history and song, will not see his name carved into madrasas and tombs, will not have the khutbah pronounced in his honor—have but to join and fight for his life, when anything less would mean death?

I look outside and, with a sinking stomach, realize that only war's aftermath remains. The dust from the broken wall has settled, caking corpses and fallen weapons like volcanic ash. Small pockets of Seljuks still fight, but the Oghuz disarm them with almost lazy quickness. The Oghuz patrol the remaining walls, stride through the bailey, and bind together Seljuk prisoners, herding them roughly around the Seljuk dead. Men's wails careen through the fortress like mad ghouls.

I think of those still sheltering in Bam, hiding in the countryside, believing that their deliverance has come, mothers and fathers, wives and lovers, sons and daughters of the wounded, of the captive, of the dead. I sift through myself, dig my fingers through the soft warmth of my heart and stomach, searching for the proper emotion: horror, grief, despair.

I find nothing.

How can I watch our Seljuk soldiers, who raced back from Palestine to reclaim our home, break their bodies and still lose, and not feel my heart shatter like dropped porcelain? I tear at the skin around my fingernail, peeling a translucent strip until it bubbles blood.

Three metallic knocks sound against the door. Bakrak straightens, and my stomach clenches. A man calls in Oghuz, "Open this door in Malik Dinar's name. The fortress is his and all who resist will die."

Quickly, Bakrak breaks apart his provisional barricade; the table screeches against the stone floor as he pulls it aside, but I think, I hope, that there is something familiar about the voice. I envisage—Atsiz on the other side, Atsiz who has somehow outfoxed the Oghuz and fought through battle to rescue me. Once my captor opens the door, Atsiz will incapacitate him with one blow, take my hand, and carry me far away from the ruins of this battle, from the ruins of Bam.

My captor unbolts the door and briefly, in hope, in fear, my breath clutches. On the other side stands a giant Oghuz soldier, the top of his head brushing the door's archway. The slender hope I had compounded from air puffs from existence.

"E—Emir Mahmashad." Bakrak jumps.

"Who is this?" Emir Mahmashad rumbles, thunder deep. His boots gleam with fresh-killed gore, his eyes shine like obsidian.

"Sh—sh—she claims she is Shaherazade Khatun. The wife of Shahr-yar. I have captured her."

Unimpressed, Mahmashad eyes me askance.

Despite the Oghuz soldier's blood on my front, the soot streaking my face, I draw myself tall. "I do not claim," and my voice is that of a story-teller's, calm and authoritative, pulled from somewhere deep and shaped into something queenly. "I am."

Thirty-Seven

◇◇◇◇◇◇

Malik Dinar is not young—hard rides in the sun have burnished his weather-beaten skin to walnut and his hair falls like thin white cotton to his shoulders, but his arms are still corded with muscle, his rough hands steady. Unarmored, he wears a sturdy crimson wool robe, a curved scimitar slipped into a polished scabbard belted at his waist. A wound at his neck has been recently stitched clean. Ay Khoda, I wish it had taken his head.

"Shaherazade Khatun." His voice is gravelly, his Oghuz pure. Lip curled, he watches me as though I am not a still-new bride of twenty, but a scorpion cradled in his palm that he is preparing to crush.

I will teach him that crushing me won't be so easy.

"Malik Dinar. You should rise in a Khatun's presence."

His chuckle is smoky; he remains seated. "You certainly are what they say."

"As are you, when I was hoping you would be so much more."

He flinches as the remark cracks like a lash, his eyes catching on my tunic, stained with Oghuz blood. I smile, sweet and soft as a fig.

"Do you have my sister?"

Two soldiers enter, and my heart clenches.

Dunya, summoned by my words.

No, it is a bruised and bareheaded Shahryar—his eye is black, his lip is split, and fresh bruises, crimson and damson, bloom along his face and neck. His left leg drags. Seeing him broken, my husband, the Malik of Kirman, the numbness damming my emotions evaporates. Grief rises from my stomach, and the bad feeling between us—my imprisonment, his cold rejection—sublimates into vapor, into the realization that we are truly defeated, that the home of my father and mother and my forebears and his father and mother and his forebears is lost to us, and perhaps our lives are as well. A deep wail assaults me like a gale. I do not care that Malik Dinar sees my sorrow. Rushing to Shahryar, I embrace him. He leans on me, and Malik Dinar and his guards disappear into the roar of Shahryar's grief-stricken heart.

Two more Oghuz soldiers appear, hefting another bruised man. As I pull away from Shahryar, my stomach flutters. Atsiz. Resting on me, his green-gold eyes soften with relief.

Have Malik Dinar's spies told him what passed when Atsiz, Shahryar, and I were last together? But Malik Dinar seems uninterested, and I doubt this man would conceal delight at his enemies' discomfort.

The tent flap ripples, a cool wind runs over my nape, and premonition stirs in my belly.

Dunyazade.

The world trembles and I think, *Is this a dream?* She is thinner, her eyes tired—in my memory, she had become once more the cosseted girl in the Arg-e-Bam and so her wanness startles me. I run to her, or perhaps she runs to me, and we collide, her embrace soft and alive. Relief, vaster even than what I felt that first night Shahryar spared me, floods me, hearth-warm.

She is here. She is here, alive. And my worst, crawling fears dissipate, ink dissolving into the sea. I hold her with all my might as though I can shatter the weeks apart, the space between us, what she has experienced imprisoned by Malik Dinar, as though, if I release her, she will vanish again. Beneath the lye of camp soap, I smell Dunya, sandalwood and rose water, and in Dunya, I smell home. I begin to weep again for all we have lost, for the feel of my sister, warm and living, in my arms once more.

Cupping my sister's cheeks, I whisper, "Oh, my mouse. It is done. You're home with me, Dunya jaan, and I will protect you."

Even as I say it, I know we are only beginning.

"You have us here." Shahryar is swollen-tongued, but he fashions his shredded kingliness into some guise of authority. Does Malik Dinar see through it as easily as I? "What do you want?"

Malik Dinar smiles, his teeth yellow but strong, like a camel's. "With all due respect, because every Turkman soldier owes a debt to the Seljuks, who were sultans and the sons of sultans, I have won all I want. Well, almost all." He stares openly at Dunya, and I shift to place myself between his greedy eyes and my sister's body.

"I am captured, I admit," Shahryar says, "but Bam's walls have never been breached. Even you, who have been laying siege for months, have not broken through." He raises his chin, proud.

Malik Dinar's steward places cups of fragrant tea in our hands. I'm tempted to sip, but I do not trust Malik Dinar to abide by the laws of hospitality. Neither Shahryar nor Atsiz drinks.

"Do you think Bam will hold when I sap its walls as I did the Qaleh Dokhtar? Do you think Bam will hold when my Oghuz, the support of the Prince of Believers at their backs, pass through it like a storm and kill your men and your women and your children?" Malik Dinar's voice is sharp and strong, wind whipping through the plain. "Do you think the city will hold when I march you and your emirs and your wife before those strong walls and take your heads?"

The cup shakes in Shahryar's hand. "Yes."

I imagine: Bam's thousand-year-old walls, the great adobe shell that safeguards all that is sweet and tender in our town, leveled asunder, split like a lightning-struck tree, and the Oghuz marauders pouring in, torching homes, killing townsfolk—Hanna, Laila, Ishaq, Ismat—all the girls that I wed Shahryar to save. I remember the destruction of the village, the burnt husks of homes, the slaughtered men, the disappeared women and children, the bodies of dead men after battle in Palestine, Ascalon ground to sand. Is this what we open Bam to if we refuse to make peace? Is this what we open Bam to if we surrender?

I cannot let that happen.

"I speak only for myself—not for Shahryar or Bam—but perhaps I can offer a solution amenable to all."

The men seem surprised, but they do not try to silence me.

"A truce between the Oghuz and the Seljuks of Kirman," I say. "Its terms: that Shahryar accept Malik Dinar as his suzerain and swear fealty. You, Malik Dinar, will reap riches and gain a governor who knows the province, but avoid the burden of governance. In this way, you may cement your victory and be more than a Malik of Kirman, but a Malik of Maliks." I bow my head humbly.

In the ensuing silence, Shahryar is unreadable. That habitual fear that I have gone too far, that I will incur his ire, rises, but before it reaches a crescendo of drumming panic in my head, it bursts, leaving only stillness.

Considering the offer like a choice leveret, Malik Dinar cocks his head, more hawklike than ever. My heart rises. If Malik Dinar accepts, then I will persuade Shahryar that this is what Baba would have negotiated, a coup to safeguard his patrimony despite defeat.

"Had you presented that offer ten years ago, Shaherazade Khatun," Malik Dinar says crookedly, "when I was a younger warrior, still thirsty for blood and battle, I would have accepted. But I am an old man, my battle days closing. I'm ready to bequeath my sons an empire, take a young wife to tend me in my home." He looks at Dunya again, and I would pierce his eyes.

"Will anything sweeten the exchange?" I ask, although I don't know what we could give.

"I want what my Oghuz have won in battle: Kirman."

"I am to simply trust that if, at my word, Bam opened its gates to you, you would not slaughter the men and take the women's bodies by the sword?" Shahryar demands.

"No."

Dunya's tongue darts over her dry lips, but she speaks firmly. "Upon the conditions that he cease his hostilities against Kirman and no harm come to Bam and its inhabitants, nor to you Shaherazade, you Shahryar, nor Shahzaman nor anyone else, I will wed Malik Dinar. That guarantee is my dower gift."

"Dunya!" I exclaim.

Shahryar's mouth draws white.

Malik Dinar smiles a smug catlike smile, and I sense that Dunya's declaration is no surprise to him. "I accept that no harm come to the people of Kirman, to Malik Shahzaman, or to Malik Shahryar's emirs, so long as they quit Kirman and do not return and do not seek to foment dissent against me. If they understand that you are the agreement's security, and that a breach of these terms would result in a breach of their . . . security."

This is madness. What does Malik Dinar think? What does *Dunya* think? That we are so craven as to secure our safety with the bride-price of a girl? In her simple clothes and braids fraying beneath her sheer saffron veil, she looks so young. I remember when Mama first placed her in my arms, red and caterwauling, thick black hair on her head and long eyes, all irises, a deep inky blue. She looked like a *pari* child and I loved her with all my heart. And to sell her off to Malik Dinar? To let crass Malik Dinar run his rough hands over her skin, force himself on her in the dark? My sister deserves a Khosrau—not him.

"What of Shaherazade Khatun and Malik Shahryar?" Atsiz asks sharply.

Malik Dinar gives Shahryar an exaggerated bow. "He would remain here, as my honored guest, and Shaherazade Khatun with him, as a wife's place is beside her esteemed husband. Although perhaps," he chuckles, "you prefer some . . . distance . . . from your wives. They certainly seem to prefer it from you."

Shahryar pales.

"No." Now, I speak not just for myself, but for Shahryar and Kirman. "We will not accept this." Not for anything, not even half the world.

Dunya rests her hand softly on mine. "Malik Dinar—will you give us a moment?"

With unexpected ease, he rises, saying to Shahryar, "Confer with your lieutenant, Malik Shahryar. With your sister-in-law, with your wife. If you do not already see it, I am sure they will persuade you of this agreement's rightness."

I look to Shahryar, but everything—his easy confidence, his brittle brilliance—is snuffed. He is swept out to sea in a storm, clutching a torn hull.

"Don't offer yourself, Dunya," I say after the grimy tent flap swings shut behind Malik Dinar. "We will continue fighting. *Bam* will continue fighting. The walls are strong, the stores are deep, fresh water flows from the mountains. They will survive."

Even if we do not.

Dunya shakes her head, her plaits swaying like windblown grain. Light falls through the tent's patched gaps, illuminating her high cheekbone, a shining eye, shadowing her lips and neck.

"Perhaps, Shahera. But the Oghuz have been preparing saps beneath Bam's walls. He can crack Bam like an egg; he does not need Shahryar's surrender. Will he then spare the townspeople? The emirs? Atsiz? Ishaq and his family? I do not believe it. Not without something more."

"Do not do this, Dunyazade, not on my account." Atsiz grasps Dunya's hand and presses his forehead to it. "I would rather meet my death as a man of war than be saved on the back of a girl's future."

Dunya gently breaks free. "It is not your choice, Emir Atsiz. Malik Dinar seeks a Seljuk bride. Here I am, ready-made, the daughter of the beloved vizier, the sister of the Khatun, the sister-in-law of the Malik, an unmarried virgin, fallen into his lap." She smiles wryly, and I think of the mountain ride my sister followed me on that brought her here. I feel a quiver of disgust at myself.

Shahryar stands and wipes his palms on his blood-and-earth-stained tunic. He paces. He looks at us, at the tent's ceiling, and his lips move softly as though in prayer. He closes his eyes. "I cannot allow it, Dunyazade. If it were solely my life, I would pay the price a thousandfold. But Atsiz is right. If the Seljuks have failed, we have failed, and if the cost is my death, then it must be paid. You are Vizier Muhammad's daughter and for his memory I cannot permit this. I remain your Malik and the terms of surrender are mine."

"You threatened my sister with death every dawn for months and now you remember to honor my father? Yours is a thin protest."

Vivid red blotches Shahryar's face.

"I do not do this for you, Shahryar. Nor you Atsiz." Dunya's voice shivers. "I cannot let Malik Dinar raze Bam, destroy our people. You did this for Bam, Shahera. Let me do it, too."

I embrace her, and her heart thumps hard and fast against my chest. "What if he harms you? What if he forswears himself?"

She is unmoved. "Then I will do what you would do, Shahera. I will be clever and I will figure it out. Men tell stories of women like Shireen, who wait to be found. Then there are the women of your stories, who bleed for those they love, who do not wait, but act." Pulling away, she cradles my cheek, and her eyes meet mine, calm and sure. "This is the only way."

Is that not what Baba did? Did he not carefully weigh the options and then, with a leaden soul, permit his headstrong daughter to do what had to be done for Bam? I can think of a thousand protests, but each thread I unspool to guide us out of this labyrinth strikes a hard wall.

"Will you do what must be done, Shahryar?" The question is the heaviest I have ever asked.

The Malik of Kirman does not hesitate even though he knows what it means. "Yes."

"But you must do one thing too, Shahera," Dunya says.

"Anything, azizem." My voice is strangled.

"You must persuade Malik Dinar to exile you from Bam like the emirs."

"Why, when I could remain with you?" I envision us walking through the Arg-e-Bam, arm in arm. Then I think of Baba, no longer there, of Malik Dinar darkening Shahryar's place. The fantasy fades.

Dunya shakes her head. "Malik Dinar has heard how you tamed Shahryar, how you assuaged Caliph an-Nasir, how you alone negotiated the Seljuk army's release from Sultan Saladin."

I try not to consider how Shahryar will take that summary. "I am a woman. Malik Dinar will not harm me."

Nervously, Dunya glances at the tent entrance as though expecting Malik Dinar to reenter. "He is violent in the face of threat, and you should not underestimate him—he does not underestimate you." She grabs my arm. "I cannot let him lock you up, cut out your tongue, strangle you with a noose. I cannot. And if you do not leave, he will."

"But we will be parted."

Who am I without Dunya, my conscience, the soul within my soul, my compass leaf pointing true north?

Who am I without my husband, who has not spoken while his wife and her sister consider her departure? He seems resigned before another loss, so small, in the face of all else. Despite everything, I ache for him, for the thought of forming a life where I am not identified by our marriage, for being another stone in the mountain of his defeat.

Then I consider exile with Atsiz and feel a jolt at the possibility of a future where my fate does not hang on a word.

∗ ∗ ∗

"We will accept your terms, but for one," Shahryar announces, eye to eye with Malik Dinar. Shahryar's black hair, overgrown from months of travel and battle, frames his grim face. "To preserve Bam and its people from further bloodshed and war's depravities, I, Shahryar, Malik of Kirman, will cede Kirman to you and your heirs. My emirs will go into exile, my sister-in-law will become your wife, and her marriage will be a surety to this treaty. I will surrender myself to your custody and you will not harm another Kirmani, soldier or civilian."

I wish I could squeeze his hand. I hope someday, somewhere, people remember the sacrifice and valor of Shahryar, the last Seljuk Malik of Kirman.

"But Malik Dinar," I say.

Malik Dinar's satisfaction at Shahryar's capitulation transforms into suspicion.

"I will not be your prisoner. I will join the emirs in exile."

Malik Dinar sneers. "You are content with your wife abandoning you, Shahryar?"

Shahryar struggles and then says, "I am not such a small man that I would control my wife when I can control nothing else."

Malik Dinar turns to me. "How would you respond, Shaherazade, if I said that I preferred you in Bam, under my eye?"

"Do you fear a woman, Malik Dinar?"

"I am an Oghuz and I fear no one save Allah the Most High."

"If you fear Him, then do as He commands and show mercy to your captives."

He is unmoved, the savage. I feel a sharp squall of anger, may Allah curse this flea-bitten, accursed barbarian. But I cannot give vent. I must entice him, sweeter than honey and palm sugar, sweet enough to curdle his tongue.

"Will anything sweeten the exchange?" I ask again.

"What could you offer me that I have not already made mine?"

He is right. He has my sister, my home, my husband, me. What can I give a man like Malik Dinar?

"This isn't a tale that you've told a sultan or caliph, Shaherazade Khatun," Atsiz says, sounding bored. "You will not persuade him." In his eyes, I read some calculation, although I cannot guess its meaning.

"Caliph an-Nasir? Sultan Saladin?" Malik Dinar inquires, piqued.

Atsiz's stratagem strikes me. "Yes, Malik Dinar. Surely you are well informed enough to have heard how I saved the girls of Bam and enchanted the greatest rulers of our time with my tales."

Malik Dinar considers. "I am canny as an-Nasir, as strong a general as Saladin, I have defeated Shahryar. I am a king as much as they. More than some." He looks sidelong at Shahryar.

"Perhaps one day," I say carefully. "But great rulers are more than a few battlefield victories."

"What are they then?" he asks with unexpected seriousness.

I consider the best of Sultan Saladin, an-Nasir, and Shahryar. "They are wellsprings of honor, bearers of innate majesty, caring custodians of their subjects, that move not only soldiers and horses on a battlefield, but all they meet, from singers to storytellers, farmers to merchants, to present the best of themselves and pay tribute."

"And you are a storyteller, who pays tribute with your tales."

I incline my head. "When the ruler is mighty, yes."

"If I granted you exile, you would offer me this . . . tribute?"

I look at Dunya and begin.

"Malik Dinar, Firdausi says, in the age before the Sassanians, where Bam and its adobe citadel now stand, there was a poor village called Kajaran. Inside Kajaran, there was a girl called Taraneh, who spun cotton. Taraneh was the eighth child of a man with seven sons called Haftvad, who paid little mind to his youngest daughter.

"Like the other girls of her village, Taraneh passed long days spinning cotton on the mountainside outside Kajaran, cutting her hands against the taut thread, blistering her fingers against the poplar spindles. At the end of each day, the girls would descend from the mountainside, bringing great lengths of spun yarn to their homes.

"One day, as Taraneh settled herself on the mountainside to spin, she found by her hand a windfall apple of the softest pink-red that cupped perfectly in her palm. Her teeth broke into the crisp, white flesh, and inside coiled a small green worm. A girl with great love for all creatures, Taraneh gently prized the green worm from the apple and tucked it in her spindle case.

"That day, with the worm by her side, Taraneh spun double her usual amount of thread. The girls gathered to marvel at the deftness of Taraneh's hands and the wonderful bob of the spindle.

"For days, with the little worm that she tended with great concern by her side, Taraneh spun mountains' worth of cotton yarn, enough that all of Kajaran could have been clothed by her product alone. Even her father wondered at his daughter's work.

"One night, Taraneh returned from the mountainside, and her parents asked how she managed to spin so splendidly. Revealing the little worm, Taraneh told them that since it had come into her care, magic had filled her spinning.

"From the worm and his daughter's work, Haftvad gained great fortune. The thread that Taraneh spun was plentiful and fine, and it filled Haftvad's coffers with gold and silver. In turn, Taraneh cared for the worm, feeding it until it grew too plump for the spindle case. With his own hands, Haftvad built a fine black wooden box for its home.

"Although few daughters were as dutiful as Taraneh, she could not but feel a flicker of resentment as her father and brothers became the spokes of civic life in Kajaran, fat on the wealth of her labor, as she spun endlessly on the mountainside until her fingertips calloused.

"Even as Haftvad and his sons grew bold, Taraneh maintained her sweet demeanor. The girls, who spun in the mountains with Taraneh and may have otherwise resented her fortune, pitied her for they saw how her father and brothers took advantage of her kindness.

"One afternoon, a girl, who liked Taraneh and worked for Kajaran's wealthiest nobleman, sat beside her. As Taraneh's spindle twirled, she whispered, 'My master is plotting against your father. I do not know what, but your father should flee.'

"Taraneh thanked the girl and spun faster, until she had produced as much yarn as every other girl combined. When she returned home, she informed her father of the whispered warning. That night, Haftvad fled, leaving his sons and wife and daughter and the worm behind.

"For months, he traveled through the countryside. With the gold accumulated by his daughter's labor and the worm's charm, Haftvad spun a great army into existence. He led this army to Kajaran, putting the nobleman who had plotted against him to the sword. In his great victory, Haftvad collected vast spoils. Soon, Haftvad was deluged by men from nearby villages who wished to tie their destinies to his. Haftvad built a great, iron-gated adobe citadel, and his seven sons commanded seven armies that gained renown for their ferocity.

"In Haftvad's citadel, the worm was housed in an immense cistern. Under Taraneh's care, it grew from the size of a horse to the size of an elephant to the size of a wealthy merchant's home, curling its fat green flesh around the cistern's corners. Taraneh, who often slipped into the cisterns to escape her braggart father and bully brothers, fed it milk and honey as she hummed folk songs. Stories of this fearsome worm deterred invaders as much as the size of Haftvad's armies.

"But there are always empires greater than our own. As Haftvad grew his wealth and grew his army and grew his worm, another, stronger empire rose, its ruler crowning himself the king of kings. For the *shahanshah*, Haftvad's defeat would be another jewel in his empire's crown. Although Haftvad had defeated enemy after enemy, had grown rich on their spoils, and could field seven armies led by his seven sons, Shahanshah Ardashir's army was greater, his spoils vaster. On the battlefield, Haftvad and his sons fell beneath a storm of arrows, and Shahanshah Ardashir split the citadel's iron gate open.

"Striding through the citadel that was now his, Ardashir took stock of the fine tapestries and gold handiwork that had once belonged to other men, then became Haftvad's, and were now part of Ardashir's kingly treasury. But though Ardashir traversed the citadel's great halls, he did not find the worm. He thought to himself that, like the tales of the strength of Haftvad's armies, the worm was nothing more than fable.

"For the final measure of his search, Ardashir descended into the citadel's chill bowels. First, he saw a young woman, little more than a girl. Then, behind her, he saw a great and helpless beast, green and squealing as Taraneh tried to shield it. But Taraneh was an unarmed girl and Ardashir a warrior king. Sliding his lance out, Ardashir bounded and slipped the iron into the worm's soft gut. But the worm was so vast that for a moment, both Taraneh and Ardashir believed that nothing had happened.

"Then, the worm ruptured with a resounding BAM so loud that Taraneh clapped her hands to her ears. As air burst from the worm, its flesh fell like sliming hail onto Ardashir and Taraneh, and Taraneh wept for the end of her friend and the end of her world.

"Seeing the thin, weeping girl, Shahanshah Ardashir felt a flash of pity in his cold conqueror's heart. 'Go.'

"Without glancing at Ardashir, but taking a final look at her worm, Taraneh dashed up the stairs, through the citadel that had been built from her work, and disappeared into the world with naught but her spindle, leaving all that she had known and grown behind.

"That is how Bam came to be."

"No."

The denial shakes Malik Dinar's tent. Dunya's eyes widen with fear and Atsiz looks ready to hurl himself at the old warrior, regardless of the Oghuz guards that stand ready.

"I am not a romantic fool like Sultan Saladin to let you run free because you told a charming story." Malik Dinar opens his rough hands wide and smiles with insincere apology. "You will remain in Bam and perhaps, from time to time, I will inveigle you for tales of my own."

Dunya's warning rings in my ears.

It does not end thus.

"You do not want me as your enemy, Malik Dinar," I say, and my voice is cold, cold as the snow capping the Jebal Barez, cold as the Dasht-e-Lut on midwinter's night. "Imprison me and I swear to you, I will weave intrigues that will sweep the Arg-e-Bam, from harem to great hall, that will leave you lifeless within the year. Murder me, and know that Bam will rise to avenge the death of the girl who walked into the lion's mouth to save the city's daughters. Deny me this and your rule will be hard and it will be short."

As I say it, the truth of the words weighs on my tongue, heavy and prophetic.

Malik Dinar sits back and his expression shifts. I am no longer a scorpion, but a viper, a leopard, a crocodile, sharp-toothed and uncontainable.

I soften, becoming a girl again. "But you wish to marry my sister, a politic move for a man who seeks to build a peaceful reign. Release me, and so long as my sister is safe at your side, I will not be your enemy. I will not be a martyr. I will not be a thorn that festers until it kills you and the empire you hope to bequeath your sons. You claim you are not a fool, O Malik Dinar? Prove it to me."

The conqueror king smiles like a wolf.

Thirty-Eight

Dunya's fingers are still tipped black, stained from the ink of her marriage contract.

Earlier, as she signed the contract before the long-bearded qazi, Malik Dinar's companions, and the remaining Seljuk nobles, her shaking hand had knocked the brass inkwell to the great hall floor. The ink had splashed Malik Dinar's madder robe, but he threw his head back at her nerves, as if they were simply those of a girlish bride. But when Dunya gave him a scythe-like grin, his face fell, perhaps, for the first time, registering the woman he had wed.

I touch her fingers in awe. With just that, she bought peace. "What a woman you are, Dunya."

Malik Dinar's burly Oghuz guards flank us as we walk through the Arg-e-Bam. *His* Arg-e-Bam. Through the stone walls, I hear carousing Oghuz: drums beating, platters crashing, songs bellowed by the untrained voices of warring men.

Just hours before, Shahryar had boomed his surrender before Bam's ravaged pistachio groves. As Shahryar's capitulation had reverberated against the walls, I'd had a mad hope that the townspeople would do what we could not: reject surrender, fly an arrow into Malik Dinar's eye, eke out victory where there was only loss.

But no storybook hero emerged. Jaw shaking, Shahryar had watched the South Gate heave open, Oghuz roars vibrating in our ears. Flanked by his emirs and cavalry, Malik Dinar had processed through Bam, from the South Gate, over the Chelekhoneh River, through the Worm Gate, and into our citadel. As Shahryar and I had followed Malik Dinar—his captives, his trophies—through Bam's deserted streets, I recalled the jubilation and raining flowers when we left for Palestine. *How quickly the world turns to cinders*, I thought.

Now, Dunya and I stand before the heavy cedar doors, carved with vines and eight-pointed stars, that lead to the rooms where we once lived with our Baba when we were girls and the whole of our world could nestle in his palm.

I close my eyes. What if Baba is waiting for me and Dunya behind those doors, arms outstretched. "My doves," he would say. "My brave, beautiful, brilliant doves. Look at all you have done, woven the world through your fingers. Vizier of viziers, Khatun of khatuns." The madrasas and charities and mosques I would endow if it were true.

Ay Khoda, if my Baba is there, waiting for me, I will devote my life to Your will, my money, and my time, I will devote to Your path.

I push in.

The blue-and-green tiles are unswept, the air stale. I bring a bronze olive oil lamp to life and it fills the chamber with a rotted sweetness. Baba's door creaks as I open it. In the stuttering lamplight, I see his books and scribbled notes blown around the floor. My last, most absurd hope vanishes.

I bury my face in his pillow, and there, just there, I detect his scent: attar and the slightest hint of brackish sweat. How adroitly his fingers braided my hair while Fataneh's secret snaked in my stomach. No more than a year gone, but the world is unrecognizable. Would Baba even know us?

Sorrow swells in my chest, so solid that if my fingers could pass through bone and tissue, they could probe it. I wish I could let it swallow me whole.

"Hurry," Dunya says. "Malik Dinar has given you the hour to gather your belongings." She begins piling Baba's notes and books, ordering the Oghuz guards to stack them carefully into a trunk. They take to her commands with surprising ease. "Baba's words are yours, Shahera. Take them. Ismat Khaleh has Mama's jewels. Take those too. I—" Her voice catches, but her eyes, before her new Oghuz guard, stay steely.

I drift to my own room, and the memory of *home*, of *safety* brushes my shoulders. I direct a heavy-footed guard to wooden trunks painted with irises and narcissus, packed by Gulnar long ago with clothing and books. "These go with me too."

"You will have a few moments with Shahryar and then spend the night under guard at Ismat's," Dunya murmurs briskly. "But you, Gulnar, Atsiz, and the rest *must* be outside the South Gate *before* Fajr."

"I will. And you? Are you ready for tonight?"

Between us hangs Faramurz. Does she resent me for the world I have wrought, where she must labor beneath an old man to save her sister and province, where the man she loved died?

Squaring herself, Dunya replies, "It will be done. There is nothing more to say."

In her clear dark eyes, there is no resentment. Only fierce resolution. I wish I could attend my sister on her wedding night as she attended me, loosening her braids and perfuming her with gentle hands, whispering wise counsel about what to expect as she passes into womanhood. I will miss so much of Dunya's life, when I thought we would be joined until death.

She grasps my hand. "Before you leave, you must bid farewell to Baba and Mama."

✳ ✳ ✳

Tall, sandstone blocks scrolled with Farsi mark the graves in Bam. In the dim torchlight, I can see the patchy grass that has sprung up. Side by side, beneath a bowed pomegranate tree, are Baba's and Mama's graves. Mama's stone is worn smooth by a decade of wind and sand, made all the softer by the sharp newness of Baba's gravestone. How bizarre that they lie here, just finger-lengths from me, the hip bones that split as Mama gave birth, the knees that creaked when Baba lifted me in his arms. Quietly, I recite al-Fatihah, the opening chapter of the Qur'an, a cool drink of water to the dead awaiting the Day of Judgment.

Somewhere, too, in this graveyard, are Altunjan, Shideh, Inanj—and Fataneh, head and body, perhaps cradled in her arm or propped against her cut neck in farcical joinder. She dissolves below, becoming once more the fermented clay from which Allah molded Adam, a Khatun decaying like anyone else. In fifty years, in a century, in a millennium, who will remember her life, let alone her death, all that preceded it and all that followed?

A blade's breadth of a man strides toward us, chain mail and swords jingling like dirhams. Red battlefield mud flakes from his boots onto the long grass. The Oghuz leers at me, and red heat flushes my neck. A reminder that I am no longer a Khatun. I give him a hard glare, and he gulps.

"Dunyazade Khatun, Malik Dinar commands your return."

Dunya's brown eyes flash with dismay. I take her hand. "You will give us a moment," I say to the Oghuz, as he follows us back to the citadel.

Here, Dunya and I slid over the glassy tiles, mischievous girls racing down the hallway. In that courtyard, coruscating with bougainvillea, Baba defeated me at shataranj again and again until I learned to overmaster him. And back in the great hall where Malik Dinar celebrates victory, I watched Shahryar fall in love with his first wife, and I became the fourth of the wives who followed whom he could never love. These memories are so grounded in place, they thin time.

Sisters often grow, entwined like vines, drinking the same water, grown from the same seeds, only to be torn apart by marriage, to never see each other again. I do not know how the vines ripped asunder do not wither. I say none of this to Dunya, who gasps into my shoulder.

Aware of the guards, I whisper, "You are Dunyazade Khatun, strong and clever—you have always been the better of us, azizem. I will be waiting for you at the end of this. And if you need me, I will come. May Allah safeguard you, tonight and all nights." I kiss her cheeks, her forehead, her temple, and clutch her neck in a child's stranglehold embrace.

Dunya's lips quiver, her eyes shine but she does not weep. I try to match her resilience but my face is damp.

"Khoda hafez, jaanem," I say.

I watch her until she disappears, but Dunyazade Khatun does not look back.

***

The Oghuz guards lead me to a small chamber at the far end of a hall. I feel time thin again, as though I have stepped into a mirrored past: this is the same room where, many moons ago, a girl saw a cornered queen and set into motion one thousand and one unforeseeable events. I feel the warm sun on my eyelids, hear the heavy breaths behind the courtyard door.

Then it disappears.

The guard opens the door, just wide enough for me to slide in. "Be quick." He locks the door behind me.

In a crisp white cotton tunic, the erstwhile Malik of Kirman hunches on a thin mattress, his eyes reddened and face hollow. I pause at his exposed grief but force myself to sit beside my husband. His breath warms my cheek. "Salaam, Shahryar."

"Durood, Shaherazade."

Shahryar meets my eyes, and I look to the mica-flecked floor, unnerved by the ocean-deep sorrow he doesn't attempt to conceal. Hesitantly, his fingertips touch my jaw, which clenches beneath his touch.

"Let me look at you, little Shaherazade," he says, no rancor in the diminutive, only a fondness that makes me ache for all that I once wanted for us.

I close my eyes and let him look.

"Look at me."

It is a soft request and I comply. I see him, each piece, layered like a stack of shadow puppets: Shahryar the abandoned prince, the lover, the beloved, Shahryar the Malik, Shahryar the warrior, Shahryar the betrayed, the mad, the murderer, Shahryar the defeated. Shahryar my husband. The pile is thick and sharp-edged, bloodstained and mismatched.

"I want to remember you, Shaherazade, brave and clever, young and beautiful," he whispers. "My wife who crossed the world with me."

I realize that after this, Shahryar, who once I had prayed would be to me as much as anyone could be, will be nothing. Less than air, less than mist. And the chains of fear—that if I misstep, he will hurt me, that if I misstep, I will never persuade him to love me, these chains that held me fast during our marriage—dissipate.

Emboldened, I touch his soft beard, stroke my thumb along the delicate ridge of his brow. I try not to think about what will happen to him tomorrow. Or in a week. Or in a month. He is like a shorn lion, and despite his sins, I feel pity. Perhaps I am a fool to feel it. Or perhaps that is humanity.

Perhaps that is even love.

"I wish . . ."

But what do I wish? Once, I would have wished for his love, as hot and blazing as it flowed for Fataneh. Yet, seeing him as he is, not as I dreamed him to be, I know that too much shadow roils between us for that to have ever been.

"I wish it were not ending this way, Shahryar."

He places his hands, which I have always thought beautiful with their long fingers, soft pink cuticles, and broad palms, over his knees. "I do not have your facility with words, Shaherazade, but I am no fool. I know what you have done for me."

I begin shaking my head, but he says, "Do not do that, Shaherazade. Let me give you your due. If you wanted to cleanse my heart of rage, it is done. If you wanted to open my eyes to the horrors I inflicted, it is done: for so long as I live, I will atone for the bloodstain of Altunjan, Shideh, and Inanj on my soul."

His voice trembles, a plea for forgiveness. But forgiveness for the murders of Altunjan, Shideh, and Inanj, for girls who deserved lives that stretched long before them, is not mine to give.

"If you wanted to salve the memory of Fataneh's betrayal . . ." He looks away and digs his bare heels into the floor. ". . . Then that is not easily done, but you have salved it."

I do not deserve this. I betrayed him with Atsiz, did what Fataneh had done, what he feared all women would do. Yet, as we stand on this precipice, he drowns that into a swamp, burying it deep in mud and sulfur, and weaves a new tale for himself.

"I have known that you wanted my love, but . . . I could not give it. Perhaps, now that we are here, that is a blessing."

His lovely eyes plead apology, and I am winded. Here are words that I have wanted to hear, confessions I have feared, but even the admission, *I could not give it*, does not split my heart. Was there a vanished point when, if our destinies had intersected, we could have grown to love together and tend a prosperous Kirman?

Yet, the path we walked brought us here and Allah does not err.

My shoulders lighten, a bundle I hadn't realized I carried blowing into smoke.

"Even if I am exiled, and you remain here, we are still bound," I say slowly, but then I pause.

I don't doubt that I am ready for this, that since we entered Malik Dinar's tent and perhaps even before, the weights of our marriage have dropped from my body one by one. Maybe tonight, I'll weep for my lost hopes for our marriage and for the girl who dreamed those dreams, but for now, I am clear eyed.

"If I could, I would return my dower gift to you, but I no longer possess its complete sum. There are two things, however, I can offer for my freedom instead."

Some of the heaviness eases from his face and he leans back with a smile as though we are still in a tent, marching through Palestine, and things between us are as they were at their best.

I present the chronicle that I fought so hard to write. The morocco leather cover is soft, and within, the letters are not perfectly formed nor beautifully illuminated. But the story is Shahryar's, and Shahryar, very soon, will no longer be mine. I pass the chronicle to him.

"How do you make me out in it?" he asks with deliberate lightness, running his fingers over the cover and opening it. His eyes glide over a page and his expression softens.

"Just as you were."

"A politician's answer, little Shaherazade." Closing the chronicle gently, he returns it to me. "Keep it. Keep it safe. Wherever you go, have it copied, placed in libraries. I . . . do not know how much longer I will be in this world, but let your words live in the chronicle and let me live in them. As I was." Shifting in the following silence, he asks, "Where will you go?"

"Maybe to Samarkand with Shahzaman, to start. After that, we will see."

And I see: mountains and deserts and far-flung cities, the places in my tales, Cairo and Fez and Tashkent and Mecca, their bazaars and libraries, histories, holy places, and storytellers beneath long-branched trees, Atsiz at my side, easy and beloved. I suppress a shiver at this intoxicating and rare liberty that is mine, frightening, confusing, and heady, all at once.

Perhaps Shahryar sees the emotion pass through me, for he gives me a wan smile. "When you see my brother, give him my blessings and my thanks for safeguarding my home. Give him my apologies that I could not do more to protect him and that I could not see him one last time." His voice cracks.

I squeeze Shahryar's hand. Tears shine in his eyes like glass, but he gathers himself and continues in a studiedly hearty voice. "Now, you said you had two offerings in exchange for your dower gift. What is the second?"

"O Malik: the second is the end of Jauhara's tale, if you will accept it."

He smiles, bittersweet. "Qubool ast."

With a physical burst, I recall my clattering nerves as I unwrapped 'Omar's story on our wedding night, knowing that if I failed, not only would I die, but so would countless other girls after me. To think that this beaten man, now denuded of that earth-shattering power we whispered around, would have murdered me if I'd faltered. Did I bleed out that evil? Or does it lurk, still integral but lulled into dormancy? And does the fate of his soul still matter, now that it is not tied to the destiny of a province?

I think yes.

And so, for the last time, I spin.

"In the Name of Allah, the Most Gracious, the Most Merciful.

"O Shahryar, they say—and Allah knows better—that there is a story of past times and past peoples, that is best suited to men of intelligence and understanding.

"As the moon waned, then waxed, shoots of limestone temples dedicated to the marid sprang from the earth, and each day new acolytes arrived, smoking the palace with incense. The crowds at the mosques thinned into wind, the call to prayer muffled by al-Maut's edicts. Jauhara feared how quickly the marid's power swelled, how rapidly the people descended into apostasy.

"Yet al-Maut declined to bring Jauhara into her confidence, and although the parrot and Kushyar hunted al-Askar for sign of Jauhara's family, their efforts bore no fruit.

"When the moon gleamed full again, al-Maut bade Jauhara join the white-swathed acolytes and follow the marid between the palace stones.

"Stepping into the strange chamber, Jauhara shielded her eyes against the torchlight's midday glare. As Jauhara's vision adjusted, a blindfolded man in fraying robes resolved before her. Hands bound and face masked by shaggy, filth-streaked hair, he knelt before the looming gold-and-ebon scales, which swayed in a breeze that touched nothing else. Something stirred in Jauhara like a long-dissolved dream.

"With nimble, twisting fingers, the falcon marid unbound the prisoner's silken blue blindfold. The man looked up.

"At the sight of her father, a black wave pulled Jauhara to her knees. She felt bubbling water pummel her, clog her ears, fill her mouth with brine. Before the dark could fully submerge her, an acolyte yanked her from the flagstones. Dazed, Jauhara blinked, and she noticed an unconscious, broad-shouldered figure, steadily breathing but gagged in the shadow of the lotus-topped columns.

"Ice crept on Jauhara's skin as al-Maut whispered, 'Did you not think I would smell a rat?'

"Jauhara tripped as al-Maut pushed her toward 'Omar. Hissing, the acolytes and marid drew a tight tether around father and daughter. 'Omar's gaze met Jauhara's and she choked down a whimper. In his eyes shone home—the home Jauhara had fled, the home she had hoped to return to, the home she had decimated by speaking magic into the air and awakening the marid. The loss of it fissured the ground beneath her.

"Al-Maut handed Jauhara an ancient dagger, its blade forged of meteorite iron and shaped like a pinnate leaf. 'You know what you must do, Jauhara,' al-Maut murmured. The soft words struck like a storm. 'Do this and I will make your dream come true—you will stand with the marid once we make Egypt ours again.'

"'And if I do not?' Jauhara rasped.

"Al-Maut shrugged. 'Then both your lives are forfeit.'

"Jauhara's fingers trembled around the dagger's gold-veined lapis hilt. Seeing the tears clouding her eyes, 'Omar choked, 'Do it, ya Jauhara.' Nodding frantically, 'Omar beckoned Jauhara, full of fear, full of mercy.

"Jauhara approached, her heart skittering. Crouching, she gently kissed her father's creased forehead and then buried her face between his shoulder and neck, where, as a child, she had rested her head and where, she knew, a great artery flowed like a wellspring.

"'Ya, Baba,' Jauhara murmured.

"'Ya, habibti.'

She thought of her father's life, the glory and miracle of it, and felt the weight and balance of the dagger in her palm. She curled her fingers around the hilt. Tightened her grip. And then Jauhara was an eagle, a hawk, and she flew, the blade pointed true north at al-Maut's cursed heart.

"Al-Maut flicked Jauhara aside, and the impact of her body striking the wall of glyphs rang like a gong through the hall. The dagger clattered into shadow. Snarling, the marid tackled Jauhara and held her down, their marble hands digging into her yielding, human flesh.

"'Abdurrahim!' al-Maut called, and a gray-haired chancellor pushed forward. Jauhara remembered what 'Omar had told her of Abdurrahim—one of the men who, long ago, had welcomed 'Omar into the governor's fold when 'Omar was but newly raised from palace sweeper.

"Al-Maut placed the blade in his hand. 'Kill him.'

"Abdurrahim turned the dagger over. Running a wet tongue over his chapped lips, he looked at al-Maut and then at the prone 'Omar. For a breathless instant, Jauhara thought he would balk.

"Abdurrahim stepped toward 'Omar, each footfall a drumbeat.

"'Watch, Jauhara,' al-Maut hissed, gripping Jauhara's jaw and turning her face toward her father. 'You will watch your father die, and then your mother, and your brothers and sisters, and your friend there too. With each death, you will see the power of the marid grow until we cannot be vanquished. In the end, I will kill you too and you will beg for it.'

"Jauhara's eyes rolled to her father and to Kushyar and she knew it was over, that this thing she had started as an adventure, without understanding mortality or loss or the ways of the world, was done.

"Abdurrahim pressed the iron blade against 'Omar's throat until blood flowered crimson across his collar. Swaying, 'Omar shut his eyes. 'I bear witness that there is no god but Allah and Muhammad is his messenger!' Each resounding word pressed the dagger deeper into his flesh, but 'Omar did not falter.

"Wresting her chin from al-Maut, Jauhara cried out, 'Ashadu anna la ilaha illa'Allah, wa ashadu anna Muhammad rasul'Allah!'

"The earth's axis wavered.

"A blazing light, radiant as the sun, filled her vision. Jauhara threw her hands up, but the light only burned brighter, a hundred thousand bonfires that filled the room with shattering brilliance and left stars in Jauhara's eyes and tears on her cheeks.

"The light spoke, and in its voice resounded trumpets and exotic birds, crashing thunder on the savanna and the opening of galaxies, great and gorgeous noises all intermixed with a purity that rang like a bell. 'In the name of Allah, the Most Gracious, the Most Merciful, release them.'

"'I will not,' al-Maut hissed, her rainbow wings shading her eyes as her marid siblings amassed behind her, their claws lengthening, teeth sharpening.

"'You *will*, for I am an angel of the Lord,' the light intoned, and the words spooned like sweet honey into Jauhara's ears, 'a sword of Allah, and I come to vanquish you in His name and cast your evil into the darkest reaches of this world—'"

The guard knocks sharply. I look at Shahryar, the remainder of Jauhara's tale pulverized into dust on my tongue. This cannot be it. Does the guard not understand that this story that he cuts short is the only fruit of the marriage of Shaherazade Khatun, daughter of Vizier Muhammad, to Shahryar, son of Turanshah, the last Seljuk Malik of Kirman?

The knocking grows more insistent.

"Let me tell you—"

Shahryar places a finger against his lips. "When I see you again, you will complete your tale. But for now, I declare your mahr is returned."

I bite my shaking mouth, clench my quaking hands, feel my very bones quaver. "O Malik, I divorce thee."

I cannot look at Shahryar. Instead, I look at his shoulder, memorize its broadness, the slight tremble, and I think: the Seljuks are ended, Bam is ended, Shahryar is ended, my own sister is ended for me. Our empire is ruptured, and the threads that bound us together have disintegrated, and in this dissolution I am unmoored.

Shahryar watches the emotions play across my face like shadows beneath a tree. I realize that I am ungrateful, that if my fate is uncertain then his fate, he, whom I once loved with all my heart, for whom I upended kingdoms and unspooled words like parasangs of yarn, is all too certain. We stand on opposite sides of a chasm, riven by fathomless loss.

But something still remains for me, even if I must leave behind all I have loved and all I have feared to have it.

I will do it because I must. Beneath that necessity, there is something more.

A fluttering candle flame of hope, of certainty, that from me, my destiny cannot flee.

Shahryar places his hand tenderly on my head like a father blessing a bride. *"In the end,"* he murmurs, *"your sorrow will be softened and what has passed will be forgotten."*

It is a verse by Nizami, but he says it like a prayer.

✳ ✳ ✳

The sun rises, a fire-washed opal that shards light over Bam and alchemizes the town: the citadel's voluptuous curved towers, the adobe-baked homes spiraling down the tel, the pistachio groves greening the city walls. Squinting, I pick out a lone figure pacing the parapet, her almond farajiyya whipping in the same wind that stirs my braids.

I turn away. I must. If I do not, I will never leave, the roots and vines binding me to this place so tight they are one with my flesh. I focus forward: Shahzaman at the Samarkandi army's head, the Kuhbonan Mountains rising sharp and frosted to my left, Atsiz to my right.

I catch my veil as the breeze gusts east to west. The wind flies past turquoise domes high as hills, sails over deserts that stretch like the sea, and flicks pages through Papersellers' Street. Finally, it snarls in the feathery leaves of a bowing tamarisk tree, whose hunched branches shade children and bazaar-goers ringing a long-braided storyteller. As she speaks, her hands flutter like swallows and the wind falls quiet.

They say—and Allah knows better—that there was once a kingdom in faraway Persia drowning in the blood of its maidens and reeling from the brutality of its mad king. The king's advisers quaked, his city boiled, and the kingdom's girls shivered each night, afraid that the bedeviled king would pluck them next. All seemed destined to burn—until the vizier's daughter, a quiet girl of little note, proffered herself to stanch the flow with tales of wonder she wove from shadow and gold. And while her tales halted the rivers of blood, yes, they also threw open doors dividing worlds, cracked the empire like an egg, and thrust the vizier's daughter into the marvelous unknown . . .

Afterword

This book is an ode to medieval Islamic history, to the diversity of culture, religion, people, art, literature, and food that powered global culture for centuries. It was a fascinating era, science and mathematics were being pushed forward, philosophy and theology deepened, and the politics! Conquests, usurpations, betrayals, and family dynamics that would make the Plantagenets blush. And it always seemed a shame how unearthed this period is in (English-language) literature.

As a Muslim kid growing up in the United States, *The Arabian Nights* (or, in Arabic, *Alf Layla wa Layla*) was a cultural touchstone for me before I'd even heard of it. Aladdin, Sindbad—the few Muslim heroes I encountered in kids' movies and books growing up, the few characters in whom I could see a piece of myself reflected—were from the *Nights*. I'm not sure exactly when I discovered that the stories of Sindbad and Aladdin were contained in a broader story of a heroic Muslim girl, but I remember wanting more of *her*.

Shaherazade has always presented an intriguing puzzle that I couldn't shake: *Why would a girl offer herself to a murderous king with only her tales as armor?* I read the original *Nights* and looked for novels that answered that question to my satisfaction, but found none that captured Shaherazade in a fully realized form. What I really wanted was a book where Shaherazade herself was spotlit, where her mind and machinations were front and center, where the historical world she would have occupied was palpable.

My Shaherazade, of course, is fictional, but she draws on real Muslim women of the premodern era, who were themselves savvy rulers, noted scholars, and renowned poets, many of whom are mentioned in the novel itself: A'isha bint Abu Bakr, Turkan Khatun, Rabia al-Basri, Razia Sultan, Safiyya al-Baghdadiyya, and Ulayya bint al-Mahdi. Despite the notion of the so-called oppressed Muslim woman, the list is long and Shaherazade is an avatar of the kind of power Muslim women have wielded through the ages. It's a power Shaherazade holds in the original *Nights*, too: she is the authorial voice, the protagonist, the hero stepping into the lion's den, and it's that power that so mesmerized me.

And because of the dearth of accurate portrayals about this period, it was important for me to be assiduous and circumspect as I created Shaherazade's world. I spent years researching the Seljuks, that period, and the regions covered in the book, relying on chronicles, medieval histories, architecture, art, literature, and modern secondary sources to create an immersive world that did not run on stereotypes and assumptions but rang as true as possible. For example, while the idea of women embarking on a military campaign (especially, for some, Muslim women) might seem fantastical, certain Seljuk queen mothers did join their sons on campaign.

As for my beloved Seljuks, the erstwhile Sultans of the East and West, their reign shepherded the building of great universities like the al-Nizamiyya in Baghdad, the work of renowned poets like Attar and Omar Khayyam, along with all sorts of bloody political maneuverings (not infrequently dreamed up by Seljuk women). Seljuk dominance in Persia came to an end in 1194 when they were effectively supplanted by the Khwarezmids, just two years after the events of this book close. Kirman itself was taken by the Oghuz led by Malik Dinar in the late 1180s. (In addition to taking artistic license by inventing a whole new ruler for Seljuk Kirman in the *Arabian Nights'* Shahryar, I also took a little license in fudging the dates. What's a decade or so between friends?) The Seljuks, however, were but one of numerous Turkic dynasties in the Islamic Middle Ages that redefined the world. Among their brethren count the Ottomans, the aforementioned Mughals, the Delhi Sultanate, the Mamluks, and the Timurids.

In September 1192, Sultan Saladin and Malikric signed the Treaty of Jaffa, ending the Third Crusade. Jerusalem remained under Muslim control but Christians secured the right to go on pilgrimage and received control of certain coastal territory. Sultan Saladin died six months later. Pope Innocent III called the Fourth Crusade in 1202.

Which is all to say—this story of Shaherazade and this slice of the Seljuks, medieval Persia, and the Third Crusade, is but a small window into this era, region, and culture. As Shaherazade would say, *What is this compared to what happens next?*

Acknowledgments

To see this story I began writing one cloudy weekend in 2008 transform into a real, published novel still feels like a delusion that has leeched from my mind into reality. This novel is so much of me, has grown and deepened as I have grown and deepened, and I am so grateful to all those who have supported me along the way:

First, of course, thank you to Ammi and Abbu, without whose fathomless love, support, and encouragement of my love of stories, reading, and writing this book would not have been possible. I am also grateful to my Dada, Dadi, Nana, and Nani, each of whom played a part in my love of language and stories. And thank you to my brother for being the archetype of the collected younger sibling who can see all the way through his big sister's BS.

I am also so grateful for my friends and family, especially those who read this book in its various iterations (including back in its "Ascending Dawn" days), who offered their feedback on the story and, more importantly, love for it: Maria, Insiya, Priyanka, Janet, and Kristin.

Thank you to those who guided me in the craft of writing, particularly my high school English teacher, Mrs. Bryson, and the writing workshops I took at Harvard University and Sackett Street.

And, of course, my utmost thanks to my agent, Stephanie Cabot (and her team at Susanna Lea Agency), who found this manuscript in the slush pile and believed in it. Whose thoughtful feedback helped me build a stronger manuscript. Who has been a smart, savvy, and supportive shepherd in this process and backed me on all my soapboxes. Thank you, thank you, thank you.

A huge thank you to my fabulous editors Retha Powers and Abi Scruby (and their respective, amazing teams at Henry Holt and John Murray). You two are a testament to the importance and power of diversity in publishing. It does not escape me that it took women of your backgrounds to see the value of a book set in the medieval Muslim world and to connect with the characters and story. I am so appreciative of your thoughtful edits, your grace for me as I juggled legal work and book work, your infinite patience with my type A self, and the beautiful book we've put together. From the bottom of my heart: thank you.

As I wrote this book over the course of fourteen-odd years, I relied on a number of primary and secondary sources to anchor and color Shaherazade's medieval world. I am incredibly grateful for these writings and scholarship. I will always have a special place in my heart for Husain Haddawy's translation of *The Arabian Nights*, which was my touchstone as I wrote *Every Rising Sun*, my jump start of inspiration for Shaherazade's stories whenever I faltered, and whose beautiful translation of Shaherazade's command to the Malik to *listen* was always a whisper in my ears.

A few other key writers and works:

- *The Life of Saladin or What Befell Sultan Yusuf* by Beha ed-Din abu El-Mehasan Yusuf ibn Shaddad (ed. Sir Charles William Wilson)

- *Shahnameh* by Abolqasem Ferdowsi (trans. Dick Davis)

- *The Annals of the Saljuq Turks Selections from al-Kamil fi'l-Ta'rikh* by Ibn al-Athir (trans. D. S. Richards)

- *A Rare Thirteenth Century History of the Seljuqs (The Notification of Kings: The Refreshment of Hearts' Sadness, and Signal of Gladness* by Najmu'din Abu Bakr Muhammad bin 'Ali (trans. E. G. Browne)

- *The History of the Saljuq State* (ed. Clifford Edmund Bosworth)

- *Women in Iran: From the Rise of Islam to 1800* (eds. Guity Nashat Becker and Lois Beck)

- *The Great Seljuk Empire* by A. C. S. Peacock

- *The Annals of the Caliphs' Kitchen* by Ibn Sayyār al-Warrāq (trans. Nawal Nasrallah)

- *Baghdad During the Abbasid Caliphate* by Guy Le Strange

And always: subhan'Allah.

About the Author

Jamila Ahmed is a Pakistani American writer and lawyer. She is a graduate of Harvard Law School and Barnard College, where she studied medieval Islamic history. She lives in Brooklyn.